Dear Reader,

The Randalls: Summ... summer days when ... and lived vicariously through ... it. I hope that's what you'll do with heroes Brett and Jake, the two remaining Randall bachelors from my original BRIDES FOR BROTHERS series. (You met their other brothers this March when Harlequin released *The Randalls: Wyoming Winter.*)

These two men, like their brothers, are dream guys. Not because they are picture-perfect. They are, of course, in my mind, but they are strong, loyal and loving, too. And maybe a little stubborn. Brett, whose story you'll find in *Cowboy Groom,* is snared by the wrong woman and then finds the right one. Now, *there's* a problem! And in *Cowboy Surrender,* big brother Jake—who has been doing all the matchmaking from the beginning—suddenly finds his own family setting marriage traps for him. Jake's brilliant solution to his difficulties provides its own complications.

Join the second half of the Randalls as they search for true love and the sweet kisses the ladies offer in return for their bachelorhood. And don't miss the next generation of Randalls as they follow in the footsteps of their parents with brand-new stories in the Harlequin American Romance line. Watch for them!

Best wishes and happy reading!

Judy Christenberry

Judy Christenberry

THE RANDALLS
SUMMER SKIES

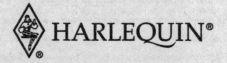

HARLEQUIN®

TORONTO • NEW YORK • LONDON
AMSTERDAM • PARIS • SYDNEY • HAMBURG
STOCKHOLM • ATHENS • TOKYO • MILAN • MADRID
PRAGUE • WARSAW • BUDAPEST • AUCKLAND

To Barbara Hunt, who, like Jake,
feels responsible for the rest of us.
No one could ask for a better sister.

ISBN 0-373-83530-2

THE RANDALLS: SUMMER SKIES

Copyright © 2002 by Harlequin Books S.A.

The publisher acknowledges the copyright holder
of the individual titles as follows:

COWBOY GROOM
Copyright © 1997 by Judy Christenberry

COWBOY SURRENDER
Copyright © 1997 by Judy Christenberry

Visit us at www.eHarlequin.com

Printed in U.S.A.

JUDY CHRISTENBERRY,
the bestselling author for Harlequin American
Romance and Silhouette Romance, has been writing
romances for over fifteen years because she loves
happy endings as much as her readers do. A former
high school French teacher, Judy now devotes
herself to writing full-time. Her spare time is spent
reading, watching her favorite sports teams and
keeping track of her two adult daughters. A native
Texan, Judy now resides in Arizona.

THE RANDALLS

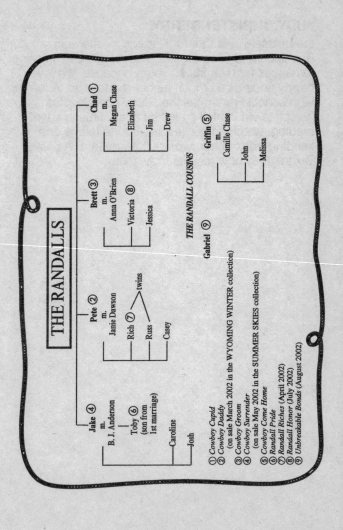

Jake ④
m.
B. J. Anderson
┬ Toby ⑥
│ (son from
│ 1st marriage)
├ Caroline
└ Josh

Pete ②
m.
Jamie Dawson
┬ Rich ⑦ ⎫
├ Russ ⎬ twins
│   ⎭
└ Casey

Brett ③
m.
Anna O'Brien
┬ Victoria ⑧
└ Jessica

Chad ①
m.
Megan Chase
┬ Elizabeth
├ Jim
└ Drew

THE RANDALL COUSINS

Gabriel ⑨

Griffin ⑤
m.
Camille Chase
┬ John
└ Melissa

① *Cowboy Cupid*
② *Cowboy Daddy*
(on sale March 2002 in the WYOMING WINTER collection)
③ *Cowboy Groom*
④ *Cowboy Surrender*
(on sale May 2002 in the SUMMER SKIES collection)
⑤ *Cowboy Come Home*
⑥ *Randall Pride*
⑦ *Randall Riches* (April 2002)
⑧ *Randall Honor* (July 2002)
⑨ *Unbreakable Bonds* (August 2002)

COWBOY GROOM

Chapter One

It felt good to be home. After several weeks in Casper, Cheyenne and Washington, D.C., Brett Randall was happy to be back on the Wyoming ranch he shared with his three brothers.

All the glittering lights and famous people he'd seen couldn't top the feeling of coming home.

And the anticipation of sharing his news.

Brett stood alone in the dark of the kitchen. His family hadn't expected him to return for a couple more days, but he couldn't wait to tell them before they read about it in the newspaper.

Just as he started toward the stairway, he heard a car coming up the driveway. Who would arrive at two in the morning? Except himself, of course.

He made it to the window in time to see a small economy car approach. Before its headlights could reach the house, the driver shut them off. The new arrival obviously didn't want to be seen. Which meant he probably wasn't up to any good.

Crime was unusual out on the ranches of Wyoming—other than a cowboy drinking too much and getting rambunctious—but it wasn't unheard-of. Brett, however, had no intention of letting anyone rip off his family if he could prevent it. He eased over to the back door, thinking he'd slip outside and follow the thief to whichever barn he intended to enter.

When he heard the intruder step on the back porch, anger filled him. This guy was brazen enough to break in to the house?

Brett stood behind the door, ready to leap on him as soon as he entered. Slowly the door opened, and Brett felt his adrenaline surge. Even as he leapt, he realized the guy was either small or hunched over. No matter. He shouldn't have tried to invade Randall territory.

With a cry of triumph, Brett landed on the thief.

And then landed on his back.

Shock left him unmoving briefly. Then, as he struggled to his feet, he found himself rolled over on his stomach, his right hand twisted behind his back.

And the intruder sitting atop him.

In spite of his embarrassing position, he noticed something strange about this intruder. Perfume. And slender thighs gripped his hips with a sensuous feel that had nothing to do with a man.

What the hell was going on?

LIGHT FLOODED the kitchen as the Randall brothers poured into it.

Anna O'Brien, holding the thief captive, was grateful for the reinforcements. She'd discovered he was a big man and knew she wouldn't be able to hold him for long.

"Anna, are you all right?" Jake demanded. The oldest Randall brother, he'd been the first through the door.

"Someone broke in?" Megan asked as she clutched the arm of her husband, Chad.

Pete stepped forward. "Here. I'll help— Brett!"

All the hubbub subsided, and everyone stared at the figure on the floor. With a sinking feeling, Anna also looked at the irate face of the man on whom she was sitting. She'd heard about the fourth brother, Brett, but she'd never met him. "Brett? This is Brett? I thought he was a thief."

"Me?" he roared. "You're the thief! Who are you?"

He bucked beneath her, signifying his desire to be released, and Anna relaxed her hold on his arm so they could both stand. "I'm sorry. I didn't know who— You came at me so suddenly, I—"

"Wait a minute," Chad, the youngest Randall brother, interrupted. "*He* jumped *you?* Then how did you end up on top?"

Anna wished the kitchen were still dark. She knew Brett Randall wasn't going to easily forget the humiliation she could see on his face. "I've taken several self-defense classes," she hurriedly explained, hoping to minimize his embarrassment.

His brothers, however, weren't about to ignore an opportunity to tease him.

"Anna? Little Anna took you down?" Jake roared, grinning at Brett. "Man, city life must've made you soft."

"It's about time he got home," Pete Randall agreed, his grin just as big.

"What's happening?" came a female voice from behind them.

"Janie? I told you to stay in bed," Pete protested. "You're not supposed to use the stairs, is she, Anna?"

Anna smiled for the first time since she'd arrived. Pete's overprotectiveness was the reason she was here in the first place. "Not often, Pete, but I'm sure one trip down them won't hurt. Are you feeling okay, Janie?"

"Wait a minute. Why are they asking you?" her captive demanded. "I know we have a female vet, but did we get a female to replace Doc Jacoby?"

Anna truly looked at Brett for the first time, noting his resemblance to his brothers. He was a little shorter than the other three, but still over six feet. And just as handsome.

"I'm not a doctor. I'm the midwife."

He seemed startled by her words, reminding her again how long it often took to be accepted. Her size, just topping five foot five, wouldn't be so bad except that she didn't carry much weight, and her hair was red with the complementary freckles scattered across her nose. Most people thought she was too young to take care of expectant mothers.

Jake filled the silence. "We told you Anna was living here until Janie has the twins, didn't we?"

"Yeah, but I pictured...someone different," Brett finished lamely.

Anna raised her chin. "I assure you I'm perfectly competent."

At her words, the Randall clan spoke en masse, their reassuring words embarrassing her. She'd only been there a little over a week, and already she knew she would miss them when she left.

In the midst of their protestations, she noticed Brett said nothing. He simply stared at her while he listened to his family.

"Why was she sneaking in?" he asked abruptly when the rest of them fell silent.

"What do you mean?" Jake asked.

"She turned off her lights before she reached the house. And she tried to be real quiet."

Anna started to answer, but Pete beat her to it. "Janie doesn't sleep well right now. The least little noise distracts her, so Anna tries not to awaken her."

"Maybe she should come home at a reasonable time, instead of staying out so late." Brett glared at Anna.

"I wish I had, but Mrs. Stokes's baby wasn't in any hurry," she replied. "The poor woman was in labor for fifteen hours."

Both the pregnant women in the room—Janie, huge with twins, and Megan, only a little over four months along—rubbed their stomachs in a reflex action.

"Don't worry," Anna hurriedly added. "She made it just fine. And the baby, too. An adorable little girl."

"Glad to hear it," Jake said, "but I suggest we all get to bed. The ladies need their beauty rest, and we have a full day in the saddle as soon as the sun comes up."

"Uh, Jake," Brett said, interrupting the general movement to the door, "don't you want to hear why I came home early? Isn't anybody interested in my news?"

"Anything wrong?" Jake asked, concern in his eyes.

"No. No, it's good news." A smile broke across his face. "I'm saving you the trouble of matchmaking for me, brother. I'm engaged!"

"Engaged?" Jake repeated, his voice disbelieving. "What are you talking about? Who are you engaged to?"

"Yeah! I thought you weren't ready for marriage." Chad slapped his brother on the shoulder. The others crowded around him, offering warm words.

Anna stood back and watched his family congratulate Brett Randall. She wasn't surprised some lucky female had grabbed him. He was handsome as sin, he and his family had one of the largest ranches in Wyoming and she expected he was as nice as his brothers.

She'd been hesitant to move to the Randall ranch, even though her stay should be less than a month. Having been raised on the "wrong side of the tracks," Anna had always felt uneasy around the wealthy. Living in their midst would be even worse, she'd felt sure.

To the contrary, she found life with the Randalls a delight. Their life-style didn't shout wealth, they all worked hard, and then shared their lives with her as if she'd been born there.

The pang of regret she felt for hearing Brett had been taken was ridiculous, of course. She would never have had a chance at one of the Randalls. Now she felt like one of Cinderella's ugly stepsisters at the ball.

"I was beginning to think your catching my bouquet wasn't working," Janie said to Brett with a tired chuckle as she leaned against her husband, Pete.

"Well, aren't you going to tell us who she is?" Chad asked. "This isn't some whirlwind romance with a stranger, is it?"

"Like you'd known Megan for a lifetime before you married her," Brett chided.

Anna had heard the story of Chad and Megan's romance, learning they'd married after only two weeks.

"Well, who is she?" Jake insisted, ignoring his brothers' argument.

"Sylvia Sanders."

The name had no significance for Anna, but it apparently did for the rest of the people in the kitchen.

"Senator Sanders's daughter?" There was astonishment in Jake's voice.

"Yeah. What's the matter?" Brett asked, edginess tinting his question.

"Nothing," Megan assured him. "She's a beautiful young woman. Congratulations, Brett." She kissed his cheek, then stepped back beside her husband and elbowed him.

"Uh, yeah, congratulations, brother," Chad said. "She's a real looker."

Everyone else crowded around Brett to offer their praises for his choice and to wish him well. Anna wondered if she was imagining their reluctance.

"Thanks. It got leaked to the papers, and I wanted to tell you before you read it like everyone else."

"So, when's the wedding?" Pete asked.

"Hey, don't rush me! I'm not diving into marriage like you two did," Brett assured Pete and Chad.

Somehow Anna got the impression Brett wasn't as sold on the idea of marriage to Sylvia as he wanted his family to believe.

Or maybe it was just wishful thinking.

"I CAN'T BELIEVE he— Oh! Good morning, Anna." Janie's expression turned guilty as Anna opened the kitchen door later that morning.

"Do I need to make myself scarce? I can catch breakfast in town if—"

"No, of course not," Janie said, waving her in. "Red left you a plate on the back of the stove."

"I could take it back to my room to eat," Anna suggested, still feeling as if she were intruding.

"Don't be silly, Anna." Megan shot her a smile. "Janie just feels guilty because you caught her gossiping. And if she doesn't finish what she started, I'm going to wring her neck."

After dramatically looking over each shoulder, Janie leaned closer to Megan and Anna as she sat down. "I was saying that I can't believe Brett is going to marry Sylvia Sanders. She is such a snob!"

"You know her?" Anna asked. The closest she'd ever come to seeing any of Wyoming's politicians or their families was on television.

"Sure. Last year Daddy insisted we go to a dinner at the governor's mansion. But she attended Kansas University the same time I did. We weren't friends, of course. She was too important."

"Maybe she was shy," Anna suggested.

Megan chuckled. "You have such a good heart, Anna. But in this case, you're wrong. I met her once. She virtually ignored me until someone mentioned that my mother's fifth husband has a title. As if that mattered."

"Fifth?" Anna asked, distracted by that detail. "Your mother's been married five times?"

Megan rolled her eyes. "Yeah. And if this marriage ends soon, as I think it will, I'm sure I'll get daddy number six. Lucky me."

"And Miss Sanders was impressed that your stepfather has a title?"

"Boy, was she. The only thing that impresses Sylvia more than a title is money. And Brett has money."

Anna blinked several times. "You don't think she's marrying Brett because he's rich, do you?" Anna wasn't so naive as to not believe a woman would marry for money. But there was so much more to Brett Randall—as far as she could tell.

She didn't really know him, but based on what she'd seen—felt—this morning, he was a great physical specimen. And if he was anything like his brothers, then he was a prize package.

"Money and power. The Randall men have a lot of influence in this state," Janie said proudly.

"Maybe, but those are added benefits to having fallen in love with him," Anna offered. For some ridiculous reason, it hurt to think of Brett's fiancée not appreciating him.

Janie shook her head glumly. "I don't think Sylvia is capable of falling in love."

"For Brett's sake, I hope you're wrong," Megan said. "But I tend to agree with you."

Anna ate her scrambled eggs and watched the other women as their expressions grew even more gloomy.

"Will they live here with everyone?" Anna had found the family togetherness charming, unheard-of in nineties America.

Janie gasped. "Good Lord, I hadn't thought of that!"

"We'll be miserable," Megan moaned.

"Why?"

"Because Miss High and Mighty will expect to be waited on hand and foot. She'd never lift a hand to help someone else. And we'll all feel bad for Brett. He's such a good guy." Janie drummed her fingers on the table, frowning.

"Yeah, he doesn't deserve Sylvia. She'll ruin his sense of humor." Megan turned to Anna. "Brett can always make us laugh when things get tough."

"And he's always on our side of any argument. He tells our husbands they're crazy to argue with us," Janie added with a chuckle.

"You wouldn't expect a bachelor to be so sympathetic with pregnancy, either. But he and Jake are both terrific about that."

"So, girls, what are we going to do?" Janie continued.

"About what?" Anna asked.

"To break them up, of course!"

BRETT HAD A BIG GRIN on his face in spite of the sweat beading on his forehead. July in Wyoming wasn't always comfortable, but he loved it.

"Feeling a little rusty?" Jake asked as he stepped up on the porch beside his brother.

"Nah. Nothing to it. Feels good to be back."

"Yeah. But we needed you to plead our case on that land-use bill. Think you made any headway?"

"Maybe. Since the senior senator is going to be my father-in-law, I think I might be able to persuade him."

Jake pulled him to a halt before he could open the back door. "Wait a minute. You didn't ask Sylvia to marry you to persuade her father, did you?"

Brett stared at his brother before laughing. "Do I look stupid? Of course not. Sylvia is beautiful, elegant, a lot of fun." He blew out a long breath before revealing a secret to Jake. "You know, we were all against marriage after your divorce from Chloe, but watching Pete and Chad with their wives, I—I was beginning to feel lonesome."

Jake put his arm around Brett. "Okay, little brother, as long as Sylvia makes you happy, I'm happy. I've been telling you you should get married like the others."

"Yeah. You've been telling me nonstop. Ever since Pete's marriage."

"Well, you did catch the bridal bouquet," Jake teased.

"That was a mistake. Janie was half-asleep. She didn't even look where she threw it."

"Looks like it worked anyway. One more marriage, and we'll have everyone taken care of." Jake grinned at his brother as he opened the door and gestured for Brett to precede him.

The rest of the family was already gathered around the table. The rest of the family and the little midwife, Brett noted sourly. Just what he needed, a reminder of his humiliation last night.

Jake took his normal place at the head of the table, leaving Brett one seat—beside the redhead.

As soon as grace was finished, Janie called for his attention.

"Yeah, Janie? When are you going to hatch?"

"Hey!" Pete protested. "That's my wife you're talking to."

"I hope so, 'cause I think she's pregnant," Brett teased.

"I don't want to discuss me," Janie protested. "I want to know when you're bringing Sylvia to meet all of us."

Brett looked at her in surprise. "I assumed it would be best to wait until after you've had the babies, Janie. I don't want the visit to be a strain for you."

Pete nodded in approval.

Janie, however, didn't seem to appreciate his consideration. "I don't think that's a good idea."

"Why not?"

"Because it may be six months before I feel halfway decent once these babies are born. I won't get any sleep, and I won't have an excuse to be fat any longer. I think she should come for a visit at once."

"Yes," Megan chimed in. "You want her to come now, when the ranch is beautiful. In winter, she might not like it as much."

"Megan, she's a Wyoming girl," Brett protested.

"Maybe so, but she's spent a lot of time in Washington, D.C."

Jake looked at Megan sharply before turning to Brett. "Megan's got a point. Have you two discussed where you'll live after the wedding?"

Brett's head shot up. "Aren't we welcome here?"

"Of course you are!" Jake returned. "You know you are.

But I got worried that Sylvia wouldn't want— She's used to a more—more exciting life.''

"Sylvia knows I want to live here."

"Then call and invite her," Janie insisted. "Tell her we're all anxious to welcome her into the family. We'll give a party to introduce her to the neighbors."

"You sure you're up to all that activity?" Brett asked Janie. He wouldn't want to do anything to interfere with the safe delivery of his first nieces and nephews.

"Tell him, Anna," Janie ordered.

Brett reluctantly turned to the one person at the table he'd been trying to ignore. He didn't want to be reminded of last night.

"I'll make sure Janie doesn't overdo it. And I can help Red with things around here."

Staring into big blue eyes that reminded him of the Wyoming sky in summer, Brett almost forgot what they were discussing. Those eyes must be the biggest part of her, he decided. Except for those red curls that seemed to have a life of their own.

"Brett? Are you going to telephone Sylvia?" Jake prodded, calling him to attention.

He reluctantly drew his gaze away from Anna. "What? Oh. Oh, yeah. I'll go call her right away." He turned back to look at Anna again. What was wrong with him? Why was he suddenly reluctant to talk to Sylvia? He was going to marry her. Wasn't he?

Chapter Two

"Hi, lover."

Her sexy voice reassured him. Of what, he wasn't sure, but Brett had been uneasy until she spoke.

"I miss you already," Sylvia went on. "When will you be back? No, Maria, put that over here."

Brett waited impatiently until he had her attention again. "I've got a better idea. Why don't you come here? The family wants you to come visit. We'll have a party to introduce you to the neighbors."

He began to wonder if he'd lost the connection because silence was his only answer. Finally Sylvia said, "I'd love to, angel, but as Daddy's hostess, you know I need to be here."

"I'm sure he can spare you for a week or two, Sylvia. After all, he'll have to get used to me coming first, won't he?" Brett chuckled. Several times his brothers had pointed out how much things changed with marriage.

Sylvia didn't laugh with him. "Of course, Brett, but— Maria! I told you I wanted lemonade with my lunch. Sorry, Brett. The woman can't get anything right. I suppose I could spare a week. Daddy's visiting with his constituents right now, nothing important. When shall I come?"

"The sooner the better. Tomorrow?"

"Darling, I can't be packed in such a short time."

"All you'll need are jeans and a party dress. We're pretty casual around here."

As if he'd never spoken, she continued, "I suppose I could leave Friday. You'll come pick me up?"

Brett never hesitated, though Casper was a two-hour drive. It suddenly seemed important that he see her again. "Of course. I'll be there about nine, and we can be back at the ranch for lunch."

"I won't be ready until about three. Daddy's having a luncheon on Friday, and I need to be here."

"Okay. We'll get back in time for dinner."

"Yes, of course. Please assure everyone I'm looking forward to my visit."

"You'll love it here, Sylvia. We're going to be very happy."

"Of course we are, lover. Bye-bye."

With a frown, he replaced the receiver. He didn't feel as satisfied as he'd thought he would. Sylvia hadn't sounded as enthusiastic as she had when he left her, either. And it seemed as if she had more important things to do than chat with him.

Of course, as her father's hostess, she lead a busy life. But things would change once they were married. Then she could be busy on the ranch.

He was smiling again by the time he reached the kitchen. Sylvia could be in charge of all the parties they might want to give. And help Red around the house. And they could start a family.

"Is Sylvia coming?" Jake asked.

Brett was surprised to discover the kitchen empty except for his brother and Red, the old cowboy who'd taken care of them for a quarter of a century.

"Yeah. Where is everyone?"

"Janie and Megan take a nap after lunch every day. Anna had visits to make, and your brothers are out saddling up."

"Sorry. I didn't mean to take so long." He was looking forward to working this afternoon. There was something so straightforward about ranch work, unlike the political scene where he'd just spent the past two weeks.

"So when is she coming?"

Brett looked at Jake, surprised that he had forgotten to tell them when Sylvia would come. He'd been thinking about the afternoon. "She'll be here Friday. I'll drive in and pick her up."

"I thought you was startin' the branding Friday," Red said, looking at Jake.

"I didn't know," Brett hurriedly said. "I'll call her back and pick her up on Thursday."

"That's all right. We'll manage," Jake assured him. "You go pick up Sylvia."

"Right," Brett agreed in a distracted fashion, and headed outdoors.

"Man," Red said, shaking his head. "He's got it bad."

Jake grinned. "He's supposed to, isn't he? If I remember rightly, once they fall for someone, they don't hardly know what's going on around them."

"I suppose. But I met that little lady once. She's not like the other two."

"Brett thinks she'll make him happy." Jake wouldn't admit that he had his doubts, too. "Are you going to be able to manage with another mouth to feed?"

"Trust me, she won't eat much. But I'm worried about getting everything cleaned up. I've been meaning to talk to you anyway. As pretty as everything is now since Megan and the other lady redid the house, I hate to see it all get dusty. But I can't seem to manage everything."

"I should've noticed we'd put too much on you. Especially since Janie can't help anymore. I'll have to think about what to do."

"I have a suggestion. We could hire Mildred."

"Mildred, B.J.'s aunt?"

"A-course that's who I mean."

"I thought you two didn't get along." B. J. Anderson, the local veterinarian, had moved to the ranch last winter, about the time his two brothers had married, bringing with her her four-year-old son and her maiden aunt. Jake had noticed that Red seemed uncomfortable around Mildred.

Red's cheeks reddened, and he looked away. "We get along fine."

"Great. I'll speak to her."

Red nodded and began scrubbing the kitchen counter, which was already spotless.

BRETT COULDN'T SLEEP.

He'd gone up to bed with the rest of the family around ten o'clock, but he was restless. Finally, after reading for a while, he pulled on his jeans and a T-shirt.

Chuckling, he went down the stairs barefoot. Things had changed. In the past, when they were all men at the ranch, he wouldn't have bothered with jeans. But he didn't want one of his sisters-in-law to catch him in his underwear.

In the kitchen, he cut a piece of Red's chocolate cake and poured himself a big glass of milk. He'd refused a helping of dessert at dinner, but it sounded pretty good now.

Just as he sat down at the table, he heard a car approaching. A sense of déjà vu stole over him. Except that the kitchen light was on tonight, and he knew who was arriving.

She hadn't been at dinner. He hadn't wanted to ask her whereabouts, sure the mention of her name would bring more teasing from his brothers. But in the course of the conversation, he'd heard Janie tell Megan that Anna was with Mrs. Cauble tonight. The lady and her husband lived on the other side of the county.

He listened as the car engine stopped, followed by the muffled thud of a door closing. When the kitchen door eased open, he stared at the slender female form.

"Don't you ever keep regular hours?" he asked softly, startling her.

Anna jerked in surprise before relaxing. With a smile, she turned to him. "Not often. But at least you didn't attack me this evening."

He found himself laughing quietly, much to his surprise. "Nope, no attacking tonight." He looked down at the cake. "Want some dessert?"

"It looks good, but I think I'd better have something a little more solid than that."

He noticed for the first time how tired she looked. "Didn't they even feed you?"

Again she smiled. "I'm afraid dinner wasn't on their minds.

Mrs. Cauble had complications, and we had to summon the ambulance and get her to the hospital for Doc to look at her.''

Brett stood and put his hands on Anna's shoulders, guiding her to a seat at the table. "Rest. I'll fix you some leftovers.''

"I can—''

"Don't move. It sounds like you've had a rough evening.'' He went to the refrigerator and brought out some of the roast they'd had for dinner, as well as leftover broccoli and carrots.

After he put a plate in the microwave, he turned to look at Anna.

"I guess you're kin to Jake, after all,'' she said.

"What do you mean?''

"Jake tries to take care of everyone.''

Brett grinned. "Yeah, he does. He's been riding herd over us for a long time. Dad depended on him to watch the rest of us after Mom died.''

"How old were you when your mother died?''

"I was three. I can't really remember her. She died giving birth to Chad.''

"Here at home?''

He sensed some urgency in her question and looked at her closely. "No, in the hospital. It was just before Doc moved here.'' He paused, but she said nothing. "Why?''

"Just wondering.''

The microwave dinged, and he brought her dinner to her. Afterward he sat across from her and began eating his cake.

"Where do your parents live?''

She chewed her food without looking up, and he thought she was going to ignore his question. Finally she swallowed and said, "They're both dead.''

He frowned. "You're not that old. Did they die in a car wreck or something?''

She shook her head no. "I'm older than I look.''

"If you weren't,'' he agreed, chuckling, "you'd still be in high school.''

"I've always had that problem.'' She smiled back at him. "People think I'm younger than I am.''

"So how old are you?''

"I thought a man wasn't supposed to ask such a personal question?" One slender brow arched over her incredible blue eyes.

"I figure as close as we've been—" he wiggled his eyebrows at her and nodded in the direction of the floor where she'd taken him down "—it'd be okay."

He liked the way her smile lit up her face.

"I guess you're right. I'm twenty-seven."

"Twenty-seven? Well, I guess that's not too old. I can still give you a couple of years. And you'll be glad you look young when you're sixty."

"Thanks," she drawled. "And do people ask you if you're still in high school?"

"No, ma'am. And all my teachers were glad to see me go, I can assure you."

"I believe you. I can't imagine those teachers facing all four Randalls."

He grinned again. "They couldn't, either." After a pause, he returned to his question she'd avoided. "So, what happened to your parents?"

His question broke Anna out of the cocoon of the intimacy in the quiet kitchen, the web of caring Brett had casually spun. She never talked about her parents, didn't want to remember those years. Maybe she should tell Brett Randall. It would emphasize the difference between the Anna O'Briens and the Randalls of the world. It would remind her that she was here for a job, not as a part of the Randall clan.

It was all too easy to forget.

Especially with the man sitting there dressed only in jeans and a snug T-shirt, his broad shoulders and chest clearly outlined. The temptation to touch him was almost irresistible.

"My mother died in childbirth, like your mother, only she wasn't in a hospital, and my father drank himself to death afterward." She stared at him, watching for his reaction.

He returned her look, concern on his face, and she had to look away.

"How old were you?"

"Six."

"And when your father died?"

"Seventeen."

"Is that why you became a midwife?"

His perception shot through her like a knife. Even Doc Jacoby, her staunchest supporter, didn't know about her mother. He thought she liked babies and pregnancy. Why was she confessing everything to this cowboy?

"It doesn't matter. I need to get to bed." She abandoned the rest of her meal and pushed back her chair to stand, but a hand on her arm held her in the chair.

"Were you with your mother when she died?"

He was getting so close, invading her private space, and she felt the familiar anger fill her again. "Yes. Were you with yours?"

"No. What happened?"

His rapid-fire response almost had her answering him, but she drew a deep breath and responded in reasonable tones. "I'm really tired, Mr. Randall. If you don't mind, I'll go to bed."

"Do you call my brothers Mr. Randall, too? If so, it must be really confusing around here." His smile invited her to forget their previous conversation and relax.

"No, but they told me to call them by their first names."

"Good. Call me Brett. And finish your dinner."

"Thank you, but I have finished."

"You didn't eat enough to keep a bird alive."

He still held her arm, keeping her in place. She knew she could get away from him, but she didn't want another wrestling match with the man. "Fortunately I'm not a bird. If you'll excuse me…" She stared pointedly at his hand.

"Just a few more bites? I didn't mean to upset you."

She was torn between escaping the kitchen and proving to Brett Randall that she hadn't let his conversation disturb her. Though she suspected she was making a mistake, she relaxed and picked up her fork.

"Good girl."

"You're trying to take care of me again, Brett. I've been on my own for quite a while."

"I guess you have. When did you move to our county?"

"Last year. After I trained, I worked at a hospital in Casper for five years while I specialized in midwifery." Safe topics.

"Why move out here, away from the big city and bright lights?" He watched her even as he took a bite of cake.

She found those brown eyes hard to resist.

"I like the country. And there's more need for a midwife out here. Doc can't cover the entire county."

"He doesn't have any problem with you working here?"

His question raised her hackles again. "Here? Do you mean here in your house or here in the county?"

He grinned, shaking his head. "Now, don't get angry with me again, Red."

"Red? Red is the housekeeper. My name is Anna."

"I know, but you have a temper. It matches your red hair."

She took a deep breath and released it slowly. "I do not have a hot temper. I'm always calm."

"Ah, my mistake."

His grin told her he was laughing at her, which only made it harder to control the emotions she'd learned to curb years ago. What was wrong with her?

"So, are you going to answer my question?"

"You have so many questions I can't remember it."

"About Doc."

"Dr. Jacoby has been very supportive," she said primly, not mentioning how the doctor and his nurse, Mrs. Priddy, had both helped her settle in and had recommended her services to patients. She'd been touched by both their responses.

"Good."

She rose from her chair and washed her plate at the sink.

"How about some cake, now that you've finished your dinner?"

"No, thanks," she assured him, and turned around, only to discover him beside her, his own dish in his hands. "Red certainly trained you all well."

"You bet. He'd wring my neck if he came in here in the morning and found dirty dishes in the sink. And he always knew who the guilty party was." He shook his head in wonder.

"Sylvia should be grateful. You'll be a much better husband."

"I don't much think Sylvia will care. She'll expect a maid to keep everything clean," Brett said, grimacing.

"You don't like the idea of a maid?"

"I don't see how she'll fit in here on the ranch."

Anna knew she should drop the subject. After all, it was none of her business. But she couldn't help herself. "Surely you wouldn't give up living with your family?"

Brett leaned against the kitchen cabinet and crossed his arms over his chest. "I don't want to. I guess I hadn't thought too much about the future."

"You have time. After all, you haven't set the date yet." She started to walk to the door, but Brett caught her arm.

"Wait a minute. What about you?"

"Me? What do you mean?"

"Which cowboy do you have tied up in knots?"

He was smiling at her, those brown eyes warm, his touch sending chills up her arm. "I—I don't know what you're talking about."

"I'm talking about your love life. After all, we've discussed mine."

She stiffened. "I didn't mean to pry." Tugging on her arm, she kept her gaze down.

"Hey," Brett said softly, lifting her chin with his other hand. "I wasn't complaining. But I'm curious about you. Thought maybe you might have wedding plans of your own."

"No." When he still didn't release her, she added, "Well? Did you want to know anything else?"

"Yeah, I can think of several things. Why are you so touchy? And what's wrong with the men around here?"

"I'm not touchy. And I'm not looking."

"Why?"

"What is this? Twenty questions?" She tilted her chin in the air and gave him an exasperated look.

"Red always said I was the curious one. Drove him crazy with that word. Guess I haven't changed much."

"You *look* grown-up." She couldn't help teasing him. He was such an easygoing, likable man. As sexy as any man she'd ever been around.

And off-limits. For a lot of reasons.

Suddenly his grip on her arm disappeared, but before she could react, he'd grabbed her by the waist, lifted her into the air and spun around. "Brett!" she protested.

"Don't let looks fool you. I'm still a kid at heart," he assured her, setting her on her feet again.

She took a deep breath, trying to slow the beating of her suddenly racing heart. "I can see."

His hands remained on her waist, and the heat from his touch was spreading all over her. She pulled from his arms and walked to the door. It was time to end this midnight visit. And she would avoid all others in the future.

"Wait. I'll walk up with you."

She wanted to run from the room, but such behavior would only tell him how much he affected her.

And he did. She wanted to touch him, to feel his muscular arms around her again. To claim his caring for her own. She was like a plant parched for water being touched by a gentle, nurturing rain. Which made her weak and vulnerable. After her stay at the Randalls', she was going to have to change her personal life. It was time she made some connections.

To put some distance between them, emotionally if not physically, as he joined her at the door, she asked, "When is your fiancée arriving?"

Chapter Three

Brett came to breakfast late on Friday morning, and he was glad he did. Anna was at the table. He'd scarcely seen her since their late-night talk three days ago.

"Anyone need any errands run in Casper?"

There was no response from his family, but then he wasn't particularly interested in one from them. His eyes focused on Anna. "How about you?"

"No, thanks," she said, never looking at him. "Though if I'd thought about it yesterday, I would've asked you to deliver my friend's birthday card for me. But I put it in the mail."

He didn't believe her. After their conversation on Tuesday night, she'd been avoiding him. Or it had seemed that way to him.

"Why not come to Casper with me?" Brett suggested, an idea forming in his head. "I'd enjoy the company for the drive, and you can take your friend to lunch."

"Thanks, but I'm sure Lisa has to work today."

Brett gave her a speculative look. He wasn't sure why he was so determined to spend time with Anna, but he was. In the past few days, he'd casually questioned his brothers about her, but they didn't know much. He'd asked a few friends around town, but no one knew whom she was dating or anything about her personal life. For some reason, she seemed to keep to herself.

Now he persisted. "She'd still get some time off for lunch. Why don't you give her a call?"

Before Anna could say no, Janie chipped in her opinion. "I

think you should go, Anna. You never take time off. You deserve a break.''

"You could at least give your friend a call. It can't hurt anything," Jake added, smiling.

Brett sat back, silent, his arms crossed over his chest, letting his family do the persuading for him. Sometimes it paid to have an interfering family.

"But I thought you were gonna pick up Sylvia at three," Red suddenly said. "You won't be there in time for lunch."

Brett held back the epithet that rose to his lips. Anna had almost been convinced. Now she stared at him, really looking at him for the first time, her blue eyes large with question.

"I decided to go in a little early, do some errands. I'll be leaving about nine. We'll be there in plenty of time for lunch. Go call your friend, Anna."

"Are you sure?" Anna asked. "Perhaps your fiancée is looking forward to a quiet ride back alone with you."

"We'll have plenty of time to be alone. Don't worry about that."

"Yes, Anna, go," Janie urged.

Brett watched Janie wink at Megan and wondered what his sisters-in-law were up to, but he really didn't care as long as it helped him persuade Anna to accompany him.

She finally left the table. Brett pretended great interest in his breakfast while the rest of the family discussed the day. He ignored their comments and questions and directed a question to Jake. "Is it okay if I take the sedan?"

Each of the brothers had his own pickup, but the family also kept a sedan for more-formal outings.

"I don't know if it's back from the mechanic. I'll check on it."

"Um, Jake," Janie said in a hesitant voice quite unlike her normal self. "I forgot to tell you Mike called about the car yesterday. He said you needed a new water pump but he had to send into Casper for the part. It won't be ready until Monday."

Jake turned to Brett. "Looks like it's the pickup. Sorry, brother."

"Sorry about what?" Anna caught the tail end of the conversation as she entered the room. After Brett filled her in, she balked. "Should I stay here, then? I don't want to crowd you."

"Don't be silly, Anna," Brett said, openly winking at her. "You won't take up much room."

"Yeah, you'll just give him an excuse to sit close to Sylvia," Jake added. Everyone laughed.

Except Brett.

"THAT WAS a brilliant move about the sedan," Megan congratulated Janie.

"It wasn't planned, honest. The mechanic needed more time. But I'd like to be there to see Brett's arrival. Can't you just see Sylvia hitching up into Brett's pickup?" Janie giggled.

Megan smiled back. "I know. She'll be horrified. She probably won't say anything in front of Anna, but poor Brett'll catch it later."

"He'll probably catch it for bringing Anna, too."

"Do you think our plan has a chance?" Megan asked after looking over her shoulder cautiously.

"I don't know why not. He's the one who asked Anna to go with him, not us. Maybe he's already interested in her."

"She'd be a perfect fit for the family...unlike Sylvia. Though Anna is right—I guess we do need to give Sylvia a chance."

"We'll see," Janie said, promising nothing.

BRETT DECIDED he must've been bad since his luck wasn't so good this morning. When he got to the garage, planning on bringing his truck to the back door, ready for Anna to join him, the truck's engine wouldn't turn over. In fact, it wouldn't do anything.

He jumped out of the truck and started back to the house to tell Red he was taking Chad's truck when Anna met him at the garage door.

"Ready?" she asked.

"Nope. Engine's dead. I've got to—"

"We could take my car," Anna offered.

In his mind's eye, Brett saw the fifteen-year-old mini-station wagon that Anna drove. "Do you think I'll fit in it?"

Anna grinned, and it seemed to him that her riotous red curls bounced and her eyes sparkled.

"We'll fold you up like an accordion," she promised.

"If you're sure you don't mind, we'll take your car, and I'll buy the gas." He liked the idea more and more as he thought about it. Anna could drive and he could concentrate on her. He wasn't sure why he had so much curiosity about the little red-head, but something drew him to her. Maybe she was the sister he'd never had.

"Let's get started," she agreed, still smiling.

With his knees pressing against the dashboard, Brett found he was more comfortable when he turned his body around toward Anna. He liked the view better, too.

"So, who is this Lisa?" he asked once they were on their way.

"A friend." She sent him a sideways glance, as if to see if her brief answer would satisfy him. When he said nothing, she added, "We shared an apartment the five years I was in Casper."

"Is she a nurse, too?"

"A dietitian, actually. But she works at the hospital."

"Don't tell me she's responsible for that terrible food they serve you."

Anna laughed, a delightful sound. "I'm afraid so. But it's good for you."

"Is that why you weigh ninety pounds sopping wet?"

She frowned at him. "I weigh more than that."

"Not by much. You need to eat regular meals." He watched the irritation build in her face.

"My eating is none of your business."

He grinned. "There's that temper again."

"I *do not* have a temper."

A chuckle was his only response.

After that, she refused all his conversational offerings for almost half an hour. Brett was content to ride beside her, studying her profile. She drove with competence and self-assurance, even when her jaw was clenched.

Today her red curls were pulled back on the sides by barrettes, leaving her big blue eyes to dominate her delicate features.

"Did you get your blue eyes from your mom or your dad?" he finally asked.

That question surprised her into answering. "My mother."

"And your red hair from your father?"

"No. My father was what they called black Irish."

"Do you have brothers and sisters?"

"Why do you want to know?"

"I was thinking about how much you work. Figured you didn't have time for family."

"No. No brothers or sisters. My—the baby died with my mother."

"So you're all alone?" he asked softly.

Her chin rose even as she kept her gaze on the road. "Lots of people are."

"Yeah," he agreed with a sigh. "I guess I was just thinking about how empty my life would be without my brothers. We're pretty close."

"That's an understatement," she said with a grin.

He smiled in return. When Anna was smiling, he had a notion he would feel the sunshine from a mile away. "Is everything going to be all right with Janie? I mean, why did Doc think you should move to the ranch?"

"He didn't. But there was a huge storm two weeks ago. It cut off the phone lines and flooded some low-lying roads. Pete got in a panic, afraid of what would happen if Janie had the babies during another storm like that. I think I'm here to reassure Pete as much as anything."

"I don't blame him. He's loved Janie for a long time."

"Yes," Anna agreed softly. "He and Janie and Chad and Megan are wonderful couples. It makes me feel good just to be around them and see the love they share."

He wished he could see her eyes as he asked, "Ever been in love yourself?"

"No."

"Why not?"

She shifted her gaze from the road to him. "Love isn't something you can order from a catalog, Brett. Why did you wait until now to fall in love? You're not exactly wet behind the ears.''

"Hey, are you calling me old?"

"If the shoe fits..."

"Well, even if I am a little past my youth, I have a good reason."

"And that is?"

"Don't tell me you haven't heard about Chloe, the Wicked Witch of the West." He felt sure Jake's ex-wife had been mentioned.

"Yes, I have. And I've also heard the theory that fear of marrying someone like Chloe kept all of you from venturing down the aisle. But I'm not sure I buy it."

"Why not?" Brett demanded, his hackles rising.

"I think the four of you used her as an excuse. You know, typical bachelor cop-out."

Only the grin she turned his way kept him from blowing up. Okay, he'd teased her. He guessed she had a turn coming. "And what do you know about bachelor cop-out?"

"Just what every single female knows, Brett. Most of us have heard all the lines." She rolled her eyes at him for emphasis.

A surge of jealousy startled him. No, not jealousy, he decided. Must be a protective instinct. Of course. He felt as if she were his little sister. If any man handed his sister a line, he'd want to punch him out.

"You mean you've already heard that your eyes are as blue as the sky on a Wyoming summer day?"

"Yes, I have."

"And your hair is as bright as the flame burning in my heart for you?" He emoted with the best of the melodramatic heroes.

"Brett, please," Anna protested with a smile.

"How about 'Your skin is as soft as a feather pillow,' or 'Your laughter is more melodious than a thousand bells'?"

She fought to hold back laughter as he continued.

"Your teeth are like pearls. Your lashes would make a mink envious. Your eyebrows are more delicately arched than the Golden Gate Bridge."

"And my freckles are like gold dust sprinkled across my nose," she added, giving in to her laughter.

He stared at her. "Someone actually said that?"

"Yes. Do you disagree?"

Pretending to consider her face carefully, he said, "Yeah. I think they're more like liver spots."

She reached over and swatted his arm. "So much for your silver tongue. You just flunked Flattery 101."

"Just kidding. Your freckles are perfect."

"Nice try, but I do have a mirror. Tell me about Sylvia."

Her abrupt change of subject told him she was uncomfortable being the center of attention. He obliged her, but he wasn't through learning about the little midwife. "Sylvia is beautiful, a good hostess. Lots of energy. I think we went out every night I was in town. I'd be ready for bed by ten o'clock, and she'd want to dance until two in the morning."

"I guess that's good. It takes a lot of energy to get everything done on a ranch."

For the first time, Brett really thought about Sylvia on the ranch. Could he picture Sylvia pitching in with the chores? Not really.

"Brett? Did I upset you?" Anna asked, a look of concern in her big blue eyes.

"No, you didn't say anything wrong. I was just thinking about Sylvia living on the ranch."

"At least she won't be intimidated by Janie's and Megan's beauty. You'll have the best-looking wives in Wyoming."

Anna smiled, and Brett felt the warmth of it. Sylvia was beautiful, but she had a different kind of beauty, he realized. A more artificial one. A cold one.

"Sometimes beauty isn't all it's cracked up to be," he muttered.

"I wouldn't know," Anna replied cheerfully, her gaze on the road.

"What do you mean?"

She took her eyes off the road to give him a look of surprise. "Isn't it obvious? *I* wouldn't be classed with your sisters-in-law."

He stretched his arm along the back of the seat and traced a finger down her cheek. "I wouldn't be too sure about that."

She gave him a look of disbelief and turned her attention back to her driving.

BY THE TIME they reached Casper, Anna was ready for the ride to be over. Brett was treating her like the other Randall men did—as their little sister.

She only wished she felt about him the way she did his brothers. But there was something different about the way she looked at Brett—and it was far from sisterly.

She'd made a mistake, accepting his invitation. After the other night, she'd avoided him and managed just fine. She'd almost convinced herself she'd imagined her reaction to him. But five minutes into their ride, she knew differently.

Why this one man out of the four should touch her senses as he did, she didn't know. Even though he was single, unlike Pete and Chad, he was as much off-limits. Whether he had a fiancée or not, he was a Randall, rich, powerful, important.

"Traffic doesn't bother you?" Brett asked as she wheeled around a corner.

"No. I adjusted to it while living here for five years." She pulled into the hospital parking lot, checking her watch as she did so. "Five before twelve. Perfect."

"Will Lisa meet us here or do we go in?"

"We?"

"Don't I get to go to lunch, too?"

She studied his face, unsure whether he was joking or not. "I just assumed— I don't mind you taking the car, Brett. You said you had errands to run."

"I lied. I just wanted you to come to Casper with me." With an angelic smile on his handsome face, he said, "Can I please come to lunch?"

Anna had been hoping for a respite from Brett's charm, but she couldn't refuse his request. "Of course you can join us, if you want. But we're not— I mean, Lisa and I are just plain folks."

"Not having met Lisa, I can't comment on her, but I don't think anyone would ever call you plain, Anna."

Fortunately Anna spotted her friend waving from the sidewalk at that moment. "There's Lisa."

Brett gave her friend a thorough male once-over. "Nope, she's not plain, either."

"You promised to behave yourself."

"No, I don't think I did," he replied, as if carefully considering her words. "But I will buy lunch since you're so nice to let me join you."

"You'll do no such thing. This is my present to Lisa."

"Well, I should give her a present, too. After all, I'm coming with you."

She stopped the car in front of Lisa, trying to ignore the man beside her. After getting out of the car, Anna gave Lisa a big hug. "I'm so glad to see you."

"Me, too. Who's the hunk?"

"A member of the family I'm staying with. Come on. He's going to join us for lunch."

Lisa crawled into the small back seat, and Anna made the introductions, then resumed her place behind the wheel.

"Hope you don't mind me horning in on your lunch, Lisa," Brett said, offering one of his charming smiles. "If you like, we can go to the Three Palms."

"I'd love to," Lisa exclaimed. "Though why they named a restaurant that here in Wyoming, I don't know."

At the mention of the pricey, upscale restaurant, Anna felt immediately uncomfortable. "Are you sure we're dressed up enough for the Three Palms?"

"You both look great. People wear almost anything there."

Anna looked down at her denim jumper and white shirt and wished she'd worn her only suit. But it was too late now.

When they arrived, Brett escorted them into the restaurant, where a snooty maître d' stood erect when Brett gave his name and requested a table for three.

"Of course, Mr. Randall. Right this way."

"We'd have been shown the door," Anna whispered to Lisa, "if we'd arrived without Brett."

The maître d' led them to an elegant table near one of the palm trees.

Anna took one look at the menu and had no doubt Brett could read the horror on her face.

"What?" he asked with a frown.

"There are no prices on the menu," she whispered, leaning toward him.

"I told you lunch was my treat."

"But I—"

A waiter interrupted her protest, and Anna gave up. She couldn't have a fight over money here. But on the way home, she would make it clear to him that she intended to pay him back. And she would.

Brett proved himself to be a wonderful host, making an effort to put Lisa at her ease and asking questions that drew her out. However, Anna began to realize that a lot of his questions included information about her.

"I bet you two must've had the busiest phone line in Casper when you were living together," Brett teased Lisa. "All the bachelors in town must've called."

Lisa giggled and blushed. "Well, we did all right. But no longer. I have news for Anna. Larry and I are getting married."

Anna, pleased for her friend, demanded more details. As Lisa told her about the wedding she'd planned for the fall, Brett didn't show any discomfort.

"You like weddings?" Lisa asked, looking at him. "You don't seem to mind our talking about mine."

"Weddings are great. We've had two already this year in my family, and I just got engaged myself."

Lisa's face fell, and Anna realized what her friend must've been thinking. She hurriedly said, "That's why Brett is here. He's picking up his fiancée to take her to the ranch for a visit."

Brett leaned over and patted Anna's hand. "That's right. And Anna came along to keep me company." He smiled teasingly.

Anna was distracted by a beautiful woman, a tall, elegant blonde, dressed in a Chanel-like suit, approaching their table. She pulled her hand out from under his. "Uh, Brett—"

"Brett, what *are* you doing?" came a caustic voice. "And with whom?"

It might be July in Wyoming, but the new arrival's words were coated in ice. And Anna had a pretty good idea who she was.

Chapter Four

Brett looked up, a smile on his face. Man, his fiancée was a beauty. He stood and hugged her. "Hi, darlin'. You're looking good."

Sylvia didn't receive his compliment with her normal flirtatious smile. Instead, she stared at the two women. "Who are your companions?"

"Let me introduce you. This is Anna O'Brien. She's the midwife staying with us until Janie has her babies. And Lisa McNabb, Anna's friend. It's her birthday."

"I still don't understand why you're here with them," Sylvia said stiffly, ignoring the greetings the other ladies offered.

Brett frowned. "The ladies said hello, Sylvia."

He was relieved to see Sylvia take the hint. He didn't think she'd be rude intentionally. Seeing him unexpectedly probably threw her off.

"Hello. Please excuse me. I was surprised to see my fiancé with someone else." She smiled, but Brett noted that the smile didn't emit much warmth.

"Anna kept me company on the drive in so she could take Lisa to lunch for her birthday. Since you were tied up with your father, I'm eating with them. Are you lunching here?"

"Obviously. I didn't realize you'd be here in time for lunch or I would've asked you to join us. Come along. I'll have the waiter find you a chair." She turned away without another word, expecting him to follow.

Brett remained where he stood. "Uh, Sylvia...?"

She stopped and looked over her shoulder. "Yes, lover?"

"I'm going to have lunch with Anna and Lisa. We'll see you back at the house later, like we planned." He smiled to ease the blow. Sylvia didn't like having her plans thwarted.

"What?" She stared at him, disbelief on her face.

"You know I don't like the political scene," he said with a grin, figuring she'd understand since they'd had several discussions about his aversion to politics.

"But, lover, there are several influential people at the table who'll do your career a lot of good." She stepped to his side to put both her hands on his arm.

"Not unless they're cowpunchers looking for a job, Sylvia. We're a little shorthanded on the ranch right now." He chuckled at his humor and noted Anna's amusement.

Sylvia wasn't smiling.

"Don't be ridiculous. I'm talking about your future."

An uneasy feeling in the pit of his stomach stiffened Brett's spine. But the restaurant was no place for an argument. "We'll discuss the future at another time, sweetheart. Go on back to your father, and I'll see you at three."

Sylvia glared at him and then directed her anger at his companions before she turned around and flounced toward the back room where private parties dined.

He resumed his seat and smiled first at Anna, then at Lisa. "Sorry about that. Sylvia doesn't like surprises."

"That's all right, Brett," Anna said quietly. "If you'd like to join her, we understand."

He liked the way Anna handled herself. She may have come from a poor family, but she was as much a lady as Sylvia. "Thanks, Anna, but I hate political groups. Sylvia knows that. She just forgot."

LUNCH WAS a drawn-out affair, partly because the service was slow and stately, and partly because they were enjoying themselves. Brett seemed to take Sylvia's snit perfectly in stride. He chatted and joked with Anna and Lisa as if his fiancée had never appeared.

But Anna couldn't dismiss Sylvia's glacial glare as easily. She was reminded of Janie and Megan's opinion of the blonde. As beautiful as she was, Sylvia didn't appear to be as close to perfection on the inside.

For Brett's sake, Anna hoped she was wrong.

"I really have to get back to work," Lisa finally said. "I've been gone longer than I should. But it's been so much fun. Thanks, Brett, for lunch, and for bringing Anna with you. I haven't seen her in such a long time."

"Actually she brought me. And I've enjoyed myself, too."

His smile was warm, and Lisa blushed. Good thing Larry wasn't here, Anna decided. He might be jealous.

Brett paid the bill, carefully hiding the total from Anna even though she tried to see it without being obvious. When her gaze met his, he was grinning at her, his eyes dancing.

After they dropped Lisa back at the hospital, he gave Anna directions to the Sanders mansion. As she carefully followed them, she asked, "Are you going to tell me how much the bill was?"

"Why would I do that?"

"Because I'm going to pay you back."

"You are a stubborn little wench, aren't you?"

"Little what?"

"Isn't that what you'd be called in Ireland?"

"We're not in Ireland, and this isn't the eighteenth century. And you're not going to distract me. How much?"

"Well, if you must know, it was twenty-five dollars," he said with a big sigh, as if he were suffering.

Anna chuckled. "That may have been the tip, but you know darn well the bill was a lot more."

"Really?" His brown eyes rounded with childish innocence. "Then I sure must've undertipped. We'd better go back!"

"Come on, Brett. Tell me how much so I can pay you back."

"Sugar, I told you lunch was my treat."

"But you don't even know Lisa!"

"Hey, I do now. I'm even invited to her wedding. You heard her." He grinned in satisfaction.

"Only because you forced her into inviting you," Anna protested.

He turned a sad expression toward her. "You mean you don't think she wants me to come to the wedding?"

"Brett Randall, quit acting so silly!"

"Now I really am hurt. I thought you liked me."

She huffed a big sigh of frustration. "You must've driven your teachers crazy."

"Nah. By the time I came along, they'd already suffered through Jake and Pete. I was a piece of cake compared to those two."

At his direction, she turned off the main road into an exclusive neighborhood. She forgot their silly discussion as her mind turned to another concern. "Brett, uh, I don't think Sylvia is going to like riding in my car. It's a little too old for this neighborhood."

Brett lifted one eyebrow and grinned at her. "I'm sure some of these houses are older than your car. It'll be all right."

"I don't think so. Sylvia wasn't too happy about your dining with us. Maybe you should rent a car to drive her back to the ranch." Anna figured nothing less than a limo would do for Sylvia.

"And leave you to drive back home alone? Don't be ridiculous. Sylvia won't mind."

Anna looked at the relaxed smile on his face and was almost convinced. Brett looked so sure of what he was saying. "Okay, but if she gets mad, don't blame me."

"I won't, Anna. Sometimes Sylvia gets upset, but I can usually talk her out of it. I'm a good talker," he assured her, his eyebrows wiggling.

She chuckled again. "I hope you're not overestimating your abilities, cowboy."

"Hey, we'll make a bet. If Sylvia refuses to go with us, I lose. But if I persuade her, I win and you lose."

"What would I win?" Not that she'd hold him to such a ridiculous bet, but she was having fun.

"The best steak dinner in Rawhide."

"Uh-nuh. I noticed you didn't offer the Three Palms again. Too rich even for your blood?" she teased.

"The Three Palms it is," Brett agreed.

"Wait. I was just joking. If I lose, I can't afford to take you there."

Brett stretched his arm along the back of the seat. "Tell you what. If I win, you can promise to deliver our first baby free of charge."

The automatic rejection that popped into her head surprised her...and told her she was in big trouble. She didn't want to think about Brett having a baby with Sylvia. "O—okay," she agreed, her voice trembling slightly.

"Hey, are you all right?" Brett asked, leaning toward her.

"Fine. Just fine. How many babies do you and Sylvia want? I might could give you a cut rate."

Brett chuckled. "We'll ask Sylvia. Maybe we can have twins, like Pete and Janie. That would save on delivery fees, wouldn't it? Especially if that was the first baby. After all, we're getting that one free."

"Don't be too confident. You haven't won the bet yet." And Anna wasn't too sure he would. He gestured to a driveway, and she pulled in, parking her rusted-out wagon right behind a silver Rolls-Royce.

"Maybe I should wait in the car," she suggested.

"Nope. I'm not going in there alone. I'd be too scared."

He laughed when she stared at him, surprise on her face.

"You're teasing me."

"Yeah, sugar, I'm teasing you. Sylvia and her dad are regular people. Come on." He slid out of her car and stood beside it, waiting for her to join him.

She wished she could lock the doors and refuse to get out, but that would be childish. Instead, she drew a deep breath and prepared for the worst.

Brett took her arm and led her up the wide steps. Punching the doorbell, he leaned against the gray stone wall, staring down at her.

"What are you looking at?"

"All that bright red hair. You're kind of like Rudolph the Red-Nosed Reindeer, aren't you?"

His reply took her by surprise, and the temper he always teased her about flared. "How dare you? My hair—"

The door swung open, and a uniformed maid stared at them. Then she recognized Brett. "Mr. Randall! Come in. Miss Sanders is expecting you."

Brett smiled at the maid before turning back to Anna. "After you, Miss O'Brien." He winked at her.

Anna suspected he'd teased her on purpose, to distract her from the nerves building in her stomach. It bothered her that her weakness was so evident to him. Raising her chin, she preceded him into the mansion.

The house on the Randall ranch was huge, but it was a home, warm and welcoming. Anna realized the decor of the Sanders mansion was elegant, but it left her feeling cold and distant. She couldn't help but wonder whether Brett noticed the difference between the two houses.

The maid was leading them into a sitting room when a tall man came down the stairs. "Brett! Good to see you again, son."

"Hello, Donald. How are you?" Brett said, extending a hand. After they greeted each other, Brett reached back to bring Anna forward. "Anna, let me introduce Senator Sanders, Sylvia's father. Donald, this is Anna O'Brien."

"How do you do, Miss O'Brien," the senator said, but there was the hint of a question in his greeting.

Anna nodded, but said nothing.

"Anna's a midwife, and she's going to deliver Janie's twins," Brett added.

"I see."

Anna felt uncomfortable. It was obvious Senator Sanders still didn't understand why she was there with Brett. She wasn't going to explain. In fact, *she* wasn't sure why she was there.

"Is Sylvia ready?" Brett asked.

"You know my little girl," the senator said, smiling at Brett. "She's prompt to a fault. I wouldn't stand for any tardiness while she was growing up."

"Yes, sir, and I appreciate that," Brett assured him with a grin.

Anna wanted to point out that the lady who was prompt to a fault still hadn't put in an appearance. But she knew better.

"Come on in and have a drink. I've got a smooth bourbon

that you'll enjoy." Senator Sanders led the way into the sitting room.

Anna again held her tongue. With a father who had been an alcoholic, she abhorred drinking of any kind. But at least Brett wouldn't be driving.

"No thanks, Donald. I'm still full from lunch." Brett looked at Anna. "How about you, Anna?"

"No, thank you."

"Well, I hate to drink alone, but you forced me into it," their host said jovially, crossing the room to a small bar built into a cabinet.

He invited them to sit down, and they chatted for several minutes. At least, Brett and the senator did. Anna kept quiet and counted the minutes until she could escape the stuffy atmosphere. And if Brett Randall ever asked her to accompany him again, she knew what her answer would be.

"Lover, I'm so sorry," Sylvia trilled as she rushed through the door. "I had to take a phone call, but I'm packed and ready now."

"Good. We need to get started," Brett said, rising. "You remember Anna from the restaurant, don't you, Sylvia?"

Anna wasn't sure if Sylvia was genuinely shocked by her presence or wanted Brett to think she was. It didn't much matter. The real shock would come when Sylvia saw the car. Anna tried to hide her grin. The thought shouldn't give her so much satisfaction, but it did.

"Anna? Oh, yes, the midwife. Are we dropping you somewhere, dear?"

"No, I'm returning to the ranch with you."

Whatever niceness Sylvia had been exhibiting disappeared, replaced by a coldness that chilled the room. "Oh?" She turned to Brett. "I don't understand."

And she doesn't sound like she wants to, either. Anna watched Brett for his reaction.

"I told you Anna rode in with me. She's here for the day, like me. So of course we'll all go home together." He offered her a warm smile and slid his arm around Sylvia's waist.

Anna sighed. The woman didn't know when she had it good.

"But, lover, I'd planned on us having a long talk while we were driving to the ranch. A *private* talk."

"Don't worry, Sylvia. Anna's like a part of the family now. You can talk in front of her. She won't mind, will you, Anna?"

Brett might be handsome, brilliant, warm, and caring, but he knew absolutely nothing about women. Not if he thought that line would work. Anna could only nod and say, "Of course not, Miss Sanders. I'll be busy driving anyway. In fact, you and Brett can sit in the back together."

"Hey, wait a minute," Brett protested. "I wouldn't be able to walk when we got to the ranch if I rode in that cramped back seat, and you know it, Red!"

"Don't call me Red," Anna protested, forgetting her grand surroundings.

Brett grinned, that twinkle back in his eye. "I think you're just trying to win that bet."

Before Anna could respond, Sylvia intervened, irritation on her patrician features. "Are you refusing to ride in the back with me?"

Brett turned his attention back to his fiancée. "Well, see, darlin', Anna's car is little. I'd be too uncomfortable in the back seat."

Anna watched as suspicion clouded Sylvia's eyes.

"What do you mean 'little'? The smallest Mercedes?"

Anna choked back laughter. Oh, this was going to be good. She had a feeling she was going to be dining at the Three Palms very soon.

Brett looked at Anna, as if expecting her to explain, but Anna only smiled and remained silent.

"Not exactly. See, I was going to bring my truck, but—"

"Your truck? You expected me to ride all the way to the ranch in your truck?" Sylvia seemed to choke out the words, then shudder as the thought sunk in. She turned to her father. "Daddy, we'll have to borrow a car. Is the Cadillac okay?"

"I'll need it during the week, but I guess I can manage."

"Yes, you can!" Sylvia practically jumped down the man's throat. "Or buy another one, if you have to. I—"

"But it won't be back here until six this evening," Senator Sanders said.

"This is a nightmare!" Sylvia shrieked.

"Don't worry about it, Donald. We can't wait until six. I'll have to be up early tomorrow morning to help with the branding," Brett explained. "I can't get back late tonight."

"Fine!" Sylvia threw up her hands. "We'll rent a car for the week. Call someone, Daddy."

The senator turned toward the phone, but Brett stopped him. "Not necessary, Donald. Unless you're not coming back with me, Sylvia. Because I'm riding with Anna in her car. Now, you're welcome to join us, but we won't be renting a car without a good reason."

The quiet authority in Brett's voice was impressive. Anna found herself wanting to jump to her feet and salute him. But somehow she didn't think he'd appreciate it. She turned to see how Sylvia was taking his ultimatum.

Sylvia's nostrils flared as she breathed deeply. After flashing a look at her father, she suddenly gave Brett a sweet, wistful smile. "Well, of course, lover, if that's what you want. I was only thinking of our comfort."

"That's what I want. I also want to get on the road, so how about we load your luggage and be on our way?"

"Of course, Brett dearest." Honey was dripping from her words. Until Brett turned and headed for the door.

Then Sylvia turned to shoot daggers at Anna. "I don't appreciate this situation," she hissed under her breath before spinning on her heel and waltzing after Brett.

Anna sat immobilized, too stunned by Sylvia's reaction to move.

"Uh, Miss O'Brien, I hope you'll excuse my daughter." The senator's voice carried sincerity. "The green-eyed monster sometimes overpowers her when it comes to Brett." He gave an uneasy chuckle. "Better not let her catch you looking his way."

Anna's stomach flip-flopped as she wondered if the man had realized how attracted she was to Brett Randall. But she hurriedly decided he was issuing a general warning. She couldn't have given herself away to a total stranger.

"Of course not, Senator Sanders. I don't believe in poaching even if I could compete with such a beautiful young woman. Your daughter is stunning." *In more ways than one.*

She must have satisfied the senator because he came to her side and gave her his arm as she stood. "Good. By the way, are you old enough to vote?"

She blinked several times before saying with a smile, "Yes, I've been voting for nine years."

"Really? It's hard to believe. Did you by chance vote for me in the last election? No, no," he quickly said before she could answer. "That's hardly a fair question. I should change it—be sure to vote for me in the *next* election. And if there's ever anything I can do for you, just let me know. I live to serve my constituents."

Anna felt as if she should be wearing an Uncle Sam hat and waving a little flag while a band played in the background. After all, she was pretty sure she'd just heard part of a campaign speech.

"Thank you, Senator. I'll keep your words in mind."

"You do that, little lady," he said, patting her hand in an avuncular fashion. "Now we'd better catch up with those other two."

When they stepped into the spacious entry hall, they almost bumped into Sylvia and Brett. They'd left the room seemingly in perfect tune with each other. Something had changed.

Brett turned around at their arrival, and Anna received a clue as to the problem. On the floor in front of them was a mound of luggage.

"Anna, look at this!" Brett gestured to the luggage. "She's packed enough clothes for a trek to the North Pole. Tell her this much luggage isn't necessary."

Making a mental notation to torture Brett sometime in the future, Anna smiled at Sylvia and said, "We're fairly casual in the country, you know."

Sylvia swept a glance up and down Anna, her expression making her opinion of Anna's fashion sense quite clear. Anna bit down on her bottom lip, struggling to keep any retaliation to herself. But more and more, she agreed with Janie and Megan. This woman would not do for Brett.

"I've agreed to ride in—in Miss O'Brien's vehicle, Brett. The least you can do is take my luggage with us. I just wanted to be sure I had the right clothes so everyone will like me." Sylvia gave him the wistful look again.

You'd better go pack more bags, then. Anna looked around guiltily, afraid she'd spoken aloud. But since both Brett and Senator Sanders were staring at Sylvia, she decided she hadn't committed such a horrible faux pas.

Finally Brett threw up his hands. "Okay, we'll load all your suitcases. Come on, Senator, grab a few of them."

The senator looked almost as shocked as Sylvia. "Uh, Maria will help you. Maria?" he called.

"*Sí, señor?*" the young maid said as she appeared.

"Help Mr. Randall with Miss Sanders's bags."

The maid bent to do his bidding despite Brett's protests. Since the young woman was smaller than Anna, she felt obligated to help her, too. While the senator and his daughter watched, the three of them headed toward the door, loaded down like pack mules.

They managed to get four of the bags in the back of the car and put the other two on the back seat, leaving just enough room for one person. Brett reached in his pocket and handed Maria some cash for helping. She tried to refuse, but he insisted. "Have a night out on me. You deserve one," he assured her with his easy smile.

"*Gracias, señor.*" She smiled shyly and slipped back into the house.

"Where is Sylvia now?" Brett complained.

"Surely you don't mean the always-prompt Sylvia?" Anna couldn't help asking. She knew she sounded catty, but she'd already endured a lot at Sylvia's hand.

Brett grinned. "She's never on time. Her father likes to believe she is, but I always end up waiting."

Anna was glad to find Sylvia failed to measure up again. She was quickly coming to dislike the woman.

But, she had to admit, revenge was sweet. Since Sylvia had

delayed coming out, they both had front-row seats to see her reaction to Anna's car.

When Sylvia spotted the car, she turned deathly pale and then looked at Brett. "Damn it, this had better be a joke!"

Chapter Five

Brett stared at the woman he'd promised to marry. She was beautiful. But he suspected her beauty wasn't as deep as he'd thought.

Carefully avoiding looking at Anna, afraid she'd been hurt by Sylvia's words, he opened the back of the car and began removing the suitcases they had just loaded. Still, no one spoke until he set the first two cases down on the flagstone entryway.

"Finally you understand, lover," Sylvia purred. "What if someone saw us riding in that—that vehicle?"

Without answering, he returned to the car to take out the other bags. When he rounded the car, he saw that Anna had removed the two bags from the back seat.

"Thanks, Anna."

With a wry smile, as if she hadn't suffered any insult at all, she murmured, "No problem. I'll see you back at the ranch."

He set the bags down with the others and reached to catch her arm. "Where are you going?"

Her eyebrows almost disappeared beneath her red curls, and Brett was surprised by the sudden urge to kiss her rounded lips. They were a natural pink that looked incredibly soft.

"To the ranch, of course."

"Well, so am I. Don't leave without me."

"Brett! What are you talking about?" Sylvia demanded from behind him. Brett turned to his fiancée. She was standing rigidly on the steps, glaring at Anna.

"I'm going back with Anna, as planned. You're welcome to

join us, of course, assuming you don't insult Anna or her car anymore. Or we can cancel the visit until a more…more appropriate time. Like maybe next year.'' Since it was the first of July, he figured Sylvia would recognize his sudden lack of interest in her visit.

The look of panic that crossed Sylvia's face surprised Brett. But he was grateful she'd gotten his message.

"I'm sorry, Anna. I didn't think about my, uh, my words upsetting you. Of course I'll come with the two of you.''

Brett didn't move. "Are you sure, Sylvia?''

She gave him one of those I'm-so-misunderstood smiles. "Why, certainly, lover. I couldn't bear the thought of you two— I mean of you going without me.'' She turned her gaze from him to Anna. "You do forgive me, don't you, Anna?''

He noticed Anna didn't smile, but she graciously nodded and murmured, "Of course.''

When Brett reached for the bags, Anna also stepped forward. "Nope,'' he said, catching her arm. He noticed his hand completely spanned her forearm. She was no bigger than a minute. "You don't need to reload any bags. You've done enough, little one.''

"Don't be silly—'' she began.

"Uh-uh. Get behind the wheel. And no pouting because I won the bet,'' he added with a teasing grin just for her.

She gave him a smile that lit up her face. "No. No pouting.''

He replaced all the luggage and then gestured to the back seat, half-full of bags. "Okay, Sylvia. Get in.''

In an instant, Brett turned away from her and, opening the front door, he slid into the passenger seat. "I'm ready,'' he said blandly. "Are you?''

In a huff, Sylvia flopped into the back seat and slammed the door. She didn't even wave to the senator as Anna headed out the driveway.

THE RETURN TRIP to the Randall ranch wasn't nearly as enjoyable as the morning ride, Anna concluded. There was too little conversation.

Anna had to admit she'd enjoyed the first few minutes as

she'd watched Sylvia slink down in the back seat and hide her face any time another car passed them. Not until they were on the freeway, out of her neighborhood, did she assume a normal position. Then she'd asked Brett to explain his comment about a bet.

"Ah, that's a surprise for you. Our first child will be delivered free of charge because of my astute bet." Brett's smile was genial, but it wasn't reciprocated.

Sylvia's reaction came as no surprise to Anna. She'd already decided Sylvia didn't have a maternal bone in her body and would welcome pregnancy as much as a beauty queen would want to wallow in a hog pen.

"I see," Sylvia said, obviously trying hard to keep her tone modulated. "The offer of free care is most generous of you, Anna. If we're on the ranch at that time, I'm sure I'll appreciate your assistance."

Brett pounced on her. "Of course we'll be living there, Sylvia. All the Randalls are born on the ranch. Even Janie, with twins, is having them on the ranch."

"Uh, Brett, that may not be true," Anna hurriedly said. "Things get tricky with twins. They come early, you know, and may need special care." She didn't want him to be disappointed if Janie and the babies had to be in the hospital. He'd spoken with so much pride.

"But that's why you're there," he replied simply, smiling at her.

The confidence in his voice warmed her heart, but she had to be honest. "Brett, I'm there to calm Pete, and to provide emergency care in case there's not enough time to reach the hospital or something else happens." She preferred not to think about what could occur. Births were unpredictable.

"You'll manage," he murmured, smiling at her again.

She could lose herself in those laughing brown eyes, she realized. Maybe Sylvia's visit was the best thing for her, whether Janie and Megan wanted it or not. Sylvia would be a constant reminder not to lose her heart to Brett Randall.

After all, he had already made his choice. While Sylvia might become her least favorite person, Anna had nothing to do with the Randall family. She ignored the sudden dip in her spirits. There was going to be another Randall wedding, this one between Brett and Sylvia.

And that was one wedding she wouldn't be attending.

"SO?" JANIE ASKED as soon as she and Megan had dragged Anna into the television room.

Brett and Jake were carrying Sylvia's bags upstairs to the bedroom prepared for her, with Sylvia following them.

"So what?" Anna stalled.

"Come on, Anna. We want to know what you think of her," Megan explained.

"She's very beautiful." Anna had already decided to stay out of Randall business. Most particularly Brett Randall business. And she wasn't going to mention to anyone her suspicion that Sylvia had future plans for Brett that didn't include living with her in-laws. It was even possible that Anna had misinterpreted her words. It could be that Sylvia didn't like the idea of Anna delivering any future children.

Janie shot her a look of mock disgust. "You're no help at all."

Megan, it appeared, wasn't as ready to give up. "Do you like her?"

Anna had always been painfully honest. How was she to tactfully answer this question?

While she pondered her words, Janie crowed, "You don't, do you?"

"I didn't say that!"

"Your face did. Don't ever play poker with the boys, Anna, 'cause you'd lose all your money."

"I'm not likely to play cards with them," Anna assured Janie, anxious to escape their private conversation. "Did I have any calls?"

"Nope. No one is in labor. Amazing, isn't it?" Janie said. "So, tell us why you don't like her."

Anna sighed. Janie wasn't going to let her get away. "It's just that...Sylvia didn't like the fact that Brett was eating with us when—"

"Wait a minute. Brett was eating with you?" Megan asked, her eyebrows rising.

"Well, yes. He would've had to eat by himself if he hadn't."

Megan patted her shoulder, a gentle smile on her lips. "Sweetie, Brett has more friends in Casper than there are people in Rawhide. He could've had companions for lunch until next Christmas."

Before Anna could say anything, Janie asked, "And you ran into Sylvia at lunch?"

Anna nodded. At Janie's exasperated prodding, she told them about Sylvia's reaction to Brett's appearance with her and then added a description of the scene at the senator's house.

Her words stunned the other two. Megan and Janie exchanged a surprised look and then turned to stare at her.

"I swear that's what happened."

Janie's shoulders slumped, and she sighed. "She must really love him, then. Otherwise, she would've pitched a holy fit about him offering to leave her behind."

"That's what I figured," Anna agreed, feeling as depressed as Janie looked.

"Then, for Brett's sake, we'll have to get along with her," Megan said, determination in her voice.

"Yeah," Janie agreed, not quite as determined.

"Yeah," Anna echoed, her heart breaking.

"WE'RE DELIGHTED you're here, Sylvia," Jake said as he set down the luggage. "Welcome to the family."

"Thank you so much, Jake. I'm delighted to visit. I've heard so much about your wonderful hospitality." She smiled warmly at his brother, and Brett breathed a sigh of relief. He'd been having some doubts about his engagement after the events of the day. But Sylvia must have just been in a bad mood.

"Get washed up, sweetheart, and we'll see what Red saved us for dinner. I know you must be hungry." He smiled and turned to follow Jake from the room.

"Wait a minute, Brett. Can't we...talk?"

"Now? Aren't you hungry?" He was. Lunch seemed a long time ago.

Sylvia stepped closer and slid her hands around his neck, leaning against him. "You haven't even kissed me today." She pouted and lifted her mouth to his.

Brett eyed her lips, covered with bright red lipstick, shiny, as if he'd slide right off if he touched them, and he thought of Anna's soft pink lips. Sylvia's were thinner, more—more precise. Disconcerting as his thoughts were, he kissed her.

When he pulled away, Sylvia complained and tried to pull his head back down.

"Anna will be waiting on us for dinner, Sylvia. We'll have some time later."

She leaned her body into his, and Brett was surprised when his didn't respond as it had in the past. He must be more tired than he thought.

"Where's your room? I thought maybe we'd share a room while I was here. You know, conserve *heat*," she added, writhing against him.

He shrugged off her invitation with a grin. "It's summer, Sylvia. No one would buy that line."

"It's the nineties, Brett. Your family would understand if we slept together." She pulled his head down for another kiss.

Brett accommodated her, but what enthusiasm he'd had was waning. He was a nineties man, true, but he still preferred for the man to do the chasing. And so far, it seemed to him, now that he came to think about it, that Sylvia had done all the pursuing.

He hadn't mentioned to his brothers that Sylvia had proposed to him. He told himself it really didn't matter. After all, he'd enthusiastically accepted.

Thinking about that moment, he realized his enthusiasm wasn't what it had been. Was he that fickle? He hadn't changed his mind, had he?

"What's wrong, lover?" she asked, pouting again. "Don't you want me?"

He noticed her lipstick wasn't as bright as it had been. That probably meant he was wearing part of it. "Do I have lipstick on me?"

"Of course. Don't you like my brand?"

The response that rushed into his head wasn't lukewarm or halfhearted. Nor diplomatic. He substituted that response with a more appeasing one. "I don't think lipstick is appropriate for any man, sweetheart. Even an engaged one."

"You're probably right. If I promise not to leave a trace from now on, will you forgive me?"

She puckered up again, and Brett began to feel trapped. He took her shoulders and moved her away from him. "It's time to eat. I'll see you downstairs."

"But what about our sharing a room? I don't want to sleep alone, Brett."

"We'll see," he promised as he escaped through the door, leaving her staring after him. As well she might. He'd never been slow to hold her, touch her. Why now?

What was happening?

Jake surveyed the table with satisfaction. They'd all decided to wait until Brett and the two women arrived to eat. Their first meal should be together.

They'd even invited B.J., Mildred and B.J.'s son, Toby, to eat with them. After all, Mildred had spent the entire day helping Red. It only seemed fair.

Conversation flowed around the table, and Jake watched the interchange. His smile gradually disappeared as he realized Sylvia seemed to be ignoring the women at the table. True, she'd been quite charming to him, and she was working hard at charming his brothers, but she seldom spoke to his sisters-in-law.

Even more troubling, she ignored Red and Mildred.

"Mr. Jake?" a little voice called, intruding on his thoughts.

He turned to the four-year-old he'd insisted sit beside him. "Yes, Toby? Need some more roast beef?"

The boy nodded, and Jake served him, then leaned over to cut the meat for him.

"I can do that," B.J. insisted. She was sitting beside Toby.

"I've got it. Enjoy your meal." After one swift glance, he avoided her warm smile.

"Brett tells me you're a veterinarian," Sylvia said with a small smile to B.J.

"Yes. We moved here around the first of the year."

"It seems an unusual occupation for a woman. So—so dirty." Sylvia shivered dramatically.

Jake stiffened, hoping B.J. didn't take offense. He might avoid the woman himself, because for some unknown reason she made him uncomfortable, but her work was excellent.

"I happen to like animals," B.J. said calmly, continuing to eat her meal. "Red, your roast is excellent. I hope you gave Mildred the recipe."

"It's not as good as that apple pie Mildred made for dessert," Red said, smiling at Mildred.

"Wait a minute. How do you know it's good since we haven't had dessert yet?" Chad demanded.

"'Cause I had an early sample, boy. Privilege of the cook."

"I need more iced tea."

Sylvia's announcement stopped the good-natured teasing. Everyone turned to stare at her. She was looking pointedly at Red, whose cheeks flushed as he leapt to his feet.

"Sit down, Red," Jake said, standing up. "You've more than done your share. I'll fetch refills for everyone."

Sylvia looked surprised. "Oh, I'm sorry. Does Red not serve at dinner? I just assumed… Please forgive me, Red."

Jake looked at Brett, and his brother didn't disappoint him.

"Red takes care of us, Sylvia, but he's not a maid. He's— he's more like a mother," Brett explained. He turned to grin at Red. "Except he doesn't wear pearls like Beaver's mom."

Laughter removed the awkwardness.

"Well, I considered them, but I figured they'd get in the way of all the cookin' I have to do to feed this bunch."

"And we're growing all the time," Jake chimed in as he moved around the table, refilling iced-tea glasses. "We might even have to add on rooms if Brett and Sylvia are as eager to begin a family as you others."

"Like you're complaining," Chad teased.

Jake grinned. Everyone knew he'd done some matchmaking so they'd have the next generation of Randalls underfoot.

"Oh, that won't be necessary," Sylvia announced, silencing the laughter. "Brett and I won't be living here on the ranch."

Chapter Six

Anna watched Brett from under her lashes. She'd been right when she'd deduced that Sylvia had no intention of living at the ranch. Had Brett suspected as much, too?

Brett sat frozen as his family stared at him. Finally he turned to look at Sylvia. "I don't think we've discussed that decision, Sylvia."

She trilled a laugh that didn't bring a smile to a single member of her audience. "Silly me. I was thinking ahead. Daddy and I made such great plans for my and Brett's future, but I forgot we haven't had a chance to talk about it."

"No, we haven't," Brett said, his voice even, but everyone could see the control it required.

When Brett didn't ask her any questions, Jake leaned forward. "What plans are those, Sylvia?"

Seemingly unaware of the wariness emanating from those around her, Sylvia beamed as she explained. "Daddy has created a position on his staff for Brett. He's going to be his personal assistant. We'll go to Washington when Congress returns to session. By the time Daddy is ready to retire, Brett will be prepared to step right into his shoes. May I present your next senator from Wyoming, Brett Randall?"

Whether or not she expected applause, what she received was a tense silence.

Brett was the first to speak. "Sylvia, I explained to you that I don't enjoy political games. I appreciate your father's offer, but I'm not going to take it. Nor am I *ever* going to run for the

Senate. I'm going to be a rancher, right here, with my brothers.''
He sat back in his chair and crossed his arms over his chest.

Intractable was too soft a word for Brett's attitude. Along
with everyone else, Anna watched Sylvia for her reaction.

"I—I'm sorry, Brett. I thought you'd be pleased— I'm so
sorry. Can't we— I mean, it's my life, too, surely— Oh!'' Covering her face with her hands, Sylvia leapt from her chair and
ran out of the kitchen.

"Damn," Brett muttered, his cheeks red. Then he, too, de-
parted the kitchen without saying another word.

BRETT HURRIED up the stairs after Sylvia. He didn't want to talk
to her right now, but he had no choice. Only a jerk would leave
her alone. She'd closed the bedroom door behind her, and he
rapped before opening it.

"Sylvia?'' Expecting her to be on the bed, crying, he was
surprised when she stepped from behind the door and wrapped
her arms around his neck.

Automatically his arms came around her, but he didn't tighten
the embrace. "Sylvia,'' he protested as she almost choked him.

"I'm so sorry, Brett. Please forgive me. I was only trying to
help, to build us a brilliant future. I thought you'd be so proud
of me.''

Brett took her shoulders and pushed her away from him so
he could see her face. She certainly sounded upset, but he noticed she hadn't shed any tears.

"Look, Sylvia—'' he began, almost ready to voice the feeling
that had been growing in him all day. She would call him fickle,
but whatever emotion had led him to accept her proposal, it
wasn't there now.

She pressed her hand across his mouth. "Please forgive me,
lover. I'll agree to whatever you want. I only want you to be
happy!'' Then she leaned into him again, her lips covering his.

Again Brett held her at arm's length. Things were growing
more awkward by the moment. How could he bring up his in-
decision when she was being so self-sacrificing? "Look, Sylvia,
maybe we'd better—''

"Make love to me, Brett. Take me in your arms and make

me forget everything. I promise to make you happy!" She pushed against his hold, reaching out for him.

"Now? Sylvia, the entire family is waiting downstairs, wondering what's going to happen. We can't—"

"Let them wait. *We're* more important right now. We're going to become one, to form a family, to have children. Don't you see, Brett?"

Brett had thought a number of times about having children, like his brothers, but this was the first time Sylvia had ever mentioned that possibility.

"You want children?"

"Of course! Don't you?"

"Yes, but—but I have to go downstairs right now. I can't leave them all thinking I'm moving to Casper."

"I know you'd like it there, Brett, if only you'd—"

"No. That's not going to happen, Sylvia."

"Whatever you say, lover," she said, uncommonly docile as she laid her head against his chest.

Brett stared across the room, confusion in his head. Finally he broke free from her. "I'm going downstairs."

"But you'll come back later? I want you so!"

He reached the door before she could grab him again and tried to leave with a noncommittal answer.

Sylvia had one last question, however. "I don't even know where your bedroom is, Brett."

It struck him as revealing that he didn't want to tell her. That was stupid. "The second on the left in the other wing."

Closing the door behind him, he headed down the hall to his bedroom. He needed to do a little thinking before he faced the others.

AN UNEASY SILENCE took over as everyone concentrated on dinner. Finally Chad asked Jake a question about the branding, and others picked up the strand of conversation. Anna, however, said nothing. All she could think about was the conversation taking place upstairs.

After the apple pie had been served, without the appearance

of Brett and Sylvia, Megan and Janie offered to clean up. They were immediately joined by B.J. and Anna.

Once the kitchen was cleared of guests and family, Janie turned a triumphant face to the other three. "See? Already we've won! I bet Brett takes her back to Casper tomorrow."

"Do you think so?" B.J. asked in surprise.

"Yes! We didn't think they'd be compatible. Anna had the idea of asking her to come here so Brett would discover it for himself, and it worked. You're brilliant, Anna!"

Anna didn't feel too brilliant. She found herself wanting Brett happy, even if it meant he married Sylvia. He deserved happiness. And it wasn't as if Brett's decision affected her, she hastily reminded herself.

"Anna?" Megan questioned, watching her, "Is anything wrong?"

"No, of course not. I'm not sure—maybe they'll work it out."

"Could be," B.J. contributed. "After all, you other two ladies went through some hard patches with Chad and Pete."

"Surely you're not hoping they'll marry?" Janie demanded. "B.J., can't you see she's all wrong for us? I mean, look at the way she's treated Red...and Mildred."

Anna saw B.J.'s shoulders stiffen. Like the Randalls, B.J. protected her own, and she loved Mildred dearly. "I don't like Sylvia, Janie, but Brett isn't going to choose his bride based on my likes or yours."

Anna carried a high stack of dishes to the sink. The sooner they finished the chore, the sooner she could retreat to her bedroom. She didn't want to be involved in this discussion.

Megan began rinsing the plates, and Janie started putting away the leftover food. B.J. joined Anna in her job.

"I know he's not going to choose his wife because of us, but you could see how upset he was."

"She did apologize," Anna murmured in spite of herself.

"Anna! You're not supposed to be on her side."

With a sigh, Megan turned from the sink. "I don't like it, but Anna's right. We shouldn't be taking sides. This is Brett's decision. But we're not doing anything wrong, B.J. All we're doing is trying to help Brett make an *informed* decision."

B.J. nodded. "And if he still chooses to marry her, you'll welcome her into the family?"

"Of course," Megan said. Janie nodded, and Anna grabbed another plate.

Just as she turned toward the sink, Anna heard footsteps coming to the kitchen. The door opened, and Brett stood staring at them. "Where are the others? Is dinner over?"

"Yes, but we saved you some apple pie," Megan assured him, smiling.

"Thanks, but, uh, Sylvia wants me to apologize for her. She didn't realize how set I was on living here at the ranch. She's agreed that we'll start our married life here."

"Oh…that's good," Janie said. Her enthusiasm sounded hollow, but Brett didn't seem to notice.

Anna hoped no one noticed her reaction, either. It wasn't that she expected Brett to turn to her if he broke his engagement with Sylvia. Of course she didn't. It was just that she wanted what was best for Brett.

Which, of course, didn't explain the depression that filled her.

Brett didn't seem any happier than the rest of them. With a dismal look on his face, he said, "Yeah. Well, I've got to find Jake." He backed out of the door, letting it swing shut behind him.

JAKE LAY IN HIS BED, his hands behind his head. It had been a long day, but he had a lot to think about. He'd had his doubts about Sylvia Sanders when Brett had announced his engagement. Her behavior tonight had done nothing to improve his opinion of her.

But if Brett loved her, wanted her, he'd support him to his dying day.

If what Brett said was true, that Sylvia had apologized and sworn she'd be happy living on the ranch, then who was he, Brett's brother, to complain? And she'd apologized to Red, too. After all, she was used to servants. He supposed her mistake at dinner was a natural one.

But somehow Jake wasn't reassured.

With a sigh, he settled down against his pillow. The sun rose early in the morning. He couldn't lie awake all night worrying about his brother's love life.

A few minutes later, just as he was drifting off, the turning of his doorknob roused him. But he figured if one of his brothers needed him, he'd make a more strenuous effort to awaken him. In the silence, he again sank into slumber.

Until cold, slender fingers ran up his back.

And warm lips traced his spine.

Man, he was having some kind of vivid hallucination, he thought with a smile. He couldn't remember the last time he'd had such a dream.

A warm body, ripe and voluptuous, rubbed against him, sending an alert signal all over his body. He was just considering turning over, to really enjoy his dream, when a sexy voice whispered in his ear.

"Brett? Why didn't you come? I've been waiting for—"

Jake almost landed on the floor beside his bed. He wasn't having a dream. Instead, he had a misguided visitor.

He reached for the bedside lamp.

"Uh, Sylvia? I think you've made a mistake."

Sylvia was on her knees on his bed, staring at him in shock. *Man, she was loaded for bear.* Jake couldn't help staring at her. Her robe was hanging open, revealing one of those black lace teddies he'd seen in the stores. Her breasts were barely covered, and the sides were cut up to her waist.

"Jake!" Sylvia half screamed.

"I think you've come to the wrong room," he said, hoping that was the explanation.

"But—but I counted! He said the second door on the left!"

Jake blew out his breath and wished she'd cover herself. He didn't like looking at his future sister-in-law in such disarray. "I imagine he forgot to mention the linen closet. He's in the second bedroom, but the third door."

"Ooh!" Sylvia exclaimed, frustration filling her voice. She scooted from the bed and wrapped her robe around her, then turned to stomp from the room.

Jake, now that he was alone and thoroughly awake, shoved back the covers and crossed over to close the door. He couldn't help looking out into the hallway to see Sylvia stomping down it in the direction of her room, not Brett's.

He guessed Sylvia wasn't the only one who'd be frustrated tonight if Brett was expecting a visit from his fiancée.

SYLVIA DIDN'T APPEAR at breakfast the next morning. Anna didn't think anyone was surprised. After all, she was pretty sure Sylvia's daily schedule didn't include breakfast at sunrise.

Brett, as he was leaving with the other men, asked Janie and Megan if they would entertain Sylvia today. They both agreed, false smiles on their faces. Brett didn't seem to suspect how little they were looking forward to that task. But Anna did.

Pete signaled for Anna to follow him to the door.

"Janie didn't sleep well last night," he whispered after she stepped outside.

"Thanks for telling me. I'll keep an eye on her today."

Brett turned back. "Hey, Pete, you flirting with Anna? I don't think Janie would approve."

Pete growled at his brother's teasing and leapt off the porch to head for the barns.

"You know that wasn't what he was doing," Anna scolded.

"I don't know. You're pretty hard to resist, little Anna."

The grin he shot in her direction had her heart turning flips. She gave herself a stern warning. "You'd better be careful yourself. Sylvia might be down to breakfast anytime now. She wouldn't take too kindly to your flirting, either."

"I'm safe. Sylvia won't be up for hours. I know her well."

He'd probably spent a few of those morning hours with Sylvia, Anna reminded herself. All the more reason to keep her own response to the cowboy under control. "Isn't Jake waiting for you?"

"You trying to get rid of me?"

"I'm trying to keep you out of trouble."

His hand came up to cup her chin. "Then we have a little problem, Anna, because I don't think about behavin' when I'm around you."

Her breathing sped up, and she scowled at him. "You're a terrible flirt, Brett Randall. Someone should warn Sylvia."

He stared at her, a wry look on his face. Finally he turned her loose and straightened. "Yeah. See you this evening."

Before she could steady her heart, he was on his way to the barn. Thank goodness he hadn't hung around. She'd have melted at his feet in no time.

She returned to the kitchen, trying to focus on the reason she was there, not on Brett Randall.

"Pete's hovering again, isn't he?" Janie asked.

"He's being a good husband." With that remark, she turned her attention to the breakfast she'd abandoned when Pete had summoned her.

"Little lady, you haven't eaten your eggs this morning," Red noted a few minutes later. "Are you feelin' poorly?"

Anna jerked her head up at Red's comment. "Oh. No, not at all, Red. I was just…thinking about my day."

"Got a busy one?"

"Well, I have a couple of calls to make. Not too bad, actually." She seemed to be going through a light caseload, with only five patients right now. Which left her too much time to stew about Brett and his fiancée.

"Well, whatever is ruining your appetite must be affectin' Janie, too," Red commented with a frown.

Anna whipped her head around to stare at Janie, sitting down the table from her. How could she have gotten so distracted by Brett that she hadn't noticed Janie's pale face?

It didn't take long to determine that Janie should spend the morning in bed. Anna felt guilty for having left her alone the day before to go into Casper with Brett.

The fact that Janie wasn't protesting going to bed told Anna that she was in need of rest. Janie usually fought any pampering.

When Anna got back to the kitchen, Megan asked the question she'd been holding back, afraid Janie might hear.

"Is she all right? Is it time?"

"Her blood pressure is a little high, that's all. I'll check in with Doc, but I don't think she'll deliver yet." Anna crossed her fingers that she was right. The babies weren't due for another four weeks. The longer Janie could carry them, the healthier they would be.

She crossed to the phone and dialed Doc Jacoby's home. Though he held office hours every other Saturday, it was too early for either him or the nurse, Mrs. Priddy, to be there.

After a brief conversation, Anna hung up the phone. "Doc agrees with me. She probably just needs rest. We'll keep her in bed all day today."

"Will you be making your calls?" Megan asked.

"No, Doc will make them. I'll stay here with Janie."

"Does that mean she's in more trouble than you're telling me?" Megan sounded anxious.

Anna smiled. "No. It means that neither Doc nor I want to take any chances with Janie. Or any of our patients. We're just playing it safe."

"I'm so glad you're here." Megan hugged her.

"Me too, Anna," Red added. "I don't know what we'd do without you."

Anna patted Megan on the back before releasing her and turning to Red. "You'd cope, Red, like you do with everything. Now, since I'm not going out, I believe I'll have a second cup of coffee."

"And finish your eggs. You'll need your strength to deal with Pete when you tell him about Janie." Red's worried expression disappeared as he anticipated that scene.

Anna groaned and sat down to pick up her fork. Red was right.

JANIE HAD FALLEN asleep at once, confirming Anna's belief that her friend had gotten too concerned about Sylvia's visit. Anna made several trips up the stairs to check on her patient.

Megan and Toby were watching a video in the television room. Mildred, after checking to be sure the noise wouldn't bother Janie, was vacuuming the downstairs while Red prepared lunch. No one seemed concerned about disturbing Sylvia.

Knowing the men would be in for lunch soon, Anna made another trip upstairs to check on Janie about eleven-thirty. She wanted to be able to present the best picture for Pete when he came in. Nothing would keep him from rushing to Janie's side, but the less alarmed he was, the better it would be for Janie.

Before going to Janie's room, Anna stopped off in her own room. She wanted to take her journal—in which she recorded the details of Janie's condition—with her.

The door that connected to the bathroom between her room and the one given to Sylvia was closed, but Anna heard movement on the other side.

Good. Sylvia needed to get up before noon. Anna sighed. She was being spiteful. It was none of her business if Sylvia slept until dinner.

How many times did she need to remind herself that Brett's engagement had nothing to do with her? Often, she guessed, since her heart beat faster when he was in the room. It was a good thing she knew he wasn't for her. But she didn't want him to be miserable.

The Randall men were wealthy and powerful, things she'd always feared. But she'd also discovered that wealth and power didn't necessarily exclude niceness, despite her experiences in the past.

In fact, it was Anna's theory that it was the niceness that had already cost the Randalls. While she'd scoffed at Brett's words about Chloe, Jake's ex-wife, she thought the Randall men were easy targets for any kind of scheming woman. Chad and Pete had gotten lucky with their wives, but Brett, even more easy-going than his brothers, was a disaster waiting to happen.

The urge to come to his rescue had to be squashed. He was a big boy and could take care of himself. Sure, he could.

She reached the hall just as the door to the room next to her own room opened. Sylvia, exquisitely made-up, dressed in a silk shirtwaist and heels, a cloud of expensive perfume around her, nodded at Anna and walked toward the stairs. "Would you tidy up the room before this afternoon? I may want to take a nap later."

She strolled down the stairs without waiting for Anna's response. Good thing. Because Anna, in spite of all her warnings to herself, was about ready to don a white hat, mount a white horse and ride to Brett's rescue.

Chapter Seven

Brett discovered a curious tug-of-war within him as he approached the house for the noon meal. He'd even offered to remain with the herd at lunchtime.

Jake, however, had insisted he come back to the house to spend time with Sylvia. And that was the problem. He didn't want to join Sylvia. He called himself all kinds of a jerk. After all, he'd agreed to marry her. He loved her. Didn't he?

"Ah, Brett?" Jake called to him as he was leaving the barn.

"Yeah?"

"I think I owe you an apology."

"What for?" Brett asked, frowning at his big brother.

"I'm afraid you spent the night alone last night because of me." Jake clapped him on the shoulder. "Or because of your poor directions, one of the two."

"What are you talking about?"

"Sylvia came to my room last night, thinking it was yours. She's, uh, a beautiful woman."

"Yeah."

When he said nothing else, Jake added, "I guess I upset her, 'cause she stormed back to her room."

"No problem." No, no problem at all. The only problem he had was that he was glad she hadn't found his room. Man, what was wrong with him?

Pete caught up with them. "I'm glad we're working close to the house so I can check on Janie. I had no idea having babies would be this hard."

Jake laughed. "Janie might beg to differ with you. I think she's doing the hard part."

"I know, but I worry all the time."

"Anna's with her," Brett assured his brother. "She'll take care of Janie."

"You've sure changed your tune," Pete challenged. "When you first met her, I didn't even think you liked Anna."

"What's not to like? She took me by surprise that first night, that's all."

"Yeah, she threw you to the floor," Jake teased with a laugh, "like that old bull of Pete's that no cowboy can ride."

Their teasing had no sting now. The longer he knew Anna, the more amazed he was that the kind, gentle young woman had handled him as she had. The memory of her hands on him as she'd straddled his back brought a smile to his face and a warmth that surprised him.

Must be overheated from the branding.

They had reached the house by this time, and Pete was the first in the door, with Brett and Jake right after him.

"Where's Janie?" Pete asked.

Brett surveyed the room, suddenly noting that the table wasn't set for lunch. "Where's Red? What's wrong?"

Even Jake frowned.

Anna stepped forward. "Nothing's wrong. Sylvia requested that we eat in the dining room for lunch. Red's getting the table ready."

The men all looked at each other. Jake was the first to speak. "Of course. Guys, I guess we'd better—"

"No!" Brett felt as if the word had been ripped from his throat. "No, it's ridiculous. We'd have to shower and change clothes just to go back out this afternoon and get dirty all over again."

"We can clean up for lunch, Brett. It won't be that much more if that's what Sylvia—"

The kitchen door swung open, and Sylvia entered. "Oh, Brett, darling, you're back." She ran to him, her arms extended.

He should've stopped her.

After all, there were things on his jeans she'd never encountered in polite society. Cow poop wasn't acceptable at cocktail parties in D.C. But then, he wasn't at a cocktail party.

"Hi, darlin'," he said, and welcomed her into a close embrace.

"Ooh!" she protested, backing from him, pushing his arms away. "You smell." Then she looked at the front of her dress. "You got me dirty! This is silk, Brett, and you've ruined it!"

He shrugged his shoulders. "I didn't ask for a hug, Sylvia. You're the one who insisted."

Red entered the kitchen as Sylvia stomped out of it. "What's gotten into Miss High and Mighty this time?" he growled. Then he saw the men standing across the room. "Uh, sorry, Brett."

Megan and Anna watched Brett, as well as his brothers. He grinned at all of them. "Hey, Red calls 'em as he sees 'em. I'm not taking offense. Do you think you girls could move lunch back to the kitchen while we clean up?"

Before they could answer, Pete repeated his question. "Where's Janie?"

"I'll set the table in here," Megan hastily said, and left the kitchen to collect the dishes from the dining room.

"Janie's in bed, Pete." Anna made a quick move and blocked the kitchen door as Pete started running. "Wait a minute. She's all right. I want you to be calm and upbeat. Her blood pressure was a little high, and she's been resting. The last thing I want is for her to worry."

Pete stared at Anna. "She's okay? The babies are okay?"

"They're all fine. And we want to keep them that way. You go up to Janie, and I'll bring a tray for both of you."

"You can stay in this afternoon, Pete," Jake added as Pete headed out the door.

"You sure you'll manage?"

"We made it all right yesterday with Brett gone. Now that he's back, we can do without you, brother," Jake assured him with a grin.

Once Pete had left the kitchen, Anna said, "Janie's fine. It's not necessary for Pete to stay here this afternoon."

"Yeah, it is," Jake replied firmly.

Both men followed in their brother's footsteps, but Anna

stopped them before they could leave. "Uh, Brett, there's one other problem."

"What's that, sugar?" He grinned at her, then realized she wasn't smiling. "What's wrong?"

She seemed to be struggling with an answer and he grew more concerned. "Anna?"

"It's Sylvia. She seems to think I should straighten up her room. With Janie not doing well, I don't have time to—"

Unexpected anger filled him. "She was out of line. I'll take care of it."

"I don't mind working around the house, Brett, but Janie is my first—"

Jake helped him out by putting an arm around Anna's shoulders. "We all know you'd pitch in, Anna. Sylvia is used to servants. She didn't think."

In Brett's mind, Sylvia hadn't been doing much thinking at all lately. Unfortunately he was beginning to believe he hadn't, either. After all, it was his fault the woman was here.

ANNA WATCHED Jake and Brett leave the kitchen with a guilty feeling in her heart. She'd just launched her first effort to rescue Brett. It didn't matter that Sylvia had handed her the bullets. She could've kept Sylvia's order to herself, simply ignored the woman.

But she hadn't. Because Janie and Megan were right. Sylvia was wrong for Brett. He deserved better.

"Did that female really ask you to clean up after her?" Red asked.

She'd forgotten he was there. "Yes, she did."

"Lord have mercy if Brett marries her," the old man muttered.

Megan entered the kitchen with plates and cutlery piled in her arms. "Everything okay?"

"Sure. I broke the news to Pete about Janie. He's with her. I need to take a tray up to them," Anna added. She'd almost forgotten her patient again, thinking instead about Brett.

Red helped her assemble a meal for Pete and Janie. She tread the stairs slowly, hoping to avoid spilling anything. When she reached the top and turned down the hall, Brett came out of his room.

"Anna?"

"Yes, Brett?" She drew a deep breath, hoping he'd think the jiggling of the dishes on the tray was from its heaviness, not his closeness.

"I want to apologize again for Sylvia."

"Please, Brett, it's all right. I just thought if you explained the situation, she'd offer to help out." She felt such a hypocrite. She knew Sylvia wasn't going to make any such offer. In fact, the woman would be furious with Anna for saying anything.

"I'm sure she will. And, Anna, thanks for all you're doing for my family."

"It's my job, Brett," she assured him, backing away. Heaping praise on her was only making her feel worse. At least she could assure herself that her motives were altruistic. She wasn't after Brett herself. She knew better.

He rested a big hand on the wall beside her. "I think you give a little extra. I just want you to know we appreciate it."

The man had no clue about women, Anna thought with a sigh. He believed Sylvia would apologize. And he believed Anna had told him about Sylvia's behavior because she didn't know what to do about it. "Thanks," she murmured.

"Where are you taking the tray? To Pete and Janie?"

"Yes, and I'd better hurry or everything will be cold." While she was getting hot just standing near him.

"I'll carry it for you. You come open the door."

When he took hold of the tray, Anna released it. After all, if she'd struggled with him, they'd have food all over the hallway.

"Is Sylvia coming down to lunch?" Thinking about Sylvia didn't reduce Anna's attraction to Brett, but it helped her remember how ridiculous she was being.

"Yeah. After she changes. Why would a woman wear silk for lunch on a ranch?"

"Brett, she was trying to look attractive for you," Anna said in exasperation. Not that she was on Sylvia's side, but Brett ought to appreciate his fiancée's effort.

"Knowing Sylvia, she was more intent on impressing you

ladies with her wardrobe. She knows I'm more interested in what's underneath the wrapping." He stopped and gave her an up-and-down look. "You sure don't need silk."

"Brett! Stop that!" She hurried on to open the door to Pete and Janie's room, after a brief knock. Then she left Brett to carry in the tray, escaping down the stairs.

The man was a terrible flirt! And she didn't want to risk her heart on a man who wouldn't want anything permanent with her. She knew from past experience that money married money. Besides, he already had Sylvia.

Her only concern, she assured herself, was to make sure Brett wouldn't end up married to Chloe number two.

AT LEAST BRETT KNEW his instincts were good. He should've remained with the cows at lunch. It would've been more peaceful.

He'd gone to Sylvia's bedroom after he'd cleaned up for lunch and explained the difference between life in her father's house and life on the Randall ranch. In fact, he'd been brutally honest about them. Guiltily he admitted to himself that he'd been hoping Sylvia would choose to leave, ultimately freeing him from the engagement.

After all, a gentleman wasn't supposed to withdraw from an engagement. Was he? But the thought of being permanently attached to Sylvia was beginning to turn his stomach.

Especially when he contrasted the time with Sylvia with the few minutes spent in the hallway with Anna. She was a sweetheart.

"Could someone please pass the potatoes…if it's not too much trouble?" Sylvia cooed, a beseeching look on her face, as if she was sure everyone was out to starve her.

Silently Anna lifted the bowl of mashed potatoes and passed it across the table to Brett so he could hand it to Sylvia.

"Thank you so much, Anna. I hope I'm not being too much trouble."

He couldn't see his fiancée's eyes, but Brett guessed she was staring daggers at Anna. To his amusement, the midwife appeared more than able to hold her own.

"Not at all, Sylvia. Red's food is so good, I can see why you'd want a second helping."

Her innocent smile had Sylvia steaming. She plopped the bowl down on the table in front of her without taking any.

"Don't you want the potatoes?" Brett asked.

"I've changed my mind."

"How's Janie?" Jake quickly asked. Brett guessed he was hoping to avert a fight.

"Fine," Anna assured him with a smile. "She's been sleeping this morning. A lazy afternoon ought to take care of things."

"I've heard walking is good for high blood pressure. You've probably been pampering her too much," Sylvia said, her voice sharp as she continued to glare at Anna.

Chad, who had his arm around Megan, raised his eyebrows. "I don't think you should prescribe for Janie, and definitely not for my wife, okay, Sylvia? I think your ideas might not work for pregnant women."

"Actually Sylvia's right," Anna said. "During a regular pregnancy, walking is good for the mother. As long as she doesn't overdo it. But in Janie's case, she's too far along for exercise. We need to curtail her activity in hopes that the babies won't come too soon."

Anna smiled at Sylvia, but Brett didn't think her generosity would appease his fiancée. It did something for him, however. In spite of Sylvia's treatment of Anna, she still could be pleasant. He smiled at her and noted her flushed cheeks in response. What a woman. They needed to look around the neighborhood and find someone for Anna. She shouldn't be alone as she was.

Too bad he was already— He broke off his thoughts to stare at her.

"Brett? Is something wrong?" Anna asked.

Darting a sideways look at Sylvia, he turned his gaze back to Anna. "No, nothing's wrong. I just had a—a sudden thought."

Like hell nothing was wrong. He'd just realized he'd much rather be engaged to Anna than to Sylvia. He'd thought himself a jerk for wanting to dump Sylvia only days after their engagement had become official. Now it was even worse, because he'd already found a replacement.

Silently he compared the two. Sylvia was beautiful, elegantly groomed, curvaceous, poised, sophisticated. Anna, her red hair in riotous curls, freckles sprinkled across her nose, slender almost to the point of fragile, couldn't compare in beauty. At least the average man would say that. Brett had trouble remembering his first impressions of her.

Now all he could see was the warm, generous heart buried in that small body, the blue eyes that a man could drown in, a smile that lit up a room. Dressed in jeans and a plaid shirt, Anna fit into his world. And his heart.

Sylvia didn't.

Now what was he going to do?

"Brett," Sylvia called, nudging him when he didn't respond.

"Yes?"

"When are you going to show me around? Can we go into town this afternoon?" She leaned toward him, exposing her décolleté.

"No, sorry. I have to work. Tomorrow afternoon, I'll be free. Right, Jake?" But Sylvia wasn't the one he wanted to spend his free time with. His gaze rested on Anna as she continued eating her lunch, seemingly unaware of the startling revelation he'd just had.

How did she feel about him? She had spent a lot of time avoiding him. Was it because he was an engaged man? Or because she wasn't interested in him? And how the hell was he going to find out? He wasn't free.

Jake's response caught his attention.

"Yeah. Sorry I can't spare you this afternoon, but with Pete staying here..." Jake shrugged his shoulders, knowing his brother would understand.

"I don't see why Pete has to stay here," Sylvia protested. "All Janie is going to do is sleep anyway."

Everyone turned to stare at her, and Sylvia stiffened. "Well, it's true. That's what she did all morning."

"How would you know?" Red asked testily. "You didn't get up until a little while ago."

No one came to her support, and Sylvia said, "I beg your

pardon. I didn't realize guests were expected to rise with the chickens."

Brett knew it was his duty to offer support, but he didn't want to. "Red didn't mean that, Sylvia, but you shouldn't have criticized Janie. She's pregnant with twins."

Sylvia's chin rose, and her jaw squared. "What am I supposed to do with myself all afternoon if you're out playing cowboy?"

"We hoped you'd help Red and Megan clean the lunch dishes while I see about Janie," Anna said softly.

There was a glint in her eyes that gave Brett pause. What was Anna up to? But he didn't have long to speculate. Sylvia grabbed his arm.

"You expect me to— What about that Mildred woman? Won't she do the cleaning up?"

"Around here, Sylvia, we all pitch in where we can. And you were complaining about having nothing to do," Brett explained. His fiancée kept revealing her selfish nature without any prodding. While Anna, on the other hand, offered a helping hand without any asking.

"After we clean up, I could take you into Rawhide if you want," Megan suggested.

"Oh, no, you don't, sweetheart," Chad protested. "You are to have your nap, just like Anna instructed."

"I see!" Sylvia said. "To be treated like a princess around here, a woman has to be pregnant! If you'd only told me of your shortage of help, Brett, I could've brought Maria with me!" Flinging down her napkin, Sylvia rose from the table and stomped out.

Brett stared at his plate, too embarrassed to look at his family. He'd definitely screwed up by getting engaged to Sylvia. What was he going to do about it?

"Who's Maria?" Megan finally asked.

"She's a maid at Senator Sanders's residence," Anna finally said.

Jake cleared his throat. "We probably need to give Sylvia a little time to adapt to our way of life. I'm sure it's quite different from her own."

Brett felt all kinds of a heel, but he didn't want to give Sylvia time. He didn't want her to adapt. He wanted her gone. But when, before lunch, he'd started to suggest they reconsider their engagement, she'd immediately become apologetic and pleading.

As she had after her announcement that they wouldn't live on the ranch. Both times he'd felt as if he would be kicking a puppy that was starving and homeless if he backed out of their engagement.

His gaze fell on Anna. She might fight back—in fact, had fought back—when he'd confronted her—but she'd never whimper. She had too much courage.

Her gaze lifted to catch him staring, and he grinned at her. She smiled in return, before reluctantly, it seemed to him, dropping her gaze to her plate.

"Why don't you plan something special for Sylvia tomorrow?" Jake suggested, continuing his train of thought. "How about a picnic after church? We could all join— No, on second thought, it might be better if the two of you had a picnic by yourselves."

"No!" Brett burst out before quickly modifying his response. "No, Sylvia and I will have lots of time to be alone. She's here to meet all of you and get to know you. I think a picnic is a great idea for all of us."

"But will Janie be able to go?" Megan asked.

Anna smiled. "If it's somewhere nearby that's easy to drive to. We could take her by car, along with a lawn chair for her to sit in. The outing would be good for her. She's beginning to feel too confined."

"Great!" Brett said with enthusiasm. And he didn't have to fake his enthusiasm. He could be a good host without having to be alone with Sylvia. And as long as Janie was going, he knew Anna would be there. Which increased his pleasure. "Let's make it by the lake. I'll take Sylvia there by horseback. She needs to get used to riding. Anyone who wants can join us. How about you, Anna? Do you like to ride?"

He didn't realize he was holding his breath until she nodded enthusiastically.

"I love to ride, but I don't get to do so often. Is anyone else going to ride?" she suddenly asked, looking around the room.

"I'll ride," Jake said, smiling at Anna.

Brett stared at his brother. Was he attracted to Anna? Brett had forgotten he wasn't the only unmarried Randall, since Jake said so often he'd never remarry.

"Maybe we should ask Mildred and her family, too. Toby would like to ride," Jake added.

"Good idea," Red agreed. "I'll ask her this afternoon."

Chad added, "I'll be the chauffeur for the pregnant ladies."

"But I wanted to ride," Megan complained.

"No way. We're taking no chances," her husband said emphatically, but he softened his words with a quick kiss.

Brett's gaze immediately flew to Anna. Her lips were pink and soft...and tempting. Maybe it was a good thing they were surrounded by family. He couldn't start kissing Anna until after he'd sent Sylvia packing. But he wanted to.

"Good. All you have to do now, Brett, is inform Sylvia of our plans. I hope they please her."

"Uh, yeah." Brett didn't think Sylvia would be pleased. Her idea of an afternoon's entertainment would be a concert, a cocktail party or going to the theater. How the heck had he ever thought she'd fit in here?

He guessed he'd been confused by how well she fit in the world of politics. He'd made the boneheaded conclusion that she would fit in well anywhere.

Tonight he'd tell her about the treat in store for her. Or maybe in the morning. It might be best to wait until they were in church. She couldn't protest too loudly if people were praying all around her. Could she?

Chapter Eight

"Have you come over to our side?"

Anna almost dropped the plate she was putting in the cabinet at Megan's question. Slowly she turned to face Red and Megan. "What?"

"You know what I'm asking. Red told me about Sylvia asking you to clean her room. He said you told Brett. And then at lunch you asked her to help with the dishes."

"I didn't think it was an unreasonable request," Anna said in a faint voice. She'd hoped her determination to free Brett from Sylvia hadn't been quite so obvious.

Megan grinned. "It wasn't, to anyone but Sylvia."

Anna smiled in return, giving up any pretense. "I know. And you're right. I've decided Brett should know what kind of woman he asked to marry him."

"How could that boy get so hoodwinked?" Red demanded. "I thought I taught him better."

Anna patted his shoulder. "I'm sure you did, Red. The problem with Brett, and all the Randalls as far as I can see, is that they're too nice. They're sitting ducks for any unscrupulous woman."

"I hope you don't mean me," Megan protested.

"No, of course not. You and Janie are terrific. But consider Chloe and now Sylvia."

"I know," Megan agreed with a sigh. "Chloe wanted the money and power. But what is Sylvia after? Her father is wealthy, and, as senator, has a lot of power. Why Brett?"

"He's handsome, good-hearted, generous and—" Anna had to force herself to stop. She could list Brett's attributes forever.

"I know. And that's why I thought we should give her a chance, but she doesn't love him."

"How do you know?" Red asked.

"Because she only thinks about herself," Megan said firmly. "Remember Solomon's test of love between the two mothers for a child? The one who put the child's welfare above her own was the true mother. Well, Sylvia puts her own welfare above Brett's every time. He would be miserable living in D.C., or even Cheyenne. But that's what she intends."

"She did apologize and say she'd live here on the ranch," Anna couldn't help reminding Megan.

"But did any of us believe her, except maybe Brett?"

"Not me," Red muttered.

Anna felt forced to play devil's advocate, if for no other reason than to assure herself she was doing the right thing by trying to expose Sylvia's behavior. "On the other hand, I think Sylvia will be miserable here, and Brett doesn't seem willing to put her welfare first."

"Exactly!" Megan said triumphantly. "He doesn't love her, either."

"Then why did he ask her to marry him?" Anna couldn't help asking the question, though she didn't want to hear the answer.

"Lust!" Megan said succinctly. "Pure and simple lust."

"Then you think they've already—"

Megan and Red laughed together, but it was Megan who answered. "Honey, the Randall men are, ahem, extremely normal. Well, not normal—I mean, they have the normal male appetites. But they're anything but normal." By the time she finished speaking, her cheeks were red and she was giggling.

Anna couldn't help smiling in return, even though she could feel her own cheeks flushing. "I think you're telling me more than I need to know."

Or wanted to know. She didn't want to think about Brett's hands on Sylvia. Especially when she compared her own figure to the other woman's. Another reason to know that Brett would never look at her. Compared to Sylvia, she was as sexy as a fence post.

"Some marriages have succeeded based on less," she said weakly, but she couldn't think of a single example.

"Oh!" Suddenly Megan gasped and put a hand on her protruding stomach.

"What's wrong?" Anna quickly demanded, moving to Megan's side, Red hovering behind her.

Megan beamed at both of them. "The baby moved! It definitely moved!" She reached out for Anna's hand to place it on her stomach.

Anna felt nothing, but she wasn't surprised. "Have you felt it before?"

"I wasn't sure. There have been little…I don't know… flutters, but I thought maybe it was indigestion. Oh, I can't wait to tell Chad!"

Anna and Red smiled at the thrill on her face.

"Why don't you go take your nap now? Red and I will finish up here."

After some more encouragement, Megan left the kitchen, her face still glowing.

Red turned to Anna. "And that's why we don't want Brett to marry Sylvia. He should have that kind of future to look forward to." He nodded to the door, meaning Megan. "I think Sylvia would expect her maid to have the baby for her."

Anna, too, wanted Brett to have the best—even though she wouldn't be a part of it.

BRETT HAD TO WORK harder that evening than he had all day during the branding. His family seemed determined to desert him. To leave him alone with Sylvia.

He didn't know if they were doing so to be discreet, or because none of them liked his fiancée. Whatever the reason, the end result was the same. So he worked even harder at roping them into activities that assured him he wouldn't be alone with Sylvia.

Anna wasn't any help because she was called out before they had come back from the pastures. She still hadn't returned. He found himself checking his watch and listening for her car instead of paying attention to the movie they were all watching.

When the movie ended, Red offered apple cobbler as a late-night snack. Sylvia turned it down, so Brett immediately accepted. "I'll see you in the morning, Sylvia," he said cheerfully.

"Aren't you even going to walk me to my room?" she demanded, a petulant look on her face that filled him with distaste.

He started to refuse, but then he discovered Jake's gaze on him. "Sure."

Sylvia said nothing as they walked up the stairs. She'd spoken little all evening, though she'd certainly cozied up against him on the sofa. The strokes she'd given his arm, his chest, his cheek, had been an invitation in which he had no interest. For some reason.

When they reached her door, she turned toward him even as her hand covered the doorknob.

"I know something more tempting than cobbler."

Since she pressed her body against him, guessing her meaning didn't take a lot of brain cells. He replied, "I'm crazy about Red's cobbler."

"Brett!" she protested, that hurt look coming into her eyes again. But he wasn't about to be dragged into her bed out of guilt. He didn't make love to a woman because her feelings were hurt.

"Sorry, Sylvia, but I've been working hard all day. A little pie, and I'll sleep like a baby."

"I bet I could help you sleep even better," she whispered, her lips seeking his.

He turned his head so that she kissed his cheek. "The cobbler will do just fine." He only hoped his brothers never found out he chose food over the sexy Sylvia.

Apparently his rejection finally got through to her because she shoved her door open and stepped inside. "Fine. Go have your stupid dessert. I'm beginning to think there's something wrong with you anyway!"

Slamming the door, an announcement to the entire household that she wasn't pleased, Sylvia ceased being a problem for Brett. For the moment.

When he entered the kitchen, his words were about Anna, still on his mind hours after he realized his interest in her. "Is Anna back yet?"

"Nope," Red said, nudging a plate across the table toward him.

Considering his words to Sylvia, Brett felt a singular lack of interest in the cobbler, in spite of the scoop of ice cream melting on top of it. He crossed to the window to stare out at the darkness. "It's pretty late."

"You know babies don't pay attention to anyone's schedule," Jake said.

"I just wonder about her driving late at night by herself." He turned around in time to see Jake and Red exchange a look. "What?"

Jake shrugged. "Anna can take care of herself. She handled you, didn't she?"

"Yeah, but...she's so little. With a heart as big as Wyoming."

"Yeah, she's a good'un," Red agreed.

Brett felt his chest swelling with pride...until he remembered Sylvia was his fiancée, not Anna.

"I hope Anna stays in the area," Jake said.

"What do you mean?" Brett felt his heart clench in concern. "Why wouldn't she stay here?"

"Doc says there may not be enough customers to keep her here. We Randalls have increased her business this year, but I don't know if you and Sylvia will be as anxious to start your family as the others."

"But she has other patients," Brett insisted, ignoring the question about him and Sylvia. "She's not just taking care of Janie and Megan."

"Nope, but Doc says these things come in groups. There are a few women expecting right now, but Doc only delivered four babies the entire past year."

"Can't she do other nursing?"

"Sure. She helps out at Doc's office or the hospital when they need someone." Jake took another bite of his dessert, and Brett wanted to grab the spoon from his hand. What did food matter when they were talking about Anna leaving?

"Aren't you gonna eat your cobbler?" Red asked as if he could read Brett's mind.

Knowing that not eating would draw more questions he didn't want to answer, Brett took his seat and began finishing off his dessert. Maybe if he drew it out long enough, Anna would come home and he could make sure she was all right. He didn't like these late-night sorties of hers, even if she could take care of herself.

Half an hour later, he could spin out the snack no longer. Red had already gone to bed, and Jake was becoming curious about Brett's lingering. He couldn't explain either reason to his brother.

Sylvia wanted him in her bed, and he was trying to avoid her.

Anna didn't want him, and he was trying to persuade her.

What's wrong with that picture? he asked himself. The fact that he was engaged to Sylvia.

He wasn't sure what he was going to do about her. He thought he should wait until her visit was over before he talked to her about calling off the engagement. But if she kept pressing him to come to her bed, he might tell her earlier.

After rinsing their dishes, he and Jake climbed the stairs together. Once upstairs, he stood in the center of his room, debating his options. Finally, feeling silly, he pulled the chair from the desk in the corner and placed it under the doorknob.

He didn't want to be surprised.

Probably he should feel flattered by Sylvia's determination to get in his bed. But he wasn't. Rather, he was growing more and more curious about Sylvia's behavior.

Eventually dismissing such strange thoughts, he stripped to his briefs and pulled back the covers. It had been a long day. He should be tired. Instead, he still found a restlessness in him that refused to let him settle down.

He leaned back against the pillows and picked up a murder mystery he'd started. He forced himself to read the words, but the story didn't take hold of his imagination.

The sound of someone in the hall had him bounding from the

bed, forgetting why he'd put a chair under his doorknob. He swung the door open just as Sylvia raised her hand to knock.

"Oh!" she gasped. Then she smiled. "I'm glad to see you're so eager, lover." She put her hands on his bare chest.

"Sylvia!" he exclaimed in surprise. How could he have forgotten? he wondered. But he knew. A vision of Anna had filled his head.

"Well, aren't you going to let me in?" Sylvia whispered, tracing the hair on his chest, pressing her lower body against his.

"Uh, I'm really too tired this evening, Sylvia."

Her eyebrows climbed even as her eyes filled with anger. "You didn't seem tired when you opened the door."

"I, uh, I don't—"

A noise in the hallway drew both their glances. Brett felt relief surge through him as Anna appeared at the top of the stairs. His defenses were forgotten, and he tried to move toward Anna.

Sylvia took full advantage and grabbed him around the neck, her lips covering his. He knew from Anna's point of view, the kiss probably had the appearance of intimacy, even though he kept his hands braced on the door frame.

"Thanks, lover. You were terrific," Sylvia said in a stage whisper before she strolled down the hall, sending a triumphant look Anna's way.

With no thought to anything but erasing the appearance Sylvia had given of their relationship, Brett came out of the doorway toward Anna. "Anna, wait!" But she turned away.

"Excuse me, Brett. I didn't mean to interrupt," she muttered, still walking away from him.

He got to her in time to grab her arm before she could reach her room. Pulling her around, he tried to explain. "Anna, it wasn't what you think."

ANNA DREW A DEEP BREATH as Brett stopped her. What was wrong with the man? She'd tried to avert her gaze, but it was hard to keep from staring at him. His broad chest, flat stomach and muscular thighs would be impressive to any woman. Late at night, when she was tired, lonely and distressed, he was almost irresistible.

Even in his underwear. Especially in his underwear.

No boxer shorts for him. He was barely covered by white briefs. She didn't care what anyone said; it wasn't as if he were wearing a swimsuit.

"Did you get any dinner?"

His mundane question disrupted her heated thoughts, and she looked up at him wide-eyed. "What?"

"Did you eat any dinner? Last time you came in late, you hadn't eaten. You didn't, did you?"

She supposed he surmised his answer from her stare. Didn't the man realize her mind was on anything but food? "I ate something." She couldn't remember what, but that didn't matter.

"Come back to the kitchen and let me fix you a snack," he suggested, reaching out to clasp both her arms.

"Brett, you're in your underwear!" she finally burst out. She hadn't been raised with boys. No matter how experienced she was, somehow standing in the hallway with Brett in his underwear seemed risky.

He frowned, as if he didn't get her point. Finally he shrugged those magnificent shoulders and said, "I'll put on some jeans. But you need to eat properly."

With Sylvia's cloying perfume clinging to him, his argument held little validity for Anna. She needed to get away from him before she did something stupid.

"No, thank you. I just want to go to bed."

He tilted her chin up. "What's wrong?"

She shook her head. If she started talking about the events of the evening, she might lose control.

"Did something bad happen?" Concern filled his eyes, making him that much more difficult to resist. "Was it the baby?"

"No, my car," she said with a sigh.

He blinked several times. "Your car?"

Yes, her stupid car. She was terribly afraid it had given up the ghost. Not that she hadn't gotten a lot of use out of it. But without a reliable vehicle, she couldn't do her job. And where was she going to get the money to buy another?

Discouragement filled her. She was just making a place for herself, feeling she'd maybe found a home. Now she might have to go back to Casper to work until she could save enough for a good car.

"Sugar, I was afraid something tragic had happened," Brett said, a relieved grin on his face.

She couldn't agree with him. "It *is* tragic!"

"Is there something you're not telling me?" he asked, bending toward her again.

She pressed against the wall. "No, just my car."

"Cars can be fixed, sweetheart. Where is it? And how did you get home?" His last question grew more urgent, as if he'd just realized she'd been stranded.

"Joe Eichorn was passing by and gave me a ride."

Brett sighed in relief. "Good. Joe's a nice old man. You were lucky. Why didn't you call me?"

Anna stared up at him. "Why would I call you?"

"To come get you. You've got a portable phone, don't you?"

"Yes, I do, but I'm not your responsibility. Besides, Joe came along almost immediately after my car died." Well, half an hour afterward. She'd been debating her options, considering walking back to the ranch, but she'd been at least ten miles away.

"I'll take you out there first thing in the morning and see what needs to be done about your car. We can go before breakfast. I'll call our mechanic and see if he can meet us there." He gave her a sheepish grin. "My heart's in the right place, sugar, but I'm not much of a mechanic."

"Call a mechanic out on Sunday morning?" she demanded, ignoring his last statement. "Do you realize what he'll charge? I can't afford that!"

"Hey, Mike owes me a few favors. He'll come without charging you."

"No! No, I don't take favors. I'll manage just fine, thank you."

She figured he'd take offense at her standoffish attitude. And that would be good, because then he'd release her and she could remove herself from temptation. Instead, he gently pushed a sprig of hair from her face, letting his fingers trail down the side of her cheek.

"And how will you manage, Miss Independent?" he asked, his voice as gentle as his fingers.

"Don't—don't do that."

"Don't do what?"

"Be nice to me. Try to take care of me. I have to stand on my own two feet."

"Everyone needs a little help every once in a while. Why shouldn't you?"

His warm breath skittered along her skin, and his body heat surrounded her. Only the lingering scent of Sylvia's perfume kept her from casting herself on his chest and letting his strong arms hold her.

"Damn it, Brett! Go back to your room and leave me alone."

His eyebrows soared. "I'm just trying to help."

"Well, help Sylvia, not me. You're engaged to her!" Using the last of her strength, Anna pushed away from Brett and tried to go to her room.

Brett, however, still held her in his arms.

Until another door opened.

"Am I interrupting something?" Jake asked.

Chapter Nine

Brett worked on catching Anna's eye as she sat in the church pew three people down from him. He'd tried to maneuver a seat beside her, but he suspected her determination was the reason he hadn't been successful. Chad and Megan sat between them.

She was upset.

And the cause wasn't the car.

She'd been embarrassed when Jake had caught them in the hallway in a near-embrace, with him in his underwear. He'd explained to Jake, or at least tried to explain. But that was after Anna had scurried to her room and closed the door.

He'd gone back to Jake's room and had a long talk with his oldest brother. It seemed to him Jake had been relieved when he'd explained his change of feelings about Sylvia.

Unfortunately, though, Jake said he should wait until Sylvia's visit was at an end to tell her he wanted to break his engagement. As a gentleman, he should give her the opportunity to announce their parting, even putting the blame on him if she chose.

Heck, Brett didn't care if she blamed the entire state of Wyoming as long as he didn't have to marry her.

He still wasn't sure how he'd screwed up so royally. Certainly his attitude toward marriage had changed since two of his brothers had successfully navigated those shark-infested waters. Janie and Megan were wonderful women.

But Sylvia? She wasn't cut out for life on a ranch. Why hadn't he realized it?

And then there was Anna. She was perfect. But there were five days to go before he could even show he was interested.

Interested? What an understatement. Jake had cautioned against moving too fast. After all, he'd only been with Sylvia about three weeks, though he'd known her for much longer.

Anna, on the other hand, was new to the area. He'd known nothing about her until the night she threw him on his back on the kitchen floor. But since then, he'd learned quite a lot about her. She was alone in the world, strong, courageous, independent.

She was also softhearted, loving, smart. And she made him feel comfortable…and uncomfortable at the same time. He loved being around her, trying to care for her, but he also wanted so much more.

Her blue-eyed gaze came up and accidentally met his. She quickly looked away.

He hadn't awakened her this morning to go find her car. Instead, he'd called Mike and met him alongside the road where she'd abandoned the little yellow station wagon. Fortunately she'd left her keys in her jacket pocket, hanging in the mud room.

After looking at the engine, Mike had shaken his head and uttered a few dire predictions about his ability to repair it. Brett's first inclination was to go out and buy her a new car, a better one that wouldn't break down. But he knew she'd never accept it. So he'd asked Mike to do his best.

So far, she hadn't let him get close enough to tell her what he'd done.

When the pastor dismissed his congregation, Brett realized he hadn't heard a word the entire sermon. It wasn't the first time, but he felt vaguely guilty.

He hurried after Anna as she slipped from the church and sought out Doc Jacoby. She was quietly talking to the doctor, her face serious, when he reached her side.

"So I don't know how I'll be able to make my calls," she said, her chin down.

Brett slipped his arm around her and interrupted their private talk. "Mike's working on the car today, Anna. And until it's ready, you can use my pickup. Hi, Doc."

"See? The problem is solved," Doc said, grinning at Brett. "Good boy, Brett. I'm glad to see someone is taking care of Anna. By the way, where's your fiancée? I thought we'd see her here today."

Anna was staring at him, her mouth gaping open, but he ignored her response. "Sylvia didn't want to get up early. I'm not sure country life agrees with her." That was enough of a hint for people to begin to wonder if the engagement would last without him coming right out and telling them.

"Better think carefully, young man. You don't want to get trapped like Jake did."

"No, I certainly don't." He stared down into Anna's angry blue eyes and smiled.

Doc gave them both a speculative look and then excused himself, giving Anna a chance to unleash her anger before she exploded. She pushed his arm from her shoulders.

"How dare you! I told you I'd take care of my business. I didn't want your mechanic coming out to look at my car!"

"Why not? He's the only decent mechanic from miles around. I can vouch for his work. So what's the problem?" He continued to smile at her, but what he really wanted to do was haul her into his arms and kiss away her frown.

She momentarily closed her eyes and then glared at him again. Through clenched teeth, she said, "No problem. Where's his shop?"

"Here in Rawhide. We can run you by now if you want, but we won't have much time. We're having a picnic, remember?"

"Since you're so generous in lending me your pickup, maybe you could catch a ride with Jake, so I won't hold you up. I may need to stay at the garage and talk with Mike for a while."

There was a determined look in her blue eyes that made Brett want to chuckle. She wasn't very big, but she was a fierce competitor. And they were competing.

"Nope. Jake and I are already riding together. Besides, if you're talking to Mike, he can't be working. And there's the picnic, remember?" he reminded her.

"I probably shouldn't go on the picnic."

"If you don't go, Pete won't let Janie, and you said she needed the break." He knew Anna's weaknesses. The welfare of her patients was important. She might deny herself the pleasure of the picnic, but she'd never do that to Janie.

"You're right," she muttered, and turned away from him.

He caught her arm. "Where are you going?"

"I rode here with Pete and Janie. I need to find them."

"You can ride with me and Jake. We've got room for you." In fact, he was looking forward to having her beside him and, if he was lucky, pressed against him on turns.

Her cheeks flamed, and she looked away. "No, thank you."

"Hey, you're not embarrassed about Jake finding us in the hall, are you?"

"You were in your underwear," she whispered ferociously, leaning toward him so no one could hear.

"But you weren't," he teased, a grin on his lips. Her flushed cheeks only highlighted her freckles, making him want to kiss each one of them.

"No, but Jake—"

"Didn't think anything about it." Not strictly true, but his warnings had been for Brett, not Anna.

"You two ready to go?" Jake called across the churchyard.

Anna turned and hurried over, her gaze lowered. "I came with Pete and Janie, Jake, but thanks for the offer."

"I sent them on ahead to get ready for our picnic. We've got plenty of room for you, Anna." He swung open the truck door.

Anna glared one last time over her shoulder at Brett and then climbed in.

He got in beside her and sprawled out so he took up as much room as possible. His left knee pressed against her slender legs as she primly sat between him and Jake. With a deceptively casual shrug, he ran his arm along the back of the seat and grinned at her again when she stared at him.

Jake got behind the wheel and started the drive back to the ranch.

"Jake, about last night..." she began, and then broke off, as if unsure what to say.

"Don't worry about it, Anna," Jake drawled. "I've already explained to my little brother that it's impolite to run around undressed when we have company. He won't do it again."

"I don't see what the big deal is," Brett protested. "After all, if I were working for Calvin Klein, I'd be paid a lot of money. You two act as if I've committed some big crime."

"You would do that?" Anna asked, looking at him without anger for the first time that day. He wasn't sure her expression was an improvement, however.

"You don't think I look good enough?" he huffed.

To his delight, she blushed again and looked away. "I didn't mean— Of course, you— Brett Randall, you're teasing me!"

"Maybe just a little, sugar," he said softly, and wished his big brother were anywhere but in the truck with them.

"Behave, Brett," Jake muttered. "Do you think Sylvia will be ready when we get back to the ranch?"

Brett knew his brother had inserted his fiancée's name as a reminder. He didn't like thinking about Sylvia, but it was probably for the best. He couldn't wait to be freed from the promise he'd given. "Probably not."

"A lot of people at church were asking about her. I guess word got around pretty fast," Jake commented.

"When doesn't it?"

"It's probably just as well she didn't attend," Jake added, his expression thoughtful.

"Yeah," Brett replied, and noticed Anna's big blue eyes filled with questions. He wasn't ready to answer any just yet. But soon.

ANNA CHANGED into her jeans and a short-sleeved shirt quickly. She wanted to make sure she was surrounded by others before Brett came down.

Of course, he'd have Sylvia with him this afternoon. Which was a good thing. It was too easy to forget that Brett was off-limits.

She should remember. His family, his wealth, his good looks, all those were the opposite of her. She knew she wasn't of the Randall caliber. Her experiences growing up the daughter of an alcoholic who barely kept food on the table had taught her the realities of life. Then, while she was in nursing school, a young doctor had underlined the lesson.

Running down the stairs, she hoped she should outdistance the truth that kept creeping into her head even with her past experience. But she couldn't.

She was falling for Brett Randall.

In spite of all the odds against her.

If she wanted to protect Brett from a divorce, she could have nothing to do with him. Just like Sylvia, Anna would be bad for him. Because he'd be ashamed of her.

The doctor she'd met at the hospital had invited her to a party. She'd been an innocent, unsophisticated. She hadn't fit in. And he'd dumped her at once, snarling something about her low-class roots.

"Ready, Anna?" Jake called as she reached the back porch.

His words snapped her from her thoughts. "Yes, I'm coming."

He was standing in the closest corral, tying the reins of several saddled horses to the railing. There was no sign of Brett.

"Need any help?" she called out as he headed back into the barn.

"Nah. We've got them all saddled."

The "we" gave her pause until she stepped into the shade of the barn and discovered Chad and Pete with Jake. "You've been working fast."

"Food always makes us Randalls get a move on. Did you bring your swimsuit?"

Anna stared at Jake in surprise. "My swimsuit?"

"Yeah. We're going to the lake. A swim will feel good after lazing in the sun for a while. You've got time to go back and get it."

Thoughts of Brett comparing her figure to Sylvia's, with hers obviously lacking, filled Anna's head. "Oh, I think I'll pass on that."

Pete stopped beside her to say, "You may pass on the swimsuit, Anna, but you won't pass on the swim. Not with these characters around. They'll just toss you in in your jeans."

Anna took him at his word and went to fetch her swimsuit. When she returned to the corral, she found only Brett waiting for her.

"What happened to Sylvia?"

"She went with the truck. Seems she doesn't like to ride." He seemed totally unconcerned with his fiancée's disappearance.

"Isn't that going to make life on the ranch a little awkward? I mean, shouldn't a rancher's wife like to ride?"

"Not necessarily. But I'm glad you like to ride."

She whipped her gaze from his smug look and stared over her horse's head. "We need to hurry." She wished she didn't sound as if she'd been running a marathon. But her heart was beating double time. And it was all Brett's fault.

"Whatever you say, sugar."

"You shouldn't call me that!"

"Why not? You're about the sweetest lady I know." He urged his horse closer to her, and she couldn't ignore the want that surged through her. He was close enough to kiss her.

"Sylvia wouldn't appreciate your saying that."

His grin disappeared as if a black cloud had passed over him. "Sylvia has other attributes. She has no cause to be jealous," he muttered.

Anna agreed. And Sylvia's best attributes would be on display when she changed into her swimsuit.

They rode in silence until Brett spoke again.

"You never did say anything about your love life. Was there someone you wanted to invite to the picnic?"

"No, no one."

He didn't complain about her answer. Instead, his grin returned, and he said, "Good."

Men! What difference did it make to him if she didn't have a boyfriend? Was he already planning on cheating on Sylvia?

She glared at Brett and urged her horse to move faster.

IT SHOULD'VE BEEN a wonderful picnic. The weather was idyllic, wide Wyoming sky, bright sun, gentle breezes. They were spread out on a grassy bank beside a deep blue lake fed by mountain streams. They'd eaten Red's good cooking until they could eat no more.

But Brett wasn't happy.

And he didn't think too many of the others were, either. Maybe Toby, since he was immune to Sylvia's petulance and complaining. The rest of them were having to suffer through her tantrums.

She complained because Janie was sitting in the lawn chair and she didn't have one. Fortunately Pete had brought several in case any other lady wanted one, so that problem was easily solved.

She'd complained because there wasn't any shade. Brett had offered to move one of the big trees a few hundred yards away, but Jake had cautioned him about his sarcasm.

A good thing, too, because with the mood he was in, he might have let the tree slip and land on Sylvia's head.

The darn woman had even complained about Red's food. Fortunately Red ignored her, especially when everyone else made it a point to tell him how wonderful his cooking was.

Any conversation they'd attempted had been ended by a rude remark from Sylvia. She seemed to think she was an authority on everything because she lived in a city. Ha!

He decided he must not be as smart as he'd thought he was for ever thinking he and Sylvia would be happy.

"Hey, Brett, come throw the Frisbee with us," Jake called out.

Brett was sitting beside Sylvia's lawn chair. He looked up at her. "Want to join us, Sylvia?"

"Hardly." The chill in her tone seemed to take the temperature down a few degrees.

"Okay," he tossed over his shoulder as he went to join in. "I'll be back later."

Fortunately the next hour erased some of the sour taste in Brett's mouth.

Especially when he tackled Anna.

Jake had divided them into teams, Brett, B.J. and Toby on one, and Jake, Pete and Anna on the other. When Anna grabbed for his Frisbee, he tackled her instead. They rolled in the grass, and he loved the feel of her against him.

The delightful scent of her enveloped him, and he wished he could roll with her to a secluded spot. Then he'd taste those soft lips, run his hands over her slender body, stroke—

"Hey! You're supposed to grab the Frisbee, not me!" she protested. She pushed out of his hold and sat up, looking adorable in his eyes.

"Wait a minute, you're covered in grass." He began running his fingers through her red hair, braided down her back in one plait. It felt like silk. When they made love—and they would, eventually—he intended to run his fingers through her hair to its very end.

"Don't. You're pulling out my braid."

He leaned closer to whisper, "Good. I've fantasized about unbraiding your hair."

"Brett!" With her cheeks flaming, Anna leapt to her feet. He hurriedly rose and pursued her. If he stayed close, he might be able to get his hands on her again.

I'm a sick person, he admitted, but he chased her anyway.

But Brett noticed she kept a constant distance between the two of them no matter where the Frisbee might be.

After having some lemonade to refresh themselves, the men announced it was time to swim.

"But where are we gonna change?" Toby asked.

Red and Jake were already busy taking care of the problem. Since they'd driven two trucks, they opened a front door on each of them and tied the blanket they'd put the food on between the two doors.

"The girls will all change behind the blanket. Then they'll come out and we'll change," Jake explained.

"I need more privacy than that!" Sylvia announced from her lawn chair, where she'd sat since they'd arrived.

Jake looked at Brett and shrugged.

Realizing Jake was telling him to deal with Sylvia's new complaint, he said, "Sorry, Sylvia, but that's the best we've got to offer. Of course, if you don't want to swim, that's up to you." Brett didn't bother to actually sound sorry. He was fed up with her being a spoilsport. "Hurry up, ladies," he added, grinning at the others.

Even Megan gathered up her swimsuit, though Chad protested. She argued, "I can paddle around in the water for a little while. Anna said it wouldn't hurt anything."

"I wish I could," Janie said wistfully.

Pete immediately plopped down beside his wife to entertain her. Brett stared at Anna as she watched the couple, a wistful look on her face.

He moved to her side. "You'd better hurry or you'll have to change with the boys."

She blushed and flounced away from him without speaking, but he didn't really think she was mad. He hoped not. He was looking forward to swimming with her.

Even Sylvia, apparently tired of being ignored, followed the other women. After a few minutes of tidying up the picnic area with his brothers, Brett whirled around when Jake let out a wolf whistle.

"What a bunch of beauties," Jake said with a grin, encompassing everyone from Mildred on down.

Brett shouldn't have been surprised to discover Anna in a utilitarian navy swimsuit, modestly cut. Megan and B.J., too, were in one-piece suits. Sylvia, on the other hand, sported a silver lamé bikini that seemed out of place. And very revealing.

However, her curves didn't excite Brett.

He was more interested in Anna's slender form as she clutched a towel close to her. "You're not going to wear that towel into the water, are you, Anna?"

"I might. The last time I swam in a mountain lake, I felt like I needed a coat."

He grinned. She was right. The water was going to be icy, in spite of the warm temperatures. But it would be fun.

"Do you mean the water will be cold?" Sylvia asked, startled.

"This isn't Old Faithful," Brett assured her as he grabbed his swimming trunks and headed for the blanket shield.

The women hadn't gotten in the water yet when he and his brothers, and even Red, emerged. Red, still wearing his boots, looked doubtful about what would come next, but Brett headed straight for the water.

In actual fact, they had built a small beach here. Jake had even had sand hauled in one year so they didn't wade into mud. With a call for the others to follow him, Brett splashed into the shallows and then dived. The bottom fell away fairly sharply.

When he came back to the surface, Sylvia was standing on the edge of the water in her bikini.

"Is it cold, Brett?"

"Sure. That's the fun of it. Come on in, Sylvia." But his gaze was on Anna. She was lingering at the edge behind Sylvia, talking to B.J. and Toby.

He should've warned Sylvia. He would've, he assured himself, but he'd been watching Anna. Sylvia, not realizing how quickly the water deepened, took several cautious steps, squealing about the coldness with each move.

Then she went completely under.

Chapter Ten

She couldn't swim.

One look at how Sylvia was floundering, and Brett swam to her. Jake and Chad hit the water at the same time, but it was Brett who reached her first, as she was going under again. With his brothers' help, he got her to dry ground.

She didn't go quietly. Sputtering and cursing, Sylvia would've put a sailor to shame.

"You tried to drown me! Damn you, Brett Randall, you tried to drown me!" she screamed after several minutes of ranting.

"Don't be ridiculous, Sylvia. I assumed you could swim."

"You didn't—" Sylvia began again, but her teeth were chattering.

Anna knelt and draped a towel around the shivering woman. Red appeared with a cup of hot coffee from the pot still sitting on the coals of their campfire. Sylvia reached out greedily for the cup, not bothering to say thank-you.

But if Brett thought such thoughtfulness was going to distract her from her accusations, Sylvia showed him differently.

"It's true. You wanted me to drown!" she screeched dramatically. "Ever since I got here, you've been mean to me." Tears pooled in her eyes.

Brett couldn't help wondering if she could call up tears on command. He'd heard of some women having skills like that. "Sylvia, you're being ridiculous."

"I want to go back to the house." She pouted pathetically and lowered her lashes.

Brett sighed and looked at his family, an apology in his eyes. His gaze rested on Anna. "Okay."

"We'll all go back," Jake said, smiling at everyone. "I imagine we're all tired."

"I'll take her back if you want to stay," Brett offered, though he'd rather share his ride back with Anna.

"I'm ready, too, Brett," Janie said from her lawn chair. "I'd like a nap out of the sun."

Pete immediately fled to his wife's side, abandoning Sylvia. Brett knew exactly how he felt. If Anna so much as stubbed her toe— Of course, she wasn't his wife. But she certainly dominated his thoughts.

He looked away only to have his gaze collide with deep anger in Sylvia's eyes. *Uh-oh.* "You want to change before we go back, Sylvia? The blanket is still in place."

"No. I want to go at once."

Pete stood. "I'll take my truck back right now, Sylvia, with you and Janie. The others can follow us later."

"I want Brett with me," Sylvia insisted, a coldness in her voice.

"But I rode over, Sylvia. I'll be there soon."

"No. If you really didn't intend to hurt me, you'll come with me. Someone can take your horse back." She was staring at him, determined.

"I'll lead your horse, Brett," Anna said quietly, and turned away to help Red begin packing up the remains of the picnic.

"Go on, Brett. We'll manage here," Jake added, a note of command in his voice.

Brett had no choice but to leave Anna. But he was going to make sure, real soon, that he did have a choice.

WHEN ANNA GOT BACK to the house, after helping to unsaddle the horses and rub them down, she was tired and ready for a refreshing shower. Megan, however, was waiting in the upstairs hall for her.

"Have you got a minute, Anna?"

"Sure, Megan. Are you feeling all right?"

"Yes, it's not that. Come to Janie's room."

"Is Janie all right?"

Megan smiled. "Yes. Stop being a midwife."

Puzzled, Anna followed Megan to Janie's door. Once they were inside, Megan and Janie urged her to sit on the bed with them.

"What's up?"

"Anna, we want to be honest with you," Janie began. "You know we've been against Brett marrying Sylvia. But we haven't told you that we want *you* to marry Brett."

"You're perfect for him," Megan chimed in, a warm smile on her face.

"No!" She almost shouted out the word, hoping it would drown out the pounding of her heart. She tried not to let herself think of her and Brett together—it was too dangerous. "No, I'm not perfect for him."

"Why not?" Janie demanded, a stubborn look in her eyes.

"Because I'm from—from the wrong side of the tracks. I've told you before, I learned a long time ago that the wealthy and the poor don't mix."

"I wasn't wealthy," Megan said.

"And my parents may own a ranch, but I don't," Janie added.

Anna laughed, a tinge of bitterness in the sound. "There's a difference. I would be as wrong for Brett as Sylvia is, just for different reasons."

"I've noticed you didn't say you weren't attracted to him," Janie argued. "Does that mean you are?"

Anna could feel her cheeks flaming, and she got off the bed. "My personal feelings don't matter. If you want Brett's happiness, you'll look around for some rancher's daughter, like you, Janie. That would be best for Brett."

"But, Anna—" Megan began.

"I have to have a shower," Anna said, interrupting her, and scurried to the door.

AFTER A SHOWER, Anna felt more in control. She had stood under the spray and reasoned with herself, squashing the dreams that Janie and Megan had nourished. She was not meant for Brett Randall. For the first time, she thought he might not marry Sylvia—but he would not marry her.

In spite of her renewed confidence, she debated going downstairs for dinner. She wasn't ready to be put to the test. However, skipping dinner didn't make much sense, either. When she discovered Red had prepared sandwich fixings, she made a plate and headed for the stairs. A reprieve.

The phone rang as she was leaving the kitchen. Something told her to wait.

Red motioned her to the phone. "It's Gabe Brown."

His wife, Carrie, was one of Anna's patients. "Hi, Gabe. What's up?"

"It's Carrie. She's not feeling well. I got her to lie down, but she keeps trying to get up again, saying she's got things to do."

"How is she not feeling well?"

"She's been throwing up."

In firm tones, she said, "You tell her I said for her not to get out of bed. I'll be there in fifteen minutes."

She hung up the phone and turned around to discover Brett standing right behind her.

"Where are you going?"

"The Browns'. Carrie's not feeling well."

"I'll go with you."

She stared at him. "Why would you do that?"

"Gabe's my friend, and anyway I think you're too tired to go by yourself."

"Don't be ridiculous. I go by myself all the time."

"But it'll be dark before you get back. And you're not used to driving my truck." Brett raised his chin and squared his jaw.

She shook her head in exasperation. The last thing she needed was Brett Randall beside her. "I've gone out in the dark before, Brett. Stay here. Sylvia may need you."

"Sylvia's already gone to bed for the night."

"Is she all right? Do you want me to see her before I go?" She didn't think Sylvia's behavior was normal—not even for a pampered rich girl.

"Nope. I think she's mad at me."

That theory held water. "Well, that may be true, but if she changes her mind and finds you gone with me, she'll be beyond angry."

"I'm not letting you go without me." He crossed his arms over his chest as if to punctuate the statement.

"Brett—"

"Why don't you let him go, Anna?" Jake's commanding voice interrupted her protest.

"I didn't know you were here, Jake," she said, catching sight of him over Brett's shoulder.

"Just caught the tail end of the argument. Take him with you, that way he'll stay out of trouble. And maybe he can be some help, too."

Anna couldn't tell Jake that Brett carried trouble with him. That being together in his truck would only create more problems. She licked her lips and found Brett's gaze pinned on them. "Fine."

She started to put her dinner plate in the refrigerator when Brett stopped her.

"What are you doing?"

"Putting this food away. I'll eat it when I get back."

"Nope. You need to eat. Wrap it up and eat it in the truck while I drive."

"What about you? Have you eaten?"

"I've almost finished. I'll grab another bite while you get your stuff." He loped off for the TV room, where he'd been.

"Don't worry, Anna. Brett will behave," Jake said with a grin.

But did Jake understand the problem? She doubted it, since the problem was her reaction to Brett. An engaged man. A man totally out of her reach. With a shrug of her shoulders, she followed directions. What choice did she have?

BRETT DROVE through the night, watching Anna eat her supper out of the corner of his eye. He drank some coffee from the thermos Red had insisted on filling.

"Is Carrie real sick?" he asked.

"It may be the virus that I heard is going around. But her pregnancy hasn't been trouble free, unlike Janie's. I don't want to take any chances."

"I ran into Gabe just after they found out about the baby. Man, he was excited."

Anna smiled, and Brett fought the urge to reach out to touch her. If he did, he might never let her go. And Sylvia waited for him back home.

"Most people are excited about having a baby. I feel sorry for the ones who aren't, though."

"Why?"

"A new baby is a miracle, a gift from God. Everyone should appreciate it."

"You're right. How many babies do you want to have?"

His question seemed to surprise her. She turned those big blue eyes on him, her brows raised. "Me?"

"Sure. Do you only deliver babies? Can't you have some, too?" He pictured Anna, her belly swollen with his child. That thought filled him with delight. Oddly enough, he couldn't even imagine Sylvia pregnant.

"Yes, of course, if—if I ever marry."

"Don't you think you'll marry?" Something in her voice told him she didn't expect to.

"I don't know. Here's the turnoff."

"I know the way. Why don't you think you'll marry?"

"I didn't say I wouldn't. And you could answer the same question," she retorted, and then blushed, the color visible even in the dashboard lights. "Sorry, I forgot you're engaged."

He laughed. "That's okay. Sometimes I forget, too." He wanted to tell her that he didn't expect to be engaged to Sylvia much longer, but that wouldn't be right. Sylvia should be the first to know that he wanted to break the engagement.

They stopped in front of the house, and Anna quickly got out. Brett joined her as they waited for Gabe to answer the knock.

"I'm glad you got here, Anna." Gabe sounded exasperated. "That crazy woman won't listen to me!" He nodded at Brett, but Brett could tell all his thoughts were on his wife. Brett didn't blame him.

All three of them found Carrie in the kitchen, seemingly going through the cabinets.

"Hi, Carrie, how are you?" Anna said in a deceptively calm voice.

"Fine. But I can't find my—my… I don't remember what I'm looking for." She whirled around and almost lost her balance. Even Brett could see that she looked pale.

"That's all right. I know just where it is," Anna said, taking Carrie's arm and leading her from the kitchen. The men trailed helplessly after them to the bedroom door.

"Wet several cloths and bring them to me," Anna whispered over her shoulder.

Gabe looked torn between doing her bidding and staying with his wife.

"I'll take care of it," Brett said, and returned to the kitchen. He found the drawer where Carrie kept her dishcloths and dunked several of them in cold water before retracing his steps. By the time he got to the bedroom, Anna had Carrie back in bed, softly talking to her.

In the same tone of voice, a lilting rhythm that almost entranced Brett, she said, "Take Gabe to the kitchen and give him some of Red's coffee."

Brett took the other man's arm and led him from the room.

"But I want to stay with Carrie," Gabe protested when he realized he was being taken away.

"I think we'd better follow Anna's orders. After all, Carrie seems to listen to her."

"When *I* talk to my own wife, she ignores me, disagrees with me." Gabe shook his head, as if unable to understand why, and Brett hid his grin.

"Women are contrary, aren't they? But what would we do without them?" He sat Gabe down at the table and got some cups from the cabinet, then poured coffee from the thermos.

Gabe accepted the coffee without comment. Finally he looked up at Brett. "I didn't tell you. Carrie was pregnant before. She lost the baby when she was about four months along. Tore her up. I was grateful *she* was okay, but she's mourned that baby every day since then."

Brett's stomach clenched. Babies seemed to arrive so effortlessly when he heard about someone having one. But he could tell now that it wasn't as easy as he'd thought. Of course, Janie and Megan would be glad to tell him that every day, but he really hadn't thought about it.

He reached out and held Gabe's shoulder. "Anna will take good care of her."

"Yeah, she's been a real help. Ever since Carrie found out she was pregnant again, she's been worrying. After she talks with Anna, she's okay for a few days. Then she frets again. And it isn't just about the baby. Some days she's sure I'm going to dump her because she's not pretty anymore." Gabe gave a disgusted laugh. "Can you imagine such silliness?"

"She really thinks that?"

"That's what she says."

"Having a baby must make a woman crazy," Brett decided.

"Yes, it does," Anna said from the doorway, a tired smile on her lips.

Brett leapt up and guided her to his chair. "Here, sugar, sit down."

She gave him a grateful smile and looked at Gabe. "I need to talk to you, Gabe."

"Shall I wait outside?" Brett hurriedly asked, but Gabe assured him he could stay. Wanted him to stay, in fact, to support him.

He pulled up a third chair and waited.

"Gabe, can you afford to have someone come in every morning and clean? Carrie is worrying because she's too tired to keep up with all the work there is to do. If you could hire a woman to work half a day and leave Carrie in bed until noon, I think some of the problems would be solved."

"Is she going to be okay?"

"I think so, if she gets enough rest."

"Well, sure, I'll hire someone. I don't know— How about Mildred?"

Brett looked up. "She's helping Red until Janie's babies are born, and maybe longer."

"I heard Betty Froman is looking for some extra work," Anna said. "You know their son starts college this fall."

"I'll call her." Gabe jumped up from the table, unwilling to wait till morning.

Anna stood. "I'll go check on Carrie again. Ask Gabe to write down all that Carrie ate today after he makes his call. Okay?"

Brett nodded and watched her leave the room. It was as if the light dimmed when the door closed behind her.

IT WAS ALMOST TWO in the morning before Anna felt safe leaving Carrie. With her history, Carrie's was a high-risk pregnancy. Because of that, Anna wasn't scheduled to deliver the baby, but she was working in conjunction with Doc to try to bring the baby to term.

Brett insisted on driving back, and she was too tired to argue. She leaned her head against the back of the seat and closed her eyes. The next thing she knew, they were turning off the road onto Randall property...and she had her head on Brett's shoulder, his arm holding her against him.

She tried to sit up, but he held her close.

"Shh, don't move. We're almost home."

"But I shouldn't—"

"Yes, you should. I didn't have to do anything back there, but you worked a miracle."

She let her head rest on his shoulder, distracted by his exaggeration. "I didn't do much."

"Yeah, you did. You not only calmed Carrie's fears, but also Gabe's. I didn't know that they'd lost a baby before."

"Gabe told you? Carrie didn't want anyone to know. She seems to feel losing the baby was her fault."

"Was it?"

"No. These things happen. A lot of times, we never know why." Her eyes drifted shut, and she struggled to open them again.

"Will she make it this time?"

Anna sighed against his broad chest. Strange that something so hard and muscular could make such a comfortable pillow. "Who can say? I hope so. I'll go over in the morning and see how she's doing. And convince her to let Betty do the cleaning."

He chuckled. "Too bad it's not Sylvia you have to convince. She doesn't have any trouble lying in bed while someone else cleans."

Anna immediately struggled to a sitting position. It was much too easy to forget about Sylvia.

"Hey! What happened? I thought you were resting."

She didn't want to answer his question, and she was grateful they had reached the Randall house. "Thanks for going with me and driving."

"No problem. Want me to carry you to the house?"

"No! No, I can make it. You're the one who'll have trouble. You've got to roll out early."

"I'll bet you won't be far behind me."

Probably not. But she'd do her best to miss him.

ANNA DID SLEEP a little later than usual the next morning. But not as late as she'd planned. She was awakened by a sound she heard a lot.

Someone was throwing up in the bathroom next to her bedroom.

Wearily she shoved back the covers and found her robe. Maybe Carrie did have a virus, and it had traveled to the Randall ranch. She knocked on the bathroom door.

The person cleared her throat and croaked out, "Yes?"

"Sylvia, is that you? Can I help you?"

There was a response of some sort, but Anna couldn't comprehend it. She opened the door to find Sylvia kneeling before the toilet. Quickly she hurried to her side to hold her forehead and brace her body.

After the bout of nausea was over, she led her to the sink and washed her face for her. "Have you been running fever?" she asked, feeling Sylvia's forehead.

"No!" the other woman snapped, showing no appreciation for Anna's assistance.

"When did you first feel nauseated?" Anna asked.

"About a week ago!" Sylvia retorted, anger on her face.

Anna felt foolish when she finally put two and two together. She should've known at once, since she was a midwife. But she hadn't expected it.

"How long have you known you were pregnant, then?"

Chapter Eleven

In the silence that filled the room, Anna feared Sylvia would hear her heart pounding. In spite of her warnings to herself, she'd hoped that Brett would break up with Sylvia. Now that hope was gone.

"I don't know what you're talking about," Sylvia retorted, but Anna noticed her gaze refused to meet Anna's.

"We both know you're pregnant, Sylvia. Have you seen a doctor?" Anna spoke with more confidence than she felt, and she hoped Sylvia didn't notice the trembling of her voice.

"No." Her response was abrupt and filled with resentment.

"How far along are you?"

"Just three weeks." She seemed to gather herself together and lowered her lashes in a modest pose. "The first time, we were so overcome with desire, it took us by surprise. We weren't prepared and—" She looked directly at Anna finally. "I'm sure you understand. The Randall men are so..." She shrugged her shoulders and didn't finish her sentence.

Not that she needed to. Even Anna, not married to a Randall man, could fill in the blanks. When Brett could turn her on without even touching her, she could easily imagine him causing her to forget anything and everything else.

But she didn't want to imagine him doing so with Sylvia.

"Are you having any pain?" Anna asked abruptly.

"Pain? Oh, no. Just this stupid morning sickness. How long does it go on?"

Anna forced herself to speak gently. "It's different with every patient. Sometimes six weeks, sometimes three months. When will you see a doctor?''

''I did one of those self-tests. I'll go see a doctor when I get back home. But please don't tell Brett you know. He wants to keep it a secret from his family until after the wedding.''

''No, I won't discuss it with Brett. But I don't think his family would object.'' In fact, a baby was the one thing that might sway his family to accept Sylvia.

''We'll break the news to them when we're ready. Besides, you have to not tell. Doctor-patient privilege.''

''I'm not a doctor,'' Anna said automatically. She guessed it was human nature to react to the smug expression on Sylvia's face. Especially when she'd just stomped all over her foolish dreams.

''Well, you just don't let on to Brett that you know, or you'll regret it. I won't stand for you messing in my business.''

Anna's cheeks flushed, and she clung to her temper, remembering Brett's teasing. ''And I don't appreciate being threatened. If you'll excuse me, I have work to do.''

She slipped from the bathroom without saying anything else. It was the only way she could control that temper she'd assured Brett she didn't have.

In her room, she sat down on the edge of the bed, staring into space. She'd actually come to believe that Brett would break off his engagement with Sylvia. She'd even dreamed that he would turn to her.

Foolish, foolish dreams. Even if Brett wanted to break the engagement, now there was a child to consider.

And after her bleak childhood, Anna would never wish the same for a baby who didn't ask to be born. She did everything she could to give each baby a healthy start in the world, but she, more than most, knew that wasn't enough.

Wearily she rose from the bed and gathered her clothes for the shower. She felt a strange reluctance to go back to the same room she'd just shared with Sylvia. But she couldn't go without a shower. And Carrie was waiting for her care, hopefully in bed.

ANNA SPENT THE MORNING chatting with Carrie and Betty, who'd been thrilled to earn some extra money.

"I feel so lazy," Carrie complained.

"Why? You're doing your job. Right now your first duty is to your baby. Gabe agrees. If that means lying in bed, eating chocolates, someone has to do it," Anna suggested with a grin.

"Chocolates?" Carrie asked, her eyes lighting up.

"A figure of speech, young lady. You get carrot sticks." She ignored Carrie's protests. "You just remember to stay down all morning. And take a nap in the afternoon if you feel like it."

"I think you're spoiling me," Carrie said with a sigh.

"Sure am. But if you're ever going to be spoiled, now's the time. Once that baby gets here, you're going to think back on these days as absolute heaven."

As she left the house just before noon, she ran into Gabe coming in for lunch.

"How's she doing?" he anxiously asked.

"Just fine. But you remember to wait on her and encourage her to stay off her feet. We need to keep that baby from delivering as long as we can."

"I'll do everything for her, I promise. Thank you so much for all you're doing, Anna. We're both so happy about the baby." His face was lit up with excitement.

"Try to stay calm, too. I don't want Carrie to get too excited." She suspected that warning would fly out the window. As she drove back to the Randalls', she thought about Gabe and Carrie and their excitement about the baby. Janie and Pete and Megan and Chad were thrilled about their babies, too. How did Brett feel?

Brett and Sylvia. She needed to start thinking of them together, permanently. The way she should've been thinking all along.

Instead, she'd cuddled up against him last night in the truck, which filled her with guilt. Even if she'd been asleep when she settled against him, she still hadn't moved away when she woke up. And Brett had encouraged her.

"Which either means that Brett's unbelievably friendly, or he's not the kind of man I thought he was."

Somehow she couldn't bring herself to believe Brett would cheat on his wife...or his fiancée. "Just goes to show what a miserable judge of character I am."

JAKE RODE to Brett's side as they approached the barn. "I hope Sylvia's okay after her dunking."

"I'm sure she is. We certainly suffered lots worse things as we were growing up." Brett couldn't keep the scorn out of his voice. He thought Sylvia was pouting.

"Brett, women are different," Jake began.

"No kidding, brother," Brett drawled. "Look, Jake, I know you said I should wait until Sylvia's visit was over to discuss ending our engagement, but I can't stand it any longer."

Jake grimaced and stared straight ahead. Brett tensed, waiting for his brother to respond. It wasn't that he couldn't break it off with Sylvia without his approval. But he'd rather have Jake's approval...and his respect.

"You're right," Jake finally said, releasing a big sigh. "I think I was wrong when I advised you to hold on for the rest of the week." He turned to Brett and grinned. "I thought you might change your mind again."

Brett rolled his eyes.

"Well, how should I know?" Jake complained. "You're the one who asked her to marry you."

"Actually she asked me. Maybe that's part of the reason I agreed. She pursued me...I mean, really pursued me. I guess I was flattered and—and thought there must be something there. She's beautiful...at least, at the time I thought so."

"I don't think she's gotten any uglier," Jake teased.

"Yeah, she has. Oh, I know her looks haven't changed, but I've gotten to know her a little better."

Jake shook his head, still grinning. "She's not exactly our kind, is she? I'm glad you woke up before the wedding."

"Me, too."

"So when are you going to tell her?"

"As soon as I can. It may mean taking half a day off to take her back home. I don't imagine she'll be any more interested in remaining than I will be in having her stay."

"I hope you're right. She's acted a little strange this week."

Brett thought of the several discussions he'd had with Sylvia when Jake wasn't present. Jake didn't know just how strange Sylvia had been. "Yeah," he agreed fervently.

After tending to their horses, the men headed for the house. As they reached the back porch, his pickup, with Anna at the wheel, came into sight. Brett stopped and watched it.

"You coming, Brett?" Pete called, holding open the door.

"I'll be there in a minute. Anna's almost here."

"Uh-huh," Pete responded knowingly, and Brett gave him a disgusted look before he disappeared behind the door. His brother acted as if he were juggling women all over the place. He wasn't doing any such thing. He couldn't help it that he'd fallen for Anna.

And still had a fiancée.

Maybe Pete had a point. And maybe it was a good thing he'd made up his mind to clear things up with Sylvia.

Anna got out of the truck, a frown on her face. He thought she looked more pale than usual and suddenly wondered if things had gone badly at Gabe's.

"Anna?" he called, leaping off the porch toward her. "Is everything all right?"

She jumped and gave a muffled cry. "You—you startled me!"

Her reaction made him even more concerned. The unflappable Anna startled in broad daylight? "What's wrong?"

"Nothing! Nothing's wrong."

"Carrie's fine?"

"Yes, of course. Why would you think she wasn't?"

"You've just spent the morning there, and you looked pale." His hand cupped her cheek before he could think about whether touching her was wise.

She jerked away from him, suddenly rigid. "I'm a redhead. I'm always pale." Her voice was almost lifeless, with none of the slight lilt that entranced him.

"You two coming in for lunch?" Chad asked, his head appearing through the open back door.

Anna responded to his question not only with a yes, but also with a quick movement that eluded Brett's hand. Before he could move, she had disappeared after his brother.

And there wasn't a damn thing he could do about it.

It was definitely time to talk to Sylvia.

When he entered the kitchen, he discovered everyone at the table except the one person he'd resolved to talk to. "Where's Sylvia?"

Red, carrying a large platter to the table, said, "She told Megan she didn't want any lunch."

Brett squared his jaw. *Good. The lady had just made arrangements for their private conversation, even if she didn't know it.* "I'm going to talk to Sylvia. Go ahead and eat without me."

NO ONE SAID ANYTHING after Brett left.

Anna avoided looking at any of them. And wished she didn't know what she knew.

Finally Jake said, "I think, when Brett comes back down, he'll have an announcement to make that will please everyone."

Anna hoped she held back the gasp she felt. Because Jake's meaning was obvious. He believed Brett was going to break up with Sylvia. Surely Brett wouldn't abandon his child. Or Sylvia, for that matter. After all, Anna had never held to the idea that only the woman had to suffer for creating an unexpected baby.

Megan let the bowl of mashed potatoes almost fall to the table, where it landed with a thud. "You think so?"

"It's about time!" Janie said.

Anna almost bit through the skin on her bottom lip. Had she been that wrong about Brett? "Why—why do you think that, Jake?"

"Brett talked to us this morning, Anna. He feels he's made a mistake, and the sooner it's corrected, the better off everything will be. I imagine Sylvia feels the same way."

"Brett said that?" Anna asked, unable to hide the dismay in her voice. She couldn't believe Brett would be so callous about the baby.

Chad, who had ignored the conversation to this point, concentrating on his food, looked at Anna. "Why do you sound so surprised? Engagements aren't permanent, like marriage. Brett has the right to break it off if he wants to.''

"I know, but— Nothing." Anna suddenly concentrated on her food.

"What's wrong, Anna?" Jake asked.

Anna peeped at him and found his gaze on her. She quickly looked away.

"Anna, I thought you didn't like Sylvia, either?" Janie asked.

"It's none of my business," Anna said quietly, wishing she'd never said anything. She put down her fork and pushed her chair back. "I—I forgot about a call I need to make. If you'll excuse me?" Without waiting for permission, she hurried out of the kitchen. If she stayed much longer, she might disgrace herself as Sylvia had this morning.

She hadn't gotten far down the hallway when Jake called her name. Dismayed, she turned to find him coming after her.

"Yes, Jake?" *Keep calm. He can't suspect anything.*

"Did I say something to upset you?"

"Why, no, of course not." She tried to keep her voice bright.

"Then why are you going upstairs instead of to the closest phone?" Jake asked, watching her closely.

"Um, I'm going to get my notes so I can make an accurate report to Doc."

"I thought your briefcase was in the kitchen."

Anna swallowed. Now what excuse could she give? She opened her mouth to try another lie, but Jake cut her off.

"Why do you want Brett to stay engaged to Sylvia?"

Anna fought to hold back the hysterical laughter that bubbled up inside her. *Want* them to stay engaged? Never! But she wanted Brett to be the kind of man who wouldn't abandon his unborn child.

"Jake, I can't— I mean, it's none of my business."

"Come on, Anna, tell me what's wrong."

With that gentle, caring voice, the man should have been a priest to listen to one's sins, except that he was too sexy to be monastic. Maybe he should've been a dean of students, facing wrongdoers in his office. Or maybe he should just be a father. He'd be a terrific one.

She couldn't break Sylvia's confidence, but she couldn't continue to pretend, either. "Jake, I can't tell you why, but I don't think it would be a good idea for Brett and Sylvia to—to break their engagement."

"And what reason would you have for saying something like that?"

Anna stared at Jake, wondering how he'd spoken when his lips hadn't moved. Then footsteps behind her gave her the answer. She turned with a sinking heart to face another Randall who spoke quite like his brother. "Brett!"

"Yes, Brett," he agreed, a smile on his lips that wasn't pleasant. He moved closer to her, and she backed away. "Are you going to answer my question?"

"N-no." She lifted her chin and squared her shoulders. "Besides, you already know the reason."

Jake interrupted Brett's steady stalking of her. "Brett, I gather you can handle this conversation. I'll be in the kitchen if you need me."

Brett nodded and took another step toward her.

"Wait, Jake. I—I don't think…" Anna protested, but without looking, she realized Jake wasn't heeding her request. Suddenly she was alone in the hallway with Brett.

"You haven't answered my question," he repeated.

She shook her head.

"Is it because you think my fiancée and I are eminently suited?"

She shook her head again. Speaking seemed beyond her.

"Or maybe you think I want a life in politics? You want to brag that you once fell asleep on the shoulder of the next governor?"

She bumped against the wall, feeling trapped. He leaned toward her, resting a hand on the wall on each side of her head.

"Or maybe, without Sylvia in the picture, you're afraid that I might take advantage of your sleepiness next time," he said slowly, his voice lowering with sensual intent.

Anna couldn't swallow, couldn't even blink, as his mouth dipped closer and closer to hers. He was going to kiss her. He was going to fill that need that had her heart hammering. He was going to…kiss her while the woman carrying his child was one flight up.

Anger surged through her, and she jerked away from him, ducking under one arm. "How could you?" she demanded, tears filling her voice.

Instead of coming after her, as she'd feared he would, he frowned, staring at her. "Anna? Why are you so upset? Surely you've realized I'm more attracted to you than to Sylvia? That's part of the problem. That's why I have to break the engagement."

"No!" she flung back at him. "You will not use me as an excuse to abandon your responsibility."

"What responsibility? The engagement? Isn't that the entire point of an engagement—to decide if the marriage will work?"

Her voice trembled as she tried to answer him. "I think your engagement has gone a bit too far for that."

"For what?" He seemed more confused than anything.

How could he be confused? How could he not understand how serious his situation was? "Brett, I know! Dear God, I know. I promised Sylvia I wouldn't let on to you, but—" She broke off and covered her face with shaking fingers.

The next thing she knew, he was cradling her against him, his touch comforting rather than sensual. "Shh, sweetheart, it's all right. Don't cry."

She hadn't even realized she was weeping until then.

"Whatever is the matter, we'll fix it, Anna. Everything's going to be all right."

He was wrong. Nothing would ever be right again, Anna suddenly realized. Because she'd made the foolish mistake of falling in love with Brett Randall.

The Brett Randall who loved his family.

The Brett Randall who was honest and true and sweet.

The Brett Randall who would never abandon his baby.

The Brett Randall who would never be hers.

"I—I have to go upstairs," she said, pushing against the comfort of his arms. But she'd been foolish again, because he had no intention of letting her escape.

"Tell me what's wrong."

How could he still sound so honest, so concerned? It seemed easier to stay in his embrace because she could bury her face in his broad chest and not have to look him in the eye.

He wouldn't even allow her that much. Strong fingers reached for her chin and pulled her face up. "I can't fix the problem if you don't tell me what it is."

"You can't fix this problem, Brett." As much as she wished he could.

He reached up to catch a tear as it struggled down her cheek. "Won't you at least let me *try* to play the knight in shining armor? It's always been a fantasy of mine."

She closed her eyes to hide the agony that filled her. The sweetness of his words reminded her of girlish dreams, dreams that could never be.

"Anna?"

He sounded almost as distraught as her. She opened her eyes. A calm descended over her, as if she'd finally accepted her fate. "I'm sorry, Brett. Babies are too important to me."

His frown returned. "What are you saying?"

"You can't break up with Sylvia."

"We're back to where we started. That's what you said earlier, but you never explained why." A rueful grin twisted his lips. "Not that it matters. I intend to break my engagement no matter what you say."

"You intend? Then you haven't yet?"

"No. Sylvia refused to talk to me."

"Brett, I know you and Sylvia have problems, but maybe if you got counseling…" she said in a rush, hoping to convince him before he could wear her down.

"Damn it, Anna!" he exclaimed, suddenly backing away from her. "Why do you keep harping on me and Sylvia?"

"I told you! Because of the baby!"

He stared at her as if she were insane.

Then he asked, "What baby?"

Chapter Twelve

Anna stared at Brett. Now she was the confused one. Finally she said, "Sylvia's baby...and yours."

"The hell you say!" Brett roared.

Before Anna could respond to Brett's reaction, one she didn't understand, the door to the kitchen swung open and Jake looked at them. The rest of the family seemed to be gathered behind him.

"Everything all right out here?" Jake asked cautiously.

Brett continued to stare at her, anger and disbelief on his face. Anna didn't know what to say. Finally she started, "I don't—"

"Tell 'em!" Brett ordered, his voice hard.

She looked at him, surprised. "What?"

"Tell 'em why I shouldn't break the engagement!"

"Brett, I promised Sylvia I wouldn't say anything." She'd already broken her promise once. Besides, she shouldn't be the one to tell them there'd be another Randall heir in the near future.

But Brett just kept staring at her, and the rest of the Randall clan did, too. Eventually, with her voice trembling, she said, "I don't think they should break the engagement, because of the baby." Then, to be sure everyone understood, she added, "Because they're having a baby."

The only sound to be heard was the ticking of the grandfather clock near the front door until someone—she thought Jake—muttered, "Damn."

"Are you sure?" Janie demanded.

S

Anna broke the hold Brett had on her gaze and looked toward the family. "Yes, I'm sure."

"I guess that changes things," Jake said with a sigh.

As if someone had sent a bolt of lightning through Brett, he turned to stare at the others. "Just like that? A few words is all it takes for you to believe it?" It hurt Brett to realize that fact. He'd sometimes felt a little inferior to his brothers because his talents were in numbers rather than more-macho areas, but he'd always thought they believed in him.

"Brett," Megan said softly, "accidents happen."

"It didn't happen to me."

Jake frowned. "Brett, are you saying you don't think this baby is yours?"

"Damn right it's not mine." Now he understood why Sylvia had tried to seduce him. And he gave thanks that he had rejected her. That Anna had already tempted him. He stared at her, still hurt that she believed Sylvia.

"How can you be so sure?" Jake asked.

"Because, big brother, I've never shared a bed with my soon-to-be *ex*-fiancée."

"A bed isn't required," Pete muttered. "Janie and I are testament to that fact."

"Then I'll be more specific. I've never had relations with Sylvia. If she's pregnant, and I doubt that she is, it's someone else's baby. Not mine."

Chad stared at him. "Why?"

"Why what?"

"She's a good-looking woman. Weren't you tempted?"

Brett could feel his cheeks flushing. "Yeah. In the beginning, I was. But I was staying under her father's roof. It didn't seem the polite thing to do to sit at his table and seduce his daughter at the same time."

"Oh, good." Chad gave him a cheeky grin. "I was just trying to decide which would be worse. You being the father of Sylvia's baby, or you being attracted to something other than women."

Brett glared at his brother, but he could tell his look didn't faze Chad. Movement at his side drew him as he realized Anna was slowly sliding down the wall.

"Anna? Are you okay?" he demanded, grabbing her arms to shore her up.

She nodded, just barely meeting his gaze before looking away. "Yes, of course. This has all been a bit of a—a shock. I apologize for causing you any…for upsetting everyone. If you want me to leave, I can—"

Several emphatic no's rang out, including Brett's.

"I think we're all a little shocked, Anna," Jake said quietly, "but that kind of sacrifice won't be necessary. Why don't we all come back into the kitchen and sit down."

Since Jake's suggestion was more of a command, everyone did as he asked. Brett found himself beside Anna. He wasn't happy with her right now, but he still wanted to be close to her.

"Anna, why do you think Sylvia is pregnant? Did she tell you?"

"Not until I confronted her. She was nauseated this morning and—and I suddenly sensed…I realized…I asked her."

"Just like that? She said, 'Oh, yes, I'm pregnant'?" Brett scoffed.

Anna looked at him for the first time since they'd entered the kitchen. "Pregnant women are my business. I won't doubt your knowledge of your stupid cows. Don't doubt my expertise."

He almost grinned at her feistiness. As serious as the situation was, he was beginning to understand Anna's behavior in the hall. And was relieved. It wasn't that she wanted him to be with Sylvia. She'd been concerned about the baby. Unbelievable relief filled him.

"Well, if she really is pregnant—and I'm not convinced she is, that would explain her behavior," he said, speaking his thoughts aloud.

"What do you mean?" Jake asked, making Brett regret his lapse of control.

He could feel his cheeks flaming, but he answered his brother's question. "Sylvia's been working hard at getting me into her bed."

Jake chuckled. "I can testify to that. When she mistook your room for mine, she wasn't hiding any weapons."

"And you resisted?" Chad asked in surprise, looking at Brett. "Man, I'm beginning to worry about you again."

Brett wanted to choke his younger brother, but he had to settle for an angry glare. "I'd already realized I'd made a mistake by the time Sylvia came here. It would've been…" He couldn't think of the proper adjective.

"Dishonorable?" Anna suggested softly.

"Yeah," he agreed, smiling at her. Maybe she had some feeling for him after all. He hoped so. He thought he was becoming obsessive over her.

"I think you need to go back upstairs and explain to Sylvia that the engagement is over. We've got time to get her back to Casper before dark," Jake said firmly.

"We?" Brett hated to think of a long drive with just him and Sylvia.

"I'm going with you. I want to be sure her father understands the situation."

"You don't have to go with me, Jake. I can tell Donald, I assure you."

"I know, Brett. But I thought you might like some company."

Brett exchanged a look with Jake that warmed him to his toes. Jake was the best brother a man could have. It went a long way to erase the hurt he'd experienced in the hall.

"Thanks."

ANNA STOOD out on the porch, one arm looped around a timber that held up the roof. Taking a deep breath, she stared out at the distant mountains.

She loved it here so much. Not just the Randalls, though she couldn't imagine a more perfect home. No, she loved Wyoming, the hugeness of it, the incredible beauty, the big hearts of the people in it.

Was she going to have to leave it?

She'd fallen in love with Brett Randall.

And he was real enough to break her heart.

Too many times in the past, she'd been snubbed because her

father was an alcoholic. Cruelly teased because she couldn't afford nice clothes. Not invited anywhere because she didn't have a home she could invite friends to.

When she'd gone to nursing school, she thought she'd left her past behind. She'd thought no one would know about poor Anna O'Brien. But she'd been wrong. Spending her meager earnings on cheap store dresses hadn't changed things.

Her taste had improved over the years, and the money she could spend had increased a little, but she didn't try to fool herself anymore.

She would always be the same person.

Surprisingly she was a person that Brett Randall wanted. That in itself was amazing.

But it was also the reason she might have to leave a place she'd been hoping to call home.

After all, she'd had trouble resisting Brett when he wasn't really trying to seduce her…and he'd been engaged. How would she manage to resist him when neither of those things was true?

He and Jake had taken Sylvia back to Casper only minutes after Anna's revelations. They were due back anytime now. Brett would no longer be engaged. And he would be trying to seduce her.

Maybe she should agree to go to bed with him. Why fight him and her own feelings when her heart would be broken either way? At least she'd have memories to dream of in her lonely bed.

She blinked back tears, knowing she was only tormenting herself. She couldn't give in to her wants. Or Brett's. Not unless she wanted to follow her father's path of self-destruction.

If she remained strong and resisted temptation, she would at least have self-respect. She'd fought her past too hard and too long to give that up for anyone. Even Brett.

She'd have to stay until Janie had her babies. She'd promised. But then she'd find a new place, start over again. It wouldn't be so hard. She'd made friends here, but she could make more friends somewhere else. It wasn't as if she had family here to tie her down. She could pick up and move whenever she wanted.

Her brave thoughts faltered at the pit of yearning that filled her. How she wanted to have roots, a family.

But that wasn't what Brett wanted. Not with her. He wanted her…for a while. For pleasure. But that pleasure would turn to heartbreak when he finally chose someone to be Mrs. Brett Randall.

The future Mrs. Randall would be like Sylvia, only with a good heart. Beautiful, refined, well educated. She'd have gracious parents, polished silver, sorority girlfriends. And she'd love babies. And, most of all, she'd love Brett.

Oh, please, let her love him with all her heart.

The sound of an engine disrupted her thoughts. It had to be Jake and Brett returning. She should go inside, hide among the others. But she didn't move.

Just this last time. In the cover of twilight, she'd let herself look at him. She'd pretend everything was fine. And she'd feast her eyes upon him enough to last her a lifetime. Just this last time.

BRETT COULDN'T IMAGINE a more beautiful sight than Anna standing on the porch, waiting for him. It was certainly more than he expected. He didn't see Jake precede him up the stairs and into the house. All he could see was Anna, her red hair lighting the growing darkness, her slender form drawing him.

Filled with a sudden elation, he leapt on the porch, grabbed her and lifted her in the air, spinning in a circle. Before she could even think of protesting, he set her back on her feet and swooped down to cover her lips with his.

Her hands were already on his shoulders, in an attempt to maintain her balance. He took it as a good sign when they linked around his neck, her fingers sliding through his hair. He'd waited forever, it seemed, to taste Anna's soft lips, but the wait had been well worth it.

The growing hunger urged him to greater closeness, and his tongue teased for her to open to him. His arms held her even tighter against him, and his fingers caressed and stroked her. He lost all sense of time and place. All he knew was Anna. And she was all he wanted to know.

Unfortunately a voice intruded on the happiest moment Brett had experienced in a long time.

"I guess I don't have to worry about my brother's sexual orientation anymore," Chad drawled.

Brett reluctantly lifted his lips from Anna, his gaze trained on her beautiful face. "Go away, bro," he muttered, wanting to be alone with the woman in his arms.

Her eyes popped open, and the pleasure on her face disappeared, replaced by a panic Brett didn't understand. She broke free of his embrace and quickly followed Chad into the kitchen. Brett hurried after her.

"Sorry, Anna," he apologized at once. "I was celebrating my bachelor status." Anything to take that look off her face.

Clearly Chad had informed the others of what he'd interrupted.

"I'm glad I wasn't on the back porch," Janie said from her seat at the table. "Pete would be upset if you kissed me like that."

"Upset? I'd take his head off," Pete agreed with a grin.

Brett ignored their teasing. He kept his gaze on Anna as she put as much distance between them as the kitchen would allow.

"I'd say that's a good way to *lose* your bachelor status. That's probably how you got into trouble with Sylvia," Chad suggested.

"No, not exactly," Brett replied. He didn't go into details, as he had with Jake, but Sylvia had been the one wanting to kiss. And her kisses had been pleasant, stimulating.

Anna's kiss was a knockout.

He didn't want dinner. He wanted Anna. If she so much as smiled at him, he'd pursue her. Hell, he was going to pursue her anyway. But it wouldn't take much of an invitation from her for him to take her to bed.

Just thinking about it was producing a result that would soon be obvious to everyone in the kitchen. He quickly sat down at the table. "I'm starving."

Chad gave him a knowing grin. "I bet."

He was going to have to beat up his brother. A quick look at Anna told him she didn't comprehend Chad's dig.

Anxious to make sure Anna had forgiven him for that kiss, he said, "Anna, you don't mind sitting next to me, do you?"

Anna gave him a quick glance and then looked away, her cheeks pink. "No, of course not, but—but I'm not very hungry. I think I may skip dinner."

Brett desperately sought a reason to keep her there with him, but Jake came to his rescue.

"I wish you'd stay, Anna. We've got something to celebrate tonight, and we'd like you to be a part of it."

"Maybe it should just be family, Jake," she offered, not looking at Brett.

"You feel like family, Anna. I wish you'd sit down and eat with us."

Anna licked her lips and then bit down on her bottom one, and Brett thought he was going melt. Damn, he'd never been this out of control, and he'd only kissed the woman. The strength of his desire was beginning to scare him.

"Besides, I bet you'd like to hear about our talk with Sylvia and her father." Jake's grin was an invitation to relax.

Brett breathed a sigh of relief as even Anna came to the table. As she sat down next to him, he took care not to touch her. After all, he didn't want to scare her away. And he'd like to ease the tightness of his jeans, which hadn't come from overeating. He had yet to take a bite. Of anything but Anna.

Jake made an amusing story of the afternoon's strife. Brett even laughed at the picture he presented. In actual fact, he hadn't enjoyed the encounter at all.

And he wasn't convinced that the story came as a surprise to Sylvia's father. The father of her child wasn't someone Donald would choose for a son-in-law.

Both Sylvia and her father had tried to convince Brett to go ahead with the marriage, offering a brilliant political future as his reward. He'd refused.

Even if he wasn't interested in Anna, it wouldn't have been a difficult choice. He had no interest in politics. Or in Sylvia.

"So you weren't tempted by a combination of the lovely Sylvia and being president of the United States?" Chad teased.

"Not even for a second," Brett muttered, and cast a look at

Anna. She concentrated on her eating, and he allowed himself the luxury of watching her.

"Does that mean you're beyond temptation, brother, or you didn't care for the bait?" Chad continued, grinning at him.

He glared at his brother, knowing Chad wouldn't hesitate to embarrass both him and Anna. "Mind your own business."

As if she read her brother-in-law's mind, Megan changed the subject. "Chad, we're going to have an old-fashioned social at church as a fund-raiser. I forgot to tell you I said we'd go."

Brett noted with relief that his wife had snagged Chad's attention.

"When is it?"

"Saturday night. It's a box social. You know, where the women bring a picnic supper and the men bid on it."

"I have to pay to eat a dinner you fixed?" Chad asked, frowning. "That doesn't make sense."

"Yes, it does, brother," Jake said, a grin on his face. "What you're paying for is the right to keep the other men from having dinner with your wife."

Chad's face clouded up. "Is that true? Another man could outbid me and eat dinner with you?" he demanded of his wife.

"Yes," Megan said serenely, continuing to eat her dinner.

"They'd better not try," Chad muttered, and then looked around the table. "What are you hyenas laughing about? Someone's going to go after your women, too."

"Well, I think I'm safe," Pete said, an amused grin on his face. "No one's going to want a surly woman about to give birth to twins." He sustained a punch on the shoulder from said pregnant wife, but she didn't really seem to mind.

Brett immediately took Chad's point to heart. As casually as he could, he asked, "You going, Anna?"

Even as Anna nodded, Megan answered, "Of course she is. She promised. After all, there's a shortage of women. We'll need everyone to participate. Both B.J. and Mildred promised, too."

Jake gave a dry chuckle. "Talk about change. There'll be five women participating from the Randall spread. Last year, we didn't have one."

Pete nodded. "Good thing only two of them actually belong to us, or our neighbors would accuse us of being greedy."

With a worried tone in his voice that surprised the others, Red asked, "But how will we know which ones to bid on? Don't you have to keep whose box it is a secret?"

Brett looked at him sharply. He'd already been reviewing his bank account, to make sure he had plenty of money for bidding. "What are you talking about?"

Megan explained. "It's part of the fun. The men aren't supposed to know whose box is whose."

"What?" Brett roared. "Then how can I—? I mean, how can the man bid on his wife's lunch?"

"That's why the bidding will be exciting," Janie said, and Brett noticed her gaze traveled between him and Anna. "Of course, some women won't follow the rules. It always happens."

"But since the money is going to be used to repair the church roof before winter arrives, no one really minds," Megan explained.

"So you'll tell Chad which lunch is yours?" Red asked Megan.

"Never," she said with a wicked smile.

Chad squared his shoulders. "Maybe I'll just bid on another lady's lunch. Maybe I'll have an even better time with some other woman."

Megan sent him a mournful look. "If you do, I'll probably go into early labor."

Chad's pretense collapsed at once, and he figuratively groveled at his wife's feet. Brett didn't even crack a smile at his brother's capitulation. He knew exactly how he felt.

Already he was trying to figure out how to identify Anna's picnic lunch.

Because he was damn sure going to be the one to share it with her.

Chapter Thirteen

Thursday night, Brett paced the kitchen floor, pausing each time he neared the window over the kitchen sink. It was after eleven o'clock. She should be home.

The kitchen door opened, and he spun around to discover Pete.

"What are you still doing up?" Pete asked as he headed for the refrigerator.

"Couldn't sleep," Brett muttered. "How about you?"

"*I* can sleep. Janie can't. She thought a glass of milk might help her. She's having a hard time these days."

Brett reached up for a glass from the cabinet as his brother brought the carton of milk over.

"Thanks." As he poured the milk, Pete added, "Maybe you should try some milk, too. Six o'clock is going to be here before you know it."

"No, thanks."

"You waiting for Anna?"

Brett jerked away from the window. "No! I told you, I couldn't sleep."

"I didn't sleep much, either, when Janie broke up with me," Pete said.

Brett stood with his hands on his hips, staring across the kitchen. He didn't want to reveal how vulnerable he was right now. But he could count on sympathy from his brothers. "She's been avoiding me," he finally admitted.

"No kidding," Pete said with a laugh.

So much for sympathy.

"Why? What did I do?"

"Well, let's see. You break your engagement with another woman and then grab Anna and kiss the breath out of her. Didn't you ever hear of subtlety?"

"At least I didn't kiss her before I broke the engagement," Brett argued.

"True, but I think at least a day's mourning period would've been appropriate before you hit on Anna."

"What was there to mourn? I felt more like celebrating." The sound of a car had him forgetting his brother and turning back to the window. Dual headlights bumping down the long driveway told him his wait was over.

"I'd better get this milk up to Janie before she gets cross with me," Pete said, grinning at Brett. "You might think about not pushing so hard, Brett. Anna's a sweetheart, and Jake will be upset if you make her uncomfortable. In fact, maybe you should wait until she's not living here to, uh, you know, make a move on her."

Pete didn't wait for Brett's reply, but Brett turned to stare at his brother as he left the kitchen. Wait until Anna left before he let her know she was driving him crazy? Not touch her, hold her, kiss her, until after Janie had her babies? That could be weeks!

When Anna entered the kitchen, Brett was in a state of confusion. Desire urged him to pull her into his arms and kiss any silliness about avoiding him out of her head. But Pete's words had struck home.

Not that he could completely ignore Anna while she was living in his house, but—but he could restrain himself. After all, that was the reason he'd given for not sleeping with Sylvia.

But Sylvia hadn't tempted him.

"Brett! What are you doing up?"

He studied her pale features, noting the alarm in her eyes. Maybe Pete was right. With a sigh, he used Pete's excuse for being in the kitchen. "I couldn't sleep and thought I'd pour myself a glass of milk. Want some?"

"No, thanks. I think I'll head for bed."

"Aren't you pushing it a little this week, filling in at Doc's office, as well as making house calls?"

She barely smiled. "I can use the money. Good night."

Before he could think of anything else to say, she was gone.

He heaved another sigh and put the milk away. Milk wasn't going to cure his sleeping problem. Only a slender, redheaded angel could do that, and she didn't appear interested.

He should've known he'd mess up on this love business. He'd always been a little different from his brothers, with a proclivity for numbers. Not that he couldn't ride with the rest of them, because he could. But numbers, computers and calculations had always been something he enjoyed.

Now Pete and Chad had found the perfect women for themselves. When Brett had tried the same thing, he'd chosen Sylvia. At least he'd gotten out of that mess. But Anna, Anna didn't respond like other women. Even he had no trouble attracting women.

Except for Anna.

And she was the one he wanted.

With all his heart. And several other active parts of him, he admitted ruefully. Well, he wasn't going to give up. Randalls weren't quitters. He'd find out which box dinner was hers, and he'd pay whatever it took to have her to himself.

But he'd be restrained. He wouldn't push her. Not yet. He would persuade her he was a nice guy. Lay the groundwork. Yeah, that was it.

And when she stopped running away, his sleeping problems would be over.

SATURDAY WAS a perfect day. The sun shone, and puffs of clouds drifted lazily by. Anna didn't even think about the box social until after she'd done some shopping in town and had lunch at the Sandwich Shop.

She'd had a tough week, doing double duty. But she needed the money to pay her car-repair bill. She'd been fortunate. When she'd visited Mike, the mechanic had handed her a small bill and a perfectly running car. She questioned him to be sure Brett hadn't persuaded him to lower his bill, but Mike assured her he hadn't.

Which was just as well, because she couldn't have paid anything much bigger. But the extra duty had helped. And gotten her away from the ranch...and Brett. She hadn't been able to relax at the Randall ranch. Brett, after that one kiss, had kept his distance, greeting her warmly but treating her like his little sister. Or maybe a distant cousin.

Even Thursday night, when he'd been in the kitchen as she returned late, he'd simply offered her a glass of milk. There'd been no attempt to get close to her.

And she was sure her heart was breaking.

"Silly girl!" she muttered as she paused to make a phone call outside the Sandwich Shop. She'd warned herself over and over again that Brett wasn't for her. She should be glad he no longer wanted to seduce her. Too bad she wasn't.

After she dialed the ranch on her cellular phone, she waited for Red to answer. Instead, Megan picked up the receiver.

"Hi, it's Anna. Is Janie all right?"

"Sure. Where are you?"

"In town. I'm going to go to my apartment to pick up my mail and fix the food for my box dinner. Then I'll be out to the ranch." She always tried to let Pete and Janie know where she'd be.

"Don't bother cooking anything, Anna. Red has fried a lot of chicken and made potato salad and stuff. He says all we need to do is pack the boxes."

"I can do my own—" Anna began.

"You'll hurt Red's feelings. By the way, how are you going to decorate your box?"

"I thought we weren't supposed to tell," Anna said. She wouldn't put it past either Janie or Megan to tell Brett to bid on her box, whether Brett wanted to or not.

"It won't hurt to tell me. *I'm* not bidding on the box dinner, silly," Megan said lightly.

"Tell Red thanks for me," Anna said, ignoring Megan's words. The two women had been prodding her all week toward

Brett. Who knew what they'd said to him. "I'll be there in about an hour, then. 'Bye."

"DID SHE TELL YOU?"

"No, sorry," Megan replied with a sigh. "I think she suspects I won't keep it a secret."

"Do you think she doesn't want me to buy hers?" Brett asked, his spirits sinking. "She's been avoiding me."

"No, Brett, I'm sure that's not true. But she said the other day she didn't think she was good enough for you."

"What?" he roared, unable to believe anyone could think such a silly thing.

"She seems pretty hung up on not being socially on the same level with us," Megan said. "Does it bother you that she has no family, no connections?"

"Of course it bothers me. I don't want her to be alone. She needs me to take care of her, to be her family."

"Whew, you had me worried for a minute," Megan confessed.

"Damn. First you all think I'm having babies indiscriminately, and now you're accusing me of being a snob?"

"Sorry, Brett. I'll try to atone for it by finding out which box is Anna's. You just bring enough money."

"Don't worry. They'll be calling me Moneybags before tonight is over."

RED VOLUNTEERED TO TAKE all the ladies' box dinners into town ahead of time. "Just so no one will know," he said with a wink. "I'll leave the kitchen until they're all ready. You call B.J. and Mildred and tell them to bring theirs over, too."

Megan had done as Red directed and then carefully filled hers and Janie's boxes. Provided by the church, the boxes were all the same—large, white and square—though each lady could decorate her own.

When she and Janie came downstairs to check on their boxes, they discovered an unforeseen problem.

Anna was completing a big red bow on one of the boxes that

matched the bows on the other two boxes, making all three identical.

"What are you doing?" Megan asked.

"Tying bows. It's one of my special talents. Shall I tie a big bow on your boxes, too?"

"But how can you tell them apart?" Janie asked, frowning.

"We put the sticker on the bottom with our names on it. Didn't you?" B.J. asked. "Come on, let Anna tie bows on your boxes, too. That will confuse everyone."

"It certainly will," Megan agreed as she surrendered her box to Anna, frantically thinking of what they were going to do now.

"WHAT ARE WE GOING to do now?" Chad demanded, frustration evident in his voice.

"The only thing we can do is make sure one of us bids on every one of those boxes with red bows," Jake said calmly. "Then we can all sit together. No one's going to pay any attention if we don't sit exactly beside the person whose box we won."

Brett looked at the only other single Randall. "I get Anna, okay? I'll pay extra."

"You're acting like I'm going to try to steal your girl from you," Jake said with a grin.

"I'll take Mildred's box," Red said abruptly. When the four brothers turned to look at him, he muttered, "She's too old for the likes of you."

Brett grinned. Everything seemed to be working out okay. "All right. I'm counting on all of you to win the bid. Who will go first? We don't want to bid against each other."

They determined their order for bidding and turned confidently toward the table.

Only to discover that at least half of the boxes were tied with big red bows.

SHE'D BEEN NAUGHTY.

But Anna was determined to save Brett from the scheming of his sisters-in-law. And herself from temptation. When she'd arrived at the church, she'd gone to the room where the box din-

ners were being stored and offered to help tie big bows on some
of the other boxes.

She'd learned the technique of making a huge, decorative bow
when she'd worked at a florist while she went to school. The
trick came in handy, especially tonight. Now, Brett wouldn't feel
he had to buy her box.

And she wouldn't have nearly as much fun.

With a sigh, she moved to her seat among the women.

"What did you do?" Megan whispered, her gaze wide-eyed.

"I helped some of the other ladies. But I fixed yours and
Janie's boxes. I painted a blue butterfly on the side of those two
boxes."

"A blue butterfly? Thanks, Anna." With relief, she waved to
her husband, and he hurried over.

After whispering in his ear, Megan smiled to reassure him.
He whispered back, then waited for her answer. All she could
do was shrug her shoulders because, Anna guessed, she couldn't
identify the other boxes.

Which was what Anna had intended.

She saw Brett among the men. He was studying the boxes
intently. Chad was beside him, saying something to him. Anna
wondered whose box Brett wanted. Some of the ladies were
gossiping in the storage room. Several single ladies, decked out
in their fanciest clothes this evening, were hoping Brett would
get theirs.

The mayor picked up the first box, and the bidding began.
When Janie's and Megan's boxes were shown off, their husbands made short work of the bidding. Several others had clearly
discovered the name of the lady beforehand also.

Anna happened to be looking at the Randall men and noticed
the look of chagrin on Red's face when Mildred's box was sold
to a neighboring rancher. Minutes boxes later, B.J.'s box was
sold to a cowboy two ranches away from the Randalls'. The
next box, held high by the mayor after he peeled off the name,
drew several bids, including Jake's. Everyone chuckled when
Jake won the bid and discovered his dinner mate was Janie's
mother, Lavinia Dawson. Her husband, Hank, shouted a warning

to Jake about trying to steal his bride and received applause for his teasing.

Brett still hadn't bid. Anna had surreptitiously watched him, wishing things were different. Wishing he really wanted to bid on her box. Wishing she were one of the Randalls, going home this evening with Brett.

With a sigh, she drew her gaze from Brett and turned back to the bidding. One of the older women discovered a distinguished-looking rancher, a bachelor, had purchased her box, and she smiled with pleasure.

Anna's eyebrows rose as she smiled, too. It was never too late, she supposed, to discover that special person. At least, she hoped it wasn't.

She was afraid she'd already found him, but he was too important for her. Which meant that she'd be lonely for a long time. She couldn't imagine ever having any interest in another man, even when Brett married.

The mayor picked up one of the red-bowed boxes. "Now, this box seems special." He paused and stared intently at the audience. "What am I bid?"

"Five hundred dollars."

Everyone gasped. The hundred-dollar bids of the Randall brothers had been the highest bids all evening. Anna stared at the bidder, the one Randall who had remained silent until now. He must know whose box the mayor had.

She steeled herself to hear the name of some beautiful young woman, the daughter of a neighboring rancher. The mayor asked for other bids and received laughs in return. With a beaming smile, he lifted the card in the air.

"A fair price, Brett. You have just purchased dinner with Miss Anna O'Brien."

Chapter Fourteen

"I'm sorry, Brett."

He stared down at Anna's sweet face, barely taking in her words. She held the big white box between them, ensuring a certain distance, but he reached out to stroke back a difficult curl that insisted on falling across her brow.

"Mmm?"

"I said I'm sorry."

"Why? What's wrong?"

"You spent five hundred dollars. You must've had a certain— I mean, you must've thought you knew whose box it was. Too bad you got the wrong box."

"The wrong box?" he repeated, frowning. He had known whose box he had. Once he'd seen all the red bows, he'd hurriedly offered the mayor a deal that would net the church five hundred dollars. Money well spent, as far as Brett was concerned.

"Do you want to invite whoever it was to eat with us?"

He studied the determined look on her face. What the hell was going on? He'd planned on a quiet dinner for two, under one of the nearby trees. But she was acting as if she didn't want to be alone with him.

Pete's words about crowding Anna while she was at the ranch haunted him. A look over his shoulder showed his entire family staring at them.

"Nah. Why don't we just join the family?"

"But, Brett, you paid five hundred dollars."

She made it sound like a fortune. To her, it probably was. To him, it was a small price to pay to share some time with Anna.

"It's for a good cause," he mumbled, and led her over to the large picnic table Jake had commandeered. "Room for us?"

"Sure." Jake moved down the bench.

One good thing about a big family, Brett discovered, was that there wasn't much room for latecomers, which meant he and Anna were close together. "Scoot over just a little, sugar. I'm about to fall off the bench." He wrapped an arm around her small waist and pressed up against her.

"Need some more space?" Jake asked, looking at him over Anna's head, a sly grin on his face.

"Nah, I think we've got enough room. Right, Anna?" He smiled down at her bright red cheeks and pulled her more tightly against him. The feel of her long legs, even through his jeans, made him think of endless nights, her legs wrapped around him, hours of incredible pleasure and mornings of no regrets.

"I—I could sit on the other side of the table. I think there's more room over there."

"Now, that wouldn't be fair. I paid for your company," Brett reminded her.

She leaned toward him, almost pushing his heart rate into the danger zone. "Yes," she whispered, "but I'm not the one you wanted."

"Ah, sugar, you'll do." His lips drifted ever closer to hers. She turned her head away, reaching for something on the table, but her breast brushed against his arm.

Instead of being affected, as far as Brett could tell, Anna turned to the picnic box. How could she remain so cool when he was on fire?

"Red made all the food," she explained brightly, "so I think you're guaranteed a good meal. What piece of chicken do you want?"

When she turned those big blue eyes in his direction again, Brett couldn't think about chicken. He sat still, hoping to remain in control, wishing he didn't have to.

"Brett, tell the lady what chicken you want." A grin lit up Jake's face.

Brett wanted to punch him in the nose, a disturbing thought, since he'd always idolized his big brother. But he was daring to taunt Brett when he knew what was on his brother's mind.

"The drumstick," he muttered, his voice hoarse.

She put the drumstick on a paper plate, added potato salad and baked beans and handed it to him.

How was he going to concentrate on eating with her pressed up against him, touching him, her scent enveloping him? Many meals like this, and he'd be skin and bones.

"Eat, boy," Red ordered from across the table. "There's gonna be dancin' in a little while. You'll need your strength."

"Dancing?" He looked down at Anna. "You like dancing?"

"I haven't done a lot of dancing. I'm probably not very good. But I don't think you have to dance with the owner of the box you bought. You can ask anyone."

"Uh-huh. But you'll dance with me?"

"Well, of course, but—"

"Good." He picked up his piece of chicken and attacked it with fervor. He wanted to finish his meal and get to the dancing. A good excuse to hold Anna against him. Lordy, lordy, it was going to be sheer pleasure. And torture.

AFTER DINNER, the ladies retired to freshen up before the dancing began. Anna needed the break. Her role of disinterested lady was wearing thin. She'd been avoiding Brett since that explosive kiss when he'd returned from the city. Tonight she could avoid him no longer.

For self-preservation, she'd played the innocent who didn't notice him touching her. *Didn't notice?* She would've laughed hysterically if it weren't causing her so much pain.

And now she had to spend the evening dancing with him.

The man was so—so handsome and sexy. And good. He could have his pick of half the women here. And probably would, she reminded herself, hardening her heart again. She mustn't let those traitorous thoughts in her head. Especially the knowledge that Brett would be a wonderful lover.

But that's all he would be. And it wouldn't be enough for her. She sighed, struggling to bring some order to her windblown curls. She pulled out her lipstick and tried to color her lips, but her hand was shaking. In disgust, she recapped the tube and put it back in her purse and went outside.

The sun was setting, the summer dusk falling, and Anna looked at the sky, seeing first one star then another light up the darkening blue. Nearby, the organizers had strung colored lights around a platform, and several fiddlers and a guitar player were warming up on one end. A perfect scene for romance.

After one dance with Brett, maybe she'd find Mildred, sit and talk with her. And then catch a ride back with Megan and Chad. She didn't think they'd stay very late. That way, maybe Brett would start looking for someone else to take to his bed.

She sighed again. Life offered hard choices. Resisting Brett Randall had to be the hardest.

"I hope that sigh means you missed me," Brett whispered, his arms coming around her.

She jumped in surprise and managed to put a few inches between them. "Actually I was thinking about how pretty the sunset is. And—and how tired I am. Maybe I should go on home now. If you want to go find someone who—"

Brett gave her a piercing stare and ignored her stumbling words. "Come on. You promised me a dance." He took her hand and started off for the dance floor.

All she could do was try to keep up. What was wrong with the man? Couldn't he take a hint? He was only going to cause them both a lot of pain.

Just as they reached the dance floor, the musicians began their first song, a slow, dreamy waltz. Brett turned around and wrapped both arms around her, scarcely giving her room to breathe.

"Brett, you're holding me too tight."

"Only because you're not doing it right."

"I told you I wasn't a very good dancer," she said stiffly.

"You dance just fine, sugar. All you gotta do is relax. Put your arms around my neck."

With a feeling of a nonswimmer diving into the ocean, Anna did as he ordered, relaxing against his strong body, laying her head against his chest, just over his heart. Its steady beat was all she heard. Closing her eyes, she gave herself to the one and only dance she would probably ever have with Brett Randall.

BRETT'S ARMS WERE WRAPPED around Anna's slim body, his hands resting on her small waist. He breathed in her scent, pure elixir as far as he was concerned. They should bottle it.

Every movement incited his body more. Her breasts were pressed against his chest, her arms around his neck. He could feel her fingers move in his hair. He was in heaven and hell at the same time.

A sudden chuckle ran through him. When *their* daughter got to dancing age, he was going to lock her up. No damn cowboy was going to hold her like this. 'Cause Brett would know exactly what he was thinking.

Anna raised her head from his shoulder. ''Is something wrong?''

He wanted to kiss her—hell, he always wanted to kiss her— but she was skittish tonight and he didn't want to take any chances. He gathered her close again. ''No, sugar, nothing's wrong. Everything's perfect.''

And it would be, if he and Anna were going home together. Of course, technically they were. But they wouldn't be in the same bed, the way he wanted them to be. They wouldn't be wrapped in each other's embrace. They wouldn't be husband and wife.

That's what he wanted. He was beginning to think that's what he'd wanted all along. From the moment he saw her. Or maybe he should say *felt* her in the dark of the kitchen. If Sylvia hadn't been around to complicate things, he would've gladly gone down for the count by the end of the first week.

Which was only a couple of days ago, he realized with another chuckle. But life before Anna didn't really seem to have existed. At least not with any importance.

When the music ended, Brett didn't hear it. He was too wrapped up in Anna. Only when a neighbor jostled him did he open his eyes.

Anna, seemingly in the same state, abruptly stepped back from him. "Oh! I didn't realize— Where's Mildred? I'll keep her company and—"

But Brett had no intention of letting Anna escape. He took her hand and put it back on his shoulder. "Don't go anywhere. They're going to play another song any minute now."

"I'm sure there are lots of other people you want to dance with, so I'll just—"

"No, you won't."

"No need to worry about me. I'll find someone to talk to."

"The only thing I'd worry about is the stampede when these woman-hungry cowboys realize you're free. I'd probably get trampled. You have to stay to protect me."

Anna's cheeks reddened, and she refused to look at him. "You're being ridiculous, Brett."

"Hey, can I have the next dance?" a cowboy asked, tapping Brett on the shoulder. He was a handsome young man, with an eager expression on his face.

Brett frowned at him. "Nope. Anna's my partner tonight. I bought her box."

"You're supposed to share for the dancing," the cowboy protested. "The mayor said so."

"Later," Brett said as the music started up. He pulled Anna close to him again, feeling a sense of rightness that filled him all the way to his toes. Anna had to feel it, too, didn't she?

"Brett," she whispered, the warmth of her breath tickling his chin.

"Yeah, sugar?" He leaned closer to nuzzle her forehead, enjoying the feel of her curls against his face.

"The music is faster. This isn't a waltz."

He surveyed the dancers over her head, a grin on his face. She was right, of course. The other dancers were spinning around the floor, moving in quick time, barely touching. He tucked her even closer against him. "Sorry, this is the only way I know how to dance."

She pulled away from him. "I don't think I believe you."

He had moved them to the side of the dance floor toward the darker end. When he stared into those blue eyes of hers, he couldn't remember his warning to himself to convince her he was a good person before making a move. All he could think about was Anna, and how perfect they were together. He followed his natural instincts and kissed her.

Her soft lips, full and warm, were heaven, and his body responded with a speed that exceeded the music. The sweetness of her filled him, and he craved more. Stroking her back, he fought the urge to lift her in his arms and carry her into the darkness.

"Hey, Brett, good thing you got rid of your fiancée!" someone called out.

The words barely registered with Brett, but Anna jerked away from him, her cheeks red again.

"Damn!" Brett muttered. Without Anna to shield him, everyone would see how aroused he was. And Anna wasn't hanging around. She hurriedly left the dance floor, leaving him standing there, still wanting her.

BRETT WANDERED AROUND the church grounds, barely acknowledging old friends. He had too much on his mind. Namely Anna. He'd really screwed up his love life, getting engaged to Sylvia just before he met Anna.

Finally he'd gotten rid of the complication of Sylvia, but Anna wasn't cooperating. Okay, okay, Pete was right. It was indecent to go straight from Sylvia to Anna. Any woman would want to be courted, to have some time before he declared he wanted her in front of everyone.

But how could he hold back? Anna consumed him. She was his missing part, his soul mate. He'd never say that to his brothers, though. They'd rib him forever about being a poet.

But for Anna, he'd even take that.

So he could be patient. Couldn't he? After all, in spite of herself, she'd shown him that, if nothing else, she wanted him as much as he wanted her. That was a start, even if she wasn't in love with him...yet.

He had at least a couple of more weeks before Janie delivered. He'd keep it casual, let her get to know him. Then, as soon as she moved back to her apartment in Rawhide, he'd camp on her doorstep.

Satisfied with his plan of action, one that wouldn't make him wait too long, he turned back to the dance floor. After all, it wasn't safe to leave the keeper of his heart alone around all those cowboys.

And if he was lucky, Janie would have her babies in a day or two, and he wouldn't have to wait as long.

That thought cheered him up, and he returned to the colored lights at a run.

"Where's the fire, Brett?" someone called out.

Brett waved and kept on going. As soon as he got close, he discovered the red curls he sought framed by the black shirt of the cowboy holding her. Roy Barnes. He was one man Brett would never let their daughter dance with, he assured himself angrily, then realized what an inane thought he'd had. By the time their daughter was interested in dancing, Roy wouldn't be around. But he didn't want Anna dancing with the man, either.

The musicians announced a break, and the dancers moved en masse to the steps. Brett hurried toward them. Time to reclaim his woman.

Anna and Roy were chatting as they came toward him, and jealousy filled Brett. It had been a long time since Anna had really talked to him.

"Anna," he called sharply.

She turned toward him, but the pleasant smile on her lips disappeared.

"Evening, Brett," Roy added, smiling. As well he might. His arm was around Anna's waist.

"I think maybe you ought to stop pawing the lady, Barnes," Brett growled, completely forgetting his plan of action.

Instead of following his orders, the cowboy raised one eyebrow and grinned. "I think Anna's old enough to make her wishes clear."

Brett swung his gaze to Anna, unable to keep from pleading with his look for her to tell Roy to get lost.

"Roy is just being polite, Brett. We're going to get something to drink if you want to join us."

At least she didn't snub him. But she didn't reject Roy, either. And Brett knew Roy wasn't being nice. He was imagining making love to her, just as Brett had done. He was hoping to keep her to himself. He was— "Anna, you don't understand!"

"Yes, I do. They're serving punch over there."

Roy didn't allow her to linger, and she went with him.

Frustrated, Brett stepped to her side and took her arm, his hand giving Roy's a quick shove that dislodged it.

"Hey!" Roy protested, coming to an abrupt halt. Brett, however, pulled Anna on, hoping to leave the other cowboy behind in the crowd. No such luck.

Roy caught up with them and took Anna's other arm.

Suddenly she came to an abrupt halt. "Look, I don't enjoy feeling like the wishbone on the Thanksgiving turkey. I can find a glass of punch by myself. If you two want to walk along with me, fine. But let's try acting like mature adults."

Roy recovered first from Anna's lecture. "Why, sure, Anna, darlin'. Whatever you say."

"I was just trying to be gentlemanly," Brett muttered as Anna pulled her arm away from him.

She rolled her eyes at him but said nothing because they had reached the refreshment table. After they each claimed a glass of punch, Anna sat down at one of the picnic tables. The two men almost collided to see who got the seat beside her.

Brett managed to slide in beside Anna by bumping Roy to the side, almost knocking him off his feet.

"You cheated!" Roy yelled, and everyone at the dance turned around to stare at the three of them.

Brett figured possession was the important thing, so he kept quiet and snaked his arm around Anna.

"Move down, Brett," Anna coolly ordered.

He stared at her, disbelief filling him. Didn't she understand? He'd won fair and square. "Why?"

"So that Roy has room to sit down. After we invited you to join us, you shouldn't take Roy's place." She stared at him, waiting for him to do as she asked.

He had an awful fear that Anna was going to offer Roy the seat between the two of them, but to his relief, she slid down the bench after him, letting Roy sit on her other side.

Then Anna began speaking in a low voice, anger lacing her

words. "For the last time, I am not some Kewpie doll to be won at the fair. I don't want either of you to put your arm around me. Nor do I intend to dance with either of you again. Do you understand?"

Brett was stunned. Here he'd returned to the dance to protect her, be there for her, and she was treating him like something to be avoided. Damn it, she was going to be his wife! Of course, he hurriedly admitted, she didn't know that yet, but when she did she'd regret what she'd just said.

Roy was quicker to respond. "I'm sorry if I embarrassed you, Anna. But you're so pretty, I lose my head."

"Thank you for the compliment, Roy."

"I've told you you're pretty!" Brett snapped. He felt like Alice in Wonderland. Everything was coming out wrong.

Anna gave a long-suffering sigh and looked away.

Roy, on the other hand, couldn't resist sending a smile of triumph in his direction.

"Anna, can I have the next dance?" another cowboy asked, having walked up behind them without Brett realizing it.

"Sure, Mike. I'd like that. Is the band ready to start again?"

"Yeah, I think so." The happy cowboy stood waiting, and Anna asked Roy to let her out. He did so, taking her hand as she stood. "If I can't dance with you again, Anna, I'll go on home. But I'll see you in the morning."

Anna smiled and walked away from the table with her new partner. Before Roy could depart, Brett stood.

"What did you mean you'd see her in the morning?" he growled at Roy.

"Just what I said. When I see something I like, I go after it," Roy announced, a self-confident smile on his face.

"Why, you jerk," Brett snarled, and reared back, ready to fight. "Anna isn't some prize to be won. She's—she's a wonderful woman."

"Watch it, Brett, or I'll break you into little pieces. There's no Randall brand on Anna. And I think she's ripe for the pickin'," Roy said, his meaning clear.

Brett grabbed Roy's shirt and jerked him toward him as he aimed his fist. But something stopped his arm in midair.

Jake.

"Brother, didn't Daddy teach you not to fight at church socials?" Jake asked.

"Yeah, but he didn't mention someone might insult a lady at a church social." He continued to glare at Roy, who didn't look any happier than him.

Jake dropped his arm and moved between the two of them. He was still smiling, but there was a steeliness in it that encouraged Brett. Jake didn't tolerate insulting any woman. But when it was one of their women, he'd explode. Jake turned his full attention to Roy. "Anna is living on Randall property...and we protect our women."

"Hell, Jake, I didn't insult Anna. Unless you call asking her out an insult." Roy turned to glare at Brett again.

"That's all he did?" Jake asked, amusement filling his smile now.

"Damn it, Jake, that's not all. He wants her!" Brett knew he was right. Roy had made his intentions perfectly clear.

"Well, hell, Brett, if that's an insult, half the men here tonight are guilty. And no one more than you!" Jake drawled.

Everyone around them burst into laughter.

Unfortunately Brett couldn't deny his brother's words.

Chapter Fifteen

By the time Jake was ready to go home from the church social, Brett was in a snit. He admitted it. He'd get over it. But right now, he was enjoying it.

Anna had slipped away an hour ago with Chad and Megan. And there hadn't been anything he could do about it.

He maintained a steady silence after Jake slid behind the wheel. When Jake didn't even notice, driving along whistling beneath his breath, Brett was compelled to speak.

"Damn it, Jake, you embarrassed me!"

"I know. And I'm sorry. But you were being a little hard on poor old Roy."

"He was trying to steal my girl."

"Oh? I didn't know you'd claimed Anna."

"'Course I have!"

"So when's the wedding?"

Jake continued to watch his driving, calmly steering the big truck.

Finally Brett broke the dark silence. "I haven't asked her to marry me yet."

"Then I guess she's not your girl. Last I heard, until a woman gives her promise, she's free to do whatever with whomever."

"I can't ask her yet. I just broke my engagement," Brett said in exasperation. "But you can't expect me not to protect her in the meantime."

"Have you let her know how you feel?"

"I've tried. But I haven't come right out and said…I mean, it's awkward. She's avoiding me."

"You can't blame her. A week ago, you were marrying someone else."

Brett let his chin rest on his chest. "I've messed up, haven't I?"

Jake reached over to slap him on the shoulder. "Not as bad as I did. I married Chloe. You only got engaged to Sylvia. And besides, Anna doesn't care anything about Roy Barnes."

Brett's head snapped up and he stared eagerly at his brother. "Did she tell you?"

"Nope. But I can tell by watching her. You two were all over each other when you danced. Roy tried, but he was the only one doing the trying."

Brett sagged back against the seat. He'd feel better if Anna had told Jake she didn't want Roy. That she wanted him. He'd feel best of all if Anna told him that herself.

"I hope you're right," he finally said with a sigh.

"'Course I am. Wait until tomorrow. You'll see."

BRETT WAS DEPRESSED.

Especially since Roy Barnes had joined Anna as she entered the church this morning. He hadn't expected that after his conversation with Jake last night. Roy and Anna were sitting at the other end of the pew, whispering to each other.

He didn't like Roy sitting that close. Or putting his arm around her in church. He was supposed to be paying attention to the sermon, worshiping. That's what church was all about. Didn't the cowboy know any better? Church was no place to romance a woman!

Brett's indignation over Roy's behavior grew with each seemingly unending minute. But when they stood, after the final benediction had been given, Brett realized he couldn't remember a single word the pastor had spoken.

And had he had the opportunity Roy enjoyed, he knew he would've been concentrating on Anna. Hell, he hadn't been nearly as close, and she was all he'd thought of.

Thinking seemed to be all he was going to get to do about Anna, because so far this morning, she hadn't spoken to him.

Looking up, Brett was just in time to see the other cowboy, his hand on Anna's arm, heading out the door of the church. Brett started after them.

"Hey, Anna, you ready?" Brett called as he got near them, his gaze narrowed on Roy instead of Anna.

"I'm askin' Anna to come with me," Roy protested. "I'm invitin' her on a picnic."

"We had a picnic last Sunday. Anna's expected back at the ranch. Janie didn't feel up to coming to church this morning." Brett felt a real sense of gratitude to Janie for her pregnancy. Whatever it took to keep Anna out of the other man's clutches.

"Thanks for the invitation," Anna said, smiling at Roy, making Brett's blood boil. "But I really do need to go back to the ranch."

"I could come there. I'll bring a couple of ponies, and we could take a short ride, close to the house."

"Thanks, Roy, but I need to stay near Janie. She's getting close to time."

"Then how about I rent a movie?"

Brett was about to inform the persistent cowboy that Anna didn't have any interest in spending the afternoon with him when Jake joined them.

"Hi, Roy. We're going to work out some of Pete's stock this afternoon. Why don't you help us out? We could turn it into our own little rodeo."

Brett glared at his brother. He didn't want to compete in front of Anna, especially with Roy, who had a reputation as a tough rider. The cowboy had been on the rodeo circuit a year or two with Pete.

"Great," Roy said. "You'll watch, won't you, Anna?"

"Of course. It'll be fun."

"You can even join us for lunch if you want," Jake added.

Brett stared at his brother, openmouthed. What was wrong with him? Brett had told him last night how much he loved Anna. Now he was inviting the competition home with them!

"I'll go home and change and be right over," Roy said, a grin on his face. "Want to ride with me, Anna?"

"I'd better go straight back to the ranch. I'll see you there."

Anna smiled and waved goodbye to the cowboy, and Brett wanted to put his arms around her and hold her tight against him. She was his. Why didn't she know it?

When they started back to the ranch, Brett was even more depressed. Anna wouldn't even ride in Jake's truck with him. She'd chosen to ride with Megan and Chad.

"Cheer up, boy," Jake said. "You haven't lost her."

"Well, if I haven't, it's no thanks to you. Why'd you invite Roy over?"

"To prove a point. Anna may have sat with him in church, but she paid a lot of attention to you. Probably because you were staring at her," Jake added with a chuckle, "but maybe because she's more interested in you than in Roy."

"So why do we need him there?" Brett growled, but he was encouraged by Jake's words.

"So she'll know which one she's interested in. How can she be sure unless the two of you are both there?"

"But Roy's much better at the rodeo stuff than I am."

"Anna's not a prize you win for riding a bucking bronco, Brett. She's a woman who can make her own choice. If she cares about you, it won't be because you're the best cowboy."

Jake's logic was all well and good, but Brett didn't want to look bad in Anna's eyes.

"Besides, it was obvious the man wasn't going to quit until he arranged something with Anna. Did you want him getting her all to himself? He can't cuddle up to her when he's riding a mad bull."

Good point. A picture of Anna and Roy next to each other on the sofa watching a movie made the rodeo idea look good. "You're right."

"Uh, Brett? Don't offer to ride too quickly," Jake advised. "You can do some watching with Anna."

Another good point.

WHEN ANNA REACHED the outdoor corral the cowboys were using after lunch, one of the Randall cowboys was already on the back of a big Brahman bull, one arm in the air as the bull bucked his way around the arena. Another cowboy on the rail blew a whistle, and the rider slid from the bull's back, landing on his feet at a run, heading in the opposite direction.

"That always scares me," Anna said, standing next to Megan.

"What scares you, Anna?" a deep voice asked from behind her.

She whirled around to discover Brett right behind her. Her breath caught in her throat, and she couldn't speak. After what had happened last night on the dance floor, she was determined to avoid him at all costs. She'd even gone to the trouble of encouraging Roy.

Megan came to her rescue. "I think Anna was referring to the dismount from an angry bull. And I agree. I was at a rodeo in Denver and saw a man get gored."

"Must not've had a good clown," Brett said casually, as if the danger were nonexistent.

"There isn't a clown here at all," Anna stated. She turned back to face the corral. It was easier to maintain her composure when she didn't have to look at him. And yearn for his kiss.

"Nope, but Jerry's on his horse in the arena. And he's good at handling the bulls," Brett explained.

One of his big hands reached out for the corral rail on each side of Anna, and she felt surrounded by him. A shuddering breath swept through her body. To know that she could turn and find her lips only inches from his was a torment difficult to bear.

If he'd never kissed her, she was sure the ache to feel his lips on hers wouldn't be so great. But he had. Twice now. And she could scarcely bear to be in the same room with him without longing for that closeness again.

But she was just as determined to resist. She was not going to have an affair with Brett Randall.

Roy was the next cowboy to burst out of the chute on the back of a bull. Brett leaned forward to whisper in her ear. "Worried?"

"Of—of course. I worry every time." At least she could still breathe as long as the cowboy wasn't Brett. She didn't think she could bear to watch if he decided to take a turn.

Roy successfully completed his ride. After he'd made it to the corral rail across from them, he turned to wave to Anna. She waved back, but she could feel Brett's scowl behind her. "He rode well," she said in justification.

"Yeah. He's good for *something*," Brett muttered.

Anna looked at Brett out of the corner of her eye. What if Brett decided to ride? Surely he wouldn't. He'd stayed beside her since the beginning.

Roy rode another bull triumphantly.

Then he, too, crossed the corral to visit.

"All you Randall men staying over here with the ladies?" he said, glaring at Brett, who still stood behind Anna, practically embracing her. "What about you, Brett? You gonna ride, or are you afraid?"

"Don't be ridiculous!" Anna protested.

But Brett pushed away from the corral fence and answered at the same time. "I'm riding."

"Brett, don't," Anna pleaded, trying to hide her distress.

"Let him go, Anna. He needs to do some hard work. He'll get soft if all he pushes around is a bunch of numbers," Roy said, grinning at her.

"Give me a kiss for luck, sugar," Brett said, spinning her around.

She couldn't have denied him, whatever the reason, but she threw her arms around his neck and fervently met him more than halfway. This kiss was brief, unlike the other two, and left Anna wanting more. Her fingers trailed down his chest as he turned away from her.

"Be careful," she called softly, and he turned to give her a cocky grin before he walked away.

"Don't worry. He probably won't last long," Roy said, an arrogant air on his face. "He's soft. He does all the book work, you know."

Anna whirled to glare at him. "He's just as strong as any of you. But he has brains, too. Which makes him twice as good as you!"

"Good for you, Anna," said Pete, who was standing nearby, and Megan clapped her hands.

Roy turned and stomped off toward the chutes without saying anything else.

Anna turned to Pete. "Can't you talk him out of this insanity? It's crazy for him to put his life in danger. I mean, don't you have cowboys who are supposed to do that sort of thing?"

"I thought you believed in him," Pete said in surprise.

"I believe he *can* do it, but I don't want him to," she explained, sure she was being completely logical.

"Don't worry, Anna. Brett's been riding bulls since he was a kid." Pete nonchalantly turned back to the ring.

At that moment, the chute burst open, drawing their attention. Anna grabbed the rail so tightly, her hands ached with the pressure.

To Anna's eyes, the bull seemed meaner than all the others put together, bucking twice as high. When the huge animal completely reversed himself in the air and landed in the dust with an earthshaking jolt, she just knew Brett was going to come flying off.

She squeezed her eyes shut, fear shattering her. The men gathered around the corral cheered, and she opened her eyes, thrilled to discover Brett still seated on the enraged animal.

Why hadn't the man blown the whistle? She wanted to run around the corral and grab the whistle from him. Roy must've paid him to make Brett ride longer. This had to be longer than eight seconds. A man could paint the Mona Lisa in this length of time!

"Oh, God, please let him be safe," she prayed under her breath. Brett didn't deserve to be hurt. He didn't—

The men around the corral cheered as the whistle was blown, and Anna sank against the rails, overwhelmed with relief. When Brett continued to cling to the bull's back, she looked around her, bewildered. "Why doesn't the bull stop?"

Even she realized the idiocy of her question. She'd seen the others dismount. It looked even more dangerous than the ride. But she hadn't worried about them.

"Can't he get off?" she gasped, her heart tripling its beat.

She held her breath as she noticed him loosening his grip and preparing to slip off the animal. At the same time, the bull gave his biggest jump, and Brett flipped in the air, landing on his back, his head slapping the dirt.

"Brett!" Anna screamed, and immediately clambered over the railing with no thought to her own safety.

Brett didn't move.

The bull came perilously close to his head as the man on horseback maneuvered him away. Anna ignored the bull and the rider and made a beeline to Brett.

She heard other footsteps, but she was the first to reach Brett's side. She fell to her knees and lifted his head to her lap, breathing a sigh of relief when his eyes fluttered and she felt his pulse.

"Brett, are you all right?" she whispered, tears gathering in her eyes.

"Anna!" Jake yelled as he reached her. "You almost got run over by the bull, you crazy girl. What do you think you're doing?"

"Trying to take care of my m—patient!" she snapped. His brother could at least have some concern for Brett.

"He's okay, aren't you, Brett?" Chad asked, suddenly appearing beside Jake.

As if answering a wake-up call, Brett's eyelids opened all the way and he stared at them. Anna gave a silent prayer of gratitude and stroked his face.

"Sure, I'm okay. I banged my head, that's all." He made an effort to lift his head, but Anna firmly held it against her. He smiled up at her. "But I rode him, Anna. You did hear the whistle, didn't you?"

She glared at the man she loved, wanting to drop his head onto the dirt and walk away, but she couldn't. He might already have a concussion. "Yes, I heard the stupid whistle. What difference does that make?"

"I wanted you to know I can ride as well as Roy," Brett explained, a wounded look on his face.

Men! How could Brett worry about such a silly thing when he'd put his life in danger? "Can you get up?"

"Of course."

But she noticed he didn't refuse the help his brothers gave him. As soon as he was upright, Anna shoved the much larger Chad out of the way and wrapped her arm around Brett's waist.

"Maybe we'd better call that a wrap for today," Jake said as she and Brett started back toward the chutes.

"Not on my account," Brett said nonchalantly. "I'm fine."

"Brett Randall, don't you dare get on a bull again!" Anna ordered, her free hand on her hip. She didn't care what anyone thought of her actions. She didn't want to live through another agonizing ride.

"You lettin' a woman tell you what to do?" Roy called from across the corral.

Anna didn't know what to expect from Brett. She hadn't intended to embarrass him. She held her breath when he stopped to look down at her.

A slow smile spread across his handsome face. "If it's Anna, I sure am," he called over his shoulder. Then, standing under his own power, he lifted her against him and kissed her.

AFTER THE EXCITEMENT of the afternoon, everyone seemed interested in an early night. Anna was glad. She and Red had helped Brett to bed, and she'd given him some headache medicine. Then, every hour she got to go into his room to rouse him just in case he'd suffered a concussion.

The sight of his big body spread out on the mattress was almost more than she could resist. It grew more and more difficult to remember why she shouldn't give in to the attraction they felt.

Oh, she knew he didn't love her. Not the way she wanted to be loved. If he did, he'd be interested in more than sleeping with her. But maybe she could convince him.

You idiot, Anna. You know better.

Yeah, she did. But her hands trembled, her heart thumped and her mouth went dry every time she went into his bedroom.

She was going to have to face the embarrassment of her behavior today, too. Fortunately none of the family had mentioned the kiss they'd shared, or her ordering Brett not to ride again, when she went down to supper.

She had no right to order him to do anything.

She knew better than to take his kisses seriously. Men liked to show off for a woman. But showing off didn't mean anything.

Certainly not what she wanted it to mean.

She'd have to stay in control until she could leave, she reminded herself after her next visit to his room. Otherwise, she might let her feelings for Brett overpower her good sense. Once Janie's babies were born, she could move back to her apartment and gain some perspective. Not seeing Brett every day would help.

"You going on up, Anna?" Jake asked as she started to leave the television room.

"Yes, I'm a little tired. But I'll continue to check on Brett."

"Thanks for caring about—I mean, for—Brett," Jake said, grinning.

"It's my job. I'm a nurse," she muttered, and hurried out the door. Did Jake know about her feelings for Brett? She hoped not. She was embarrassed enough as it was.

She dressed for bed, then slipped on her robe. Time to check on Brett again.

Slipping into the dimly lit room, she sat down on the edge of his big bed and lightly shook his shoulder.

"Brett? Brett, can you wake up?"

Earlier he'd barely roused and then fallen back asleep. This time, however, he opened his eyes wide. "I guess I can, since you're so determined."

She sat up straight. Her visit suddenly took on the aura of a much more dangerous event. He was wide-awake. "Do you still have a headache?"

"Nope. I don't have a headache, and I don't need to go back to sleep. How about you?" He gave her that endearing grin she found so hard to resist.

"I believe I do need to sleep, so—"

He swung back the covers. "Come on in. I've got plenty of room."

The brief glimpse of his long, muscular legs, his briefs, his broad chest, was almost more than her poor heart could bear. "Brett!" She pulled the covers back in place.

"Ah, don't get upset, Anna. I was just trying to take care of you."

"Don't expect me to fall for that line."

"Well, maybe I was looking for a little congratulations for riding the bull," he added, a twinkle in his eye.

Definitely no concussion.

"I believe I, uh, congratulated you in the corral."

"That puny kiss? It didn't even last as long as my ride. I think I deserve another."

She thought he did, too. Forget her sage advice to avoid the man, to keep her self-respect, to move away at once. All she could think about was Brett.

"All right," she calmly agreed.

He stared at her, almost in shock, and she lowered her lips to his before he could move. It didn't take him any time to come around, however. His arms went around her like a vise, hauling her against the entire length of his body as his mouth consumed hers.

Anna poured all the fears of the afternoon, all the longings of the night, into her kisses, opening her lips, her tongue dueling with his.

She stroked his body, running her fingers through the dark hairs on his chest, feeling the hard muscle beneath the warm skin. Exploring his back, the nape of his neck, she wondered if she could ever get enough of touching him.

To her surprise, Brett broke off the kiss.

"Listen, sugar, we have to talk."

He still held her against him. When Anna, realizing he now didn't even want her, tried to pull away, he refused to let her go.

"You want to talk?" she demanded, regretting that she sounded like a tragic heroine. But she was upset. She'd just decided to settle for his lovemaking if she couldn't have his love, and he'd changed his mind.

"Yeah. I wanted to tell you Sylvia didn't mean anything to me."

"I know." That was it? He thought she didn't know that, by the time Sylvia left, he'd almost hated her?

"I didn't want you to worry about her."

"No," she agreed even as her lips were descending to his again. She was relieved when he met her more than halfway. And maybe their brief conversation was beneficial. It made her long for his touch, his taste, more than ever.

There was nothing tentative in Brett's response. Somehow Anna ended up under the covers with him, and he'd rolled them over until he was on top of her. She wasn't sure how because she'd been distracted.

Then he lifted his lips from hers...to talk again.

"Anna, I can't wait," he whispered, his breathing ragged.

Anna's lips sought his, willing to accommodate him. After all, she hadn't put up any resistance the past few minutes. In fact, she'd been encouraging him. When he resisted, she tugged on his shoulders.

"No, wait, you don't understand," Brett whispered.

Before she could figure out what he meant, someone knocked on the door.

"Anna? Are you in there?"

Chapter Sixteen

Anna couldn't believe it. She'd finally decided to sleep with Brett, but first he wanted to talk. Then Jake arrived at the door.

In spite of Brett's reluctance to release her, Anna scrambled out of the bed, pulling her robe around her. "I'm coming, Jake," she called as she rushed to the door.

"Gabe's on the phone. He says it's an emergency." There was an unspoken apology in Jake's voice, as if he knew he'd interrupted something.

Anna hoped her embarrassment didn't show on her face.

Jake gestured to his bedroom next door, and she hurried to the phone beside his bed. "Gabe?"

"Anna? It's Carrie. She's hurting real bad. And bleeding."

Anna didn't waste any time. "I'll be right there. Call the ambulance." She hung up the phone and sprinted for her room. It only took a couple of minutes to change into jeans and a shirt. She stepped into loafers as she ran out the door.

She found Brett waiting for her at the bottom of the stairs.

"I'm coming with you."

"No, I don't have time for you," she muttered, rushing past him. She didn't need to be distracted, either.

By the time she backed her car out of its place, though, Brett slipped into the front seat, startling her.

"What are you doing?" she demanded, throwing on the brakes.

"Going with you. Come on, what are you waiting for?"

She didn't know. Ramming her foot down on the accelerator,

she roared down the driveway. As the ranch house lights dimmed behind them, she caught her second breath.

"Why are you here?"

"To take care of you."

She took her gaze off the dark road only momentarily, but she muttered, "That's crazy. You're the one with a concussion."

"I don't have a concussion. It's late at night. I don't want you out alone."

"I can take care of myself," she protested. "Don't you remember the first time we met?"

"Yep. You threw me on the floor."

"Well, then? You should've stayed in bed."

"Nah, I've been sleeping. I don't need to rest."

She growled in protest even as they sped through the night. "I don't have time to play, Brett. Carrie is having problems."

"I'm not here as a playmate. I'll do what I can to help, and if I can't help, I'll stay out of your way."

One of his big hands pushed back the riotous curls from her face and then settled on her shoulder. It felt so good she had to protest again. "This is foolish behavior."

"No more foolish than you jumping into the corral with a mad bull romping around. In fact, I'd say my accompanying you is a lot less dangerous. Wouldn't you?"

She glared at him before turning back to her driving. She didn't want to discuss her behavior this afternoon.

As THEY SPED through the night, Brett kept his gaze on Anna, taking in her uncombed hair, no-makeup face, thinking how beautiful she was. How natural and basic her approach was, putting others first, racing to give help.

Sylvia hadn't even been willing to help do the dishes. What Anna would face at the Browns' would be a lot more difficult.

Anna braked and pulled into the driveway that led to a small house, its porch light blazing.

"Is there anything you need carried in?" he asked as they came to a halt.

"My bag is behind the seat. If you'll bring it, I'll go on in. Both of them need some reassurance, if nothing else."

"I'm right behind you," he assured her. And he was, as soon as he removed her keys from the ignition and grabbed the medical bag. She'd left the door open, and he didn't bother to knock.

Following the sound of voices, he reached the open doorway to the bedroom where Carrie Brown and her husband were. Both of their faces were white, fear written in their eyes.

Brett didn't know much about having babies, but he knew the situation was dangerous. And having already lost one baby, he knew Gabe and Carrie were afraid tragedy might strike again.

"Anything you need?"

"No. Carrie, do you mind the company? Brett could hold your other hand. Maybe tell you a few funny stories," Anna suggested with a smile. Brett could tell she was worried and was trying to hide it from her patient.

"Anna, is the baby all right? When the bleeding started, I was afraid— I felt it move!"

"Of course you did, Carrie. Now, I need to take your blood pressure and temperature before the ambulance gets here. You let these men do the talking while I do, okay?"

"Oh. But—"

"Brett, did you tell Carrie about our rodeo today? He turned a flip in the air. Almost broke his head," she said with a smile.

Brett understood Anna's silent command and began relating little stories from the rodeo, hoping to distract both Carrie and her husband. He even talked about Roy competing with him for Anna's attention, and bragged shamefully of his success.

In the meantime, Anna worked quietly, taking Carrie's temperature, her blood pressure, and then listening to the baby's heartbeat.

Brett admired her strength and control. Even in the few minutes since they'd arrived, he could see Gabe relaxing a little. Carrie, however, was strung tight as a wire.

"Can you hear the baby's heartbeat? Can you?" she demanded.

"Hey, Carrie, she can't hear you and the baby, too," Brett teased. "As soon as they finish their conversation, she'll talk to you. And if that child's as long-winded as Gabe, she'll get back to you around Christmas."

"Hey, I'm not talkative!" Gabe returned, surprise on his face.

"I know," Brett muttered, "and I could use some help distracting your wife."

Gabe took Brett's not too subtle hint and began asking Carrie about what she wanted him to pack for the hospital. He even went so far as to get a pen and paper to make a list. Brett almost lost his control when Carrie explained about the baby clothes they'd need. He only hoped they were right.

The wail of the siren came through the night. He'd always considered that sound alarming, but now it was a comfort. It gave knowledge that help was on the way.

"Perfect. They're almost here," Anna said, putting away her stethoscope.

"Is everything all right?" Carrie asked anxiously, forgetting the list.

"Anna?" Gabe asked, too, his voice shaking.

Brett wondered how he'd feel if his woman, Anna, were in Carrie's position. He probably wouldn't hold together as well as Gabe was.

"Everyone's safe for the moment. We'll know more when we get you to the hospital and can hook up the ultrasound. They'll have alerted Doc, and he'll be waiting for us."

Gabe went to the closet and grabbed the suitcase and began throwing things from the list into it. By the time the ambulance attendants entered the bedroom, the suitcase was full, though who knew if any of it would be useful.

Anna turned to Brett as they put Carrie on the stretcher, Gabe walking beside her holding her hand. "Can you follow with the car?"

"Yep. Gabe with me or you?"

Anna took a deep breath, worry all over her face. "He'd better come with me."

When they reached the ambulance, she said to Gabe, "Go sit up there by Carrie's head." Then she turned to Brett. "I'll see you at the hospital?"

"I'll be right behind you."

To his surprise, she lifted up on her tiptoes and gave him a brief kiss that had him wanting more. "Thanks."

Before he could respond, she was in the ambulance, closing the back door, and the driver raced off into the night.

He went back and closed the front door, then got in Anna's car and followed the ambulance into town.

Man, Pete was right, he thought as he drove along. Having a baby was hard. Maybe because the whole thing was beyond any man's experience. Not knowing what was happening was the hardest thing of all.

When he reached the hospital, he found Gabe pacing the waiting room. "Did Doc come in?"

"Yeah. He was waiting for us. They won't let me in there."

"They'll be out to talk to you soon, Gabe. They're just trying to do the best they can for Carrie."

"But if she's having the baby, I'm supposed to be with her. I promised her I'd be there for her," he said, his eyes wide with panic. He took a turn about the room, then came back to Brett to confess, "Sometimes I pass out if there's much blood."

Courage had a lot of definitions, Brett decided, including Anna ignoring a big bull to run to his side. But poor old Gabe was showing some courage, too. He didn't want to be anywhere near an operating room. But for his wife, he was pleading to be beside her. Brett clapped him on the shoulder and paced the room with him.

Five minutes later, Doc came into the waiting room. "Gabe, we've got a little problem here. We're going to have to take the baby, do a cesarean. You understand?"

Brett braced the other man, his heart aching for both Gabe and his wife.

Gabe jerkily nodded his head. "The—the baby?" he whispered.

"We're going to do everything we can to take care of the little tyke. It's early, of course, but babies usually make it at thirty-four weeks."

Gabe sagged against Brett. Bracing his friend, Brett studied Doc. "Anna? Is she going to help you?"

"Yep. She's scrubbing now. I've got to go. Gabe, you want to be in the operating room with Carrie?"

Brett felt the shiver go through his friend, but Gabe nodded. "Yeah," he said hoarsely. "I got to be there with her."

"Good boy," Doc said, patting him on the shoulder. Then he nodded to Brett. "It'll take about an hour or so."

Gabe followed Doc down the hall on wobbly legs. Brett remembered to call to Gabe as he walked away. "You need me to call your parents?"

"Uh, yeah," Gabe agreed before he went through the double doors.

Brett fished in his pockets for a quarter and called Gabe's parents, who lived there in Rawhide. Carrie's parents lived in Cheyenne, several hours away. Brett figured Gabe's parents would know how to get hold of them.

After Gabe's parents' arrival, Brett had company in the waiting room as he waited for Anna. She'd had a long day, with no chance to rest. Unless you counted the few minutes in his bed, and resting hadn't been on his mind. She'd be exhausted. But he was proud of her.

When Doc came out again, he was alone. Gabe's parents rushed to him, and Brett followed, looking for Anna.

"Carrie is fine. A little weak. She lost quite a bit of blood, but we're giving her transfusions. The baby is a boy. He's a little puny, of course, but he's holding his own."

Now that he knew everyone was safe, Brett waited patiently for the eager questions to be answered. He had one of his own. He was ready to take Anna home.

"Anna?" he asked as Doc turned to go.

Doc's eyebrows rose. "You her official keeper, young man?"

Brett never hesitated. "Yes, I am. She's bound to be exhausted. I'm waiting to take her home."

Doc nodded, grinning. "Good choice, Brett. But it'll be a while before she can go, 'bout half an hour. She's settling Carrie in."

Brett nodded. He knew Anna wouldn't leave before everything was taken care of. She never put herself first. That was why she needed him.

Not that he would interfere with her work. But she needed someone to pamper her a little when she wasn't delivering babies. She needed someone to let her know how special she was. And that someone was him.

He'd been encouraged at the corral when she'd kissed him back. Of course, he'd said it was for luck. But she didn't shy away. Then, when she'd run to his rescue, he'd figured that was a good sign.

Jake had visited him before he'd drifted off to sleep earlier, and he'd related what he'd heard about how Anna had told Roy off for criticizing Brett. He'd fallen asleep figuring how he'd tell Anna first thing this morning that he loved her. That he wanted to marry her, to hold her close to him all his life.

When she'd woken him up that last time, and he'd come fully awake, he'd intended to take advantage of the situation, glad he wouldn't have to wait until morning. But they'd gotten distracted.

It looked as if that declaration would have to wait until they'd both had a little sleep.

When Anna appeared, Brett reminded himself again that now wasn't the time for a proposal. Her pale face made the freckles stand out. He wanted to haul her into his arms and kiss each one of them. And any other part of her that wanted loving.

"How's Carrie and the baby?" he asked softly.

She didn't smile, but she nodded as she pressed her lips tightly together. "I think they'll both make it. Carrie's stabilized."

"Ready to go home?"

His words brought a faint smile, pleasing him. "Yeah. It's been a long night."

He took her arm and led her to her car, the passenger side. "I think I'd better drive. I haven't been working the last couple of hours."

Anna didn't make any argument. When he got in on the driver's side, he reached out and slid her over the bench seat until she was sitting next to him. Her head fell naturally to his shoulder.

Starting the car, he backed out of the small hospital parking lot and soon had them on the road back to the ranch.

"I want to thank you for helping tonight," Anna whispered, not moving as she leaned against him.

"No problem. I was real proud of you," he added, turning to kiss her brow.

She swallowed noisily, then seemed to struggle to say, "There wasn't a lot I could do. I wasn't s-sure the baby would make it."

"It must be hard for you when something goes wrong." He couldn't imagine having to face the death of a baby. Or a young woman in the prime of her life. His arm tightened as he thought of Anna in Carrie's place.

She was pressed against him, one hand clutching his shirt. It made him feel good to know that she wanted him to hold her close. That she depended on him. As tired as he himself was, however, it took a few minutes to realize that Anna had begun to tremble.

"Anna, are you all right?"

She didn't answer except for a low sob.

He pulled the car to the side of the road and shut off the engine. "Sugar? What's wrong? Is she not going to make it?"

Though he tried to see her face, she buried it in his shirt. He was relieved when she shook her head, but her sobs were deeper. He ran his hands up and down her back, unsure what to do.

"Anna, what—?"

"It's my mother all over again," she cried. "Only there wasn't anyone to help *her*. Just me…and I couldn't!"

"Of course you couldn't, Anna. You were only six years old. It's not your fault. And you saved Carrie tonight. And the baby."

She gulped several times before she rubbed her hand over his shirt. "Sorry. I've got your shirt all wet."

He didn't mind. Especially since she stayed pressed against him. He brushed her hair back and stroked her cheek. "No problem."

"It's just that…every time, I see my mother. I feel that panic rise up in me, as if I were six years old again." Her sob turned into a hiccup, and she buried her face again.

"Mercy, sugar, you go through this every time?"

She shook her head. "Only when—when it's bad, like tonight. And usually I'm by myself when I fall apart. Sorry, Brett. Guess now you know what a coward I am.''

He wrapped both arms tightly around her. ''I don't know any such thing. I know you're brave, and skilled, and caring. I know that you care more about other people than you do about yourself.'' He tilted up her chin to kiss her trembling lips, trying to restrain his urge to devour her.

Those soft lips molded themselves to his, and she pressed even closer. Her need only fed the fire burning inside him. He loved her response. There was nothing coy about Anna O'Brien. She made him feel good all over...in more ways than one.

He only hoped he did as much for her. He worried that she would later think he'd taken advantage of her emotional needs. ''Anna, are you sure?''

She looked up at him, her eyes wide. ''I'm sure. I was sure earlier, in your bed. I've fought what you do to me for too long. I need you, Brett. I need to feel you inside me, around me. Don't stop.''

Whatever the lady wanted, he readily agreed, his lips returning to hers. As if it were a sacrifice. He would've died if she'd backed off.

She was such a little thing, and yet she held his heart in her hands. His lips left hers and trailed down her neck, tasting her soft skin.

Just like this afternoon and earlier tonight, he was claiming her, and she wasn't saying no.

His hands slid under her sweatshirt as his mouth devoured her. He had to touch her skin, to feel her warmth. He came to an abrupt halt, however, when he realized she wore nothing beneath the sweatshirt. If he'd known that earlier, he wouldn't have been able to think of anything else.

Pulling his lips away, he gasped, ''You're not wearing a bra!''

Embarrassed, she pulled her shirt down and tried to sit up. ''No. I'm—I'm not very big. No one can tell.''

Brett pulled her back across his chest, his mouth returning to hers and his hands sliding up her slim form. His hands eagerly slid under her shirt again, cupping her breasts.

Several minutes passed before he lifted his mouth to respond to her comment. "You're perfect, Anna O'Brien. Absolutely perfect."

He began pushing the sweatshirt up, unable to wait to see her milky skin in the moonlight, to touch every part of her. He'd forgotten his exhaustion, and hers, too.

When he'd removed the shirt, he paused in reverent awe before his hands cupped her small breasts again, his thumbs gently stroking. Her breasts were the most beautiful he'd ever seen.

She gasped several deep breaths but didn't protest him having pulled her sweatshirt from her slim, lithe figure. His lips sought hers as his hands stroked her.

He was pleased when she began unbuttoning his shirt. The feel of her fingers on his skin set him on fire. Soon he was bare-chested, too, and she ran her fingers through his chest hairs, sending shivers all over him.

In spite of the small space in her front seat, Brett was eager to completely disrobe. All his plans for a beautifully romantic seduction, which he'd almost achieved in his bed earlier that evening, had flown out the window.

All he knew was that Anna was his. Forever and ever. And he was going to get around to informing her of that fact in case she had any doubts. Soon. Right now he had other things on his mind.

He did have a momentary thought about a condom, since Jake had always preached responsibility, but he couldn't stop now. It didn't matter, since he and Anna would be married right away.

When he entered her, Brett felt the most incredible sense of peace and homecoming, of rightness, that he'd ever felt. It was immediately replaced by intense excitement, a driving urge to completion that consumed him. Fortunately Anna was urging him on, crooning to him with a sweetness that made the final explosion all that much more powerful.

As silence and stillness fell in the little car, he twisted the pair of them so he was on bottom and she could rest atop him.

"We should—"

"Rest, sugar. Rest. We'll deal with everything later." He knew how tired she was and, more than ever, he wanted to take care of her. Soon he'd take her back to the ranch and they'd sleep in his bed, but for a few moments, he needed to hold her here.

He kissed the top of her head and held her against him, feeling her relax, sinking onto him, making him feel even more that they were one.

Anna let a small sigh of contentment escape as she snuggled into Brett. She wasn't willing to debate her behavior tonight. She'd tried too long and hard to resist this man, but tonight she couldn't. Tomorrow she'd face the pain of loving him. Tomorrow she'd worry about the future. Tonight she'd just love him.

With a grand, glorious, incredible love.

Chapter Seventeen

The ringing bothered her.

It wasn't close. Muffled. That was how it sounded. She should answer it. If she knew where it was coming from.

But she was so comfortable, so warm, so...content.

The ringing came again. She opened one eye, expecting to see her bedroom. Instead, she saw the car dashboard.

About the same time, she realized she was stretched out stark naked on top of Brett Randall.

"Dear God, what have I done?" she said with a gasp, her words as much a prayer as anything.

The ringing of the phone again sent her diving over into the back seat, scrambling for her bag. She kept the cellular phone there and only used it in emergencies.

"Hello?" she gasped.

"Anna? Where are you? It's time!" Pete's voice was frantic, and he didn't bother to take time to breathe. "She's in labor. Hurry, Anna."

"I'm on my way. Ten minutes at the most."

Brett's head appeared above the seat. "Anna? What's wrong?"

He looked groggy, but Anna couldn't spare the time to be concerned about him.

Or about what she'd done.

"Janie's in labor." She twisted and turned, trying to find her clothes. Her jeans were in the back seat, but she couldn't find her panties or her sweatshirt anywhere. "Damn it, where are my clothes?"

Brett held out her panties, and she snatched them from him. "Is my sweatshirt up there?" Later, she was going to be horribly embarrassed about her situation. She didn't have time now.

"Get dressed, Brett," she snapped as she grabbed her top from him and shrugged into it. By the time she had her clothes on, Brett had pulled on his jeans and was buttoning his shirt.

She clambered back over the seat and slid behind the wheel, shoving Brett's leg out of the way. Without looking at him, she started the car and rammed her foot on the accelerator.

Dawn was just breaking, but there wasn't much light because a thunderstorm was building all around them. "This storm is going to panic Pete."

"He'll be all right. But what about Janie? She's not due yet, either."

"She's thirty-three weeks, only three weeks early. That's fairly normal for twins," she said tersely, staring at the road ahead of her, checking her watch.

He didn't ask any more questions. Much to Anna's relief. She was focused on getting to Janie. But on the fringes of her mind, she was replaying what had taken place in her car a few hours ago.

Their lovemaking had been unbelievably wonderful...and incredibly stupid. She wasn't the kind of woman who slept around. But Brett wouldn't know that.

He probably thought they would have an affair.

She couldn't do that. She couldn't offer him casual sex when the urge overtook him. All she had to offer was her entire being, in particular her heart. And when he rejected it, she would be devastated.

The lights of the ranch house drew her thoughts, but she took one last look at Brett, one lingering look of love, before she faced what lay ahead. Both for Janie and herself.

When they reached the ranch, Jake was on the back porch watching for them. Anna didn't ask Brett to bring her bag this time. She didn't want him anywhere near her.

"I'm here," she announced unnecessarily as she ran past Jake.

Within seconds she was in Janie's room, reassuring both Pete and Janie that everything was progressing as it should. She sent Pete out to call Janie's mother and Doc, and she drew her first deep breath since the phone had awakened her.

"WHERE HAVE YOU TWO BEEN?" Jake asked as he led Brett into the kitchen and poured him a cup of coffee.

"Uh, I went with Anna, remember? Carrie and Gabe Brown. If it hadn't been for Anna, Carrie and the baby might not've made it."

"Everything's okay now?"

"Yeah." Brett cleared his throat. Yeah, everything was great. He and Anna had worked out their differences. Hadn't they? He only knew they belonged together. No question about that now. He grinned, his gaze dreamy.

"So you just left the hospital?"

Jake's question brought him back to reality. He looked at his sharp-eyed brother and dismissed any idea of lying to him. "Uh, no, not exactly. When we left the hospital, Anna seemed okay, but after a few minutes, she started crying. I stopped the car to console her and—and we decided to rest for a while. And—and we fell asleep."

Kind of an expurgated version of the truth, but—

"I guess that would explain why your shirt is buttoned up crooked," Jake said, a grin on his face.

Though he felt his cheeks heating up, Brett couldn't hold back a smile. Damn! Being with Anna felt so good he wanted to tell everyone. "Yeah, I guess it would."

"She's a good woman," Jake said softly. "You got lucky, brother."

"Yeah."

JANIE WAS TAKING HER TIME.

Brett felt sure he was going crazy. Several times, he'd gone upstairs and rapped softly on the door of Janie's bedroom. Each time, Janie's mother, Lavinia, opened the door to tell him Janie was doing fine. When he asked about Anna, she told him Anna was doing fine also.

"But she hasn't had much rest," he whispered back the second time.

"She's taken several naps."

"Can I bring her some food? And you, too, of course," he hurriedly added, remembering his manners.

"Red has brought us some food, thank you, Brett. Why don't you get Pete to go downstairs for a while?"

So instead of getting to see Anna, he escorted his brother downstairs. And paced with him. And listened to him talk.

"I think Janie should go to the hospital," Pete burst out.

"Want me to call an ambulance?" Brett offered.

"No, she won't go. She wants the babies to be born here. Like we were. And Anna says there's no reason to transfer her to the hospital right now."

"Did she talk to Doc?"

"Yeah. They're talking all the time. I'd better go back up there."

As Pete headed for the stairs, Brett grabbed his arm. "Your mother-in-law told me to keep you down here for at least half an hour, and it's only been five minutes. Let's go to the kitchen and get something to eat."

He watched the struggle on Pete's face, knowing his brother couldn't think of eating while Janie was in labor. He could sympathize with him.

And he hoped his and Anna's…activity only a few hours ago didn't result in a pregnancy. Not that he didn't want babies. Of course he did. But he wasn't ready to face what Pete was going through just yet. He wanted some time with Anna. Just the two of them.

Chad and Jake, along with Janie's father, were in the kitchen with Red when they entered. All conversation halted as Pete and Brett entered.

Waiting was difficult, Brett decided, but having family around certainly made a difference. He thought about how hard it must've been on Anna, being all alone. But she wasn't anymore.

She was going to be a Randall. And their family was growing every day.

"Does this ever get any easier?" Pete asked as he plopped down beside Jake.

"Don't look at me," Jake returned. "You're the first one to go through this fathering business."

"But he's not going to be the last," Chad said.

No, he wouldn't be the last, Brett agreed silently.

"It never got any easier for me," Hank muttered.

Everyone remembered that he and his wife had suffered several miscarriages.

"It was pretty hard for Gabe and Carrie last night," Brett said. "Looks like she and the baby will be all right, but I'm not sure about Gabe. He passes out at the sight of blood, but he went into the operating room to be with her."

Pete nodded grimly. "I'm going to be there for Janie. It's not fair to let her be alone."

As he finished speaking, Doc came in the back door and hurried past them without a word. Pete watched him, his eyes large as he straightened in his chair. "Maybe I should—"

"They'll call you, boy," Hank assured him.

Pete had just subsided against the back of the chair when the door swung open and Anna appeared. Brett leapt up, but he wasn't the one she wanted.

"Pete, it's time," she announced.

Without waiting for him to respond, she turned and ran out the door. Pete almost beat her to it.

ANNA HAD MADE A DECISION while she helped Doc deliver Janie's twin boys. She had to leave. Obviously she couldn't be trusted to resist Brett's charms. Indeed, resisting them now would be almost impossible, now that she knew how powerful and wonderful those charms were.

She should never have lost control.

"Brilliant conclusion!" she muttered as, having reached her bedroom, she began pulling open drawers and dumping her clothes on the bed. She slid the suitcase out from under the bed, threw it open and placed the stacks of clothes haphazardly into it.

She wasn't aware she was crying until a big, fat tear landed on her hand. She swiped her cheeks and kept on packing. The sooner she got away from the Randalls', the sooner she'd be back in control.

Why had she been so stupid? She'd told herself all along that Brett wasn't for her. She'd known he wouldn't choose someone like her. Of course, that wouldn't stop him from sleeping with her. Especially when she threw herself in his arms and encouraged him.

But when he kissed her, she forgot all her warnings.

And never would she forget the moments spent in his arms this morning. But he hadn't spoken of the future, of love.

Her hand stole to her stomach as she realized they'd taken no precautions. The thought that she might even now hold Brett's child inside her both thrilled her and brought a dose of despair. If that were true, she'd have to move away. She wouldn't fall to Sylvia's level, trying to trap Brett with a baby, even if it was his.

With a sob, she admitted she'd have to move away whether she was pregnant or not. She couldn't remain in the area, watching Brett from a distance. Possibly running into him on the street. Watching him eventually marry and have his own children.

She sniffed and wiped her face again. Then she fastened the suitcase and hefted it off the bed onto the floor. She had to get away. She couldn't think this close to Brett. The lack of sleep and emotional stress made a coherent thought impossible to find.

Taking a deep, shuddering breath, she straightened. Returning to Janie's bedroom, she whispered a goodbye to Mrs. Dawson, checked on Janie and the babies one more time, then slipped from the room. Returning for her suitcase, she then started down the stairs.

She could hear voices from the kitchen and knew, as always, the family was gathered in their favorite room. Which was why she headed for the front door. She'd have to walk around the house to her car by the back porch, but no one would notice her departure. They were too busy celebrating the two newest Randalls.

She stowed away her suitcase and slid behind the wheel. As quietly as possible, she started the engine and eased down on the accelerator. In seconds she was leaving the Randall ranch behind.

And tears were rolling down her cheeks.

"DID I HEAR A CAR?" Brett asked, thinking they were having company as word spread about the babies. Maybe B.J. was coming to see Janie.

Even as he casually rose to go to the window, his brain registered that the sound was getting fainter rather than louder. Curious, he leaned toward the window.

Just in time to catch the taillights of Anna's car.

He whirled around to glare at Doc. "Where's Anna going? She's too tired to take another call."

"Anna?" Doc asked, sitting up straight. "What call?"

Brett didn't ask any more questions. He raced for the stairs. He slowed down to quietly open the door to Janie's room, and Janie's mother met him.

"Where's Anna? Did she say where she was going?"

Lavinia stared at him as if he'd lost his mind. "She said she was going back home," she whispered. "I thought everyone knew."

Panic filled Brett. Gone home? She was home! He'd been congratulating himself all day that Anna was now his, a part of his family, the center of his heart. Without a word, he left and ran to Anna's room. The open drawers and empty closet told their tale.

With no logic or discernible thoughts, Brett ran back down the stairs, through the kitchen, ignoring the questions shouted at him, and out to his pickup. Fortunately he'd left the keys in it. Within seconds he was spinning out of the yard, chasing Anna.

She couldn't leave him. She loved him. He knew she did. And if she didn't, he'd teach her to love him. Because he couldn't live without Anna.

Her little yellow car was pulling onto the highway when he

first saw it. She wasn't traveling very fast. Brett pressed down even more on the accelerator and began honking the horn.

He knew the moment she became aware of him because her car slowed, as if her foot had slipped from the accelerator. But instead of pulling over, as he'd hoped she would, she sped up.

Damn the woman! What did she think she was doing? He whipped onto the highway and charged after her. Though he'd had Mike tune her car to good condition, it didn't have the power of his pickup. In a minute, he'd passed her. Then, after he'd gotten a little way ahead of her, he jammed on the brakes and slewed his truck across the two-lane highway, blocking Anna.

She had no choice but to stop.

He jumped out of the truck and reached her car door by the time she'd come to a halt.

"Where the hell are you going?" he demanded as he yanked open the door.

"Home," she said, but she didn't look at him.

He took her arm and pulled her from the car. "Look at me!"

Instead, she tried to turn away. He took her chin between his fingers and pulled her face around. The tears streaking down her pale cheeks almost broke his heart.

"Sugar, what are you doing to us?" he asked as he lifted her against him.

"Put me down. I have to g-go—"

"Where? Where do you think you can go so that I can't find you?" He buried his face in her neck, breathing in the scent of her.

"I—I can't stay, Brett. I'm not what you need. Megan and Janie pushed you into—into thinking you might like me. You haven't had time—"

He slid her down his body until her lips were even with his. His mouth covered hers, swallowing the words that were spilling out. Later there would be time for explanations, arguments. Now he had to persuade her that she wasn't going anywhere.

And he was persuading as hard as he could.

She pulled away, her fingers slipping between their lips. "Brett, you're—you're not listening to me."

"Because you're talkin' nonsense, sugar. No one persuaded me to 'like' you! Damn it, I love you!" He dipped his head and trailed kisses down her neck. He heaved a sigh of relief when her arms went around his neck and she buried her head on his shoulder.

"That's it, sugar. That's it. We're together. Forever and ever," he crooned, as if he were comforting a baby. Indeed, her body trembled against him, and he felt her sobs. "Don't you love me, Anna? Even a little? You tried to save me from a bull. I thought that meant you cared about me."

"Of course I do!" she almost screamed, rearing back from his embrace. "I love you, you idiot!"

"Then why were you leaving?"

"Because I'm not right for you, just like Sylvia. I know we— we strike sparks off each other, but you need someone appropriate, someone important—"

"Strike sparks?" Brett shouted. "Damn it, we're a nuclear warhead! I've never felt anything like I felt this morning, in this little bitty car."

"We shouldn't have— I lost control," she confessed, collapsing against him again.

"I think that's my line, Anna darlin'."

"No, it was my fault. I threw myself at you. But it's okay. I don't expect anything—"

"Well, I do! If you don't promise to marry me right away, I'm going to tell everyone you seduced me and then abandoned me. And after I paid five hundred dollars for your company, too."

Her head popped up again. "Brett, don't be silly. Men don't— What? Paid? You didn't know it was my box."

"Yes, I did. I bribed the mayor. I need you, Anna O'Brien. No one else will do. You're perfect for me."

"Oh, Brett…" Anna whispered, her gaze roving his face as if searching for the truth.

"Anna, my love, I can't live without you."

"Are you sure?"

"Let me show you how sure I am."

"DAMN IT, SUGAR, some day soon you're going to have to give me time to get you to a bed before you attack me like that," Brett complained as his heart returned to its normal speed. His smile of contentment stretched from ear to ear before he leaned down to kiss her again.

Anna loved him. All was right with the world.

She lay beneath him, her arms linked around his neck. "Me?" she complained with a grin. "You're the one—"

A horn honking interrupted their soft teasing.

"Oh, mercy, I'm blocking the road," Brett exclaimed, and began grabbing his clothes. Anna tried to help him even as she was pulling her sweatshirt over her head. "Hurry, Brett. Oh, this is so embarrassing."

They heard a car door close and realized someone was coming to investigate. Brett zipped up his jeans and stepped out of the car to shrug on his shirt. Barefoot, he hurried to his truck, while Anna pulled the door closed behind him.

"Brett Randall, what are you doing blocking the—?" His first-grade teacher, Mrs. Renniker, asked as she peered at him through her glasses. She stopped her question when she saw Anna in the car behind him. Then she stared at his bare feet.

When her gaze traveled back up to his face, Brett knew it was beet red. He expected her to blister him with some sharp words.

Instead, she smiled. "I guess I'll be getting an invitation to another Randall wedding soon." She looked at Anna again. "Very soon."

Brett turned back to look at Anna, too, his heart in his eyes. Then he beamed at Mrs. Renniker. "Yes, ma'am," he agreed. "There'll be another Randall wedding any day now."

Epilogue

The hastily planned wedding was wonderful. Doc Jacoby gave the blushing bride away, and Brett thought she'd never looked more beautiful. Her red curls were subdued beneath the white veil, but he knew the fire in her was as strong as ever. And would be in their children, too.

The entire community once more came to the Randall ranch to enjoy another reception. There was a lot of talk about Jake's plan, and the success he'd had.

Janie and Pete showed off their new sons from the top of the stairs. Janie wasn't about to let anyone get closer and expose her babies to any germs. She took them back to their nursery, where their grandmother was waiting.

Megan and Chad were teased about their baby's arrival. And Brett and Anna beamed at everyone. Several women grew teary eyed just watching Brett hover over Anna, not letting her out of his sight for a minute.

Jake raised a glass of champagne to toast the new couple. "Here's to the latest Randall lady. My brothers have all been fortunate in their brides. May they all be happy and, of course, have lots of babies."

His audience chuckled.

"What about you, Jake?" someone shouted. "Aren't you gonna do your share to carry on the name?"

Several suggestions were shouted out for Jake to follow, but he shook his head, grinning.

"Not me, Miller. My job is to be the best damn uncle in the world. My brothers are taking care of the marriage duties."

Everyone drank to his toast, and conversations continued.

Janie, Megan and Anna all stared at Jake, then looked at each other. First Janie, then Megan and Anna, raised their glasses and had a private toast.

Brett, catching sight of their action, slipped an arm around his wife. "What was that all about?"

Anna turned in his arms, loving his touch, the feeling of never being alone again, of belonging to Brett Randall. She reached up and kissed him softly. "Nothing, sweetheart. Just girl stuff."

She winked at her new sisters-in-law before allowing her husband to carry her over the threshold of her new life.

COWBOY SURRENDER

Prologue

"You need to sell your cows and replace them with ostriches."

Jake Randall's head jerked up, and he stared at the woman sitting to his left at the kitchen table. "I beg your pardon?"

"Ostriches are the latest thing. I'm sure you would do well with them. And you should paint your barns red. That's the color people expect to see."

Even as he spoke to his guest, Jake turned to glare at his sister-in-law Janie, seated halfway down the table. "I didn't realize you were an authority on ranching, Miss Quentin."

"Just a case of using common sense. I think the ranch would be more attractive if your employees wore uniforms, too. Maybe black pants and turquoise shirts."

Jake swallowed carefully before saying, "Thank you for the suggestion. Are you going to be in Wyoming long?" He hoped not.

Janie spoke before her friend could answer. "Allison is thinking of settling here."

"Oh, really," Jake sent a silent prayer upward that she chose another part of the vast state of Wyoming, far away from the Randall spread he and his brothers owned.

"It all depends," Allison Quentin murmured, suddenly batting her eyes at Jake. "I'm in Wyoming to find a husband. I've heard women are scarce out here."

Not that scarce.

"MR. RANDALL, I'm so glad you could join Megan and me for lunch," the blonde gushed, patting his arm with a soft hand capped with bright red talons that any self-respecting wolf would've been proud of.

"My pleasure, Miss Baker," he said politely, but he shot a look of frustration at Megan. His sister-in-law had asked him to accompany her shopping for a present for her husband, his brother Chad. She had neglected to mention a previous lunch engagement until a couple of minutes ago.

The blonde's statuesque figure was encased in a tight black dress, cut low to expose her charms. When she leaned toward him to talk, Jake had a fascinating picture in his mind of her popping out of the dress like a hot dog bursting from its skin when it was cooked.

"I'm thrilled to meet a real live cowboy," Mindy Baker cooed. Her hand traveled up and down his sleeve, as if seeking entrance to what lay below the fabric.

"You've never met Chad, Megan's husband?"

She giggled, her bosom shaking like gelatin. "Well, of course I have, silly, but he's married."

"Cowboys can't be married?"

"Of course they can, but I'm not interested in married cowboys." She batted her fake eyelashes at him.

Uh-oh. Not again!

JAKE LOOKED FORWARD to dinner with his family. His three brothers and their wives were pleasant company, and his new twin nephews were special delights.

Yeah, life was good.

He swung into the kitchen, a smile on his face, only to find his favorite room in the house empty, the table not set for dinner. What the hell…?

"Jake?" Red called, following him into the room. "We're eating in the dining room tonight."

A sense of foreboding filling him, Jake asked, "Why?"

The cowboy-turned-housekeeper walked directly to the oven, not even glancing at Jake. "We have company tonight, a friend of Anna's."

"An unmarried friend of Anna's?" Jake asked carefully.

"How would I know?" Red answered, again not meeting his gaze. "Come on, everyone else is ready to eat."

Jake followed Red into the formal dining room, but he would've preferred retreating to his bedroom. He was beginning to feel hunted.

Anna, his newest sister-in-law, a petite, red-headed whirlwind, met him at the door. "Jake, I hope you don't mind, but I've invited one of my nursing professors from Casper to stay a few days with us. She's never been on a ranch before."

"It's your home, Anna. Of course you can invite your friends to stay."

"Janice, let me introduce you to Jake, Brett's brother. Jake, this is Janice Kobell."

"How do you do, Miss Kobell. It is 'Miss,' isn't it?" he asked a trifle grimly.

"Yes, it is, though, of course, I'm always hoping to find that special man. I can't tell you how frustrating and difficult it is to find any kind of man in the city. They're all so wimpy. That's why I decided to accept Anna's invitation. She assured me the Randall men would never be considered wimpy. And she was so right. You are a wonderful specimen, Jake. I can't wait to observe you in…action."

Her eyelashes blinked so furiously, Jake wondered if she had something in her eye.

"You're welcome to watch all of us work," he said, taking a step back.

Janice stepped closer to him, her nostrils flaring, as she reached out to stroke his chest. "Oh, Jake, I'm not talking about work."

Jake lost his appetite.

Chapter One

"Crazy women!" Jake Randall muttered as he charged into the barn.

There was a sharp wind blowing outside, foretelling the cold winter that would soon follow. But it was only October and Jake, a veteran of thirty-four previous Wyoming winters, hadn't been chased inside by the weather. No, his problem was women.

"Something wrong?" a cool feminine voice asked.

Jake spun around in surprise. He had supposed he was alone. Instead, he found himself facing B. J. Anderson, the local veterinarian who lived on his and his brothers' ranch.

"I didn't know you were here," he said abruptly, and stuck his hands deep in his back jean pockets.

B.J. rolled her eyes and turned her back on him, continuing her examination of the mare in the stall with her.

Jake studied her. She'd been around since the first of the year, arriving, with her young son and aunt, almost simultaneously with the influx of women to the Randall family.

Women he'd wanted for his brothers.

Women he now wanted to strangle.

It wasn't that he didn't love his new sisters-in-law—or the changes they'd brought to the Randall ranch. And he adored his twin nephews, born in July. But he needed some relief from their female scheming.

"B.J."

She'd finished her examination of the mare and was packing up her kit. "Mmm-hmm?"

She didn't sound interested in a conversation—or anything else—with him, he thought in irritation. Not that he could blame her. She was a damn good vet, in spite of being female. He'd doubted her abilities at first, but now he backed her one hundred percent...as a vet.

It was as a woman that he had problems with her. Something he hadn't exactly kept to himself.

She came out of the stall, her long legs encased in slim-fitting jeans. She was a tall woman, strong, lithe, but no one ever mistook her for a man. In fact, Jake was amazed, now that he thought about it, that she hadn't married since her arrival.

There was a shortage of women in Wyoming. Even ugly ones were snatched up. Not that anyone would ever call B. J. Anderson ugly. Not with her beautiful body and long dark hair, usually braided, her smooth, creamy complexion that urged a man to touch it, her—

"Did you want something, Jake, or were you just passing the time?" she finally asked, interrupting his thoughts.

He turned away from her, hoping to clear his mind of the strange thoughts suddenly running rampant. "I've got a problem."

"Only one? Then you're ahead of the rest of us." She started walking past him.

Desperate for someone to talk to, he reached out and caught her arm—and then dropped it. The awareness that filled him the minute he touched her was part of the problem he had with B. J. Anderson.

"Can you spare me a minute?" he asked.

She shrugged her shoulders and sat down on the bench that ran along the back wall of the barn.

Jake considered sitting beside her, then thought better of it. He paced across the aisle between the stalls several times.

"Jake, are you going to talk, or parade back and forth?"

"You're friends with the girls."

His abrupt statement didn't seem to faze B.J.

"Girls?"

"Janie, Megan and Anna."

"Your sisters-in-law? Yes, I think I can safely say they're my friends."

"So what are they up to?" He watched her, anxious to see if she would cover up what he suspected was going on.

Her eyebrows rose, but she didn't look away. The smooth perfection of her face was enhanced by the hazel eyes that dominated it. "About what?"

"Me."

Her gaze traveled slowly up and then down him, taking in every detail before returning to his face. "I haven't a clue as to what you're talking about." She leaned back against the wall, crossing her arms over her chest, and extended her boots, crossed at the ankles. The picture of ease.

He raised his hands to his hips and scowled at her. Any other woman would be running for cover about now. B.J. stared at him, not moving.

"Don't you?"

"No, I don't, and I don't have time for twenty questions." She stood and picked up her bag.

"It's Friday night. What's so important that you can't take a few minutes to chat?"

Her mouth hung open, showing her surprise, which pleased him for some odd reason.

"To chat?" she repeated, an underlying current of humor in her words.

"Yeah, to chat."

"Jake, I've been living a few yards from you for about nine months now. You have never 'chatted' once in all that time. You have spoken to me only when necessary, and even then you never smiled. "Chatting involves smiling, friendliness, common interests—"

"We have common interests," he inserted sharply, glaring at her.

"Oh, yes, you own animals, and I work on them. You want to discuss the latest breeding information?"

"No! I want to discuss what my new family members are up to." He paced back and forth again before facing B.J. "Maybe I haven't been as friendly in the past as I should've been, but—"

She turned away from him and sat down again. "What do you want to know?"

He frowned at her, surprised by her behavior. In the past, in spite of his attitude, she'd always been unfailingly polite. "Do you really need to go?"

"No."

This time he joined her on the bench. "I think the girls are up to something."

She rolled those hazel eyes and leaned her head against the wall. "Like what? Are they teaching Red some new recipes? Putting flowers in your room, lace ruffles on your bed? What, Jake?"

"So you really don't know?"

"Jake Randall," she said, sitting up and blowing out a deep breath, "I have had a hell of a day. I will answer your questions if I can, but I won't play games. Get to the point."

"I think they're matchmaking."

He sat tensely in the silence that surrounded them, waiting for her response.

A low chuckle, throaty and sexy, drew his gaze to her face.

"How appropriate." With a smile on her lips, she stood and started out of the barn.

"Wait! B.J., is that what they're doing?" He wanted confirmation. He hated to accuse them if he was imagining things.

She turned around, one eyebrow slipping up.

He acknowledged again that she was one beautiful woman. Sexy as all get-out in jeans, a flannel shirt and denim jacket. Menswear that he'd like to peel off her, layer by layer, until she was all woman.

"How would I know, Jake?" Her smile widened. "But if they are...how appropriate," she repeated. Then she headed toward the barn door.

"What do you mean by that?" he asked as he got up to follow her.

"Don't act the innocent. Everyone in the county would know what I meant. You were the matchmaker for all three of your brothers' marriages. Why not turn the tables on you?"

"That's not true." Before she could object—and he could tell she was going to—he added, "Besides, it was for their own good. They're all happy now, aren't they?"

Surprising him, she leaned forward and patted his cheek. "And now it's your turn. You can be happy, too." Then she turned her back on him again.

He circled her and stood in front of the door. "Look, B.J., I'm not asking you to stop them. I'll deal with the problem. I just want to be sure that is the problem. I don't want to upset everyone for no reason."

Sighing, she leaned against the wall. "But how would I know, Jake? I haven't talked to any of them for several days."

"I think they started their—their plan a week ago when that airhead from Kansas City visited Janie. The one who wanted me to sell the cows and buy ostriches."

Laughter trembled on B.J.'s lips, and Jake's mouth went dry. For someone who didn't mix a lot with the opposite sex, she had very kissable lips, soft, full, generous.

"Did you agree? Are you trying to tell me I'm out of a job unless I bone up on ostrich anatomy?"

"Don't be silly," he growled.

"Well, it's the only thing that makes sense. Why would someone touting ostriches make you think Janie was matchmaking?"

"Because the woman then announced that she'd come to Wyoming to find a husband," he explained, a triumphant look on his face.

"Probably just a coincidence."

"Then Megan took me to lunch after drafting me to help her pick out a saddle for Chad. And we were joined by a Marilyn Monroe wannabe, falling out of her dress. She informed me she was looking for unmarried cowboys."

B.J. frowned slightly, then shrugged her shoulders.

"Still think I'm imagining things? Tonight I come down for supper only to discover Anna has invited a friend, a *single* friend, to visit for a few days. She's looking for a man, preferably someone not too wimpy."

"And you think you're the only nonwimpy man around?" Her eyebrows arched again, and Jake blinked. He wished she wouldn't do that. It made him want to trace their path with kisses.

He shook his head. "No. But I think I'm the only unmarried nonwimpy man in my own house."

"There's Red," she offered, her smile widening.

"Not unless Miss Janice Kobell wants to go one-on-one with Mildred."

He'd shocked her. Jake realized B.J. had no idea what was going on under her very nose. Well, maybe not her nose because her aunt Mildred and Red were together at his house, not hers.

"What are you talking about?"

"Sorry, B.J. I didn't realize that information would come as a surprise."

"What information?"

"That Red and Mildred...hell, they're hot for each other."

Her cheeks flooded with color, drawing Jake's gaze. "Don't be ridiculous! Mildred has no interest in— She's never indicated— She's never married!"

"So her life is over? Or do you not think Red is good enough for her?" He was growing irritated by her attitude.

"That's not— Mildred can— I think you're making this story up."

"Ask Mildred. She may even deny it, but she'll blush from here to high heaven if she does."

B.J. walked away from the door, a frown on her face, pacing back and forth as he had earlier.

"You're serious about this?"

"Yeah."

She paced some more, giving him ample opportunity to admire her body. Something he didn't need.

"Could we get back to my problem?" he asked abruptly, determined to end their conversation before he got as hot and bothered as Red.

She spun around and stared at him. "What problem?"

"The matchmaking thing, damn it. Have the girls said anything to you?"

"No. I told you I haven't talked to them in several days."

He sighed. "And I told you they must've been planning this

scheme for several weeks. Have they said anything to you about finding me a wife?''

''No. Nothing. Maybe they placed an ad for you in a lonely-hearts club magazine.'' She reached out for the door, but he put his hand against it, holding it shut.

''What, Jake?'' she demanded, frustration in her voice.

Clearly his revelation about her aunt Mildred and Red had distracted her. But he had his own problems to deal with. ''Could you ask them?''

''You mean, could I spy on my friends for you? No, I couldn't.''

''You'd better rethink your decision.''

''Why?''

''Because if they managed to get me married off, who would be their next target?''

A wary look filled her eyes. Slowly she said, ''Why would they choose another target? Maybe they're only interested in marrying you off.''

''I don't think so. Success goes to the head. They'll start thinking they're invincible, that they can play God. And the next unmarried person in their target range is you, B. J. Anderson. They'll start on you next.''

''Then I'll just have to hope and pray that you hold out against them, won't I?'' She tugged on the door again.

''You could help me.''

''I won't spy on my friends.''

''It's not spying. You could just ask them if that's what they're doing. A simple question.'' He was close enough now to smell her, an earthy scent that made him think of summer. He'd better end this conversation soon.

''And they would tell me the truth, Jake. Right after they asked me to give my word not to tell you. So what would my asking them accomplish?'' He opened his mouth, but she spoke before he could. ''No. Don't ask me to break a promise.''

''But, B.J.—''

''No. I'm not going to help you out, Jake. You're on your

own.'' This time when she tugged on the door, he let her open it.

Within seconds he was alone in the barn.

Time to think up a new plan.

Chapter Two

B.J. crossed the yard to the neat little house off to one side. Lights were burning in the windows, welcoming her as they always did.

What was she going to do about Mildred?

Every since Darrell, B.J.'s husband, had died, Mildred had been there for her and Toby. Her aunt had kept house and helped raise Toby from the time he was a year old.

The three of them had shared a good life.

Now Mildred was keeping part of her life a secret. And it had to be because she thought she didn't have a choice.

Damn Jake Randall's hide.

The man had been the one drawback in her move to Wyoming. He hadn't wanted her here. Even when he finally accepted her skills, he still hadn't wanted her here. She didn't know why. She just knew he didn't.

The rest of the Randalls had been delightful, making her feel a part of the community, even a part of their family, her and Mildred and Toby. She'd tried to accommodate Jake's aversion to her. She'd avoided him, and she'd tried to keep Toby out of his way.

Tonight had been different.

Because he wanted something. She opened the door of the house, still undecided about what to say to Mildred. The thud of little feet took her mind off her problem. She opened her arms wide, dropping her kit as Toby rounded the corner of the hall.

"Mommy!" he called as he launched himself toward her.

"Toby!" she responded. It was a game they played each evening as she came in. He was already in his pajamas, reminding her that she was later than usual.

Spot, the dog Jake had given her son, stood at her feet, barking as she hugged Toby. Then Mildred came toward them.

"Land's sake, girl, were you planning on working all night? You haven't had your dinner yet. Toby, get down and let's take your mom to the kitchen and feed her."

"Okay! There's chocolate pie tonight. Mr. Red sent it home with Aunt Mildred."

"How kind of Red," B.J. said, watching Mildred. Sure enough, just as Jake predicted, even that mild comment had Mildred's cheeks pinkening.

With loving concern, the two most important people in her life settled her at the kitchen table. Toby, almost five years old, carried a plate of biscuits to the table and proudly set them in front of his mother. Mildred added a plate filled with delicious food.

"Well, did you have a good day today?" B.J. asked her son, putting off talking to Mildred.

"Yeah! I learned to write my name." In a flash, he was down from the table and out the kitchen door.

"I believe he's going to demonstrate his miraculous feat," Mildred said, her lips curving into a tolerant smile. "He only wrote it for us ten or twelve times."

"Is he getting in the way?" Several months ago, just before the birth of the twins, Jake had hired Mildred to help Red out with the housework. Each afternoon after preschool, Toby spent his time at the Randall house.

"Not at all. Red and the ladies love on him so much, it's a wonder he's not spoiled."

"Mildred—"

"Watch, Mommy!" Toby exclaimed, running back to the table, a crayon and paper clutched in his hands.

After several repetitions of his new talent, Toby allowed his mother to finish her dinner. Then she took him to bed and read him a story, as she always did.

When she closed the door behind her drowsy son, she returned to the kitchen to find it sparkling clean and no Mildred in sight.

She tracked her down to the living room, where Mildred was watching a favorite TV show. Patiently B.J. waited until the commercial break.

"Jake and I were talking—"

"You and Jake? That's something new, isn't it? Maybe he's gotten over whatever has kept him kind of standoffish," Mildred said with satisfaction. "Want more pie?" she asked, standing.

"No, I don't. And I don't want to discuss Jake."   "I always thought you had a problem with him as much as he had with you," Mildred said, a teasing light in her eyes. "Like maybe he was a bit too much man for you."

"Mildred! What are you saying?" B.J. thought she'd kept her reaction to the oldest Randall brother carefully hidden. She should've known Mildred would see through her.

"Nothing to be ashamed of. A woman can't help her reaction to a man. And Darrell's been gone almost four years now."

"Mildred, this has nothing to do with Jake Randall! Or me, except— It's about you. And Red."

The easy grin left Mildred's face. "What are you talking about?"

"I'm asking what's going on between you and Red."

"Nothing! Nothing at all. I work with him, that's all." In spite of her protests, Mildred's face filled with color. Just as Jake said.

"Mildred, there's nothing wrong with l-liking a man. Red's a true gentleman."

"He certainly is. But that don't change the fact that there's nothing going on." Mildred sat down abruptly, as if she could no longer stand.

B.J. licked her dry lips and wished she could choke Jake Randall. "All I want to say is Toby and I want you to be happy. There's no reason to—to hold back if you and Red—"

"How many times I gotta tell you, girl? There's no such thing going on. I'm an old woman!" Mildred, belying her words, jumped to her feet and ran from the room.

The television program started again, and B.J. stared at it

blindly. If Jake was right and Mildred was lying, B.J. didn't want her aunt to give up a chance at love because of her and Toby.

What was she going to do about it?

Damn Jake Randall's hide.

JAKE MADE SURE he was out of the house before anyone reached the kitchen the next morning. It wouldn't be the first time he'd gone without breakfast. Since Janice had made a point of informing him that she was an early riser, he had no choice.

Last night, after he returned from his "chat" with B.J., Anna's friend had sat beside him and talked nonstop until he'd been able to excuse himself and go to bed.

Today he intended to make another effort to find out what was going on.

When his brothers joined him in the north pasture, they made several comments about him missing breakfast. Then Chad pulled a napkin out of his jean jacket. "Red was worried about you and sent these biscuits."

Jake grabbed them.

"So it wasn't lack of appetite that had you out early? Was it the boys' crying?" Pete asked, referring to his twins' nocturnal habits.

"Nah . That's music to my ears," Jake assured him.

"Unlike a certain lady's conversation?" Chad asked.

After a quick look at Brett's guilty face, Jake shrugged and said nothing.

Brett spoke up. "Sorry, Jake. I didn't know Anna's friend was such a chatterbox."

"I can put up with a little talk," Jake finally said, "but I'm beginning to think the girls are trying to marry me off."

Jake was convinced at once that none of his brothers suspected the same thing. It bothered him. Was he so conceited that he thought every woman was after him?

"Why do you think that, Jake?" Pete asked.

Jake enumerated the three encounters that had convinced him.

"I hadn't heard about the lunch," Chad said, frowning.

"Janie never said anything to me," Pete protested.

Brett just chuckled.

His brothers stared at him, Jake with a ferocious frown on his face.

"What? It's funny. I mean, it's poetic justice, isn't it? After all, that's what Jake did to us," Brett explained.

"I don't find it funny at all. And you sound like B.J.," Jake growled.

He realized what he'd said when his three brothers exchanged startled looks.

"You talked to B.J. about this?" Chad asked cautiously.

"Yeah. I figured the girls might have said something to her about their plans."

"And?" Chad persisted.

"And nothing. She refused to help me."

"That shouldn't be a big surprise," Pete drawled, wrapping his right leg around the saddle horn and resting his elbow on it. "The two of you haven't exactly been friendly."

Jake ignored Pete's comment. "Listen, I want each of you to tell your wife to leave well enough alone. We all know marriage isn't a good idea for me. Okay?"

Brett grinned at his oldest brother. "We may tell 'em, Jake, but that doesn't mean they'll do what we say."

"Just tell 'em!" Jake shouted, and rode off to chase a cow, leaving his three brothers behind.

"Do you think he's right?" Pete asked, watching Jake.

"Could be," Chad said, frowning. "And frankly I wouldn't mind. I'd like Jake to be happy. But Megan's friend wasn't right for him at all."

"Neither was Janie's," Pete said.

"Well, Anna's friend sure isn't," Brett added. "The woman is driving me crazy. I can't imagine what she's doing to Jake, drooling all over him."

Pete swung his leg back down and slid his boot into the stirrup. "Okay. We'll each talk to our brides and see what we can find out." He nudged his horse and, as he set out in a gallop, called over his shoulder. "And maybe give them a few suggestions along the way about who might attract Jake."

IN THE NORMAL COURSE of work, B.J., who covered the entire county, didn't see Jake more than once or twice a month, unless her family received an invitation from the Randalls. So she was surprised to run into him at lunch.

"B.J.?" he called to her as she was about to get into her truck.

"Yes, Jake? You need something?"

"I just wondered if you'd thought over our conversation last night."

Yes, she had. She'd tossed and turned all night, wondering what to do about Mildred. "Yeah."

"Good. You willing to help me now?"

She frowned. Was the man still going on about the matchmaking? "No. I thought you were talking about Red and Mildred."

"Red and Mildred? There's nothing to do about those two. Unless you intend to object."

"Of course I don't intend to object. But Mildred won't even talk about it. I'm not sure you're on the right track here."

"Did she blush?" he asked, a grin on his face.

She wanted to smack him. Instead, she turned away. "Yeah."

"Well, there's your answer."

"Red's not trying to take advantage of her, is he?" she suddenly asked, squaring back around to face him.

"Take advantage of her? Come on, Anderson, that's even outdated for Mildred to say, much less you."

"I'm an old-fashioned girl. Is he?"

"No!" he returned, his good humor disappearing. "Red is as much a gentleman as I am."

"Some reassurance!" she muttered sarcastically.

"When have I ever been less than a gentleman to you?" Jake demanded, his pride seemingly hurt.

She shrugged her shoulders. "Forget it."

He clenched his jaw. "So, have you changed your mind about helping me?"

"No. I think you can protect yourself without me coming to your rescue."

Jake whipped off his hat and ran his hand through his thick

hair. B.J. followed his movement, wishing she had the right to—
She put her wanton thoughts out of her head.

"I'm not sure I can. Someone came to my room last night
after I'd gone to bed."

"Someone? Didn't she introduce herself?"

She watched in amazement as Jake blushed.

"I had a chair under the doorknob. She couldn't get in."

"Maybe it was one of your brothers."

"I don't think so."

"My, my, my. Maybe you're right. Maybe these women are
desperate for a husband," she teased, grinning at him.

He reached out and grabbed her arms. "You're not going to
think this is so funny when they start in on you."

Her breath caught in her throat. She'd never been quite this
close to Jake Randall before. His brown eyes held her gaze, and
he moved closer still.

"Maybe you're looking for a husband. Is that the reason
you're not worried?" he whispered.

"No. No, I'm not looking for a husband. But I don't have to
start worrying until they take you down. So don't give in, Jake.
Resist temptation."

"Those women don't tempt me," he muttered, and pulled her
closer still until her body was pressed against his.

B.J. felt her mouth go dry as his hard muscles were imprinted
on every inch of her. She needed to protest, to move away, to
do something. Quickly.

"Hey, Jake!" a cowboy called from the steps of the bunkhouse. "You eatin' with us?"

"Yeah," Jake yelled back as he released B.J.

She took a step away from him, drawing a deep breath.

"See you around, Doc," he muttered, and walked away.

As B.J. watched his arrogant stride eat up the distance to the
bunkhouse, she whispered, "Not if I see you first."

"SWEETHEART, I HEARD you took Jake to lunch the other day
with a friend of yours. Was it Mindy?"

"Yes, it was. Jake didn't mind, did he?" Megan asked, turning innocent eyes on her husband.

"Um, well, he sort of got the idea you might be trying to marry him off." When she said nothing, he added, "And Mindy's just not his type."

"I know. Wouldn't it be awful if he fell for someone like her? It'd be Chloe all over again," she said with a shudder, naming Jake's ex-wife.

"Yeah," Chad agreed, but he watched his wife closely.

"JANIE, ARE YOU up to anything?"

Looking up from the baby bed where Nathan was having his diaper changed, Janie stared at her husband. "What are you talking about? Oh, honey, would you change Neal's diaper?"

Pete moved to the other bed. "Hey, there, little guy. Is that why you're fussin'?" He started the change but he didn't drop his questioning. "I asked if you were up to something. Jake's got a bee in his bonnet that you might be matchmaking."

"What? Who would I match him with?"

"Allison."

"Good heavens, Pete, she's not Jake's type. That would never do. Besides, she'd drive us all crazy in a minute."

The grin she sent in his direction had Pete thinking of doing some matchmaking of his own, as soon as the boys were tucked in for their nap. Some matchmaking between him and his lovely wife. His favorite kind.

"UM, ANNA, could I speak to you alone?" Brett whispered in his wife's ear after lunch.

With a smile that set him on fire, she took his hand and led him into the television room. "Yes, husband mine?"

His only answer was to cover her soft lips with his.

Several minutes later, her cheeks flushed and her hair in disarray, Anna pushed back from his embrace. "Was this what you wanted to talk to me about?"

He nibbled on her neck, wishing he could forget working this afternoon and carry his bride up the stairs. But that wouldn't be fair to everyone else. "No. Jake wants you to stop matchmaking."

Anna's eyebrows soared. "What are you talking about?"

"Janice. And when is she leaving?"

Anna giggled. "Soon, I hope. I had no idea she would set out after Jake like that. Wouldn't it be terrible if she caught him?"

Brett shuddered. "Yeah. I wouldn't mind if Jake married. Only I'd like him to marry someone nice. Someone who'd make him happy."

"Or someone he could make happy?"

"Whatever," he muttered, and returned his lips to hers. She was too distracting for any coherent conversation.

JAKE CONVINCED HIMSELF his brothers would take care of his problem. And when Janice left the next day, he felt confident everything was taken care of.

Until Friday night.

He came down from his shower to find the kitchen quiet. Warily he headed back toward the stairs, but before he could retreat, Pete and Janie met him.

"Hi, Jake. We're going to town tonight to celebrate Pete's new contract with the Cheyenne rodeo," Janie announced.

"Great . I'll keep an eye on the babies for you."

"Not necessary. We're taking the entire family. Mrs. Mott is coming in to watch the babies and Toby," Pete assured his brother.

"Toby?"

"Yes, B.J. and Mildred are going with us," Janie explained, smiling before she suddenly turned serious. "You don't mind, do you, Jake? Pete told me that you thought we were, uh, but—"

"Well, I am a little worried about Mildred," Jake responded, trying to ease the awkward moment. After all, he had nothing to worry about with B.J. along. The woman would scarcely talk to him, much less think of him as husband material.

"I'll warn her to keep her hands off you," Janie agreed, laughing.

They divided into groups, six of them in the sedan they kept for family trips, and four of them in one of the pickups with a crew cab.

B.J., thrust into the back seat with Jake, leaned over and whispered, "If you're worried about them matchmaking me with you, don't. I'll keep my distance."

He breathed in her perfume, felt her warmth down one side of him and decided her keeping her distance would be a good idea.

He'd known all along why he'd avoided B. J. Anderson the past nine months. He just hadn't wanted to admit it to himself or anyone else. But he'd better face it now and prepare his defenses.

She disturbed him.

She made him entertain thoughts he shouldn't be having.

She made him want to throw her on a bed and fall on top of her so fast she couldn't get away, and make slow, mad love to her.

"Here we are," Pete called out as he parked the car in front of the steak house in Rawhide.

"I hope they've got a table big enough for all ten of us," Janie said as they piled out of the car.

"Uh, sweetheart, we'll need a table for eleven," Pete corrected.

They were joined by the others from the pickup and Megan said, "Better make that twelve."

"Wait a minute. What's going on?" Jake asked, the hairs on the back of his neck rising.

"Sorry, Jake, but Bill Morris called. He helped me get the contract, so I didn't think any of you would mind if he joined us." Pete looked directly at B.J. with a smile of apology.

Jake almost chuckled aloud as he noticed B.J.'s reaction, her hazel eyes widening in alarm. Bill was good with cows, but he left a lot to be desired in his social skills. Served B.J. right, after being so unsympathetic to his plight.

But he'd forgotten Megan's words.

"Hey, that works great," Megan said. "I ran into Ceci Holmes. When I told her we were celebrating Pete's contract, she asked to come along. I couldn't say no. This way, neither Jake nor B.J. will be by themselves. So…you don't mind, do you, Jake, B.J.?"

That suspicion that he'd almost quieted roared back, and Jake

wasn't about to be a patsy a fourth time. Without looking at
B.J., conveniently standing beside him, he said, "Sorry to disappoint you, but Ceci and Bill will have to console each other.
B.J. and I are together tonight." Then he wrapped an arm around
her shoulders and squeezed. "Right, sweetheart?"

Chapter Three

B.J. couldn't have been more on the spot if she'd been standing in the center of the arena of the National Rodeo, all eyes trained on her. She knew what Jake wanted her to say. And the picture of Bill Morris sitting next to her, trying to paw her under the table, as he'd done once before when she'd found herself beside him, weighed heavily in Jake's favor.

At least she knew he didn't have any interest in her.

She slid her arm around Jake's waist and leaned against him, finding her five-ten height fit perfectly against his six-four frame. "Jake's right. We're together." She felt a sigh of relief travel through his body, sending tingles through her own.

"Really?" Megan asked, her eyes big. "Then I guess Bill and Ceci can entertain each other."

"I guess so," Jake drawled, then to B.J.'s surprise, turned his head and kissed her.

It was a brief kiss, his lips just brushing hers, but it shot through her like an electrical charge. She was glad he still had his arm across her shoulders, otherwise, she might have fallen.

When she gathered herself together enough to look at the group, she discovered them all staring at her and Jake, bemusement on their faces.

Pete spoke up. "Well, let's go inside, shall we? I'm starving for one of those thick steaks."

There was general movement, but Jake held her back. When the others were several steps away, he whispered, "See? I told you they'd start on you next."

"They weren't matchmaking," she muttered, ducking her head, hoping he wouldn't notice her reaction to his warm breath skittering across her skin. "But I've dealt with Bill Morris before. I don't want him touching me."

Jake frowned and lifted her chin so she had to look at him. "He's bothered you?"

She shrugged, not wanting to tell tales out of school.

"B.J.?"

"He tried to paw me under the table."

"I'll take care of it," Jake growled, and started into the restaurant, his arm still around her.

"No, wait," she protested, forced to walk with him. "I didn't tell you that so you could do something to the man. I dealt with it. I told you so you'd understand why I went along with your—your lie."

"It's not a lie. We are together," he replied with a grin.

When they reached the tables the waitress indicated, they discovered Bill and Ceci already with the others. Bill immediately moved toward them.

Jake pulled B.J. along with him, rounding the table to whisper something to Pete. Pete took Janie's arm and moved her down a couple of chairs, leaving a place for Jake and B.J.

"B.J., how you doin'?" Bill asked, coming to stand beside her, leaning close to her.

Jake immediately pulled B.J. to his other side, putting his left arm around her and sticking out his right hand to Bill. "Hi, Bill. How you doing?"

"Fine. Looking forward to visiting with B.J. Pete said she'd be here this evening. I never see you, B.J. Every time I call, Mildred says you're busy."

"I've had a lot to do lately," she said, but didn't smile. She didn't want to give the man any encouragement.

"And I've taken up the rest of her time," Jake drawled. He let his arm slide from her shoulders to her waist and turned to pull her against him, and he kissed her again.

He was going to have to stop that, B.J. reasoned, because it left her dizzy. And wanting more. She'd have to remember to tell him when they were alone—no, not alone. She didn't need to be alone with Jake.

Ceci appeared beside Bill. "What's going on? Are you two an item? Is there going to be another Randall wedding?"

"No!" B.J. protested, but her voice was soft, hoarse.

"Who knows?" Jake replied heartily, his voice easily covering hers.

Was the man crazy? Ceci was a nonstop gossip. She'd be spreading rumors all over the county.

Before B.J. could protest again, Jake pulled out her chair. "I think the waitress is waiting to take our orders. There are a couple of chairs over there," he said, pointing out two places on the other side at the end of the table.

"Beside Red and Mildred," Ceci noted with a smile. "Don't they make the cutest couple? I was talking about those two the other day. Everyone's betting they'll marry. I swear, you Randalls are certainly marriage minded these days. What a change!"

Bill pulled the bubbling Ceci after him, but he was frowning in B.J.'s direction. Not that she cared. She owed the man nothing. But she was concerned about the impression Jake left.

"Don't you think you overdid it?" she whispered, leaning toward him so no one else could hear.

"Do you want that...man calling you?"

"You know I don't."

"Well, I took care of it."

"But, Jake, Ceci will tell everyone—"

"So no one will call. Is that going to bother you? You got a hot romance going?" His voice had sharpened, and he leaned closer.

She swallowed and turned away, reaching for the glass of water the waitress had just placed in front of her. Not only should they avoiding kissing, but also they should keep a lot of space between them. No close quarters.

"Don't be silly," she finally managed to respond, mumbling into her napkin.

"So what does it matter?"

"I thought it mattered to you. I thought you didn't want to consider marriage."

"I'm not!" he said sharply, drawing everyone's gaze. He nodded and smiled, but B.J. could tell it took some effort. Without losing his smile, he muttered, "Don't get confused. I have no intention of marrying ever again. We're just pretending."

B.J. pasted on a smile, too, but she ordered, "Don't you dare insinuate I'm trying to trap you into marriage. I'm not the one who created this—this situation."

"Fine! " he snapped, his false smile still on his lips.

"Fine!" she returned, and picked up the menu.

JAKE COULDN'T ENJOY his steak because he knew what was coming next. And wondered if B.J. had thought about the dancing that would follow. Maybe dancing with him wouldn't bother her.

But it was going to be hell on his nerves.

He was only playing a role, of course. That's why he'd kissed her. Twice. Once to convince his family. And once to warn off Morris. He'd never particularly liked the man, but now he despised him. He'd have to warn Pete not to have much to do with him in the future.

He looked sideways at B.J., calmly eating and chatting with Janie, who sat on her other side. No sign of nerves there. Of course, B.J. could handle emergencies. She had to in her line of work.

His gaze encountered Bill's as he looked away from B.J. The man was glaring at him. With grim satisfaction, Jake put his arm along the back of B.J.'s chair, his fingertips caressing her shoulder. Bill smoldered.

B.J. turned to look at him, a question in her hazel eyes. "Did you want something?"

"No. Just making sure Bill gets the picture."

"I think you're getting carried away, Jake. I told you I took care of the situation."

"But he's been calling you, so you must not have done a thorough job."

"Then I'll handle it."

"You're not dancing with him."

"Jake," she said in irritation, "I am not one of your brothers. You can't order me around."

Amused by her indignation and fighting the urge to kiss those tempting lips again, he leaned closer. "No, but I'm with you tonight. You agreed. So you dance with me."

"So you're only going to dance with me? Do you realize how much you're limiting yourself?"

"Not much. You're the best-looking woman here. Dancing with you won't exactly be a hardship." He gave her his best smile, one that had charmed many a woman.

His compliment received a glare before she turned back to talk to Janie.

"Jake?" Bill called from down the table.

"Yeah, Bill."

"How long have you and B.J. been seeing each other? I hadn't heard she was taken."

With his fingers still stroking her shoulder, he leaned back in his chair and drawled, "Long enough."

"Not long," B.J. said immediately after. "We have a lot in common."

"Yeah, we like to chat," Jake added, grinning wickedly at her, daring her to recall their earlier conversation.

She rolled her eyes at him and then returned to her meal.

"There's been so much happening around our place, it's hard for anyone to keep up," Janie said. "Or maybe I'm saying that because the twins keep me so busy. You're going to have to come visit, Ceci. I don't think you've seen them yet."

"I intended to, though I'll have to admit I was a lot more enthusiastic before I realized Jake was taken. All us girls have been talking about it now being Jake's turn to marry." Ceci giggled and then added, "I guess you've been thinking the same thing, Jake."

Red stood suddenly and raised his glass of iced tea. "A toast to Jake and B.J."

Jake almost choked. Maybe he had gone a little overboard. B.J. was right about gossip spreading fast. If he wasn't careful, he was going to be married to the woman before the end of the week. At least in the minds of his neighbors.

"Uh, thanks, Red, but I don't think we're to the toasting stage yet," Jake said after they all had put their glasses down.

"Then we should probably drink a toast to Red and Mildred," Ceci suggested.

Both Red and Mildred blushed a bright red, and Jake hastily intervened. "I think that's enough toasting for now. I hear the music warming up. Let's do a little dancing before it gets crowded."

Red and Mildred responded to his suggestion with enthusiasm, probably glad to get away from Ceci and her ideas. Jake noticed B.J. watching Mildred. He guessed Mildred was going to get a few questions from B.J. later.

Grinning, he decided the next time B.J. thought he was bossing around his brothers, he'd remind her of her interest in Mildred's activities. Maybe he'd been more accurate than he thought when he'd said he and B.J. had a lot in common. They both tried to take care of their families.

They all rose and moved in the general direction of the dance floor. He rested his hand on the small of B.J.'s back, guiding her, but his touch became more possessive on her waist as Bill waded through the crowd.

"B.J., how about a dance?" he asked as he reached them.

"Sorry, Bill," Jake replied before B.J. could. "I've staked my claim on all her dances this evening."

"What's wrong, Randall? Afraid of a little competition?" the other man snarled.

"Not any you can offer," Jake said softly, fighting to hold on to his temper.

As if aware of the tension, Pete turned back and put a hand on Jake's shoulder. "Any problem?"

"No, I don't think so," Jake assured him, but he continued to stare at Bill. "Is there, Bill?"

"No, no problem…yet."

Jake smiled at his brother, grabbed B.J.'s hand and led her to the dance floor. With perfect timing, the music started and he swung her into his arms.

Tonight she was dressed in a soft denim skirt, with a blue-green blouse that made her eyes sparkle. Feminine clothes that made her more attractive, if that were possible, than her blue jeans.

"Why haven't you dated?" he asked abruptly.

She looked up. "Why are you asking?"

"I hadn't thought about it until the other night."

Her lips twisted in a half smile. "I know. You've basically ignored me for the past nine months."

"With good reason," he muttered and then wished he hadn't spoken.

"What good reason?"

"I didn't figure I had any business with you."

He thought he'd come up with a good substitute for the truth—that he was too attracted to her for his own good. Her response smashed that idea.

"And you have business with me now?"

"Yup. We're together. Remember?"

"Mmm."

They danced in silence as he became more and more aware of her. His embrace grew closer, and she surprised him by laying her head on his shoulder. He glanced down to discover her dark lashes resting on her soft cheeks.

"So you're not going to tell me?" he whispered, his cheek touching her silky dark hair. It wasn't braided tonight, but she'd pulled it back with combs. He wanted to take them out and run his fingers through it.

She didn't answer, only shaking her head against his chin. He smiled and closed his eyes, too. This closeness was too nice to waste. He hadn't enjoyed a woman as he was enjoying B.J. in a long time. Or maybe never.

RED AND MILDRED CIRCLED the dance floor, not talking.

Finally Red said, "I don't think you're going to have to tell her now. Ceci made things pretty clear."

"I don't know."

"Millie, I don't want to wait." He tightened his hold on her, even though he knew she would protest. She wanted everything circumspect.

"Red, I can't just leave her and Toby. They need me."

"Leave her? You'd only be moving a few yards away. You'd still be there for both of them." They'd had this argument for several weeks now, ever since he'd gotten up enough nerve to tell Mildred how he felt about her.

It hadn't been easy. He'd never proposed to a woman before. And the hardest part was that he understood her feelings about B.J. and Toby. After all, he'd been there for the Randall brothers for as long as he could remember. Even now he wouldn't be able to walk away.

But he wasn't asking that of Mildred.

"You could ask her, see what she says," he pleaded.

Mildred looked up at him, her hazel eyes quite like her niece's. "I've been thinking."

To Red's surprise, her cheeks were bright red.

"What have you been thinking?"

"Maybe—maybe we should…" She sighed.

"Should what?"

"Have sex instead of marryin'."

Red came to an abrupt halt, throwing off several couples around them. He made his apologies and then led Mildred from the floor. At the table, he pulled out her seat.

"Mildred, if you're ashamed of me, just say so. But I'm too old to sneak around. I want you, but I want you forever, not in the laundry room when everyone is gone."

With those words, he sat down beside her and crossed his arms over his chest.

TWELVE TIMES TWELVE *is one hundred forty-four. Twelve times eleven is—*

No use. For the past ten minutes, Jake had run through the multiplication tables to help keep his mind off how close. B.J. was, how soft she felt. But even the twelves weren't enough. He simply gave up and took her back to the table.

She paused when she discovered Red and Mildred sitting down, not speaking to each other.

"Is everything all right?" she asked her aunt.

"Of course. You two dance together real well."

"Nope. It's not all right," Red retorted.

"Red, if you say anything, I'll never forgive you." Tears pooled in Mildred's eyes.

B.J. left Jake's side and hurried around the table. "Let's go powder our noses."

Jake watched the two of them cross the room before he turned back to Red. "Anything I can help you with?"

"Jake, I want to marry her. It won't stop me from doin' my job. You okay with that?"

"Of course I am, Red," Jake said, grinning. "Congratulations, you old geezer!"

"No need to congratulate me," Red said, his expression glum. "The woman won't say yes."

"You've asked her?"

"Yup. But she insists she can't leave B.J. and Toby."

"Hell, you're not moving to Alaska, are you?"

"That's what I told her." Several of the rest of the family began to drift to the table. "Walk outside with me."

Jake couldn't refuse to follow the older man. After all Red had done for their family, the Randalls owed him their complete support.

Jake listened to Red for several minutes, commiserating where appropriate, advising where he could. Not that Jake was an expert on how to deal with women. But just being there for him seemed to ease Red's tension.

When Jake led him back inside, he hoped B.J. talked some sense into Mildred in the ladies' room. The music was playing again, but he ignored the dancers and headed for their table.

Megan and Chad were sitting there, Megan's head on her husband's shoulder.

"Tired, Megan? Do you want to go home?" Jake asked, concerned about her and the baby she was carrying.

"Soon. But everyone's having such a good time."

"Yeah. Have B.J. and her aunt come back?"

"Oh, yes. She's dancing. So is Mildred."

Both Red and Jake spun around to stare at the dancers. It didn't take Jake long to find B.J. She was dancing with Bill Morris. He had his hand clamped on her, and even from where he stood, Jake could tell they were in a tug-of-war.

B.J. certainly didn't have her head on the man's shoulder, he realized with satisfaction. With a sure stride and a lot of determination, Jake crossed the dance floor.

"Take your hands off her, Bill," he announced calmly.

"She agreed to dance with me," the other man insisted, turning a triumphant glare on Jake.

"But she's not enjoying it."

"No, I'm not," B.J. said, and broke Bill's hold. "I wanted to be polite, Bill, but you're making it impossible."

"Hey, I'm just dancing."

"No. You're holding me too close. I told you." B.J. started to walk away, but Bill reached out to grab her arm.

"I want to finish the dance."

"I don't."

"Turn her loose," Jake ordered.

"Jake, I'll handle this." B.J. said, turning to face him. "Stay out of it."

"You're with me. I protect my own."

"I take care of myself. I don't need a man to protect me."

"Sweetheart, it's my right if you're with me."

"You're not listening to me, Jake," B.J. insisted.

"Hey, what happened to me? Argue with me, B.J., not Jake." Bill seemed affronted by them ignoring him.

Jake grinned at the man's distress. He guessed it was pretty sad to be ignored by the woman you'd set your sights on. He reached out to grasp B.J.'s arms. "Sweetheart, I'm listening. But you've got to understand how things work around here. If you're with me, then I take care of you."

"Great! Then I won't be with you, because I don't need a macho man throwing his weight around."

"Too late," he muttered, and it was. He'd watched those soft pink lips for too long without tasting them again. Besides, he wanted everyone to know she was his.

For tonight only, of course.

As a pretense, of course.

In the center of the dance floor, he pulled her into his arms and kissed the living daylights out of her.

Poor Bill Morris just stood there and watched.

Out of sheer panic, B.J. ripped herself out of Jake's embrace and swung her fist. She realized she'd made a mistake too late. Her knuckles had already connected with his jaw. And Jake stood there, his hand on his mouth and shock on his face.

Chapter Four

"Lady, you pack a mean punch," Jake drawled after the shock wore off.

Chad came up behind her and put his arm around her shoulders, startling her.

"Need any help, B.J.? We Randalls have had a few fights around here, but none of them with a woman. I don't want people to get the wrong idea." He grinned at his brother.

"Watch out, little brother. You're choosing the wrong side."

"Aw, Jake, you know it wouldn't be a fair fight. I've got to go for the underdog."

"She'd still be the underdog with you on her side," Jake returned, a rueful grin on his face.

The music started again, and B.J. turned toward the table where Megan was waiting. All she wanted to do was return to the table and hide. But there in her path was Bill Morris.

He sported a tentative look on his face as he started, " B.J., I'm—"

B.J. shot him a glacial stare that stopped him cold. "You'll be the next one with a bruised jaw if you ever touch me again."

Bill hurriedly moved away and B.J. walked on. When someone caught her arm, she whirled around, ready to do battle again, only to discover Jake.

"What do you want?" she asked, her cheeks red, sure everyone was watching them.

"A dance."

She stared at him, confused.

Without waiting for an answer, he pulled her into his arms. "If we don't make up, everyone will be gossiping about us for weeks," he whispered in her ear.

She heard his words, but her body couldn't respond to his warm embrace. He pulled her closer, forcing her to move her feet. "Relax, B.J. Everyone's watching."

It didn't take but a second to verify his warning. With a shuddering breath, she gave in to his persuasion and moved to the music.

After several minutes, he whispered, "Why did you hit me? I kissed you earlier, and you didn't seem upset."

"Not like that," she replied, her voice sharper than she intended. His earlier kisses had been mere brushes of their lips, not a soul-searching invasion. She didn't want to explain that she'd panicked. That she'd never been kissed like that, even by her husband. That she'd been ever so close to forgetting anything and everything but Jake Randall. No, she couldn't explain those things to Jake.

He pulled his head back to stare down at her.

She determinedly looked away. Holding her breath, afraid he'd ask more questions she didn't want to answer, she tried to follow his lead but hold her body apart from his.

"Relax." His order was delivered in a soft voice, but she recognized a note of inflexibility in it.

With a deep breath, she tried to resist, but his warm body was tempting, inviting. He pulled her closer, giving her no option about the distance between them. Then he dropped her right hand and linked his hands behind her back. Without conscious thought, her hand joined with the other behind his neck, and they danced slowly about the room, pressed one against the other.

As the music ended, awakening her from the dreamy state she'd been in, Jake whispered, "I think we should kiss again, just to convince everyone we've made up."

"But, Jake—" B.J. started to protest, but he did as he said he would, briefly tasting her lips. Then he lifted his head and smiled into her eyes.

"See? If you could smile instead of looking so stricken, I

think we'd be able to convince everyone that you slugged me in a moment of passion.'' A laughing twinkle in his brown eyes invited her to smile.

She managed a small one, but she also couldn't help asking the question she'd tried to ask when he kissed her. ''Jake, why do we want them to think we've made up?''

''That way, they won't talk about you beating me up.''

''Wouldn't it be better for them to think we fought? Then they won't expect anything else from the two of us.''

''But then my family will go back to matchmaking,'' he said as he wrapped his arm around her shoulders and directed her back to the table.

''Jake, I didn't agree to—to help you avoid the matchmaking.''

''You sure did. When you agreed that we were together, you signed on, B.J. Unless you want to come right out and tell them we were lying.''

She stared at the eager faces of Jake's family, her friends and her aunt, and swallowed. No, she didn't want to tell them she'd lied. But she couldn't keep up the charade if it meant spending time with Jake.

''At least let them believe it for tonight,'' he whispered. ''We don't want to spoil their evening.''

She tried to think clearly, but her sensory nerves were on overload and it was hard to clarify anything. They reached the table, and much to her relief, Jake suggested the evening come to an end.

Everyone seemed in agreement. As they stood, B.J. caught sight of Mildred and she remembered the other problem she needed to solve. Mildred and Red.

''Jake,'' she hurriedly whispered to her escort as they started toward the door, ''can we take the pickup with Red and Mildred?''

She reconsidered the wisdom of her request when Jake stopped to stare at her.

''Good idea,'' he murmured, a look in his eyes that gave her pause. ''That will really convince everyone.''

If it hadn't been for Mildred, she would've protested and

changed her mind. But she had to do what she could for her aunt.

It took only a couple of whispered conversations on Jake's part before the four of them got into the pickup and headed toward the ranch.

B.J. waited at least five minutes before she ended the tense silence that had prevailed. "Red, Toby and I are the only family Mildred has, and Toby is a little young to assume his responsibilities as the man of the family. So I hope you'll forgive me for asking this question." She paused and studied the man's wary expression. Then, with a big smile, she asked, "What are your intentions toward Mildred?"

"Barbara Jo!" Mildred exclaimed.

Red looked at Mildred and then back at B.J. "I asked Mildred to marry me, B.J. But she turned me down."

"Did she?" B.J. slanted a quick look at Mildred's burning cheeks. "I'm sorry. I would've liked to welcome you to our family, Red. It's too bad she doesn't care enough about you."

Mildred gasped and turned to look out the window.

Red stuck out his chin. "That's not the reason she turned me down."

B.J. was distracted by the truck slowing to a stop on the side of the road.

"We're almost home," Jake said softly. "I thought you might need a little more time."

With a nod, she turned her attention back to the couple behind her. "It's not, Red? Why did she turn you down?"

"That's between me and Red," Mildred protested.

"Normally I would agree, Mildred," B.J. said quietly, "but I suspect Toby and I play a role here. Am I right, Red?"

"You're right," he said succinctly.

B.J. reached over the seat to touch Mildred's hands, clenched tightly in her lap. "Mildred, I can't ever repay you for the support and love you've given me and Toby. Especially right after Darrell died. But we would never want you to sacrifice your happiness for ours."

Mildred lowered her head but said nothing.

"Besides, it's not like you'd go very far," B.J. teased softly. "You could still keep an eye on Toby for me."

"That's what I told her," Red said, hope lightening the expression on his face.

"And what happens when someone calls you in the middle of the night?" Mildred asked forcefully, staring at B.J.

"We'd work something out, Mildred. Surely that's not enough of a reason to deny Red's happiness. And think how much Toby would enjoy having another man in the family," B.J. added, grinning at Red.

When she looked at Mildred, B.J. felt her heart lurch. Tears were streaming down the older woman's cheeks. Had she gone too far? Would Mildred forgive her?

"Mildred, don't cry. I didn't mean to upset you." She cast a frantic look at Jake, who sat silently beside her. "I think we should go on now."

Without any argument, Jake started up the truck. B.J. turned toward the front, leaving Mildred to Red's whispered reassurances. She only hoped he was able to make Mildred's tears stop.

When they stopped by the ranch house, B.J. spoke again. "Mildred, I'll take Toby home. You and Red may need a little time to talk."

"That boy's getting too big for you to carry. You'll need help," Mildred insisted.

"She's got me." Jake offered. "I can handle Toby, Mildred,"

B.J. opened her mouth to protest, but she paused as she noticed Mildred's acceptance of Jake's words. She could carry Toby. He was only a little boy. But if Jake's offer satisfied Mildred, B.J. wouldn't say anything.

Toby had fallen asleep, of course, and B.J. reluctantly allowed Jake to carry him the short distance to her house. The sight of her little boy wrapped in Jake's strong arms unexpectedly moved her. Perhaps it was because of all the stress of the evening, the assault on her senses.

Whatever the reason, her eyes filled with unshed tears as she watched Jake hold Toby against his broad chest. Her child would never know a father's touch, a father's guidance, as he grew to manhood.

She squared her shoulders. It didn't matter. He would be loved.

"His bedroom is the last one," she whispered as she held open the door for Jake. Toby's bed was ready. She'd turned down the covers before they'd left.

After Jake laid him on the bed, she murmured her thanks, hoping Jake would leave, and tucked the covers around Toby, gently touching his flushed cheek as he lay sleeping. When she straightened and turned around, she discovered Jake leaning against the door frame, watching her.

He stood back to allow her to precede him, then followed her down the hall to the front door.

"Toby's a lucky boy," he said softly as she stopped.

"What do you mean?"

"His mom loves him very much."

"And yours didn't love you?"

His brows arched, as if he were surprised by her response. "Of course she did, but she died."

"How old were you when she died?"

"Eight."

"Toby's father died when he was one. So he's only had one parent—and who knows what the future holds?"

"That's kind of morbid."

"No, realistic."

"I was trying to pay you a compliment, B.J.," he said with exasperation.

She shrugged her shoulders and looked away. The tenderness in his voice was too much to bear after the events of the night. "Sorry. It's been a difficult evening."

"I appreciate what you did for Red."

"I didn't do anything for Red. I was trying to help Mildred. She deserves to be happy."

"Doesn't everyone?"

Sighing, B.J. gestured to the door. "It's late, Jake. Too late for a philosophical discussion."

"Okay. I can take a hint." He reached out toward her, but she jerked back. "I was only going to touch your cheek, B.J., not retaliate." His lips curved in a teasing grin.

"I've already apologized," she returned abruptly.

"But not explained." Something in her expression must've warned him to save his breath. He held up his hands in surrender and backed out the door. "Okay. I won't mention it again. Good night...partner."

She ground her teeth as she watched his long stride cover the distance between their homes. No, she hadn't explained—and she wouldn't. But she intended to make sure she never got that close to Jake Randall again.

JAKE WAS FEELING pretty pleased with himself as he walked back to his house. He'd foiled the plans of the females of the house. Ceci was as wrong for him as all the other women they'd pushed forward. But thanks to B.J.'s and his fast thinking, he hadn't had to spend the evening avoiding Ceci.

As an extra bonus, he'd shared some interesting moments with B.J. She was sexy as hell—which he'd known the first moment he'd met her. But he'd never been this close to her before. Or tasted those soft lips.

With a rueful laugh, he rubbed his chin. He'd never paid such a price for a kiss before, either. The memory of the emotions that filled him when he'd held her in his arms chased away his amusement.

It was just as well she'd hit him. It was a good warning to keep in mind. He should keep his emotional distance from B.J. But he might forget that fact if he spent much more time kissing B. J. Anderson.

As he stepped up on the back porch, the door opened and Red and Mildred emerged. The only light on the back porch spilled out from the house, but it was enough for Jake to see the bemused expressions of happiness on the couple's faces.

"I'm gonna walk Mildred home," Red said, his gaze meeting Jake's only briefly. The man could hardly keep his eyes off Mildred, whose cheeks were bright red.

"Good. See you in the morning."

The couple passed him, their arms wrapped around each other, and faded into the night. Jake stood there, his hands on his hips, his eyes staring at nothing in the darkness. Looked like Red, too, would be joining the married state. Pretty soon he'd be the last bachelor on the Randall spread. Quite a change from last year at this time, when they'd been all men, all bachelors.

Jake dismissed the feeling of loneliness that assailed him. He was happy. He didn't need the complication of a woman to make his life worthwhile. In fact, in his experience, contrary to his brothers', adding a woman to his life would only bring misery.

Some men weren't meant to be married.

He was one of them.

"MOMMY, YOU DIDN'T KISS me good-night last night," Toby protested from the door, rubbing sleep from one eye.

B.J. smiled at her little boy, in his pajamas, still young enough to enjoy a cuddle from his mommy. Her heart swelled with love as she opened her arms to him. When he raced across the kitchen, she lifted him up and pressed her lips to his cheek.

"Oh, yes, I did. But you were sound asleep." And she'd been glad. After that kiss she'd shared with Jake the night before on the dance floor, she hadn't wanted to face either Toby or Mildred.

"Where's Aunt Mildred?"

B.J. took a deep breath. It was unusual for her aunt not to be in the kitchen first thing in the morning. Was she angry about last night? "I'm not sure."

Toby didn't show much concern for Mildred's absence. His mind still seemed to be occupied with the previous night. "How did I get in my bed last night? I went to sleep on Mr. Jake's couch."

According to Toby, everything on the Randall ranch belonged to Mr. Jake. B.J. had tried to explain that all four brothers shared the ranch, but Toby knew who was boss.

"Mr. Jake carried you to your bed."

"He did?" Toby asked with awe in his voice. "Just like he was my daddy?"

"No!" B.J. answered sharply, and then regretted her response. Hugging her little boy to her, she kissed him again and said, 'Like a friend, Toby. Mr. Jake is a friend."

"I guess he is," a familiar voice said.

B.J. whirled around to find Mildred standing where Toby had been when he first claimed her attention. Thankfully Mildred had a smile on her face.

"I was afraid you were angry with me."

"I should be," Mildred said, but she was still smiling.

Pudgy little hands covered each of B.J.'s cheeks as Toby turned her face to him. "Why would Aunt Mildred be mad at you, Mommy? Did you do something bad?"

B.J. laughed, relief filling her. "Nope." She kissed his nose and then set him down. "But if I don't turn the bacon, I'll burn it, and you wouldn't like that."

Mildred joined her, apologizing for oversleeping, and together they finished breakfast and sent Toby off to get dressed.

Mildred said nothing about the previous evening, and B.J. hesitated to ask. She'd interfered enough in her aunt's life.

But the look on Mildred's face told of her happiness. B.J. hoped that meant Mildred and Red had worked out their differences. Before she worked up her nerve to ask, Toby burst back into the kitchen in jeans and shirt, his sneaker laces flopping.

"Whoa, young man, you're going to trip if you don't tie your shoes," she warned, and knelt down to provide some motherly assistance.

"Have you told Toby yet?" Mildred suddenly asked.

"Told me what?" Toby asked.

"I thought your mommy might have told you that you're going to have a grandpa." Mildred's cheeks were bright red, but a big smile was on her lips.

"A grandpa?" Toby asked, his eyes round with surprise.

"Would you like that?"

"I guess so," There was doubt in his voice. "How would I get a grandpa?"

"Well, I'm not really your grandma, but that's how I think of myself. So when I marry Red, I guess he'll be your grandpa."

Toby's eyes got even bigger. "You're gonna marry Mr Red?"

Mildred nodded and let her gaze meet B.J.'s for the first time since she'd announced her intentions.

Still seeing the hesitation in Mildred's eyes, B.J. gave her her biggest smile. "I'm so happy for you, Mildred."

"You're sure we can work things out?"

"Of course we can."

"If you marry Mr. Red, Mr. Jake will be part of our family, too, won't he, Mommy? Will he be my brother?"

B.J. leaned over to smooth Toby's dark hair from his face. "No, sweetie, Mr. Jake won't be your brother."

"But we have the same birthday, and he's my bestest friend. Mr. Jake said he's going to teach me to be a cowboy. The other day he showed me how to rope," Toby said, his face beaming, "'cept I didn't learn too good. But Mr. Jake said—"

"I think maybe we've heard too much about what Mr. Jake said," B.J. said. "But I didn't know your birthdays were the same. Are you sure?"

Toby nodded vigorously.

"Well...that doesn't mean anything. Mr. Jake isn't kin to Red," B.J. hastily explained.

"Don't worry, child," Mildred said, still smiling. "Mr. Jake may be part of your family before you know it."

"Yippee!" Toby shouted.

"Mildred!" B.J. protested.

"Now don't go all coy on me, young lady. I wouldn't have accepted Red's proposal if I hadn't seen the way the winds were blowing last night."

Chapter Five

Last night all Jake's problems had seemed solved. But this morning he wasn't so sure.

B.J. had cooperated, but she'd also indicated her cooperation was a one-shot deal. Jake had thought last night that he could go along with her decision. After all, he wasn't looking for anything permanent.

Now he realized he was going to look like an idiot.

Ever since sunup, his men had been teasing him about B.J. He'd tried to make light of his behavior last night, telling them he still intended to play the field.

They'd laughed at him.

He'd told them he'd never marry.

They'd agreed, then winked at each other.

He had in mind to tell them that B.J. was nothing special.

They wouldn't have believed him. And he didn't blame them. That's why he couldn't say those words. Because he knew B.J. was special. She was a beauty. She was intelligent. She was a great mom.

And the best kisser he'd ever run across.

"Still daydreaming about B.J., boss?" one cowboy called out, and then maneuvered his horse to the other side of the herd they were moving, to make sure he kept some distance between himself and Jake.

"Get to work, you mangy cuss," Jake called back, but he couldn't be angry with the man. He'd brought the teasing on himself by the show he'd put on last night.

Pete pulled up beside him. "The boys are having a lot of fun at your expense, brother. You okay with that?"

"I've teased a few of them in my time. Turnabout is fair play."

"You're better at this game than I am. I guess I was pretty hard to live with before Janie married me."

Jake chuckled. "I believe you could call that an understatement, Pete. You were meaner than a mama bear protecting her cub."

"Aw, I wasn't that bad."

Before Jake could assure his brother that he had been impossible to live with, they were distracted by a shout from one of the cowboys, pointing into the distance.

What had drawn his attention was a truck crossing the pasture, heading in their direction.

"Something wrong at the ranch?" Pete wondered aloud, watching the truck.

Jake frowned as he stared at the approaching vehicle. He was pretty sure he'd identified the driver. He couldn't figure why B.J. felt they should settle their differences in front of his entire staff, but he was afraid that was what she had in mind.

He cleared his throat. "That's B.J. She probably needs to talk to me. You wait here with the boys."

"But it might be something about my herd for the rodeo," Pete said.

"Then I'll call you. Wait here," Jake barked. If he didn't start toward B.J. now, she'd have her truck right next to the herd before she stopped, and they'd have an audience interested in whatever she had to say.

He eased his horse into a lope toward the approaching truck, but he could still hear Pete as he hollered, "I guess you're not as calm as I thought."

He was calm, he assured himself. He just didn't want B.J. telling everyone he'd drafted her into playing a role last night. That was all.

She pulled the truck to a stop and waited for him to reach her. She must not be any more interested in an audience than he was. He swung from the saddle and strode the couple of feet to the door of her truck as she opened it.

"Good mornin', B.J.," he drawled, but his heart sped up as she looked at him, her hazel eyes wide, an anxious look in them. "Everything okay?"

One thing he'd always given B.J. credit for: she was a straight shooter whether you liked it or not. Now his heart double-clutched when she looked away from him.

"Um, not exactly."

"What do you mean? Do they need us at the house?"

"No! Everything's fine." She flashed him a quick look and then stared at the cattle behind him.

"Something wrong with the herd?"

"No."

"Then what in blazes are you doing here, woman?" he asked in exasperation. She was driving him crazy with her evasions…and her soft lips. The urge to kiss her, in broad daylight, startled him.

"I need to talk to you."

"You don't seem to be doing much of that."

Finally she turned to look at him, but anger drove her if her expression was anything to go by. "Give me a break. This is awkward."

"Couldn't it wait until this evening?" he asked testily, figuring he knew what was coming. But he darn sure couldn't see any urgency.

"No! Tonight might be too late."

He cocked one eyebrow at her and took a step closer, moving almost inside the door where she was standing. Just close enough to catch her scent.

"Too late for what?"

"Jake, I have to ask a favor," she said, her voice low, that throaty purr that drove him crazy. She reached out and caught the front of his jacket.

His hand closed over hers, feeling the soft warmth of her skin, wishing she'd slide her hand inside his shirt. Clearing his suddenly hoarse throat, he muttered, "Yeah?"

She drew a deep breath, and he watched the rise and fall of

her bosom, feeling like a seventeen-year-old boy, afraid to breathe in case he completely lost control.

"Could we—could we pretend a little longer?"

His mind was so clogged with sensations it took him a minute or two to understand what she'd said. "You want to continue pretending to date?" He shot a quick look over his shoulder to make sure no one could overhear their conversation.

Every man in the saddle was staring at them.

He turned back to B.J., realizing she hadn't answered his question. "Well?"

"Not...exactly."

He released her hand to capture her shoulders. "What are you asking?"

"I need us to pretend to—to be an item."

"An item?" He wanted to be sure he understood what she was asking.

"Stop being obtuse, Jake!" she shouted, and struck his chest.

"Whoa! For someone asking a favor, you're being a little aggressive, aren't you, sweetheart?" He was beginning to enjoy their conversation. He had a feeling he was about to get the upper hand.

"The favor isn't for me, you jerk. It's for Red and Mildred."

Her lips were pressed together, flattening out their fullness, but he still wanted to feel them beneath his, to taste her sweetness. He was filled with a hunger that had nothing to do with food.

"Well? Will you agree?" she prodded.

"Why do Red and Mildred care if we... date?"

"Because Mildred won't agree to marry Red unless she thinks—" B.J. broke off and sighed. "I feel utterly outdated by saying this, but Mildred wants to be *sure* I have a man to take care of me before she'll marry Red."

Mentioning marriage in the same sentence with him made Jake nervous. He stepped back. "What do you mean, *sure?* Are you asking me to marry you?"

He hadn't meant to sound as if that prospect ranked lower than being bucked off a bronco onto sharp rocks. But he must've. Her cheeks whitened, and she abruptly slid back into the truck. He grabbed the door before she could slam it shut.

"Wait! I'm sorry, B.J. I didn't mean to—"

"Turn loose!" She tugged on the door, and he instantly remembered how hard she had hit him last night.

He managed to slip his body between her and the door. "No fair running off without finishing our discussion."

When she realized she couldn't budge him, she stared straight ahead, her hands gripping the steering wheel.

"I just wanted to be clear on what you were asking," he said, watching her closely.

With her jaw unclenched just enough to form words, she muttered, "I wanted you to pretend we were serious about—about each other until Red and Mildred get married. Once they're legally tied, we can have a fight—which shouldn't be difficult to arrange—and break it off."

He should have felt relief. He did, he assured himself. She wasn't setting a trap for him. She didn't want marriage any more than he did. It was all pretense.

"Okay."

His brief answer didn't seem to have an effect on her. She continued to stare straight ahead over the steering wheel.

"Well?" he said, hoping for some reaction. "Is that all you wanted?"

"Yes, that's all I wanted. Thank you."

She didn't sound grateful. In fact, she sounded as though she'd prefer to rub his face in the mud of a pigpen. Hell, he was taking a risk just for her. She ought to at least appreciate it!

He remembered that he'd asked her to take the same risk last night without giving her much of an option. But that wasn't the point.

"So you can move now," she ordered, anger still lacing her words.

"Not quite yet." He might as well get some pleasure out of their agreement, especially since he wasn't getting any appreciation. Without any warning, he reached inside the truck, grabbed her by her jacket collar and pulled her from the truck into his arms.

Then his lips did what they'd been wanting to do ever since she arrived. They covered hers, molding her flesh to his, tasting her sweetness. In spite of her anger, her mouth opened to his, welcomed his tongue as he entered, joined in their mating. Her arms encircled his head, her fingers weaving through his hair, knocking his cowboy hat to the ground.

She was wearing those sexy jeans again, and his hands cupped her bottom, pulling her tightly to him, feeling her breasts against his chest. He wanted her naked, wanted to forget everything but her.

But the cheering in the distance brought both of them back to reality. They broke apart simultaneously. Her face was red, and she hid it on his chest.

"I forgot about our audience," he muttered.

"We—we don't need to get so realistic in our pretense in the future," she returned, raising her gaze to his. "Kissing isn't a good idea."

"You weren't objecting a minute ago."

"Well, I'm objecting now." This time when she got into the cab of the truck, he stepped back and she slammed the door.

Then she rolled down the window. "Promise you won't tell anyone what we're doing. Please."

"No one?"

"No one."

He shrugged his shoulders. "Okay, I promise."

She stared at him intently, and his shoulders stiffened. Was she questioning his word? But all she did was nod and throw the truck into reverse.

He watched her drive away, reliving the kiss as he did so. The cool October wind interrupted his pleasure and reminded him that his hat was missing. When he found it on the ground, it had been pancaked by B.J.'s tire.

Shaping it as best he could, he jammed it on his head and turned around to face an appreciative audience.

Somehow he didn't think he and B.J. were going to have to work very hard to spread the word about their...agreement.

B.J. DROVE RAPIDLY across the pasture, bouncing on the seat, too disturbed to slow down. She'd known the conversation would be difficult. Damn that sexy man's hide.

She should be used to the Randalls' handsomeness. Those lean cowboy hips, broad shoulders, all that muscle, topped by warm brown eyes, a lazy grin. One man fitting that description would be spectacular. Four men, each with a big heart and a bright mind, were almost more than a woman could comprehend.

And why one of those men, only one, should have the effect on her that Jake had was inexplicable. She'd known right away that her nervous system went on overload whenever she was around him. Fortunately he'd avoided her.

Until last night.

And look what she'd gotten herself into now. More time spent with Jake. But it was for Mildred's happiness. Once she married Red, then B.J. and Jake would return to their distant relationship. Which would be much easier on her nerves.

THE THREE RANDALL LADIES gathered in the living room, seated close together so as not to be overheard.

"What do you think?" Janie asked, watching her cohorts.

"He certainly took the bait," Megan said, "but will it last?"

"Maybe…if we keep the pressure on. Do we know any more disasters?" Anna asked.

"Just a few," Janie assured her as she rolled her eyes. "And they'd all leap at the chance to spend time with Jake."

"Well, you can't blame them," Megan said with a self-satisfied chuckle. "These Randall men are really something."

"And that's why we've got to marry off Jake. He's too attractive. We'll have a constant stream of women in here trying to attract him. Or any other man they can find."

"You can't fool us, Janie," Anna said softly. "You want Jake to be happy as much as the rest of us."

"Yeah," Janie agreed with a sigh.

B.J. DROVE HOME, contented. She'd just spent the afternoon at the Winstons' helping Grey Winston deliver the first foal bred from his prize stallion. The birth had been difficult, but mother and baby were doing well now. Grey had insisted on opening a bottle of champagne to celebrate.

After a sip, B.J. had excused herself. It was almost six. She tried to be home by five each day, but her job wasn't one for a clock watcher.

Which gave her a good excuse to avoid Jake.

Last night, after her morning talk with him in the pasture, she'd gotten home after eight. Mildred had asked her if she wasn't going to call Jake, but she'd told her she'd talked to him earlier.

If Mildred assumed they'd spent time on the phone exchanging words of love, it wasn't B.J.'s fault. She hadn't said anything like that.

As she pulled up to her house, she checked the rearview mirror, making sure Jake wasn't coming out of his house or the barns. If her luck held, maybe she wouldn't see him until Red and Mildred's wedding.

The only problem was she hadn't gotten a definite date out of Mildred. She'd tried last night, but Mildred had concentrated on feeding her and avoiding an answer.

She opened the door of her truck and got out. Tonight. Tonight she'd press Mildred to set a date for the wedding.

"Anyone home?" she called as she opened the door, expecting Toby's usual greeting.

Toby exploded down the hall. "Mommy! Guess what! We're eating dinner with Mr. Red and everyone."

"We are?"

"You're not," Mildred said, appearing next with a beaming smile on her face.

"I don't understand."

"Red and I know you and Jake don't get too much time together, so we're going to take care of Toby tonight. We're going to watch a movie after dinner. Then Red and I will come back here and put Toby to bed so you and Jake can stay out as late as you want."

B.J. swallowed, frantically trying to find a way to change the plans. "Jake may have already made plans."

"Red checked with him this morning. Didn't he mention our idea when you talked to him?"

"Uh, no. I guess he forgot." Did Mildred think she and Jake were in constant communication?

"Why can't I go with you and Jake, Mommy?" Toby asked, his arms still around her neck.

Inspiration struck her as she stared into Toby's eager eyes. "I think that's a great idea, Toby. After all, Mildred, you and Red are the couple getting married. You need the time alone."

"Nonsense. Red and I are too old for gallivantin' around. We'll leave that up to you young ones."

"But I don't get to spend much time with Toby. I don't want—"

"We've already got everything arranged. And you'd better head for the shower. Jake will be here in half an hour."

"Half an hour?" B.J. asked in shock.

"You'll want to look your best for him. After all, there's lots of women chasing after Jake Randall." Mildred stepped forward and pulled Toby out of her arms. "Go figure out which story-book you want to take to show Mr. Red how well you can read, young man. I don't want to be late for dinner, either."

Toby immediately set off at a run for his bedroom, leaving B.J. standing by the front door still looking for a way out. "But, Mildred—"

"Don't you want to spend time with Jake? I thought you two—"

"Of course I do!" B.J. exclaimed. "You took me by surprise. And—and I worry about Toby."

"Nonsense, child. He'll be fine with me and Red. You go make yourself pretty for that hunk you've snared." Mildred pushed her toward her bedroom, her serenity restored.

But B.J. could barely walk. Her insides were churning, and she was grateful she didn't have to continue her conversation with her aunt. She could scarcely think, much less talk.

And in half an hour, not only did she have to make herself presentable, but she also had to regain her composure. She didn't want Jake to realize how much he affected her.

"YOU'RE NOT GOING to wear that," Red said the moment Jake walked into the kitchen.

Jake came to an abrupt halt and looked down at his jeans and plaid shirt. They looked clean to him. "Why not?"

"'Cause I think B.J. would expect you to dress up a bit. After all, you two haven't gotten away from the family much. Give you a chance to, you know, cuddle." Red dug his elbow into Jake's side.

Jake grabbed Red's arm. "What are you talking about? Is B.J. coming— I mean, are Mildred and B.J. and Toby coming here for dinner?"

"Weren't you listening this morning, boy? I told you Mildred and I were taking care of Toby so you could take B.J. out."

"No, you didn't! I would've remembered—besides, it's too late. I didn't know, so I didn't ask her. B.J. would slug me again if I asked her out to dinner at this late date. Even *I* know that much about women."

"Not to worry," Red assured him, and calmly returned to the stove. "Mildred took care of it for you. Better go change."

"Change? Change into what? Since you arranged this date, just where am I taking her?"

"There's this new restaurant in Wyndom. It has candles and tablecloths and everything."

"Wyndom? That's fifty miles away."

"That's right. That gives you a nice, long ride home with the little lady." Red winked. "Now get back up those stairs and put on some fancy duds."

Jake did as he was told...this time. But he was going to have to get a handle on this pretense. No one was going to lead him around by the nose.

Chapter Six

Jake knocked on the door and then stepped back, drawing a deep breath. Under Red's orders, he'd changed into a tweed sports jacket and white shirt. But he'd kept on his jeans.

After all, this night was B.J.'s idea. So she owed him. And if he wanted to wear jeans, instead of a suit, it was okay.

The door swung open, and Mildred beamed at him. "Come in, you handsome man. Don't you look fine!"

"Evenin', Mildred. Is B.J. ready?"

"I'll go see."

As she turned away, Toby came tearing down the hall, followed by his dog. "Hi, Mr. Jake!"

Jake squatted to the little boy's eye level. "Hi there, Toby. How are you?"

"Great! We're going to eat with Mr. Red. I asked Mommy if I could eat with you, but she said no."

He wouldn't have minded if the little guy came with them. He may have avoided B.J. the past nine months, but he and Toby had become fast friends.

"Next time we'll include you, buddy, okay? I heard they're building a McDonald's in Rawhide."

"Wow! I love McDonald's! Do they have a playground?" Toby asked, his eyes wide with excitement.

"I don't know. We'll check it out."

"Okay! Wait till I tell Mommy."

"Does your mommy like McDonald's?" He didn't know much about B.J.—except that she made his temperature rise.

Before Toby could inform him of B.J.'s tastes, Jake caught movement at the other end of the hall out of the corner of his eye. He looked up and almost fell flat on his back. He'd seen B.J. in snug jeans and a flared denim skirt and blouse, but he'd never seen her dressed in a silk sheath.

He cleared his throat, wondering if she'd intentionally forgotten to fasten the last two buttons on the dress. "Hi, B.J. You look nice."

"Thank you." She came down the hall and knelt down next to Toby and Jake. "Give me a goodbye hug, sweetie. And be good for Aunt Mildred."

Toby slung his arm around his mother's neck and hugged her, leaving Jake an unobstructed view of the top of B.J.'s dress, too. He swallowed, his mouth suddenly dry, as he eyed the shadowy V formed by the valley between her breasts.

B.J. stood and called down the hall, "We're leaving, Mildred."

Jake stood and stepped toward the door.

"Bye, Mr. Jake," Toby said.

The touch of sadness in the little boy's voice had Jake flashing a look of alarm at B.J. "We could change our plans, go somewhere—"

"I already tried. Besides, I can't let Toby con me. He wouldn't have any respect for me. Right, Toby?"

"Aw, Mommy," the little boy protested, but he grinned.

Mildred joined them. "You two get along, now. You don't want to miss your reservation."

Jake stepped aside for B.J. to precede him out the door. Then he followed to open her truck door, receiving a raised eyebrow but no comment from her. Once he got behind the wheel, however, she had a question.

"Reservations? I didn't know there was a restaurant around here that took reservations."

"There's a new restaurant in Wyndom."

"Wyndom? That's fifty miles away."

"I know." He hadn't meant to sound irritated, but he'd already put in a long day. To drive almost an hour just to eat made him weary.

She stared at him, her face expressionless, before saying, "This evening wasn't your idea, was it?"

"Did you think it was? You're the one who asked that we continue the charade. I figured you planned the evening." A quick glance at her had him adding, "Not that I object to spending an evening with a beautiful woman, but..."

B.J. bit down on her bottom lip. "I think I've been had."

"What do you mean?"

"I don't think Mildred believed our story."

Jake shrugged. "It was kind of sudden."

"It was your idea. I guess it wasn't such a good one."

"You didn't think it was at the time. I didn't expect you to want to continue with it." If she was going to criticize him, he wanted to remind her that they were together tonight because of her, not him.

It was dark in the truck, but he could feel her embarrassment. "I didn't know what else to do," she explained stiffly.

He felt like a heel. "Hey, it's no big deal. Relax and enjoy the evening. I owe you one for Friday night, anyway. It would've been a miserable evening with Ceci in pursuit."

B.J. said nothing.

It was going to be a long drive.

BY THE TIME THEY REACHED the restaurant, B.J.'s stomach was tied in knots. A combination of worry about Mildred and worry about resisting Jake's charm made conversation almost impossible with the incredibly handsome man next to her.

"We're here. Let's see if this dinner is worth the drive," Jake drawled, smiling at her, inviting her to share his amusement.

"Yes," she agreed, clearing her throat. She didn't wait for him to come around and open her door. Sliding down from the pickup, she straightened her skirt and turned toward the restaurant door.

"I've never seen you dressed so, uh, nice," Jake said, placing his hand in the small of her back to guide her.

She pulled away.

"B.J., you're going to have to stop acting like I'm poison. Otherwise, people will never believe we're dating."

"I'm not sure that's what we should be doing," she whispered.

He clutched her waist and pulled her to a halt. "Now, wait a minute. Is this the same woman who drove all the way out to the pasture to ask me to cooperate? Isn't that why we're here tonight?"

"I don't know, Jake," B.J. wailed softly. "I'm confused. I think Mildred doesn't believe our story. But should we try to convince her? Or should we give up? I don't know what to do."

Jake tipped up her chin. "We should go inside and enjoy a nice dinner. That's what we should do. We'll decide how to proceed after we eat." He brushed her lips with his. "I'm no good making decisions on an empty stomach."

As if he were sure of her agreement, Jake took her arm and led her toward the door.

Maybe he was right. All this stewing would do her no good. And why waste a good evening? After all, ever since arriving at the ranch, she'd dreamed of a date with Jake Randall.

Not that this was really a date. But she could enjoy it, even so if she'd relax. With a deep breath, she stepped into the restaurant. This far from the ranch, they'd be truly alone, and she planned to enjoy the evening.

Jake echoed her thoughts as he whispered, "We probably won't see anyone we know, anyway."

To their surprise, the lobby of the restaurant was filled with prospective diners. Jake stepped forward and gave his name to the maître d'.

"Of course, Mr. Randall, your table will be ready in just a moment."

Before Jake could turn away, another man approached the maître d'. "Look, we've been waiting for forty-five minutes. Are you sure you don't have anything?"

"Not yet, sir."

"Ben?" Jake recognized his neighbor and longtime friend.

"Oh, Jake, I didn't see you." It was Ben Turnbull, a rancher from near the Randall spread.

"You waiting for a table?"

"Yeah. I hope you don't have much of an appetite, 'cause we've been waiting more than three-quarters of an hour."

"Your table is ready, Mr. Randall," the maître d' said, interrupting them.

Ben shrugged and turned back to join his wife.

"I'm glad Red made a reservation for us," Jake muttered, taking B.J.'s arm as they followed in the wake of their guide.

"That was Ben Turnbull, wasn't it?" B.J. asked. She'd met the man once before, but not his wife.

"Yeah. They've been waiting for a table for forty-five minutes."

They reached a secluded table for four.

Jake's gaze met B.J.'s, a question in it.

She frowned, sure it wouldn't be a good idea to offer to share their table, but like Jake, she couldn't refuse. "Of course."

Jake smiled and turned to the maître d'. "Would you ask Mr. Turnbull if he and his wife would like to join us?"

The man nodded and hurried back to the front of the restaurant. Almost immediately the Turnbulls joined them.

"Jake, are you sure we're not intruding?"

"Not at all. Hello, Lucy. Have you met B. J. Anderson?"

The two women exchanged greetings and sat down. B.J. liked the friendliness of the other woman. Though she'd met most of the men in the county, she hadn't come into contact with many of the women.

"We're celebrating our wedding anniversary," Lucy confessed shyly after their orders had been taken. "We've been married three years."

There was a glow on her face that told B.J. the romance certainly hadn't gone out of her marriage. It gave B.J. an unexpected hunger for that contentment. Her own marriage had been a good one, the short time it had lasted. But she and Darrell had been friends more than passionate lovers.

Ben reached out and took Lucy's hand. "We're celebratin' something else, too. Can I tell 'em, sweetheart?" She nodded, and Ben added, "We're going to have a baby. We just found out today."

"Congratulations," Jake offered, a big smile on his face. B.J. added hers, also.

"I guess you know a lot about babies now, Jake, don't you? What with all your brothers' doings."

"Well, Ben, I know a lot more than I did last year at this time. We've got the twins, you know, and then Megan's expecting in about six weeks."

"How exciting," Lucy said softly.

"Yes, ma'am, it's exciting, all right. The next generation of Randalls. Our ranch has been passed down from father to son for four generations. I didn't want that to stop."

"That's why Jake set out to matchmake," Ben added, a grin on his face. "Right, Jake?"

B.J. watched Jake, fascinated with the man beside her. She hadn't seen him interact with others much, just his brothers.

Now his cheeks reddened, and he looked hurriedly at B.J. before turning back to Ben. "I don't know that I'd call it matchmaking, Ben. Just a little nudge in the right direction. And Pete managed on his own."

"Yeah, with Janie's help," Ben agreed with a laugh.

"Are you and B.J. celebrating something?" Lucy asked.

B.J., thinking about the Randall brothers, froze, almost choking on the drink of water she'd just taken. "No!" she protested.

"Yeah," Jake contradicted. "We're celebrating getting away from the family." With a grin, he added, "They're a great bunch, but at the rate we're growing, they're a real crowd."

"Ah. You two wanted to be alone, and here we are horning in," Ben concluded.

"No, no, that's not a problem," B.J. hurriedly said. "It was the lure of real tablecloths that got me." She offered a smile and desperately tried to think of a change of subject.

Ben roared with laughter. "Yeah, I bet! I can just see Jake Randall yearning for real tablecloths."

"Now, Ben, stop teasing. These two should be able to enjoy a night out without having to offer an explanation. I'm just glad you decided to share your table. I get tired so quickly these days," she said, smiling at B.J.

Seizing the topic of pregnancy, B.J. talked to Lucy about the difficulties of having a baby, and the two men dealt with ranch topics.

Just as B.J. was beginning to feel comfortable, Lucy leaned closer and asked, "How long have you two been dating?"

"N-not long," B.J. stammered. "We're really just friends."

Lucy smiled. "That may be true, but I haven't seen Jake out with a woman since—why, I guess, since his divorce, five years ago."

"I'm sure he's, uh, dated some since then. Probably in Casper or—or somewhere."

"Jake?" Lucy asked, leaning toward the men and interrupting their conversation. B.J. wanted to shush her, but she couldn't figure how to do it without calling more attention to the topic.

"Yeah, Lucy?"

"I don't recall you dating anyone since your divorce. Until tonight, that is. Am I right?"

B.J. wanted to die of embarrassment as Jake stared at her. She knew he must be wondering what she was doing.

"I think you're right, Lucy. I was kind of snake-bitten after Chloe."

"I don't blame you," Ben said with a shudder. "Beautiful woman, but not our kind."

"Nope. Not our kind," Jake agreed, his gaze still on B.J. She shrugged her shoulders, trying to tell him she hadn't intended to put him on the spot.

"You've made a better choice this time around. B.J. is a great lady," Ben added with a grin.

"She's no slouch in the looks department, either," Jake said. He, too, was grinning, and B.J. wanted to strangle him.

She murmured a thank-you and said a silent prayer of gratitude that their orders arrived to end the conversation. Perhaps if she ate in a hurry, the evening could end before any more damage was done.

After a few minutes, Lucy brought the conversation around to Anna, Jake's sister-in-law. "Do you think Anna will take me on as a patient?"

"I'm sure she will."

"I heard she was cutting back since her marriage to Brett."

Jake answered. "You're close by. I'm sure she'll want to help you out. Unless she's expecting herself."

"Oh? You wanting more babies, Jake?" Ben asked.

"You can't have too many babies. We want the Randalls to continue for generations to come."

"Good thing the first two were boys, then. What if you had all girls? I hope ours is a boy."

B.J. wondered what Jake's response would be. Not that it mattered, but she hated the way some men only wanted sons.

"Same blood, whether it's a boy or a girl, Ben. It's your family. That's what counts." With a sigh, Jake added, "In fact, I think I might like a little girl. They're awful sweet."

"Maybe you should have one yourself," Lucy suggested, with a sly look at B.J.

Though his gaze settled on B.J.'s red cheeks, Jake said, "Nah. I'm not suited to marriage. We've already proved that the hard way."

"Jake, you just made the wrong choice," Ben insisted. "B.J.'s not like Chloe."

"The weather has certainly been nice this fall," B.J. said in strangled tones. Her attempt to steer the conversation in another direction was a total failure.

Ben grinned at her. "Sorry, B.J. I didn't mean to embarrass you, but this guy deserves happiness like the rest of us."

She was at a loss as to how to respond.

"B.J.'s a little shy," Jake said, grinning. "I don't think she's dated much since her husband died."

B.J. almost groaned out loud. Jake had managed to shift the conversation from himself to her, but the topic remained the same.

"When did your husband die?" Lucy asked.

B.J. couldn't refuse to answer, not with the sympathetic smile Lucy offered her. "Four years ago. About six months after our son was born."

"You have a little boy? I didn't know that. So he's four?"

B.J. nodded.

Jake joined in. "Yeah, Toby's a neat kid. And growing like

a weed. Did you notice, B.J.? I think he's grown almost a foot since you moved in.''

She nodded again.

''I gave Toby one of Molly's pups, and you never see one without the other except for the hours he's at school.''

''It's hard being an only child,'' Lucy said. ''I was so lonely until I started school. We don't want our baby to be an only.''

B.J. hadn't wanted Toby to be an only child, either, but sometimes life had other plans than the ones you made. She looked up and realized Jake's gaze was on her. She looked back down at her food.

''It's not too late for B.J. to have more children, either,'' Ben offered, as if that idea had just occurred to him. ''After all, you're not exactly over the hill, B.J.''

''Thank you,'' she murmured. ''This food is certainly delicious. Jake, I hope you think it was worth the drive. He was questioning the wisdom of driving this far for a dinner just before we got here.'' This conversational gambit was more successful than the weather had been earlier. But B.J. was beginning to wonder if their dinner companions would discuss anything but weddings and babies.

Just as they took up the topic of food, they were interrupted by several older couples from Rawhide who were leaving.

''Jake! Good to see you. Well, hi, Ben, Lucy. And B.J., what are you doing— You and Jake are together? Good job, Jake,'' Henry Pollard roared with a voice loud enough to imitate a bull-horn.

B.J. cringed and tried to appear indifferent to the announcement. Probably no one else knew them here. But she felt the center of attention.

''Just having a meal out, Henry,'' Jake responded, standing, as did Ben, to shake their hands.

B.J. recognized the other couple and felt her heart sink. Mr. Miller ran the feed store, and his wife was the postmistress for the county. She handed out gossip with the stamps she sold.

''Well, I declare,'' Mrs. Miller said, smiling at B.J. ''I knew the Randall ranch was a hotbed for Cupid, but I never suspected Jake would fall to one of those little arrows.''

"We're just having a meal out," B.J. said more forcefully than she should have.

"Oh, of course," Mrs. Pollard agreed, and winked at Mrs. Miller. "Nice choice of companion, though. He's number one on the bachelor list, now that his brothers have been taken."

Before B.J. could protest again, which was probably just as well, Mrs. Pollard turned to Lucy.

"And how are you, Lucy, dear? I heard you were in town today. Everything all right?"

"You were in town and didn't come to see me?" Mrs. Miller asked.

B.J. knew the woman hated to be the last one to know something. She wondered if Lucy would share her news.

"I had to make a quick trip. I'll be back in next week for a real shopping trip and I'll stop by then, Mrs. Miller. I need a new supply of stamps."

"Good. I'll look forward to a little chat. Well, we must go now. Come along, dear," Mrs. Miller said, tugging on her husband's arm.

B.J. had no doubt she was anxious to get outside, where she and Mrs. Pollard could discuss Jake's venture into the dating game. Poor Jake. She remembered his suggestion that they eat and *then* decide whether to continue the charade.

Now it appeared the decision had been made for them.

When they finally left the restaurant, after Jake and Ben amicably argued over who should pay the bill, B.J. breathed a sigh of relief. But she was worried about Jake's reaction to the events of the evening.

He might not have wanted to continue pretending to be involved with her, but rumor would link them together for months to come. Unless he took up with another woman.

That thought bothered B.J., but she didn't want to examine why. Jake wasn't her property.

What would he say about tonight?

They settled into the pickup. Instead of driving off at once, however, Jake sat back and let the engine warm up. B.J. said nothing, waiting for him to speak.

"Interesting evening," he finally murmured.

Warily she nodded, taking one hurried glance at his face before staring out at the cars around them.

He turned toward her, and she held her breath. But the words
that came out weren't what she expected.

"Do you want to have another baby?"

Chapter Seven

He watched her reaction to his question. In the dim light provided by the neon sign outside the restaurant, he saw her cheeks flush. Her wide stare quickly shifted to the cars in the parking lot.

"Why—why do you ask?"

He gave an uncomfortable chuckle. "Don't get me wrong. I'm not volunteering. It just struck me that— Never mind." He put the truck in gear and began driving out of the parking lot.

Out of the darkness, B.J.'s soft, sexy voice answered, "Yes, I did want to have more children. I love Toby, and as Lucy said, it's hard to be an only."

"You were an only child?"

"Yes."

"You and your husband planned on a big family?"

She shifted in her seat, as if she were uncomfortable. Jake stared at her in the darkness, trying to see her face.

"We really hadn't planned that far ahead," she finally said, her voice calm, emotionless.

He frowned, suddenly filled with a lot of questions about B.J.'s marriage. But he couldn't ask them. Finally he cleared his throat and said, "Toby's a great kid."

"Thank you."

They rode in silence until Jake introduced the subject he figured B.J. wanted to avoid. "So, I guess we're going ahead with the pretense?"

"Do we have any choice? By noon tomorrow, Mrs. Miller

will have told everyone in the county that we were out together tonight.''

''We could have a big fight, break up.''

''We tried that Friday night.''

He chuckled. ''No, *you* tried it Friday. It wasn't a joint effort.''

''True. You were too busy polishing your image as a Romeo,'' she said stiffly.

''Hey, I had to do something. You slugged me in front of everyone. And then drove all the way out to the pasture to argue with me in front of my crew.''

''I didn't come out to argue with you,'' she protested. ''I came out to ask for your cooperation.''

''Humph!''

They covered a few more miles in silence.

''I'm sorry, Jake,'' she finally said, her voice low. He leaned toward her, not sure he'd heard her.

''What?''

''I said I'm sorry. I didn't mean to—to argue with you. I'm not used to negotiating with anyone, much less…a man.''

''Did you and your husband always get along?''

''No. But it's been a long time. And—and we don't have a relationship, you and I. There aren't any rules.''

Yeah, he knew. He didn't have the right to haul her into his arms and kiss the daylights out of her because he was frustrated. And he was frustrated.

''Guess we'd better work out the parameters fast,'' he drawled.

''I think it would be best to avoid kissing from now on,'' she said hurriedly, as if she'd thought of that idea for a while.

''Why? No one will believe we're—how did you put it, an item?—if we don't.'' And he'd lose out on a lot of pleasure. Kissing B.J. was quickly becoming addictive.

''Yes, they will. You've kissed me enough in front of people that they will assume we're kissing in private.''

''Nope.'' He spoke firmly, determined not to lose this battle. ''I'm the kind of guy who touches people. Everyone knows that. If I don't touch you, kiss you, no one will believe our story.''

She didn't speak, and he wondered why. He actually began to slow down, considering pulling off the road to check on her when she said, "All right, but keep it to a minimum."

"Why? Don't you want to convince Red and Mildred? Red knows me better than anyone."

"Jake, you're being difficult. You can see that our kissing all the time could cause problems. You're not a child."

"Are you telling me that my kissing you gets you stirred up? Heats your blood to a boil?" He was grinning, enjoying her discomfiture. Glad he wasn't the only one turned on.

"And I suppose it doesn't bother you?"

"Lady, one kiss from you and my jeans are too tight. I lay awake at night thinking about you in bed beside me. I'm losing sleep and my appetite just thinking about kissing you."

A car passed by them, and he saw the stunned look on B.J.'s face. She was surprised? He must be a better actor than he'd thought.

"Then why—"

"Why kiss you any more? Because I'm a kissaholic when it comes to you. I can't resist. Besides, we'll never convince Red and Mildred without some kissing." He kept his hands tightly grasped around the wheel. All this talk of kissing made him want to reach out and pull her to him, to pull to the side of the road and follow his talk with action.

"I don't think I can do this."

"Why?" he snapped back, afraid she was getting cold feet.

She didn't answer him.

"You afraid you'll lose control and go too far?"

"Yes! Yes, that's exactly what I'm afraid of."

"So what if you do? You're not a cowering virgin, B.J. Do you intend to go the rest of your life without sex? Sounds mighty sterile to me." His heart was beating faster. He hadn't thought about an affair with her, but now that the possibility had entered his head, he couldn't see any reason not to.

"I don't have affairs," she said icily.

"Have you noticed a parade of women going in and out of *my* bedroom? If you're concerned about a disease, don't be."

She gasped. "You think that's the only reason not to fall in bed with you? That disease is all I have to consider?"

"What else is there? We're attracted to each other. We'd be discreet."

"Everyone in the county already knows we're dating. Is that being discreet?"

"Probably not, but they're going to think we're doing something anyway. We might as well enjoy it." The more he thought about it, the more perfect it sounded. Except...

For the very reason that he hadn't had an affair since his divorce.

Could he handle it? That question stopped him cold. What was he talking about? Of course he could. Couldn't he? He wouldn't get emotionally involved. It would just be sex. Plain and simple.

Only sex was never plain and simple.

And as badly as he wanted her now, was it possible he could become addicted to holding her, touching her, kissing her?

Yup. Entirely possible.

He began to sweat.

"Having second thoughts?"

Her soft, sultry voice only underlined his thoughts.

"Maybe. We might get in over our heads."

She responded by laughing, only there wasn't much humor in the sound. "What you're really saying is you're afraid I'll trap you into marriage. That the great Jake Randall might fall into the very trap he set for his brothers."

"Not going to happen, B.J. And you need to understand that up front. Whatever pretending we do, it's not going to lead to marriage," he assured her harshly.

"You sound like you think I *want* to marry you! I can assure you I have no intention of marrying." She crossed her arms under her breasts.

Jake took a deep breath and turned his gaze on the road. Otherwise, he might run them off into a ditch, just thinking about touching that part of her anatomy. Unbuttoning that silk dress, button by button, peeling back the—

"Jake! What's the matter with you?"

"Nothing. I'm not used to having serious discussions while I'm driving." He couldn't come up with a better excuse on short notice.

"But when else can we come to a decision? There's always someone around at the ranch."

"What decision are we coming to?" he asked, distracted every time he looked at her. "Pretending to be together...or being together."

"Temporarily," she added, imitating his slow drawl.

"What?"

"Being together temporarily. In other words, having an affair."

"Is that what we've decided?"

"No! I meant those were our choices. And I refuse to have an affair. I told you."

"So we have no choice. Discussion ended." He figured he was the more frustrated of the two of them, but she didn't sound very happy.

"No, we have another choice. We can choose not to—to pretend. We can stop this nonsense."

"Aren't you forgetting something?" He realized abandoning their scheme would be best. Already he'd discovered she was too potent for pretense. But somehow he couldn't quite give up touching her.

"You mean Mildred and Red?" she asked, her voice falling.

"Yeah. I thought you said they deserve happiness." He slanted a glance her way. "Mildred really made a difference when your husband died, didn't she?"

B.J. didn't say anything for several miles, staring out the window into the darkness. Finally, tucking her chin down, she said softly, "She did. I owe her a lot."

"Then I reckon maybe you owe her our little pretense. It's not going to hurt anyone. The two of us may have to exercise a little extra control, but that's no big deal. I can if you can." He hoped like hell he was right.

Or maybe he hoped he was wrong and *she* couldn't control herself. It wouldn't be his fault if she asked to have sex with him.

That thought brought a big smile to his face.

"What's so funny?" she demanded.

"Nothing," he assured her as a big truck blew past them. He pretended to concentrate on his driving. When she said nothing else, he asked, "So, did you decide?"

"I guess—I guess we should pretend. For a little while longer. As long as it doesn't hurt anything. Don't you think?"

That was the most indecisive he'd ever heard B.J. be. Usually she made quick decisions. He'd admired that in her. But there was something about B.J. tonight, her softness, her sexiness, that was lighting him up. He couldn't really see her in the dark, but her image was imprinted on his brain.

"Okay." He affected a nonchalant tone.

"But you promised to keep the kissing to a minimum," she hurriedly added.

"Right. We don't want anyone to get the wrong idea."

"Right."

But there was a breathless quality to her answer that told him she couldn't help thinking about their kisses.

Silence reigned until they reached home.

Jake parked the truck in its customary spot, rather than parking in front of B.J.'s house. It was only a matter of a few yards. "I'll walk you home," he said as they both got out of the truck.

"That's not necessary." She hurriedly rounded the truck.

"Yes, it is. Red and Mildred are going to be waiting."

"But surely…do you think they'll be watching?"

"Could be. Come here," he ordered, but he actually crossed the distance between them before she could move. He draped his arm across her shoulders and began walking slowly toward her house.

"I'm not sure this is necessary."

"I believe it is. And I think you should wrap your arm around my waist. Red insinuated we should've cuddled in the truck on the drive home. If we'd done that, you wouldn't be standoffish."

"Oh?" she asked, turning to look at him. "All your dates cuddle readily?"

"Yes, ma'am. Satisfaction guaranteed," he assured her, a broad grin on his face. "Want me to demonstrate?"

He lowered his head toward hers, but she pulled away and ran the few short steps to her house.

He caught her hand as she reached the steps, pulling her off balance into his arms. She settled against him as her breath escaped. "Sorry, didn't mean to take your breath away," he assured her, still grinning. In truth, that's just what he wanted to do.

The door opening stopped him from kissing her.

"Have a good time?" Mildred asked from the door, with Red standing beside her.

"Yes," B.J. answered as she pushed against Jake's chest, trying to signal him to release her.

He ignored her and smiled at the other couple. "It's a nice restaurant. You should take Mildred there sometime, Red."

"I'll do that." Red leaned back and chastely kissed Mildred before coming down the steps past them. "Don't mind me. Go ahead and kiss her a time or two." With those instructions, he headed for the Randall house, and Mildred stepped inside and closed the door.

Jake immediately bent to act upon those orders, but B.J. put her hand between their lips just in the nick of time. "They're gone. We don't have to kiss."

Oh, yes, they did. With her pressed against him, kissing was the least of what he wanted to do. "They're probably watching. By now Red's reached the window over the kitchen sink." He glanced toward B.J.'s. "I just saw the lace curtain twitch in your house. Want to bet Mildred's not watching?"

She started to turn her head, to see if she could see the curtain moving, but he stopped her by catching her face in his hands and lowering his lips to hers. Heaven. The long wait since yesterday morning in the pasture was over.

Her soft, warm lips molded to his, and he let his hands wander down the silk that covered her, memorizing the wonderful curves. He deepened the kiss, wanting to touch and feel every inch of her. It was like a craving he'd had for chocolate ice cream as a boy. He'd almost made himself sick eating it, but he'd still wanted more.

And he wanted more of B.J.

HE'D PROMISED!

B.J. kept repeating that protest in her head. But her heart wasn't listening. Or maybe it was her body that urged her closer and closer in Jake's embrace. Her arms stole around his neck, and she opened to his urging.

His kisses were like bolts of lightning running through her, electrifying her body. His hands set her on fire, doubly so when he covered her breast with one of them, massaging and stroking her until she thought she'd explode.

When his lips left hers to trail kisses down her neck, one of his hands began unbuttoning her dress. She covered his hand with hers, knowing she couldn't let him disrobe her outside her house, and lured his lips back to hers.

Only as a distraction, of course.

Only to keep him from venturing other places.

Only to keep her sanity.

"Let's go inside," Jake whispered between kisses.

Inside. Inside with Mildred. And Toby.

"No! No, *I* have to go inside, but you should go home. I—I think we've been more than convincing," she whispered, pressing her hands against his chest, urging him to let her go.

Before she forgot she had to go.

"We need to rethink things," Jake whispered. He wasn't attempting to kiss her lips again, but he hadn't released her either. In fact, he was kissing her neck again.

"R-rethink what?"

"The affair."

"We're not having an affair!" she quickly reminded.

"That's what we need to rethink."

This time she shoved harder and gained a couple of inches as he looked at her. "No. No, we can't rethink that. And we can't k-kiss like this."

"But we have to convince Red and Mildred."

"Did you believe Red loves Mildred?"

"Yes, of course. You know he does."

"Have you ever seen him kiss Mildred like—like you just kissed me?" She sure hadn't.

"No, but I imagine they do when no one's looking. Just because they're older than us doesn't mean—"

"I'm not talking about their age! I'm saying we don't need to kiss like you just kissed me. You could just hug me or something."

"Hug you? I hug Janie and Megan and Anna. I hug Mrs. Miller sometimes, too. I hug Toby. I hug my brothers. How is that going to make someone believe I'm having an affair with you?"

"I don't *want* them to think we're having an affair!" she said, almost choking on her words. The man was going to give her a heart attack.

"You're asking an awful lot, B.J."

"What do you mean?"

He lifted his hand from her shoulder and stroked his thumb across her cheek. "You want people to believe that we, uh, care about each other…but we're not doing anything about it? We're not inexperienced teenagers."

"We're not animals in heat, either!" she returned hotly.

He looked as though he might argue that point, and she held her breath. She wasn't sure she could come up with logic after the way she'd reacted to his kiss.

A lopsided grin covered his face, making her want to kiss him again. "Well, now, the problem is my reputation is going to suffer."

"What are you talking about?"

"I haven't had a girlfriend in a while. People are going to think I've forgotten what to do with one."

"Jake, you're being ridiculous!"

"Maybe. Maybe I'm trying to figure a way out of our situation without going crazy. Holding you like this and not doing anything about it isn't easy."

She tried to put more space between them, but he resisted. "Wouldn't it be easier if you turned me loose?" she whispered.

"Yeah." His grin widened. "But not near as much fun."

"Jake, you're impossible," she protested, but she couldn't help smiling back at him.

"Yeah, I know. My brothers have told me."

He still held her against him, and she was reluctant to break contact with him, in spite of the shivers that were coursing through her. Finally she pulled away again, and this time he let her go.

"Are we going to be able to do this?" she asked, drawing a deep, shuddering breath, feeling the cool night air now that she was no longer pressed against his heated body.

Again he ran his thumb over her cheek. "Yeah, baby, we can do this. For Red and Mildred, we can do this."

She nodded, unable to say anything.

He leaned over and briefly, oh so briefly, kissed her again. A kiss almost as chaste as the one Red had given Mildred.

When he pulled away, several feet away this time, he gave her another lopsided grin. "I think we just need to practice, that's all."

Then, with a wave, he turned away and strode across the yard to his house.

B.J. stood there, in the deep Wyoming night, watching him walk away. Wondering how she'd survive any more practice as potent as tonight's had been.

Chapter Eight

Jake was late down to breakfast the next morning, an unusual occurrence. But he'd had trouble sleeping after his evening with B.J.—and his night without her.

"Gettin' lazy in your old age, brother?" Chad asked as he entered the kitchen.

"It's not his old age," Pete drawled. "It's starting up with a woman again. You know how that cuts up your peace, Chad."

The three women at the table, Anna, Megan and Janie, protested Pete's words, but Jake ignored all of it. He was busy filling a coffee mug. He needed some caffeine.

"Jake, Halloween's almost here," Janie suddenly said.

He approached the table, his coffee in his hand, and raised one eyebrow at his sister-in-law. "And?"

"I wondered about a Halloween party."

"A party? Haven't we entertained enough this year with all the weddings?" He sat down and began heaping his plate with scrambled eggs and sausage.

"But, Jake," Megan protested, "we could combine Halloween with your birthday."

His head snapped up. "My birthday?" He stared at his three brothers. "Who's been talking?"

"Is it a secret?" Anna asked. "I think it's nice to celebrate together."

Jake couldn't complain after Anna's words. They all knew she'd had no family until she joined theirs. "No, Anna, it's not a secret, but, well, I guess I'm getting to the age that celebrating a birthday isn't that important.''

"But it would be fun. Couldn't we have a party?''   Jake groaned. He couldn't say no. "If you want to, I don't mind. But I don't see any reason to include my birthday.''

"Well, we were going to celebrate yours and Toby's birthdays together. They're the same day. That's how we knew. Toby told us,'' Janie explained.   Jake grinned. He'd told Toby a month ago that they shared the same birthday, October 27. He enjoyed the time he spent with the little guy. "He's young enough to be excited about birthdays.''

"But he's even more excited about sharing his day with you,'' Megan explained. "If we celebrate his birthday without celebrating yours, he'll be upset.''

Jake sighed and chewed his eggs. Finally he swallowed and looked up to see his family watching him. "Fine. Have a party.''

"Thanks, Jake,'' Anna said with a grin.

His brothers stood up, ready to go to work, and he hastily took another bite before joining them. At least he wouldn't have to worry about matchmaking since he and B.J. were pretending.

He'd just have to worry about staying in a state of frustration and getting no sleep.

When the door closed behind the four brothers, the three women grinned at each other.

"Perfect. He agreed. Does everyone have a list ready?'' Janie asked.

"Yes, but Jake's not going to want to see Mindy again,'' Megan said.

"We can't worry about what Jake wants,'' Janie said. "We have to keep the pressure on so he'll hold on to B.J.''

"I agree,'' Anna said. "They're so cute together.''

"All right,'' Megan agreed. "We all invite every bachelorette we know.''

"Yeah,'' Janie agreed, a grin on her face, "it's going to be a real scary Halloween for Jake.''

"Have you and Red set a date yet?'' B.J. asked her aunt the morning after her dinner with Jake.

"Not yet. I guess we'd better hurry before you and Jake beat us to it. Last night it looked like the two of you were gettin' pretty cozy."

"What's 'cozy' mean?" Toby asked as he scooped his cereal into his mouth.

"Don't talk with your mouth full," B.J. immediately said, casting a warning look at Mildred.

Toby chewed and then repeated his question.

"That means they're being friendly," Mildred explained.

"Then me and Mr. Jake are cozy, too," Toby said with satisfaction. "He's going to take me to McDonald's."

"I'm not sure—" B.J. began. She thought it would be a good idea to cushion her son, in case McDonald's didn't work out.

Toby interrupted her. "Mr. Jake always does what he says, Mommy. Mr. Red told me."

She immediately thought of the good-night kiss last night. He'd promised to keep the kisses to a minimum, but she didn't think that kiss could be considered minimal in any way. She sighed. Maybe next time he would—

"You okay?" Mildred asked, watching her.

"Yes, of course. Well, it's almost time for school. Better go get ready, Toby."

"Okay. Don't forget about making cupcakes for my birthday at school, Aunt Mildred. And make an extra one for Mr. Jake, 'cause it's his birthday, too."

"Land's sake, boy, we've got more than a week before your birthday. I'll get those cupcakes made on time. Don't you worry about it."

Toby grinned and rushed from the room.

B.J. realized she'd have to pull herself together and plan a party for her little boy. And figure out what to buy him for his birthday.

"When are you going to go shopping?" Mildred asked.

B.J. smiled. Trust Mildred to read her mind. "I don't know. And I don't have any idea about what to get him. Got any suggestions?"

"How about a sexy nightgown?"

B.J. stared at her aunt, wondering if she'd lost her mind.

Mildred grinned. "I'm not talking about Toby's birthday present. I'm talking about Jake."

"You think I should get *Jake* a sexy nightgown?"

"I think that's what he'd like...as long as you were wearing it."

"Mildred!"

"Don't you go playing the innocent with me, Barbara Jo," Mildred said, her cheeks almost as red as B.J.'s. "I peeked at the two of you on the porch."

Flashes of the time spent outside with Jake last night did nothing to ease B.J.'s embarrassment. Desperately she sought for a reason to dismiss Mildred's assessment of their relationship. "Jake isn't—"

Footsteps sounded on the porch steps. Mildred leaned back to look out the window. "Jake is here. Guess he couldn't wait to see you."

B.J. jumped up from her chair, her mind frantically looking for reasons for Jake's arrival. "Probably there's a problem with the herd." She tried to ignore Mildred's knowing smile as she left the kitchen.

She swung open the door just as Jake had raised his fist to knock. "Hi. Is something wrong?"

"Nope. How did you know I was here?"

"Mildred saw you. She thinks— Never mind. What is it?" She gnawed on her bottom lip, anxiously waiting his response.

He reached out and ran his thumb along her lip. "Don't do that. Or I'm going to swallow you whole."

Jerking back, she pressed her lips together, hoping to convince him that his words didn't affect her at all.

"I needed to talk to you," he finally said.

"Now? Here? But—"

"Why don't you walk over to the barn with me? You can tell Mildred I wanted you to look at one of the mares."

Grateful for his suggestion that implied a return to normalcy, him the rancher, her the veterinarian, she slipped through the door and closed it behind her.

Silently they crossed the yard and entered the horse barn. As soon as the door closed behind them, she whirled around and asked again, "What is it?"

"I just thought I'd tell you that the girls are planning a Halloween-birthday party. I'm sure they think we're together and will expect you to-to look forward to the party."

"Okay." She kept trying to figure out why he thought it necessary to tell her that first thing this morning. It wasn't as if she'd throw up her hands in horror if one of her friends mentioned the party. "Is that all?"

"They may expect you to buy me a birthday present," he added, seemingly a little embarrassed.

B.J. knew her cheeks were bright red, but she couldn't help thinking about Mildred's suggestion. "I've already discussed that with Mildred." Then she wished she'd kept her mouth closed.

"Oh? Did Mildred have any ideas?"

"Nothing that would work. I don't suppose you could give me any ideas?" That would be a help, since she couldn't think of a single thing to get him. And she hoped her question would distract him from what Mildred had suggested.

"Anything will do. I'll pay you for it as soon as you buy something."

She stared at him. "Why would you do that?"

He shrugged his shoulders. "No reason for you to waste your money on a gift for me."

She was amazed to see his cheeks redden, as if her buying something for him would embarrass him. "Do your brothers give you presents?"

"We never did much for birthdays. We were a houseful of men, you know. Dad usually gave us each a savings bond."

B.J. stared at him, picturing a little boy Toby's age receiving a savings bond as his only birthday present. "Toby wouldn't be satisfied with a piece of paper," she murmured, smiling wryly at Jake.

"I need some ideas about a present for Toby," Jake immediately said, a smile lighting his face.

"He likes toy trucks." She couldn't help smiling back. "How about you? Do you like trucks?"

"Only big ones."

"Mmm," she said, chuckling. "I think a big one is out of my price range."

"That's okay. Mine is in good shape. And I think I'd rather have something else from you." The light in his eyes gave her a hint of his meaning.

"Like what?"

"Let's go back to what Mildred suggested."

"What are you talking about?" she said, but she turned to study the saddle hanging on the wall rather than look at him.

"I'm not sure. But whatever it is sure makes you blush. I figured it must be pretty good."

"Jake, you're teasing me. Don't you have to get to work?" One thing she already knew about the big, handsome cowboy— he loved to tease.

"I guess you're right. My brothers were already curious when I told 'em to go on without me."

"Then I'll be on my way, too. I've got some calls to make."

When she started to move past him, he reached out and caught her shoulders. "Wait a minute. I've been good. I think I deserve a goodbye kiss."

She swallowed, her throat suddenly dry. "There's no one around to impress. I don't see any reason to—"

"I do."

His lips covered hers. Groaning, she gave herself up to the magical touch that always sent her heart soaring. She slid her hands across his chest, beneath his jacket, indulging her needs.

"Mommy, Aunt Mildred said—"

Toby's piping voice intruded upon her bliss. She ripped herself from Jake's embrace to find her little boy staring up at the two of them.

"Hi, Mr. Jake. Why are you kissing my mommy?"

JAKE ALWAYS ENJOYED spending time with Toby. But he wished the boy had arrived five minutes later. That might've given him enough time to enjoy B.J.'s kiss.

Instead, he noticed the stricken expression on B.J.'s face. Squatting down, he scooped Toby up in his arms, bringing him to his eye level. "Well, Toby, that's something men do when they think a lady is pretty."

Toby gave him a doubtful look. "I think Amber Lloyd is pretty, but I don't kiss her."

"Right, son. That's because you're not grown-up. When you're a man—" he paused and looked at B.J., then turned back to Toby "—you sometimes kiss a lady because she's special."

"Mommy's special," Toby said, nodding.

"My thoughts exactly," Jake agreed.

"Why are you here, Toby? What did Mildred want?" B.J. said abruptly, avoiding Jake's eyes.

"She said I should see if you're taking me to the bus stop this morning. If you're busy, she said she could." Toby didn't even bother to look at his mother. He was examining Jake's hat.

"I'll take you."

"Okay. What happened to your hat, Mr. Jake?" His little finger reached out to trace a crease B.J.'s truck had pressed into it.

"Um, it got run over, Toby. Looks kind of bad, doesn't it?" Jake asked, but he looked at B.J. Sudden recognition appeared in her eyes, and she stared at his hat.

"I like your hat. When I grow up, I'm going to have one just like it."

"Don't you have a hat now?" Jake asked, an idea forming in his head.

"I have a baseball cap, but I don't have a cowboy hat."

"Toby, I think we'd better go," B.J. snapped, as if she were angry with her son.

"Wait a minute, B.J.," Jake said, stopping her. "I've got an idea. Why don't the three of us go hat shopping this afternoon? I'll get me a new one, and Toby could pick out a hat for his birthday. Would you like a hat as your birthday gift from me?"

"I can't go this afternoon," she immediately said.

Jake didn't know if she didn't want him to buy Toby a hat or if she was genuinely busy, but he wasn't going to give up. "How about tomorrow afternoon?"

"Please, Mommy?" Toby added.

Jake almost burst out laughing. If he'd asked B.J. to go shop-

ping, just the two of them, he knew she would've turned him
down flat. But when it involved Toby, her determination wa-
vered.

"There's no need for you to buy him a hat, Jake."

Toby's face fell, and he hugged the boy closer to him. "I
want to buy him a present he'll enjoy. A hat's a lot more prac-
tical than a toy truck."

Suddenly she capitulated. "Fine. Tomorrow."

"Great. What time do you get out of school, Toby?"

"At lunchtime. What time is that, Mommy?"

"Twelve o'clock. But there's no need to interrupt your day,
Jake. We can meet you some place in town at four," B.J. suggested.

"That's no problem. Why don't you and I meet here at
eleven-thirty, drive to town and pick up Toby and have lunch
at the sandwich shop? Then we'll go shopping."

"That's not necessary. You've got lots to do and—"

"Everyone's been riding me about not ever taking time off.
If I want the afternoon off, then I'll take it. See you then." He
set Toby on the ground and then leaned over to kiss her, briefly
this time. It wasn't nearly as exciting as their earlier kiss, nor as
satisfying, but it beat nothing at all.

Before she could protest or change their plans, he left the barn.
He strode over to the indoor arena, figuring to check on the
hands working there. As he opened the door, he heard Toby's
little voice shouting a goodbye. He turned to wave at the pair.

B.J. didn't respond.

But the thought of the next afternoon kept a smile on Jake's
face all day. He was pleased to have found such a good gift for
Toby. Heck, the kid had lived on the ranch almost a year. He
needed a cowboy hat.

Maybe some chaps, too. And a good pair of leather gloves.
After all, he'd probably grow up and work on the ranch during
his teen years for spending money. Might as well equip him
right.

"Hey, Jake," Brett called to him as he was heading into the
house that evening.

He turned around to await Brett. A feeling of satisfaction filled him. A good day's work, a good meal awaiting him and a lot to look forward to.

"You look mighty pleased with yourself," Brett commented, watching him as he stepped onto the porch.

"Yeah," Jake agreed with a grin. "It was a good day."

"Great. Uh, is it okay if I take tomorrow off? Anna and I thought we'd spend it together."

"If you don't mind, why not wait until Wednesday? I've got plans for tomorrow afternoon, and we don't want to leave the place too shorthanded."

Jake opened the door and strolled into the kitchen, knowing Brett would follow.

"Plans? What are you doing?"

"Birthday shopping with Toby."

The rest of the family was already in the kitchen, and Jake's words stopped all conversation. Suddenly everyone was staring at him.

"What?" he demanded, frowning.

"Is B.J. going?" Anna asked.

"Of course she is. I'm buying Toby a cowboy hat, and we have to try them on, find one that suits him." He ignored his family's intense interest. "I'm going to clean up. I won't be long."

"Take your time," Red said.

Once Jake was out the door, everyone started talking about his announcement.

"I wonder when he and B.J. decided this? Last night?" Janie asked.

"Probably this morning," Red said.

"This morning? When did he see B.J. this morning?" Pete asked, frowning.

"When he left you, he went straight to B.J.'s house, then the two of them walked over to the barn," Red reported, continuing to work at the kitchen cabinet, pouring green beans into a serving bowl.

"You spying on Jake?" Chad asked.

"Nope. Just working here at the sink, looking out the window. Couldn't help but see."

"Great," Janie said, enthusiastically. "Let us know if you see anything else."

JAKE STRODE from the house after dinner, wanting to check some supplies before he went into town the next day. Movement out of the corner of his eye caught his attention.

He turned toward B.J.'s house and saw what had distracted him. Toby.

His smile broadened. In Toby's hands was the rope he'd given him last week to practice.

"Hold still, Spot," Toby called to his dog as he swung the rope.

Jake realized he'd neglected an important detail in his roping instructions.

"Hey, Toby, how's it going?"

"Mr. Jake! Look! I've been practicing."

"I can see." Jack squatted down and scratched behind Spot's ears after the puppy wriggled his way to Jake. "But I forgot to tell you something."

"What, Mr. Jake?" the little boy said, raising his gaze anxiously. "I'm holding it just like you said."

Jake couldn't resist giving the boy a hug. He'd enjoyed teaching Toby to rope last week. The boy's serious concentration, emphasized by a frown on his forehead, had tickled him.

"You're doin' fine. But I forgot to mention that you shouldn't use Spot as a target. You might hurt him."

Toby's eyes widened in alarm. "Oh, no!" He reached for his dog, clutching him to his chest. "I wouldn't hurt Spot, Mr. Jake."

"I know you wouldn't. How about we set up a post over there—" he gestured toward the barn "—and you can practice on it? Then, when you've got it down, we'll take you out and let you try to rope a real cow."

Toby's eyes widened again, this time in excitement. "Gee, Mr. Jake, that'd be neat! I'll practice all the time!"

"But not tomorrow. We're going shopping for a hat, remember?"

"I remember. I want a hat just like yours."

"Not like this one," Jake said, fingering his cowboy hat. He forgot Toby as he remembered how his hat had been flattened. And the kiss that had preceded it. B. J. Anderson was some kisser.

"Mr. Jake?" Toby tugged on his jacket. "Why are you smiling?"

Jake stared at the boy, trying to collect his thoughts. "Uh, I guess I was thinking about your mom."

"Mommy?" Toby paused and then said, "Do you like my mommy?"

"Of course I do." Jake's mind flashed back to his previous thoughts. Yeah, he liked Toby's mother. B.J. was a very attractive woman.

"I like you teaching me things. Mommy doesn't know how to rope." Toby leaned against his knee, and Jake put his arm around him.

"You've got a good mom, but there are some things that only guys know about."

"Yeah," Toby agreed. Then, with some hesitation, he continued, "Can I ask you a question?"

"Sure, Toby. You can ask me anything."

"What's a ho?"

Jake frowned. "Well, it's a tool for digging in a garden."

"Oh."

"Why, Toby? Are you planning on planting a garden?" Not that there was anything wrong with putting in a garden, but cowboys weren't farmers, and he'd thought Toby wanted to learn to be a cowboy.

"No. But when one of the boys at school called a girl that, our teacher made him go to time-out and told us not never to say it 'cause it was naughty." Toby's voice sounded puzzled.

Jake could understand his confusion. "Sorry, Toby, but I thought you meant a different word. The word you're asking about *is* bad. Your teacher was right."

"But what does it mean?"

Jake was tempted to tell Toby to ask his mother. But he couldn't do that. "Uh, it's a name men call women when they think they're too—too friendly with other men. But a gentleman doesn't use it, and he wouldn't let anyone else use it if they're talking about his woman. I mean, his friend.''

"He'd punch him in the nose!" Toby said with relish, his eyes lighting up.

"Yeah," Jake agreed. "And don't ever use that word yourself."

"No, I won't." Toby put his hand on Jake's cheek. "Mr. Jake, if someone called my mommy that word, would you hit him?"

"Is that who they were talking about?" Jake demanded, surprising emotion filling him.

"No. But if someone did, would you hit him?"

"Yeah, I would," Jake admitted. "I'd flatten him before he knew what hit him." He realized his hold on Toby had tightened, and he forced himself to relax. Then he thought about what he'd just said. Maybe that hadn't been the best response to give an impressionable child.

He tried again. "Uh, Toby, fighting in school isn't a good idea, you know."

"I know, Mr. Jake. Our teacher told us."

"Great. Well, I've got to go check on some things."

"I have to go take my bath. Mommy makes me," Toby said in disgusted tones.

"That's what moms are for, Toby. Besides, ladies like us to smell good."

"Do you take lots of baths, Mr. Jake?"

"Well, usuallly I take showers, but, yeah, I take my fair share of them."

With a resigned shrug, Toby replied, "Okay, then I won't complain."

"Good boy," Jake said as he stood, patting Toby on the head.

"Mr. Jake?"

"Yeah?"

"If I have any more questions I can't ask Mommy, can I ask you?"

Jake grinned. He kind of liked playing the role of mentor to the four-year-old. He only hoped B.J. wouldn't mind. "Sure, Toby. Any time."

The two parted, and Jake headed toward the barn with a smile on his lips.

Chapter Nine

B.J. had changed her mind the next day, deciding going into town with Jake wasn't a good idea. When she tried to persuade him to her way of thinking, however, she met with solid resistance.

"No way. You're just trying to steal my idea for a present, but I thought of it first."

"Jake, that's not it. You can buy him a hat, but I don't think our appearing in town together is a good idea."

"Why not?"

"We're just trying to convince Red and Mildred, not the entire community. You know how fast gossip spreads around town."

"It doesn't matter."

B.J. crossed her arms and gave him an exasperated look.

"If you don't want to go, fine. I'll pick Toby up from school, and we'll go without you," Jake said, a stubborn look on his face.

"No, you're not going without me," she protested, unable to face remaining at home while Jake took Toby.

"Then let's go."

She did as he said, but she wasn't happy about it. They had a silent ride into town.

Any tension was dispelled as soon as Toby saw them waiting. He broke into a run, his face beaming.

"Now, aren't you glad we didn't cancel?" Jake murmured.

B.J. shot him an irritated look, but he was right. She hated disappointing her son. She knelt for Toby's hug and was surprised to discover Jake beside her. After Toby hugged her, Jake held out his arms.

"I should get a hug, too, shouldn't I?"

Toby didn't hesitate, but B.J. stood, her heart churning. Toby already had put Jake on a pedestal. How much was their pretense going to hurt her son?

"Mrs. Anderson?"

She turned to see Toby's preschool teacher coming toward her. "Hello, Mrs. Bell. How are things going?"

"Just lovely. I wanted to be sure that Toby found you. He told me he was supposed to meet you and Jake today instead of taking the bus."

Jake stood with Toby's arms around his neck. "Mornin', Loretta."

"Mornin', Jake. I see Toby found his hero. You're all he's talked about all morning."

"Must've been a pretty dull morning, then," Jake returned with a laugh.

B.J. sighed. Mrs. Bell was approaching retirement, but she could no more resist Jake Randall's charm than any other woman. The teacher laughed and reached out to touch Jake's arm. "You've been good for Toby. Now when the other boys talk about their daddies, he always mentions you."

B.J. froze, dismay filling her. "You never mentioned a problem, Mrs. Bell."

The woman's gaze flew from Jake's to hers. "Oh, there isn't a problem, Mrs. Anderson. At least not one that you could help. Toby sometimes felt a little left out because he only has one parent. He's not the only one with that problem."

B.J. had known, once Toby started school, that he would feel the loss of his father. But she hadn't planned on Jake being the substitute. "I hope you will remind him that Jake is a friend, not—not his father."

Very gently, with a sympathetic smile, Mrs. Bell said, "Toby doesn't get confused, Mrs. Anderson. He's a very smart little boy."

B.J. nodded and avoided Jake's gaze. "Thank you for check-ing on Toby, Mrs. Bell. He's enjoying your class very much."

They said their goodbyes and got into Jake's truck, Toby be-tween them. Jake helped him fasten his seat belt before B.J. remembered. Her mind was too occupied with Toby's teacher's words.

"Quit worryin'," Jake said softly over Toby's head.

Her gaze met his, but she couldn't respond. Not worry? About her only child and how she might be hurting him? Nothing could keep her from doing that.

"I told everyone about my birthday present," Toby an-nounced brightly. Then a shadow fell across his face. "But Larry said I shouldn't tell. That it had to be a secret. Does it have to be a secret, Mr. Jake?"

"No, Toby. I'll get you something else as a secret. Then—"

"No!" B.J. protested. "No, Jake, only one present. You'll spoil Toby if you're not careful."

"Are you only going to buy him one present?" Jake chal-lenged, squaring his jaw and staring at her.

"That has nothing to do with it. I'm his mother." And Jake Randall wasn't his father. She had to make that point, even if she didn't say it out loud.

Instead of responding, Jake put the truck in gear and headed toward the main street of Rawhide. "Are you hungry, Toby?"

"Yeah! We had juice and cookies, but I dropped one of mine on the floor and it broke into little pieces. Mrs. Bell wouldn't let me eat it."

"Thank goodness," B.J. said with a laugh, reaching over to push back his hair, which always flopped onto his forehead. "I think you're about due for a haircut."

"Hey, me too. How about we get our hair cut before we buy our hats, Toby?"

B.J. bit her bottom lip. Toby was still a little leery of barber-shops. Until a few months ago, she or Mildred had usually trimmed his hair. But when Mr. Jake suggested something, Toby, it appeared, had no doubts.

She was going to have to get the man to recommend baths.

Though she had to admit Toby had been amazingly compliant last night.

"Yeah, that'd be fun," Toby agreed.

"Okay with you, Mom?" Jake asked, surprising her with the familiar term.

"Yes, of course, if Toby doesn't mind."

"That way our hats will fit better, right, Toby?"

"Right, Mr. Jake."

Lunch was a revelation to B.J. All her admonitions to Toby about manners seldom had taken hold in his consciousness. But today, when Jake took his napkin and spread it across his lap, Toby immediately did the same. When Jake said thank-you to the waitress, Toby did also.

Of course, Jake's words had the young woman blushing and batting her eyelashes. Toby's earned him a pat on the head.

"So, what'll you have, Toby?" Jake asked.

"What are you having?" Toby asked.

Jake looked over the top of the menu, sharing his amusement with B.J. She supposed, if her son was going to have a hero, Jake Randall wasn't a bad choice. But she was worried about how far the hero worship would go. Even so, she smiled at Jake.

"I'm thinking of having a big, fat, juicy hamburger."

"Me, too."

Surprise, surprise, surprise.

"B.J.? You made up your mind yet?"

She turned her attention to the menu instead of the two males at the table and quickly made a decision. "Yes, I'll have the chicken-salad sandwich."

"Humph! Girl food," Jake said with a teasing grin.

"Yeah, girl food," Toby agreed.

This hero worship could get tiresome.

"I am a girl, after all," she contended.

"The prettiest one I've ever seen," Jake said, his grin widening.

"Yeah, you're pretty, Mommy," Toby seconded.

Maybe she could stand Toby agreeing with Jake after all.

The next stop was the barbershop. Al, who had cut Jake's hair since he was a little boy, trimmed first his hair and then

Toby's, following Toby's directions to cut his hair just like Mr. Jake's.

B.J. sat along the wall, watching the three of them as they indulged in man talk, feeling a little excluded. It was a new experience for her. She and Mildred had formed Toby's world for almost all his life. She wasn't used to sharing him.

She thought again about what Mrs. Bell had said. She'd have to have a talk with Toby, make sure he understood that Jake was a friend.

Jake insisted on paying for Toby's haircut. B.J. would've argued more, but she didn't want to draw attention to Jake's action. Looked as though she needed to have a talk with Jake, as well as Toby.

"All right, let's go buy us a couple of hats, Toby my boy," Jake said, grinning at first Toby and then B.J. He seemed to be enjoying his afternoon in town.

He grabbed Toby's hand and then, to B.J.'s surprise, reached back for hers. "Come on, B.J. You're not feeling left out, are you, 'cause you didn't get a haircut?"

"No, I'll get one later."

He came to an abrupt halt. "You're going to get your hair cut? I was just teasing. I don't think—"

"Trimmed, Jake. I'm going to get my hair trimmed. I'm not going to cut it short, because it takes too much time to style a short hairstyle."

Toby apparently felt left out, because he turned in front of Jake, still holding his hand. "I like Mommy's hair. Sometimes she lets me brush it."

"You've got good taste, Toby. Do you think she'd let me brush it?" His gaze left her son to stare at her hair.

"Jake!" she protested. Somehow the picture of Jake brushing her hair, feeling his hands slipping through the long strands, sensing his big, warm, hard body near hers, stirred her more than the compliments he'd paid her.

He grinned and leaned down for a quick kiss before she could protest. "And that doesn't count for the one you tricked me out of," he muttered as he started walking again, pulling her and Toby along with him to the store two doors down.

"Why not?"

"You know why. Here we are, Toby." He held the door open for Toby and then her.

"Hey, Jake, haven't seen you in a coon's age," Harvey Holmes greeted him. "And you brought along Miz Anderson and her boy. How you folks doing?"

Fortunately the store was almost empty, since B.J. figured no one would've missed Harvey's booming voice.

Harvey showed them to the hats and left them alone to make their selections, promising to help if they had any questions.

"Aunt Mildred said the good guys always wear white hats," Toby said, studying his choices.

"In the movies, they do, but that's because they don't have to worry about them looking clean." Jake was studying the different colors and styles seriously.

B.J. saw one that looked Toby's size and picked it up. The Resistol brand was a good one, she knew, but she had no idea how much the price would be. With a gasp, she put the hat back down. "Jake," she whispered, moving closer to him.

"Yeah, honey?" he answered in a distracted fashion.

"Jake, these hats are too expensive."

He gave her a surprised look. "I always buy Resistols."

"It doesn't matter what you buy. I'm talking about for Toby. They have some hats at the grocery store that will do just fine for him." She turned to explain to her son, but Jake grabbed her arm.

"You buy him all the hats you want at the grocery store, but *I'm* buying him a Resistol. He needs to learn about quality. This hat'll last him for years." His jaw was squared again, a sure sign that he had the bit in his teeth.

"The hat will last, but Toby'll outgrow it in a year."

"Great. I'll know what to get him next year," he said calmly, and took a hat, quite similar to the one she'd flattened, off the wall and set it on his head. "What do you think, Toby?"

"That looks like your old hat," the boy said, staring up at him, studying the hat from several different angles.

"Yeah, it does, doesn't it? I don't change my mind much," he admitted with another grin. "Which one do you like?"

Unerringly Toby selected a miniature version of the dark gray hat Jake was wearing. "I like this one."

Jake led him over to a mirror and set the hat on the little boy's head, squatting down beside him to compare the hats. "Hey, we look just alike, don't we?"

Toby made an adjustment in the angle of his hat so it more correctly reflected Jake's and sighed with pleasure. "Yeah, just alike. Right, Mommy?"

Their satisfaction with what they saw in the mirror would've been humorous if B.J. weren't filled with worry. But she smiled at Toby, agreeing that he and Mr. Jake were almost twins.

In truth, they did look alike, even without the hats. They both had dark hair and a similar build. Her husband had been tall, even if he hadn't shown the muscle Jake had. He'd been a law student when they met, spending his days indoors.

"You folks found what you need?" Harvey asked, approaching them again.

"I believe we have. Toby and I like these."

"I'm not surprised. You've bought the same hat since you were a boy, Jake. Starting Toby off right, I see."

"Yeah. And pretty soon I'll be buying hats for the twins, too." A satisfied smile crossed his lips.

"I'd better lay in some smaller sizes, the way the Randall clan is growing," Harvey said with a laugh. The sly look he sent B.J.'s way wasn't missed by Jake. He turned to her, too.

"How about you, B.J.?" he suddenly asked.

"What?" she asked, looking up from Toby, who was staring at himself and Jake in the mirror.

"You need a hat?"

"No, it's not my birthday. That's why Jake is buying Toby a present, Mr. Holmes. It's his birthday."

"Make it Harvey. We're not formal here. So, it's your birthday, young man?"

"In a few days. The twenty-seventh, the same day as Mr. Jake's," Toby said proudly, as if he'd planned his arrival on such an important day.

"Yeah, we're twins," Jake said with a wink to the store owner.

"I can see the resemblance," Harvey agreed solemnly, putting an extra shine on Toby's grin. "Come on over here, and I'll ring you up."

They were almost finished with their purchase, with B.J. reminding herself to discuss money with Jake, when the door opened, the bell above announcing a new arrival.

They all looked up, but Jake was the only one who recognized the man who arrived.

"Butch Gardner!" he exclaimed, and left the counter to greet the man with his hand out.

"Jake!" the man returned, pumping Jake's hand with pleasure. The two men exchanged greetings and questioned each other about what had happened the past few years. It seemed Butch, who'd lived near Rawhide most of his early years, was returning to town.

After the first wave of words had passed, the man looked past Jake and saw B.J. and Toby waiting for him. Jake turned, too, and B.J. assumed he intended to introduce them, but before he could, Butch spoke.

"Jake, you old sneak. You've done gone and got yourself that son you always wanted! And a beautiful wife, to boot. Congratulations, man."

There was a moment of silence when B.J.'s alarmed look met Jake's. She didn't want to look at Toby. She opened her mouth to correct the man, but Jake beat her to it.

"Sorry, Butch, but you're wrong on both counts. Toby is B. J. Anderson's son, and neither of them belongs to me." Jake's easy smile relieved some of Butch's embarrassment.

"Sorry, ma'am. It's an old habit of mine, leaping to conclusions. Hope I didn't offend you." He doffed his black hat as he apologized.

"No, of course not." She put her hand on Toby's shoulder. "Shall we wait for you out in the pickup, Jake?"

"No, we won't be a minute," Jake assured her before he turned back to his friend. "You'll have to come out to the place, Butch, and see everyone. All three of the others are married now, and Pete has two sons."

"No kidding? Man, I didn't think any of you would ever try

marriage again. And two boys? Then the Randall ranch is safe
for the next generation? That was always your concern," Butch
reminded him.

Harvey laughed. "Everyone knows how worried Jake was
about not having any kids. He didn't want different blood taking
over at the Randalls'."

Different blood. B.J. turned that phrase over in her head. Apparently Jake was big on bloodlines. He'd talked about that at
their dinner in Wyndom, how thrilled he was to have the next
generation of real Randalls. B.J. didn't need a sack of grain to
hit her in the head. She got the point.

"Nope, no problem now. There'll be Randalls on the place
for a long time," Jake said, his grin even broader. "We've got
to go, but the family's having a party for Halloween. Where
shall we send the invite?"

"Mrs. Potter's putting me up at her bed and breakfast until I
get settled some place."

"You looking for a job? We could use someone right now,"
Jake said, as if he'd suddenly realized his friend might be looking for work.

"I don't need any pity hiring, Jake," Butch said, squaring his
jaw.

"Man, with all we've had going on, none of us puts in a full
week anymore. And Lefty died last winter, before Christmas.
We've never replaced him."

"Lefty? That's too bad. But are you sure you need someone?
'Cause I can—"

"Jake's been asking for most of the year, Butch," Harvey
said. "There's not a lot of good help around."

Jake shot the store owner a grateful look. Then he quickly
worked out the details with his friend before sweeping B.J. and
Toby out the door.

Once they were in the truck, B.J. started to ask Jake about
the man, but Toby had another question in mind.

"Why can't I be your little boy, Mr. Jake? Is something
wrong with my blood?"

Chapter Ten

B.J. sucked in a deep breath.

Jake spoke before she could think of what to say.

"Nah. There's nothing wrong with your blood, Toby. They just meant we're not kin to each other. You know, like you and your mom."

"Oh."

B.J. desperately sought a change of subject. "How did you do in school today, Toby? Did you learn to write any new words?"

Her little boy turned and frowned at her, his look distracted. "Mm-hmm. Mr. Jake?"

"Yes, Toby?"

"How——?"

"Toby, did you know the Randalls are having a Halloween party?" B.J. asked, hoping to distract him again. She didn't think it would be a good idea to pursue the idea of Toby being Jake's son.

This time she was more successful.

"A Halloween party? With masks and everything?" Toby demanded. "Can we go?"

"It's bad manners to invite yourself to a party," she gently reminded him.

"Don't worry about it, Toby," Jake assured him. "Of course you're invited. And you can wear a mask."

"I'm going to be a monster!" Toby assured his hero. "Right, Mommy?"

"We'll see," she said, offering a mother's standard fare.

"You won't scare me, will you?" Jake asked, pretending to shake in fear.

"Nah," Toby replied, imitating Jake's way of answering. "'Sides, you wouldn't be scared. Maybe Mommy would." Toby cut his gaze toward his mother, a grin on his face.

B.J. was willing to play along, as long as it kept her son happy. "I just might be. Promise you'll tell me it's you?"

"Yeah, Mommy."

"And if she gets scared, I'll comfort her," Jake added, and shot a teasing look at B.J.

The thought of Jake's big arms wrapped around her, his hands stroking her, sent shivers through her body. His brown eyes caressed her over Toby's head, and she broke away from his gaze.

"I won't scare you, Mommy," her son promised.

"Doggone it, Toby, why'd you promise that? I was going to get to hug your mom."

"I saw Bobby's mommy hugging."

B.J. frowned, unable to follow her son's comment. Before she could ask about his words, Jake did.

"Was she happy about it?"

"Uh-huh. She was hugging Bobby's new daddy."

"Good for her," Jake said, smiling at B.J. over Toby's head.

"Yeah. Bobby says he's his real daddy. But they don't have the same blood. Do they?"

"Probably not," Jake agreed.

"Then how come he's his real daddy?"

B.J. could think of nothing to derail the conversation. Even the subject of Toby's monster costume probably wouldn't distract him.

"Because his mom married the man. That would make him his daddy."

"Even if they don't have the same blood?"

"Well, he wouldn't be his *real* daddy, but he'd be his step-daddy."

"Oh."

B.J. decided the all-male conversation had gone on long

enough. "Did you tell Jake that Aunt Mildred is making cup-cakes for the class for your birthday?" she asked. "And that she'll make one for Jake, too?"

"No. Do you like chocolate cupcakes, Mr. Jake?"

"You bet. I'll be looking forward to one of your cupcakes. Maybe I could come over and eat it for breakfast."

"Yeah!"

B.J. breathed a sigh of relief. At least Toby didn't seem upset about anything. She took a deep breath and leaned back against the seat.

Then Toby calmly announced, "Bobby said he thought I was going to have a new daddy."

B.J. felt the blood drain out of her head. She was so shocked, she didn't realize Jake had slammed on the brakes until he'd stopped the truck on the side of the road.

"What are you talking about?" he demanded harshly.

B.J.'s arm immediately went around her son's shoulders. She didn't want anyone speaking so cruelly to her little boy, but she knew how devastated Toby would be to find his hero unhappy with him. "Jake—" she began.

"Why did Bobby say that?" Jake ignored her warning.

"I told him about you kissing Mommy, and he said that's what his new daddy always did." Toby squared his shoulders and lifted his chin to stare at Jake. "Are you mad?"

B.J. didn't realize she was holding her breath until Jake ex-pelled his own.

"No, son, I'm not angry. But Bobby was wrong. Men and women kiss without getting married. You know, I've been mar-ried before, and I don't intend to marry. Your mom and I were just being friendly."

Friendly. Of course, that was the correct explanation. She was glad he'd done away with poor Toby's dreams. If he hadn't, Toby might have really been hurt.

"Never?" Toby whispered.

"No, never."

Toby turned a troubled glance to B.J. "Is that okay, Mommy?"

"Of course, sweetie," she replied, swallowing inexplicable

tears in the back of her throat. "I'm sorry if you're disappointed,
but when Mildred marries Red, you'll have a grandpa. Then
when they have—have things at school for daddies, Red can
come with you."

"Sure. I like Mr. Red."

She'd never been so proud of her child. He was hurting inside.
And it was her fault. She was going to have to tell Mildred the
truth—and let Mildred make her own decision. But she couldn't
hurt her son any more.

Hugging him closer to her, she leaned over and kissed the top
of his head. "Mr. Red likes you, too. I think we should ask
Mildred if you can walk her down the aisle when she marries
Mr. Red."

While Toby, distracted again, excitedly asked B.J. what she
meant, Jake pulled the truck back on the road and continued on
to the ranch.

DAMN! HE HADN'T MEANT to hurt the kid's feelings. Jake looked
sideways at the other two in the truck. They made a tender
picture, mother and son, her arm around him.

If Jake were ever going to marry again, it would be to someone like B.J., warm, loving, caring.

If? What was he thinking? There was no question of him
marrying! Never!

He glared at B.J. as if she were responsible for the shocking
thought that had intruded into his head. It was those kisses of
hers. The unexpected hunger he'd discovered for touching B. J.
Anderson was the reason. For only a second, he considered being married to the woman beside him, having the right to touch
her whenever he wanted.

Having her touch him.

He hurriedly sent those thoughts out the window, before his
body could show the effects of the warmth that filled him. Lately
he'd felt out of control too often.

By the time he'd parked the truck in its usual place, he'd
concentrated his thoughts on more-mundane things and convinced himself everything was okay. He turned off the engine

and turned to smile at his passengers. The sight of Toby whispering to his mother puzzled Jake.

"Everything all right?"

"Yes," B.J. said, giving Jake a brief look before turning back to her son. "It's all right, Toby. Just be sure you say thank-you."

"Thank you for my hat, Mr. Jake," Toby said. The serious look on his little face worried Jake.

"You're welcome. Happy birthday, pal. You like it, don't you?"

"Sure. It's just like yours." His smile this time wasn't his best, but Jake was pleased.

"Sweetie, run on over to the house and tell Mildred I'll be there in a minute. I need to talk to Mr. Jake." B.J. didn't look at Jake as she spoke, her gaze focused on her child.

But Jake felt anticipation build in him. Time alone with B.J. meant the possibility of a few more of those drugging kisses. He couldn't afford too many, but already his body was revving up with the thought of holding her again.

"See ya, Toby," he called out as the little boy slipped past his mother and out the door on her side. Toby waved but said nothing. Briefly Jake was distracted from thoughts of B.J. as he watched the child jog to their house, clutching the bag containing his new hat.

"Everything all right with Toby?"

"No," B.J. said, and he could hear icicles hanging off that one word.

"What's wrong?"

"We can't pretend any longer." She was staring straight ahead.

Jake studied her face, wishing she'd look at him. He was confused. "I thought we were talking about Toby."

"We are. Toby is believing our pretense. And I don't want him hurt."

"I told him we were just being friendly." In Jake's mind, his explanation would take care of the problem.

"It's not enough, Jake. Soon he'll hear rumors from other

kids. Because—because it's what he wants, he'll ignore your explanation.''

"What do you mean, it's what he wants?"

Now she looked at him, but her expression was a mixture of anger and disgust, and he almost wished she were staring straight ahead. "Come on, Jake. You must realize Toby has a bad case of hero worship. And since he's seen us..." She paused and Jake watched her swallow. He wanted to stroke her throat as he traced the movement with his gaze.

He leaned toward her, not even realizing it until she jerked away from him. Pulling himself together, he asked, "After he's seen us what?"

"Kissing! After he saw us in the barn, he obviously felt our—our relationship has changed."

"Yeah. We recognize each other now," Jake drawled at her obvious understatement.

"We always recognized each other," she said indignantly, looking at him again.

That indignation made her lips form a sexy pout that drew his lips like a magnet. But she only allowed a brief touching before she put her hands on his chest and pushed.

"Don't.''

"Sorry. I couldn't help myself."

She glared at him.

"So what are you saying? Around Toby we don't pretend? I think that might be—"

"Impossible. That would be impossible. I'm saying we shouldn't pretend anymore. At all." She pressed those lips tightly together.

"What about Mildred and Red?" He wanted to protest more, to tell her she couldn't stop what had already been set in motion. But he was afraid she'd question his motives. Red and Mildred were safer.   "I'm going to tell Mildred the truth."

Jake frowned. "Do you think that's fair? They've made plans." So had he. For a little more closeness with B.J.

"I won't risk my son's happiness."

"Aren't you being melodramatic? I'm not going to hurt Toby." He wouldn't do that. He and Toby were pals.

She lifted her chin. "No. Our pretense is over, Jake. You're on your own in the future."

"Hey, don't act like I begged you." His pride was hurt. She thought he couldn't manage on his own? He conveniently pushed aside that Friday night in Rawhide. *She* was the one who'd wanted to continue the charade.

"I know." Her words came out with defeat, and she sagged against the car seat. "I made a mistake. I'm sorry I asked you to do this—" she waved one hand distractedly "—and—and I hope you don't have any unpleasant repercussions from it."

"Hey, B.J., I don't have anything to complain about," he said softly, fighting the urge to gather her against him.

She shook her head no, her chin lowered. Before he could think of anything else to say, she slid from the truck and hurried to her home.

Damn! That made two Andersons he'd upset this afternoon. He slapped the steering wheel, angry with himself and with the events of the day. Which had started off with such promise.

His original idea had been so simple.

A little friendliness to scare off scheming women.

But things had gotten complicated.

He threw himself from the truck, not wanting to think about what had happened. When he reached the kitchen, he didn't slow down, in spite of the fact that Red and his three sisters-in-law were there.

"Jake!" Janie called out. "How did the day go?"

"Fine! Damn fine! In fact, outstandingly damn fine!"

He realized he hadn't been as tactful as he'd intended when a stunned silence followed him from the room.

B.J. ENTERED THE HOUSE and squared her shoulders. She couldn't put off her talk with Mildred. It was going to be hard enough without time to think about it.

"Mildred?"

"In the kitchen," Mildred called back.

As B.J. entered the most popular room in the house, Toby was showing Mildred his hat.

"It's just like Mr. Jake's," he explained, but the excitement that had earlier filled his voice wasn't there.

"That's a mighty fine hat. A fine birthday present." Mildred shot B.J. a puzzled look over Toby's head.

"Why don't you go find a place in your room to keep it so it won't get messed up, Toby. And then lie down for half an hour. You've had a big day."

"Aw, Mommy, I'm not tired," he protested.

"In half an hour, 'Popeye' will be on television. You can get up then and watch it."

After the little boy had left the kitchen, Mildred spoke first. "What's wrong with Toby? Did everything go all right?"

"No, it didn't." With a sigh, B.J. sank into one of the chairs around the breakfast table. "Sit down, Mildred."

When Mildred had joined her, B.J. said, "Jake and I aren't going to get married or have an affair or even be friends."

Her stark announcement didn't cause Mildred to fall over in a dead faint, which was good, but it didn't make her happy, either. "What do you mean?"

"I mean I've lied to you, Mildred. Jake and I were playing a game. At first we pretended because Jake didn't want Ceci chasing him around the restaurant, and I wanted to keep Bill Morris at bay. Then—" she drew a deep breath before continuing "—I wanted you to think that Jake and I were serious because I knew you would agree to marry Red."

Without another word, Mildred rose from the table and returned to the dinner preparations Toby had interrupted.

"Mildred? What are you going to do?"

"About what?"

"Red. You are still going to marry him, aren't you? Please don't give up your happiness. I don't need a man to take care of me. You know that." B.J. studied her aunt, her best friend, her biggest supporter, with pain in her heart.

"I don't know what I'm going to do. I have to talk to Red." She kept her back to B.J.

Getting up, B.J. crossed the room to Mildred's side, trying to get a glimpse of her face. "I'm sorry I lied to you. I thought I was helping you."

"I'm sorry, too. You and Jake seemed so right together."

"No. No, we're not."

"So what I saw on the front porch was an act?" Now Mildred looked at her, her eyes piercing in their intensity.

"Yes." She couldn't keep the blood from her cheeks, but she returned Mildred's gaze.

"You must be one whale of an actress."

Could her cheeks get even redder? B.J. wondered. "Jake's a very sexy man, Mildred. I'm not made of stone. But that doesn't mean—"

"Uh-uh. I know what that means."

B.J. closed her mouth. She did, too. It meant she'd have some lonely nights. She muttered "Sorry," and left the room. She *was* sorry. Because from now on, she was going to avoid Jake Randall if it was the last thing she did.

JAKE WATCHED the unloading of Pete's new purchase with a jaundiced eye. The gelding was reputed to be one of the meanest around, perfect for the rodeo circuit. He attempted to justify his reputation by flashing his teeth toward the cowboys who each held a rope tied around his neck. Then he lashed out with his back hooves, barely missing Pete.

"Damn it, Pete, I don't think you made a good buy."

Pete, a little breathless from his fast retreat, grinned at his brother. "Why not?"

"He's out of control."

"Nah. He's just mean and ornery."

"I think you should get rid of him," Jake insisted.

"Why? We're keeping *you* around." Pete's grin widened as Jake stared at him.

"What do you mean?"

"Since you spent the afternoon with B.J. and Toby, you've been in a worse mood than this horse could ever have. You've snapped everyone's head off. Janie was even fearful of letting you hold the twins, afraid you'd stand them in the corner for not drinking all their milk."

Jake stared at his brother, shock filling him. "I haven't— I mean, I wouldn't ever do anything to— Janie didn't say that!"

he finished indignantly, reading the teasing laughter in his brother's eyes.

"Nope, she didn't. But she might."

"No, she wouldn't. I've been in a bad mood lately, that's all. There's lots of headaches on a ranch."

"Yeah. And the only time they bothered me was when Janie had left me." Pete leveled a look at Jake that spoke volumes.

Jake didn't want to have a discussion, out loud or with stares, about women. Women had no place in his life. He was lucky to escape that little game he'd played with B.J. with no problems.

That's what he kept telling himself. He was lucky. He didn't have any interest in women. Especially B.J.

And his heart told him he was a liar.

"No one left me, brother. Got that? If I've been short with anyone lately, it's because my mind has been on—on the rising feed prices."

"Yeah, right," Pete agreed, but the sarcasm in his voice indicated the opposite. Before Jake could protest again, Pete turned to one of the cowboys standing watching the horse struggle against his captors and ordered, "Go see if B.J. is here."

Jake felt his gut clench. He hadn't seen her in a week. He'd looked for her, waited for her, but he hadn't seen her. Anticipation began building. It was ridiculous that they never saw each other when they lived only a few yards apart. "B.J.'s coming?" He tried to keep his words casual.

"Yeah. She's going to check out Testosterone, see if he's healthy."

"That's a damn odd name for a— What?" Jake roared as the realization sat in. "You're going to put B.J. in a pen with that monster?"

"I think the name is quite appropriate," a sexy voice said behind him.

Jake spun around to discover B.J. watching him. As soon as they made eye contact, she shifted to Pete. "I'm here. Are you ready for me?"

Jake's gaze hungrily traveled over her. She didn't look any different than he remembered. Sexy as hell in her jeans. She was wearing a denim jacket to protect her against the crispness in the air. Her hair was braided as usual, with dark wisps that had escaped to frame her beautiful face.

"Hey, B.J.," someone called, and she looked away. Lifting a hand, she acknowledged Butch Gardner.

He trotted over, an admiring look on his face.

Jake frowned. Shortly after Butch had arrived on the ranch, he'd questioned Jake about B.J. Jake regretted now that he'd told his friend B.J. wasn't his woman.

"I enjoyed last night," Butch said, a big smile on his face.

Jake caught Pete's sharp look at him, but he ignored it. "Last night?"

"Yeah. I ran into B.J. and her aunt and boy at the steak house, and they invited me to join them," Butch said, but his gaze never left B.J.'s face.

"Yes, it was fun," she said, but purposely turned her attention back to Pete. "I'm ready to check out your new star."

"Great. We'll put him—"

"No! You most certainly will not!" Jake roared. "You're not getting anywhere near that monster."

Chapter Eleven

Even the cantankerous horse came to a standstill at Jake's protest. Certainly the cowboys gathered around stared at him, including Pete and Butch.

B.J., however, was determined to minimize the embarrassment. "Don't be silly, Jake. Surely you approve of my work, if nothing else." With a stiff smile, she turned toward the animal.

A powerful hand clamped down on her arm. "I meant what I said. You're not getting close to that horse." This time his voice was low, quiet...and as hard as steel.

B.J. stared down at his hand. She'd missed him this past week, had dreamed of seeing him again, having him touch her. But not like this. "I don't think my doing my job has anything to do with you. Pete is the one who asked me to come."

Jake faced his brother, but he didn't turn loose of her. "Pete?"

"Jake, I wouldn't let B.J. get hurt. We're going to—" He broke off and stared first at B.J., then Jake. Finally he looked at B.J. again. "Hell, I'm sorry, B.J. Bill me for the time."

B.J. stared, openmouthed at the two Randall brothers. She and Pete had worked well together in the past. Now, like Jake, he was losing faith in her? "Do you realize that I can't sign the health certificate if I don't examine him?" She didn't have to add that Pete couldn't send the animal to any rodeos without the certificate. Pete knew that.

Pete shifted his weight, clearly uneasy. "I'll get him checked out at one of the rodeos. There are always vets hanging around."

"And waste the space in the truck if he's not okay? And what about your sale? Wouldn't it be too late to return him if you wait until then?"

"If the horse is no good, I'll personally make up the difference," Jake promised, nodding at his brother.

B.J. wrenched her arm from Jake's hold, taking him by surprise, and faced him. "Why don't you just come out and say what you're thinking? I can't handle my work because I'm a woman!"

"You know I think you're good at what you do. But this horse is a mean one. I don't want you hurt...on Randall property."

"Afraid I'll sue? I absolve you of all responsibility. Did everyone hear that?" she asked, looking at their audience, which was paying rapt attention. She received a few nods. "See, Jake, you're home free." She whirled around, ready to go to work, but Jake seized hold of her again.

"We'll be back in a minute," Jake muttered to his brother, and started off in the direction of the nearest building, pulling her behind him.

"Jake Randall, turn loose of me!" she protested, but those words didn't stop her progress. When she dug in her heels, he turned to look her in the eye.

The expression on his face told her he wasn't going to give in easily, but it didn't prepare her for what followed. Without saying another word, he slung her over his shoulder and turned back to the barn.

Stunned by the suddenness of his move, it took B.J. a little time to compose herself, if that was possible hanging upside down staring at his rear end.

"Jake Randall! Put me down!" she protested, trying to keep her voice down, hoping to draw less attention to the pair of them. Then she thought about the ridiculousness of that idea. Everyone on the ranch was watching them!

She got no response from Jake. Pushing against his back, she tried kicking him, but he held her legs tightly against his chest. "Jake!" she protested again.

He ignored her and opened the barn door.

Inside, he slammed the door shut and then dumped her on her
feet. She almost lost her balance but quickly recovered, outrage
stiffening her spine.

"How dare you, Jake Randall! You've embarrassed me in
front of the entire ranch!"

"Better to embarrass you than to let your skull get cracked
open with a vicious kick from that horse."

His grim words should have invited thanks, she supposed, but
he wasn't about to get off that easy. "All you've done is tell
everyone you have no faith in me as a veterinarian. And it's
because I'm a woman!"

"Don't start that sexist crap, B.J. That horse is dangerous."
He stood there, his hands on his hips, a righteous expression on
his face.

"Then why are you letting the cowboys deal with that horse
if he's so dangerous?" She put her hands on her hips, matching
his stance. Let him get out of this one if he could.

"Because—because they're used to dealing with difficult animals." The righteous expression had fled, replaced by some
uneasiness.

"And as a vet, I'm used to dealing with what, exactly? Kin-
dergartners?"

"Don't be sarcastic!"

"What do you expect me to be? You've made me look like
an idiot!"

"I'm trying to protect you!" He paused and then added, "For
Toby's sake. He doesn't have a father. Do you want him to be
without his mother, too?" He stopped and put his hands back
on his hips, again sounding righteous.

"You think I can't check out that horse without being hurt?
For heaven's sake, we're going to put him in a chute and tran-
quilize him. Did you think I was going to walk up and let him
kick me from here to Cheyenne?" She imitated his stance, taking a step forward this time, tossing her braid over her shoulder.

"Okay, okay, so you've got a good plan. But you could still
get hurt."

"So could you, every day. I could get hurt driving down the
road. Anyone could. But you don't stop doing your job, and I'm

not going to stop doing mine. Unless you refuse to use my services anymore.'' She paused and prayed he wouldn't go that far. "If you do that, I'll have to leave. Because no one else will hire me if the Randalls won't.''

She wasn't sure how long they stared at each other, only a couple of feet between them. With her chin raised in challenge, she couldn't look away. But he didn't look away, either, frowning at her, studying her. When he finally spoke, it wasn't about the horse.   "Damn, I want to kiss you.''

"Jake!'' she protested. She'd been holding her breath for his cooperation, and all he could think about was kissing.

"How's Toby?'' he finally asked.

She shook her head, trying to follow the disjointed conversation. "He's fine.''

"I haven't seen him since we went shopping for his hat. Has he been wearing it?''

"No, he thought he should wait until his birthday.'' She didn't want to tell Jake how upset Toby had been that Jake could never be his daddy. She and her son had had a long talk about Jake Randall. She thought Toby understood now.

"Doesn't he like it?''

"Of course he does. He'll wear it in two days.'' She bit her bottom lip, worrying about what he'd say next.

He stepped closer and rubbed his thumb across her bottom lip.

She gasped and pulled her head back. Anything to break contact with his powerful touch. "We—we can't do that, Jake.''

"Yeah, but—''

"Jake?'' Pete called through the door. "Everything all right in there?''

B.J. felt the heat flame her cheeks as she realized half the ranch had been waiting outside the barn door to see what would happen. "Oh, no! Jake! Everyone's been waiting, thinking— Who knows what they're thinking. You've got to let me inspect the horse, or I'll be ruined!''

"You're being too dramatic,'' he protested, but she read comprehension in his eyes. "Come on,'' he growled, and turned to unbolt the door.

Pete moved back abruptly, almost as if he'd been listening. Over his shoulder, B.J. could see all the cowhands staring at them. She closed her eyes briefly and then tried to look cheerful.

Moving past Jake, she nodded to Pete. "Well, let's get that ornery horse in a chute. I've got other animals to see when I finish here."

"Jake?" Pete asked, looking over her shoulder.

"Yeah, it's okay. She explained what she was going to do."

B.J. pasted a smile on her face. "His majesty has decided I know my business after all." She walked over to the cowboys holding the horse, their ropes taut.

"You'd better get him in a chute before your arms give out," she recommended. "Or before Jake changes his mind."

One of the cowboys grinned. "Aw, you can't blame him, B.J. A woman as pretty as you, it'd be a shame to leave any scars."

She glared at him. As she turned away, she caught a curious stare from Butch. He didn't return her smile. Instead, he walked over to Jake.

She turned her attention to the horse. She'd made up her mind she was only going to concentrate on animals. She didn't want anything to do with cowboys, even one as nice as Butch.

And some of them, not to name names, could be as ornery as that horse. And just as hard to understand.

"I THOUGHT YOU SAID there was nothing between you and B.J.," Butch said in a low voice.

Jake, watching every move B.J. made, his mind concentrating on her safety, scarcely heard him. "Hmm?"

"Did you two have a fight? Is that why you told me she wasn't your woman?" Butch persisted.

Jake jerked around as Butch's questions finally penetrated his head. "Why do you say that?"

Butch gave him a look of disgust. "Because you came out of the barn without a black eye. I figure there's something going on if she let you get away with slinging her over your shoulder."

Feeling the blood heat his cheeks, Jake aimed for the simplest answer. "Yeah, we had a fight."

Butch nodded stiffly and walked away. Jake turned his attention back to B.J., following her and the men leading the difficult horse to an outdoor corral with a chute. But he saw Butch talking to several of the other hands. One of his men grinned and gave him the high sign, and he wondered what Butch had told them.

After B.J. had completed her examination, she walked right by Jake without saying a word. But Jake had had time to think about something that had been said earlier.

Reaching out, he again pulled her to a halt. "Aren't you going to say goodbye?"

"I thought we'd probably spoken too much to each other already today," she said, not looking at him.

"Or maybe not enough. What's this about you dining with Butch?" He knew he didn't have the right to question her movements, but he had to know.

As he expected, she stiffened beneath his hold. "I don't think that's any of your business."

He sighed. "I know. But Butch is an old friend who just ended a messy relationship. He's vulnerable right now." He got her attention; that was for sure. She swung around to face him, putting her hands on her hips, which pulled apart her jean jacket. He couldn't keep from staring at her breasts beneath her plaid shirt.

"All he did was sit at our table for dinner so he wouldn't have to eat alone!" she protested indignantly.

"Just be careful. It doesn't take much heat from you, lady, to start a forest fire." He reached out and traced the curve of her cheek, unable to resist touching her.

She stepped away. "Jake, don't," she whispered. "Everyone is watching."

"I know. And that's why I'm going to give you a little kiss— just a friendly one—so everyone will know the Randalls and the Andersons are on good terms. Don't make a scene."

That really was his intent. After all, she had expressed concern about how the county might perceive their relationship. But once his lips met hers, all caution, all planning, all good intentions went out the window. Desire, lust…good feelings replaced them, and he deepened the kiss, sweeping her into his arms.

His uninhibited crew cheered, as they had that first morning out in the pasture, and B.J. wrenched her lips from his. She didn't leave, however. Instead, she buried her face in his shirt and muttered, "I'm going to kill you, Jake Randall. That wasn't a *friendly* kiss."

"Well, sweetheart, it sure wasn't hostile...on either of our parts."

His sarcasm accomplished what his kiss hadn't. She jerked away from him and quickly strode to her truck parked near the barn. The dust flew as she backed up, then roared down the driveway.

Jake stood staring after her, knowing that he should've apologized instead of upsetting her even more. He almost jumped out of his skin when one of the cowboys slapped him on the back.

"Glad to see you and B.J. made up, boss. We were all pulling for you. She is one fine lady."

The man moved on without waiting for a response, but several other men grinned and waved as if agreeing with him.

"Quite a little show this morning, brother," Pete murmured as he came up beside him. "The girls are going to love hearing about this."

Jake grabbed his brother's jacket front. "You can't tell them!"

"Oh, yes, I can. When they hear about this—and you know they will—and realize I didn't tell them, Janie will have my head. Or even worse, make me sleep on the couch." Pete paused to grin. "As much as I love you, Jake, I'm not willing to make that big a sacrifice."

No, and Jake couldn't blame him. If Jake had the right to sleep with B.J., he wouldn't give it up, either.

"Besides," Pete added, distracting him, "maybe this news will cheer up Red. His biscuits were so flat and hard this morning, I almost broke off a tooth."

Jake watched his brother saunter away, a grin still on his face. He had a point. Red had been depressed ever since B.J. had told Mildred the truth. Red wouldn't talk about any decisions he and Mildred had come to, but it was obvious things weren't as rosy as they had been.

But B.J. wouldn't be happy that the two of them were the hot topic of gossip in the county. Even if that hadn't been his intention, he knew his behavior this morning was responsible for everyone thinking they'd had a fight and then made up.

Man, she really was going to kill him.

EVERYWHERE B.J. WENT that afternoon, she faced knowing smiles and sly innuendo about her and Jake. As best she could, she discounted any talk of the future, but frequently the best thing she could do was say nothing. Otherwise, it would be a case of protesting too much.

When she stopped by the post office to buy stamps, Mrs. Miller beamed at her.

"I hear things are looking up at the Randall spread," the woman said, grinning from ear to ear.

B.J. smiled and asked for two books of stamps.

"A big thaw has set in, I hear," the woman said, trying again.

"Really? I heard we've got a norther heading our way, the first real big one of the season." She waited impatiently for Mrs. Miller to count out her change.

"Oh, you are a sly one, you are. But don't let Jake Randall slip through your fingers, young lady. There's too long a line waiting in case you blow it."

"Thank you for the stamps, Mrs. Miller." It was hard to return the woman's smile, but B.J. did. After all, at least things were better with this new rumor. For the past week, everywhere she went, she'd received comforting, sympathetic smiles, as if Jake had dumped her.

Her heart was not broken!

Not really. After all, she had no intention of marrying again. Her first marriage had been…nice, but her husband had been driven by the urge to make money. He hadn't been all that interested in Toby or spending quiet evenings at home. There was a fear buried deep inside her that if Darrell hadn't died so young, she would be a divorcée now rather than a widow.

She shook off her disturbing thoughts and tried to figure out what could be done about the situation she was now in, playing the role of Jake's lover. Because there was no doubt that was

what the community thought. The men had given her knowing
grins, and the women's remarks, about Jake and his reputed
prowess with women, were downright embarrassing.

Especially when truthfully, she could only agree with them.

The moment he touched her, she melted like a Sno-Kone in
the middle of a hot summer day.

It hadn't been that way with Darrell. Sex had been a part of
their marriage, but B.J. hadn't hungered for his touch as she did
for Jake's.

"It's probably because you haven't had sex in four years,"
she told herself in disgust.

Maybe she should go ahead and have an affair with him, as
he'd suggested, and get him out of her system.

She almost drove off the road as she realized what she'd just
thought. She must be losing her mind. An affair with Jake Randall could only bring heartache.

And what would it do to little Toby? His hopes would be
raised again. And then dashed. Because Jake Randall wasn't
misleading her. He didn't intend to marry again, and he'd made
that fact perfectly clear.

Besides, as much as Jake valued the "right" blood inheriting
his family's ranch, even if he wanted to marry her—a joke if
there ever was one—she couldn't accept. She wouldn't allow
Toby to be considered a second-class citizen, not in his own
home.

She pulled the truck to a halt in front of her house, weary
from her mental debates as much as from her work. And now
she had to face the troubled looks Mildred gave her. Ever since
she'd told her the truth, Mildred had refused to talk about her
marriage to Red.

B.J. didn't know if she'd told Red she couldn't marry him or
if she was going ahead with the marriage. Unhappily. B.J. hoped
Red and Mildred would marry. But she hated herself for taking
away Mildred's joy about her union.

Swinging open the door, she was stepping out of the truck
when the one person she wanted to avoid appeared beside her.

"What do you want?" she snapped quickly, almost getting
back in the truck again.

"I need to talk to you before you go in," Jake said. He kept a circumspect distance of several feet between them, but B.J. could feel the pull his presence always brought.

That was the major problem with Jake. It wasn't that he touched her. It was that she *wanted* him to touch her. Desperately. Now she could understand addiction. She had the same problem, only her addiction was for the touch of a sexy, hard-headed cowboy.

"What about?" she asked cautiously, determined to keep her head.

"Lucy called," he said, naming their dinner companions of last week. "She, uh, she's invited all the Randalls over for dinner tonight."

"You need me to baby-sit the twins?" That was the only connection she could make. After all, she wasn't a Randall. And wasn't likely to become one.

Jake took his hat off and ran a big hand through his hair. "Not exactly. Mildred and Red are going to be the baby-sitters."

"Fine. Toby and I can manage without Mildred. I've been telling her that for the past week." She hadn't meant to sound so irritated, but she did.

"B.J., I'm sorry about this morning."

His apology surprised her. And made her feel sad. She didn't want him to be sorry he'd tried to protect her. "It's okay. I should've explained right away."

He grinned, and she had to fight the urge to trace his lips with her fingers. When Jake Randall smiled at her, she had trouble thinking.

"We both know there's some kind of weird chemistry going on here. Like magnets or something. We don't always act rational around each other."

She nodded. What could she say?

"Look, B.J.—Ben and Lucy are friends. We've known Ben for forever, and Lucy almost as long."

She nodded again. Where was this story going?

"Lucy was all happy. She's pregnant, you know."

"I know, Jake. I was there when they told us, remember?"

He put his hat back on his head and grabbed her hands. "This

is kind of hard to explain.'' His gaze didn't meet hers, and she
felt her stomach turn into knots.

"What is?"

"What happened. You see, she and Ben wanted to have us
all over to—to celebrate the baby, and my birthday, and all the
changes going on over here. Kind of a party.''

B.J. wasn't sure she could take being this close to him much
longer. In an attempt to hurry his story along, she said, "I get
the picture. What's the problem?''

"One of the things she wanted to celebrate was…us.''

B.J. stared at him. "Us? As in you and me?''

"Yeah.''

"Jake, there is no you and me. Remember? It was a silly
game that we agreed not to play anymore.'' Panic was filling
her. She'd fought this battle, mostly with herself, once before.
She didn't want to go through it again.

"Honey, I couldn't tell *her* that. And after this morning,
everyone believes we had a fight and then made up. I didn't
know what to say.''

Drawing a deep breath, praying for control, she asked, "And
what exactly did you say?''

"I said we, you and me, would be happy to come to dinner
tonight with the rest of my family.''

Chapter Twelve

B.J. gasped, her mind skittering in a dozen different directions as she tried to think of a response. "You didn't— Jake, that's impossible."

"No, it's not."

"Don't you get it? If we go over there as a couple, we'll be right back where we were a week ago." And she'd have to resist temptation all over again. The past week may have been dull without Jake, but at least it had been simple.

"We're already there."

"What do you mean?"

"I told you, everyone thinks we had a fight and now we've made up." His gaze didn't quite meet hers, and his cheeks were flooded with color.

"Why does everyone think that? I know you—we kissed this morning, but—"

"I was watching you, and Butch asked me if we'd had a fight and then made up." He ducked his head before finally meeting her gaze. "I told him yes, without thinking."

"But that was before you kissed me in front of everyone. Why would he ask that question?"

Jake grinned, even while he still appeared embarrassed. "'Cause the man said he figured I'd come out with a black eye unless you...cared about me."

"I—I— He's wrong!" she protested, but she knew her cheeks were even redder than Jake's. Because Butch's words were true.

"Is he? Want me to show you?" He tugged on her hands to pull her toward him.

"No! I don't need a demonstration. I was there the first time, remember?" She pulled her hands free and put them on Jake's chest to keep him apart from her.

"Yes, ma'am, you surely were," he drawled, his grin widening.

"Jake, you're getting off the subject here. What are we going to do? Stage another fight? If I go with you tonight, everyone will assume..." There was no point in saying it. Jake knew as well as she did. "I just can't go."

"Well, I'm not telling Lucy. She's been cooking all day and is excited about the party. And Mildred is the one who said you'd go."

"Mildred?" B.J. gasped, feeling betrayed. "Why would she do that? She knows we were only pretending."

"I reckon she heard the same gossip my sisters-in-law did. And they all believed it."

B.J. closed her eyes in despair. "You mean they *wanted* to believe it. Didn't you tell them we were pretending?"

"Nope. It's none of their business."

Her fingers were still resting on his hard chest, growing warmer each minute. She wanted to splay her hands against his muscles, feel him pressed against him. When she realized where her thoughts were taking her, she jerked her hands away. "Jake—"

"Hi, Mr. Jake."

They both looked to the porch, to discover Toby leaning against the post, a wistful look on his face.

"Hi, sweetie, I was just coming in," B.J. said, and tried to move past Jake.

He blocked her way, his hands going to her waist. "How are you, Toby? Your mom said you were waiting until your birthday to wear your hat."

"I didn't think I should since I'm not five yet," Toby said soberly.

Jake grinned that lopsided smile that always caused her stomach to flip over, and B.J. knew her son wouldn't be able to resist it. "I think you're being a really good boy, Toby. I don't think I showed such discipline when I was your age."

Toby, as B.J. expected, returned Jake's smile. "I've been really good, Mr. Jake. I haven't had to stand in the corner or anything."

"Good for you, son. Will you be ready for the Halloween party on Friday? Got your monster costume ready?"

Before Toby could answer, B.J. whispered, "Jake, let me by."

She was a little surprised when he readily stepped aside, but he immediately looped an arm around her shoulders and walked with her to the porch.

"Yeah. I'm gonna be *real* scary!"

"All right! And you're going to stay with Red and Mildred again tonight?"

Jake ignored B.J.'s attempts to shrug off his arm, but she saw Toby staring at them. She'd explained so carefully that she and Jake wouldn't be kissing again. How would Toby interpret Jake's behavior?

"Mommy said she wasn't going to go places with you anymore," Toby said slowly, continuing to stare at them.

Jake looked down at her, one eyebrow sliding up before he turned his attention back to her son. "Well, Toby, it's like this. Your mom was unhappy with me. But ladies change their minds all the time. I told her I was sorry."

"Oh. Like when I've been bad and I say I'm sorry?"

Jake nodded, still smiling.

Toby really grinned. "Oh, good. 'Cause Mommy always kisses me and forgives me."

"Exactly." He came to a stop, pulling B.J. around to face him. Leaning closer, he whispered, "We'll figure out what to do later. But you'll have to come tonight if you're not going to upset Lucy." Then he brushed his lips across hers, lightly this time. "I'll be back in an hour."

He waved to Toby and strode across the yard, leaving B.J. standing like a statue, her mind seething with ways to punish the man. He was driving her crazy!

AFTER DINNER that evening at the Turnbulls', B.J. followed the rest of the women into the kitchen. Though Lucy protested she didn't need any help, they ignored her.

B.J. wasn't reluctant to help, but she was hesitant to be alone with her friends. She'd felt all of them watching her and Jake all evening. If he so much as touched her hand, everyone's eyes had been trained on them.

To be alone with the women now meant she would have to answer questions. And she had no answers. None at all.

She'd tried to come up with a reason for refusing to attend, but Jake was right. She couldn't refuse without appearing terribly rude. And she couldn't be angry with Mildred. After all, she had been told about the morning's events. It was B.J.'s fault, hers and Jake's, that everyone thought they were dating again.

That stupid kiss.

The one in front of everyone.

She'd told Mildred again this evening, before she left, that the kiss was a mistake, that she and Jake weren't—whatever. Mildred had apologized for accepting the invitation for her, but there had been a look in her aunt's eyes that told B.J. she hadn't convinced her.

"What a lovely dinner, Lucy," Megan said as she carried dirty dishes to the sink. "I'd love the recipe for that casserole. Did you see the way Chad ate it? I don't dare tell Red."

"I'd be glad to give you a copy of it. It's one of my mother's." Lucy began organizing the dishes and rinsing them.

"This has been so much fun," Janie said.

"We don't socialize enough," Lucy agreed. "But we have the party at your house in two days. Are you all ready ?"

"Almost," Janie said. "Of course, we have Red and Mildred to handle a lot of the work." She looked at B.J. out of the corner of her eye. "Mildred is a godsend."

"Yes, she's wonderful, isn't she?" B.J. agreed, hoping the conversation would stay on the party.

"Yeah. Will you miss her when she and Red marry?" Anna asked.

Uh-oh. B.J. got nervous whenever the subject turned to marriage. "Of course we'll miss her, but we'll manage. We want Mildred to be happy."

"It's so nice, the way things have worked out," Anna said with a happy sigh. "No one's alone while the rest of us are happy."

Stark silence followed her words. B.J. was careful not to look at anyone.

Finally Megan said, "Anna didn't mean to leap to conclusions, B.J., but you know we're all hopeful that you and Jake—"

"Jake and I are friends, that's all. It's awkward around here not to be a couple." B.J. hoped they believed her.

"Then you're not—" Lucy began, and then halted, blushing. "I mean, the other night we got the impression that the two of you— That is, you seem to make such a nice couple."

"No! No, we're not a couple. There's nothing between us. In fact, I would describe our relationship as a, uh, professional one. I work as Jake's vet, and that's all."

B.J. was standing with her back to the door to the dining room and didn't realize anyone was entering until strong arms wrapped around her and Jake kissed her cheek.

"Hi, honey. You got dishpan hands yet?"

Closing her eyes, B.J. fought to hold back a groan. Had he heard her words? Or was he still role-playing? She'd noticed during the dinner he had treated her much as his brothers treated their wives, but he hadn't caressed her in any way. There had been a gentle playfulness, but no actual flirtation. Until now. How could she explain this?

"Jake!" she protested even as the others chuckled.

"What?" he asked, turning her around to face him. "I just explained to the others that we're not—not a couple! Now what are they going to think?" Better to face him than the knowing smiles on her friends' faces.

"Probably that I can't keep my hands off you. That's what the guys are saying." He grinned as if he were happy about their conclusion.

"Stop acting!" She spun around to the women. "Really, Jake's just teasing. We're not a couple."

Instead of backing her up, Jake drawled, "Well, honey, we're a couple in the sense that there's two of us. But we're not a couple who's going to get married. We've both tried marriage, and I, for one, can do without that complication in my life.''

B.J. should've been pleased as she watched the happiness fade from her friends' expressions. After all, Jake had done a good job of explaining their situation. But her heart felt heavy. Probably because Jake had kind of left it hanging that they might have a relationship, just not a legal one.

"Sometimes it's awkward to be alone when everyone else is a couple. Jake and I are helping each other out," she added, stepping away from him before her body gave her away.

She sat down at the kitchen table and looked at Jake. His eyes narrowed, as if in challenge to her words. She couldn't imagine what he had to complain about. She'd only echoed his sentiments.

"But, Jake, surely you don't compare B.J. to Chloe? Can't you see that B.J. is our kind? That she'd make a wonderful wife?" Janie insisted.

"Janie!" B.J. protested.

"Janie," Jake joined her in saying, but he continued, "I told the boys to warn you about matchmaking. I'm happy the way I am. There are enough happy couples and babies at our house. Leave well enough alone." By the time he finished, his voice was stern.

Turning to Lucy, he said, "I apologize for letting family things intrude, Lucy. You fixed a wonderful meal, and we all enjoyed ourselves. I came in here to ask if you ladies weren't going to join us. We're lonesome."

His dramatic complaint raised laughter that eased an awkward moment, and there was a general movement toward the door.

"We've finished," Lucy said. "We wouldn't want you men to be lonesome."

B.J. moved faster than the others. Right now she didn't care if Jake was lonesome or not. In fact, she would like him to be lonesome! But she also didn't want to be alone with him.

An hour later, she couldn't avoid him, since he'd driven the two of them to Ben and Lucy's. She'd tried to catch a ride with one of his brothers, but Jake made sure she didn't succeed.

Once they were alone in the truck, he turned to her. "What

are you trying to do? Embarrass me in front of my brothers?" he demanded, anger in his voice.

"Why not? You embarrassed me in front of my friends." She refused to look at him.

"What are you talking about? I didn't do any such thing." He gunned the engine and roared down the driveway to the road.

"You *implied* that we were going to have an affair, or were already. I don't appreciate my reputation being smeared."

"Maybe your reputation wouldn't be smeared. Maybe it would be boosted if everyone thought you were having an affair with me."

There was a challenge in his voice, but B.J. wasn't intimidated. "How arrogant! Do you think you're that wonderful?"

"Nope. But I think you've gotten a reputation for being a cold fish."

She was stunned by his words. "What are you talking about?"

"A lot of the guys have asked you out, flirted with you, but you haven't responded."

"How can you—?" She turned bright red as she thought about her response to this man.

"Hey, I'm not complaining, lady. If you responded any more to my kisses, we would know each other a lot better than we do. But you'll have to admit you don't usually let anyone get that close."

Now her cheeks were flame red, and she stared straight ahead of her into the darkness. "I didn't think it would be a good idea to mix business with—with pleasure. I don't like to date my customers."

"I think maybe you're just afraid to get close to anyone. I'm wondering if maybe your marriage wasn't as good as you'd like people to believe." His voice cut through the shadows, making her angrier.

She wasn't interested in discussing her marriage with Jake Randall. It was none of his business. Going on the attack, she said, "I don't think you have any room to talk, Jake. Your marriage wasn't a blue-ribbon winner."

"Nope. But I never pretended it was. That's why I don't intend to marry again."

"I think you've made that abundantly clear. And I'd appreciate it if you'd keep your distance. That flirting routine you pulled in the kitchen has to stop!"

"Hey, I thought you wanted people to think we were dating. I was only playing the game."

"The game is over. I told you!"

He turned off the road onto Randall property without responding to her curt words. She didn't care. Too many times she'd let him touch her, even encouraged him, but now the touching had to stop.

Everything had to stop. No more pretense.

No more Jake.

"Just like that?"

"Yes, just like that. If anyone has the audacity to ask what happened, just tell them you dumped me." She didn't care if people thought Jake didn't want her. It was the truth. He didn't want her forever, and that was the only way she could consider— She shook her head to dismiss such silly hopes.

"I'm not sure they'll believe me, since I haven't been able to keep my hands off of you," he growled.

"They will if you'll keep your distance."

"Hey, I'm not the only one who needs this lecture. You didn't exactly fight me off, honey. Maybe I wouldn't keep coming back if you ever said no." He pulled his truck to a stop. His brothers and their wives were right behind them in the sedan. When B.J. reached for the door handle, she discovered Jake's hand over hers. "Wait," he said in a low voice.

"Why?"

"Because I don't think we've finished this discussion."

"Yes, we have, Jake. There's nothing more to discuss, nothing more to do. I'll keep my distance. You keep your insinuations to yourself. It's over."

"Fine!" he snapped, releasing her hand. "And next time don't involve me in your schemes!"

Her mouth worked as she tried to find the words to lambast him. Finally she sputtered, "You started it!"

"You continued it!" he returned.

In the light from the porch, she could see his eyes snap with anger. She pretended she didn't care. After all, she was fighting for survival, hopefully with her heart intact. "So we'll *both* finish it. Good night, Jake!"

This time he didn't stop her from opening the truck door. She slid out and ran the short distance to her house and safety.

AS SOON AS the Randall men left the house the next morning, Mildred and Red joined the female side of the family at the breakfast table.

"How did it go last night?" Red asked.

Anna sighed. "It was a nice evening, but…"

"Yes?" Mildred prodded, leaning forward eagerly.

"Jake admitted he's attracted to B.J., couldn't keep his hands off her, in fact, but—"

"Good!" Red interjected.

"Nope," Janie said. "It's not good. He announced, in front of B.J., that he had no intention of marrying. But he wasn't averse to anything else she would agree to."

Mildred gasped. "B.J. is a nice girl!"

Red squared his jaw, clearly intent on defending his own. "B.J. is a woman, Millie, not a girl, and Jake wouldn't do anything she didn't agree to."

"Whatever they do, that's not the point," Janie quickly said before an argument could break out. "We want them *married*. We want Jake to have kids, too. We want Toby to have a daddy. We want—"

"But it has to be what *they* want, too," Megan said.

"I think it's what they both want, but they're afraid," Anna said softly. "Jake's always touching her and watching her. And B.J. blushes every time he gets near."

"That's sex, not love," Red said.

"Well, then, you and Mildred must not love each other," Janie argued, "because those words describe the two of you." She stared at his arm on the back of Mildred's chair, his hand touching her shoulder.

Red jerked his hand away, and Mildred blushed.

"We're different! We care about each other. We're not just out for what we can get," Red assured them.

"Isn't that what Jake was doing yesterday morning when he didn't want B.J. working on Pete's horse? Caring for her?" Anna asked.

"That's right," Mildred seconded. "He was trying to protect her. And he spends a lot of time with Toby."

"So how do we convince bullheaded Jake that he needs to get married?" Janie asked.

Silence fell as they each contemplated the question. Finally Anna said, "We've invited all the single women we know to pursue Jake, so he'll turn to B.J."

Janie shook her head. "I know, but— Of course! Why didn't I think of it before?"

"What?" Megan demanded. "Don't keep us in suspense."

"We need to invite all the single *men!*"

Red frowned, staring at Janie. "But won't they just flirt with all the single women? Cancel each other out?"

"Some of them, yes. But B.J. is a beautiful woman. With the right encouragement from interested parties—" she winked at the rest of them "—some of the men will pursue her. I think Jake might not like sharing B.J."

Recognition dawned on all their faces.

"Good plan, Janie," Red agreed. "Jealousy always works."

"At least it can't hurt," Mildred agreed. "And if Jake isn't interested, maybe B.J. will find someone else to plan a future with."

Loud protests rose from the rest of the conspirators.

"We've already claimed B.J. as a Randall," Janie said, speaking for everyone. "And we'll convince Jake of that fact, come hell or high water." She raised her coffee cup. "Here's to Operation Halloween. May Cupid plant an arrow in Jake's heart."

"Here, here!" the others agreed in unison, raising their cups.

Red had the last word, however. "I just hope Cupid can recognize him under his mask."

Chapter Thirteen

Jake was appalled.

"You're kidding me, Anna!" When she continued to stare at him innocently, her blue eyes wide, he added weakly, "Aren't you?"

"No, Jake," Anna replied. "I picked it out especially for you. You'll look great in it."

"Anna," he began in frustration, staring at the costume waiting on his bed, "it's a dress!"

"No, Jake, it's a toga. You're going to be Mark Antony." When he didn't show any appreciation for her explanation, she added, "And you get to carry a spear."

"Anna, I'll be the only man there in a skirt." Jake had a terrible time denying Anna anything, but he'd be damned if he'd strut around in a skirt in front of his neighbors.

"No, you won't. Brett is going as a Scot. We're wearing matching kilts."

She beamed at him, and Jake felt his resistance slipping. Desperately he said, "I'm the host. I don't think I should wear a costume."

"Jake, you have to!" she pleaded. "We told everyone they had to wear a costume. Your brothers will be furious if you didn't have one. Besides, I picked this one out special for you."

He gave up. He should've known from the beginning that she would win. "Okay, okay. But the first guy who laughs at me goes home with a broken nose."

"Thank you, Jake," Anna said, and reached up to kiss his

cheek. Then she slipped from his bedroom, leaving Jake wondering how he'd gotten himself into this situation.

His sisters-in-law had announced last week that they were going to Casper to find costumes for everyone, but he hadn't paid much attention to their plans. He hadn't been in the mood to care. Besides, he figured he'd be a ghost, or maybe a pirate.

He stared at the sandals that were supposed to crisscross up his leg to his knee. Sandals in October in Wyoming? His toes might freeze off tonight.

Eyeing the toga, which would stop just above his knees, he realized he might be concerned about more than his toes freezing off.

"LAND'S SAKE, CHILD," Mildred fussed, pushing B.J. down the hall, "of all nights to be late. We're supposed to be at the party right now. Toby and I are dressed already."

B.J. didn't need her aunt to tell her. Mildred didn't normally dress as a Gypsy dancer. "What's Red wearing?"

Mildred grinned, but her cheeks were pink. "He's a Gypsy, too."

"Ah. Well, you and Toby can go on over as soon as I've seen his costume. I'll find something to wear and be over in a few minutes." She was tired. A quick appearance at the party would satisfy courtesy and then, when it was Toby's bedtime, the two of them would slip away. B.J. had no intention of spending any more time at the Randall house than she had to.

"Oh, you don't have to worry. You already have a costume. You're going as Cleopatra."

B.J. frowned. She hadn't given much thought to her costume, but she'd certainly never considered the Egyptian queen. "Why Cleopatra?"

"The girls found it in Casper. It's perfect for you with your hair unbraided and the snake thing across your forehead."

B.J. just stopped herself from asking why a snake thing was perfect for her. With a sigh, she agreed, "Okay, but I have to shower first."

"I know. Just hurry."

Twenty minutes later, B.J. stared at herself in the mirror. The one-shouldered white dress, with a gold belt in a snake motif that matched her headband, flowed flatteringly to the floor with a discreet slit on one side to midthigh.

But she felt overexposed with her bare shoulder.

"You look beautiful," Mildred said, a reverent tone in her voice.

"Don't be silly, Mildred. I think I look ridiculous."

Mildred laughed. "We'll see. Put on that bracelet and those gold sandals while I turn off the video Toby's watching. Do you have the gifts ready?"

"Yes," B.J. said, but she bit her lip as Mildred turned away. She had debated long and hard over what to get Jake. He was a man who had just about everything he wanted.

Only a chance remark by Megan about Jake's fascination with the Western writer Zane Grey solved her problem. Instead of buying Jake something he didn't need, she'd wrapped up a copy of *Riders of the Purple Sage,* autographed by the author himself. Her father had long cherished the book, and it had come to B.J. upon his death. She knew her father would be happy to have his treasure go to someone who would appreciate it.

Now, however, she had no intention of giving Jake Randall a gift. Especially one he might think was too personal. One that might make him think she cared about him.

She started to leave the bedroom without the present for Jake when her son met her at the door.

"Where's Mr. Jake's present? I want to carry it."

"Um, I don't think we should take it to him tonight, sweetie. We'll give him a present another time." She'd buy him a box of candy or some other impersonal gift.

"No, Mommy, we have to give it to him tonight. Please?"

B.J. stared down at her son. How could she disappoint him? How could she teach him about generosity, kindness, thoughtfulness by her petty behavior?

With a sigh, she turned back into her bedroom and picked up one of the wrapped presents, one for Jake and one for Toby. "Okay, Toby, here is Mr. Jake's gift."

For Toby, who'd already opened several presents, she'd

bought indestructible plastic trucks. She figured all the children present could play with them without their being destroyed.

"Come on!" Mildred called. "We're late."

"Coming," B.J. returned. With reluctance, she picked up the other gift and started toward the door. At the last minute, she remembered the cold air that had escorted her home. A front was supposed to move in tonight.

"Mildred? You'd better grab a coat. It's getting cold outside."

"A coat? Is the weather changing?"

"Yes. I wouldn't be surprised to see snow by the time we start home." At least, by the time Mildred started home. B.J. and Toby would already be snug in their beds.

"Mommy," Toby called from behind her, "I forgot to scare you!"

He looked quite different in his Batman costume, but she knelt to give him a hug anyway. "Oh, my, yes, I'm scared. You'd better hug me so I won't be."

"I'm not supposed to hug you. Mr. Jake is. I'm the one who's *scaring* you, Mommy," Toby complained even as he threw his arms around her neck.

"I know, but thanks for the hug anyway. Ready to go? Get your coat."

"But it'll cover up my costume."

"As soon as we get in the door, you can take it off."

"Okay." When he appeared only seconds later, he not only had on his coat, but also atop his Batman ears sat his dark gray cowboy hat.

"I'm wearing my new hat. Mr. Jake will like that, won't he?"

B.J. couldn't deny her son's words. She knew Jake wanted Toby to like his new hat. She just didn't think it would be a good idea for Toby to concern himself much with Jake. "Yes, sweetie."

Mildred opened the door. "Ooh. You're right about that norther, B.J. It's much colder out there. Come on. We'll want to walk fast."

"Aunt Mildred, how come you make noise when you walk?" Toby asked as he followed her to the door.

"It's these beads. They rattle against each other. Good thing I'm not planning on sneaking up on anyone. Oh, I almost forgot! Here's your mask, B.J."

"Mask? Isn't the costume enough?"

"Nope. You have to wear this gold mask, too. At least for a while. I bet a lot of people won't guess it's you. They've never seen you with your hair down."

"Yeah. Your hair is pretty, Mommy."

"Thanks, Toby. But I think everyone will know who I am."

"What will Mr. Jake be wearing? Will he come dressed as a cowboy?"

"Probably," B.J. said, finding it difficult to imagine Jake as anything but himself.

Which made the first thing she saw when she entered the living room at the Randalls hard to believe.

JAKE HAD WON a promise from Anna that he could change into jeans once the party was under way. Because one look at his bare knees was enough to make him want to hide in the bathroom and never come down at all.

In the meantime, however, he'd had to don the fake laurel wreath, strap up the sandals and greet his neighbors in the short toga. He'd received some wolf whistles from the men, grinning from ear to ear and, even more embarrassing, some ogling from the ladies.

"Hey, Jake, I hear they need some more contestants in the Miss Wyoming contest," Ben called from a short distance away. He knew better than to get close.

"I'm paying you back, Ben. I'm paying all of you back for your words this evening. You won't know when to expect it, but you can be sure it's coming." He added a smile to his warning, but it was fiendish rather than friendly. Some of the women clapped at his words, and he swept a bow, keeping his back to the fireplace. He didn't want to bend over in front of anyone. He'd embarrass himself.

As he rose, he stared at the most beautiful creature he'd ever seen, standing in the doorway of the living room. Cleopatra, a gold snake coiled about her head, black hair spilling in a glorious cloud almost to her waist, her tall, willowy form clad in a flowing white robe caught around her small waist with a gold belt, stared back at him. Her face was covered with a gold half mask.

"Mark Antony, it's your Cleopatra!" Chad called out.

Jake hadn't made the connection between their costumes. Nor had he consciously identified the woman. Until now.

But everyone else in the room had.

He crossed the room and took her hand, raising it to his lips. Then he lifted his gaze, leaned over and murmured, "I'm going to wring Anna's neck. Sorry, I didn't plan this."

"I didn't think you had. As usual, our families are one step ahead of us," Cleopatra, aka B.J., murmured. "All we can do is smile and put the best face on it."

"That's easy for you to say. At least your costume shows off your beauty."

She gave him a cool stare. "Your costume shows off...a lot of you."

"Don't you start, too, B.J. It's been downright embarrassing, the way the women have been looking at me. I feel like a slab of beef at a barbecue."

One slim brow arched up toward the gold band on her forehead. "Now you know how women feel."

He was tempted to slide his arms around her and pull her against him, but he could tell she was still angry with him. So he settled for leaning near her and saying, "Yeah, I've felt a few, but none of them have felt as good as you."

Her full lips tightened, drawing his attention, and she started to move away.

"You're still mad at me, aren't you?" he asked under his breath, aware that everyone was watching them. For the past several days, he'd done nothing but think about the dissolution of their...whatever it had been. Their pretense. He'd missed it. He'd missed seeing B.J. He'd missed touching her.

"No, not at all," she said calmly, nodding and smiling at their guests over his shoulder. "Excuse me?"

He caught her arm as she tried to move away. "There's no need to act as if we've never even spoken to each other," he protested. "We're friends, aren't we?"

Her gaze returned to his face, and he almost shivered from the coldness it showed. "No, Jake, I don't think we're friends. We used each other, but it's over. That's all."

This time, when she tried to move away, he let her go. As she strolled across the room, he got a glimpse of long leg through the slit. "Is that dress legal?" he muttered, thinking aloud.

Butch must've just walked up beside him, because he cleared his throat. "I don't think so. It's enough to make you salivate, isn't it?"

When Jake glared at him, he held up a hand. "Just thinking out loud."

Just as Jake relaxed, turning his gaze back to Cleopatra, Butch spoke again. "But I'm a little confused."

"What do you mean?"

"Janie told me there was nothing between you and B.J. She suggested I cozy on up to the lady, ask her out."

"Janie did what?" Jake whipped back, his eyes blazing. He couldn't believe what his friend was telling him. He'd begun to suspect that his sisters-in-law had been setting red herrings with those other women, intending him for B.J. all along.

That had been one reason for him announcing at Ben and Lucy's what his intentions toward B.J. were. He didn't want any misunderstandings.

Which didn't explain why he was upset now.

"You heard me. So, tell me, boss, is she yours or isn't she?" Butch waited, his gaze clear, for Jake to stake his claim on B.J....or back off.

Damn. Jake knew he couldn't honestly claim B.J. as his own. That would involve commitment, and he wanted none of that. Commitment meant you put your heart on the line, and risked it getting trampled.

But he sure as hell didn't want every man in the county thinking B.J. was fair game. In spite of what she'd just said, he knew they had unfinished business to work out. But he couldn't lie to Butch.

He finally muttered, "B.J.'s a free woman."

"May the best man win?" Butch probed.

"Yeah." He didn't have to wait long for Butch's reaction. The cowboy made a beeline for B.J.

And Jake decided to have a little chat with Janie Randall.

He didn't see her in the living room, so he headed for the kitchen. Red was preparing another plate to take to the dining room for the buffet.

"You seen Janie?"

"Nope. Not in the last few minutes. I bet she's upstairs getting the boys ready. She said something about dressing them up for Halloween."

Jake wandered back to the living room. His gaze immediately flew to B.J., holding court much as Cleopatra might have done, surrounded by handsome men.

Staring, Jake realized just about every single man in the county was there, some of them even sitting on the floor, at her feet. She had removed the gold mask and, as he watched, she threw her head back and laughed at something one of the men had said. Jake ground his teeth.

Unable to stop himself, he crossed to the group. "B.J., Mildred needs to see you in the kitchen."

As he'd known she would, she rose at once. "Of course. Excuse me, gentlemen."

He followed her from the room, down the hall, admiring the way the silky costume clung to her, enjoying the occasional glimpse of leg as she walked. Red was coming out as they entered.

"Oops. Excuse me," he said, juggling two plates. "I'll be right back."

B.J. smiled at him and then pushed the door open. "Why are you following me?" she asked Jake as they entered the kitchen. Then, a frown on her face, she turned back around. "Mildred isn't here."

"I know."

Staring at him intently, she said, "She never asked me to come here, did she?"

"Nope."

"What's going on, Jake?"

"I'm not sure, but I think we're being manipulated again."

He watched her carefully and was relieved to see she had no idea what he was talking about.

"Explain yourself." She crossed her arms under her breasts and looked every bit the autocratic but always sexy Cleopatra.

"Butch told me Janie encouraged him to ask you out."

He couldn't tell what she was thinking, though there was a tinge of surprise on her face briefly.

"And?"

"Well? Isn't that enough? Suddenly you're surrounded by every eligible bachelor within a hundred miles, and you don't put two and two together?"

"Are you saying those men are only paying any attention to me because your sisters-in-law encouraged them? Or maybe even bribed them? That I'm so unattractive no man would come within a mile of me unless one of the great Randalls told them to? Thank you very much, Jake. You've just made my night!"

She immediately turned to take flight, but he caught her arm. "Don't be ridiculous!" He couldn't conceive that she could possibly believe what she'd just said. Didn't the woman know she made him go weak in the knees, just looking at her?

"Turn loose of me!"

"B.J., you're the most beautiful woman here tonight and you know it! Even the married men can't keep their eyes off you and that blasted costume. Do you realize how high that slit is?"

Though her cheeks turned a little red, she looked him up and down and said, "About as high as *your* skirt."

"Aw, now that's hittin' below the belt, Barbara Jo," he said, grinning.

"No one but Mildred ever calls me that." She raised her chin in challenge.

He moved a little closer and tried to put a smile on her face. "I was trying to distract you from my knobbly knees."

"You're being ridiculous, Jake." She tried to push past him, but he blocked her way. "I need to get back to the living room before people start remembering that we left together. They'll think the worst."

"Which is?" he probed.

Her cheeks flushed, and she took a step backward. "That we're having a romantic interlude somewhere."

He almost salivated at the thought. Why did this one woman stir his senses? Why did this one woman drive him crazy? Why did the thought of other men—Jake stood, turned to stone. The answer was more than he could understand, accept. Because it meant he'd gone back on the promise he'd made to himself when Chloe had left.

He'd sworn he'd never love another woman. He'd never put his happiness in another's hands. And most certain of all, he'd never marry again.

It was too late. That was the most amazing part. He'd already broken those first two promises. And he wanted to break the other as soon as possible.

He wanted to marry B. J. Anderson.

"Are you going to let me by?" she asked, her voice tense.

Panic filled him, mixed with desire, and he had no answer for her. All he could do was stare at her.

The sound of the door opening behind him stopped him from answering B.J. He turned to face Janie, with Pete right behind.

"Uh, are we interrupting something?" Pete asked.

"No," B.J. quickly replied. "I was just leaving."

"Don't go on our account," Janie quickly said. "And if you're wanting to be alone, we can tell you a few good places." She grinned at both of them, as if they were all coconspirators.

Jake sneaked a look at B.J. Her cheeks were flaming, and she wouldn't look at him, even though he willed her to.

"No, thank you. I was looking for Mildred. I think it's about time for me and Toby to go home," B.J. muttered, not looking at anyone.

"Wait, B.J. I think we need to have a little discussion with Janie before you go." Anything to keep her there, near him.

"What about?" Janie asked.

"I think you, and probably the other two female Randalls, have been interfering again," Jake said, trying to keep his voice stern.

"Interfering in what?" Janie asked, not looking the least bit guilty, as Jake expected her to.

"Yeah, Jake," Pete seconded. "Interfering in what?"

Well, now, there was the problem. Exactly what should Jake call this situation. His romance with B.J.? It wasn't really a romance. At least, he'd suddenly realized it was on his part, but he hadn't broken the news to B.J.

"Uh, mine and B.J.'s lives."

Anna raised her eyebrows. "Just how am I interfering with your lives?"

"You encouraged Butch to ask B.J. out." His voice was surer now. After all, he was quite clear about that fact.

"All I did was *suggest* Butch ask B.J. out."

B.J., who'd been edging toward the door, smiled at Janie. "Thanks, Janie. He did. We're going to dinner next weekend." Then she walked out the door.

Jake stared after her, his heart contracting. Had he blown his relationship with B.J.? Had he realized too late that life without her was not worth living?

Chapter Fourteen

Ranch people weren't prone to staying up late. By ten o'clock everyone was saying his or her goodbyes. Their leaving was hastened by the storm that blew in. The first snow of the season was dusting the landscape with whiteness.

Jake, still in his toga in spite of his plans, waved the last of their guests goodbye, except for Mildred, B.J. and Toby. He had made Janie promise to keep the Andersons there until he unwrapped his gifts.

He'd been helped by Toby, even if the boy didn't realize the favor he'd done him. B.J. had tried to leave early, but Toby had pleaded to stay until Jake opened his presents.

He knew B.J. wouldn't have stayed willingly. After that little scene in the kitchen, she'd avoided him. And flirted with the men crowding around her.

With gritted teeth, he'd tried to ignore her. As he'd visited with his friends and neighbors, however, he hadn't been able to keep his gaze from straying to her. And he'd provided an entertaining evening for his audience.

They hadn't hesitated to let him know about it, either. Ben had clapped him on the shoulder and warned him he'd better stake his claim before she escaped. Mr. Miller asked him when he'd be shopping for a ring. The pastor had hinted about another Randall wedding.

Only one thing had kept him from losing his mind.

B.J. couldn't keep from watching him, too.

Ceci and some of the other ladies had pursued him, teasing

him about his costume. Every time one of them got close to him, he'd catch B.J. watching.

Now, as he entered the living room, she stood. "We really should be going."

"Jake has to open his birthday presents," Megan said. "You have to stay for that."

"It should just be family. We're—"

"Going to be family. After all, Red and Mildred are engaged," Pete said. "And it's not as if you have to drive a long way in the snow."

B.J. didn't speak, only shrugging her shoulders. Since one of them was bare, that movement heightened Jake's blood pressure considerably. He wanted to touch her bare skin, to slide his hand—

"Well, Jake, aren't you eager to open your presents?" Anna asked.

He stopped staring at B.J. and smiled. "Sure. Where are they?"

He soon had several small boxes in front of him. Inside one of them was a pair of good leather work gloves from Red and Mildred. "I've been needing a new pair, but these are almost too nice to mess up. Thanks." He smiled at the couple, sitting together, their hands entwined.

The next box was extremely light. When he opened it, he discovered it was empty. Raising one eyebrow, he said, "Are you trying to tell me something?"

"Nope, but the real present was too big to wrap," Pete assured him, and left the room. He returned only seconds later with a saddle slung over his shoulder. The leather was elaborately cut with flourishes, and the name Randall was carved into the back of the seat. Toby, half-asleep next to his mother, came awake and knelt on the floor beside Jake, running his fingers over the polished leather.

"Wow, Mr. Jake, it's beautiful!"

"Yeah, it is," Jake agreed. He looked at his brothers and their wives, fighting to hide the emotion that filled him. "Toby's right. Thank you. I've never seen anything so beautiful."

Toby, still rubbing the leather, said, "Someday I'm going to have me a saddle, too. And a horse. I'm going to be a cowboy, too." He beamed up at Jake, hero worship on his face, and Jake felt his heart turn over.

He didn't care much for what he'd heard about B.J.'s husband, but he couldn't help but feel sorry for the man. He'd fathered a terrific boy, and he didn't get to be around to see him grow up.

He pulled the little boy to him and hugged him.   "Those are great plans, Toby. Maybe tomorrow we'll try out my new saddle together."

"Really, Mr. Jake?" Toby asked, slinging one arm around Jake's neck and leaning against him.

"Really," Jake agreed, grinning. Until his gaze collided with B.J.'s.

She was staring at him, her hazel eyes dark with some emotion he couldn't read. But he didn't think it was approval, because those full lips that fascinated him were turned down on the edges.

"There's another present," Anna urged.

Jake picked up the last box.

"It's from me and Mommy!" Toby informed him, bouncing on his toes beside him. "I told Mommy we should buy you something, but she said you'd want this."

"Toby," B.J. said softly, "I think you need to give Mr. Jake some room. Come back over here."

"He's all right, B.J.," Jake said, keeping Toby beside him, his arm around him.

He watched Toby look at his mother for her approval. She gave a brief nod and a smile for her child, but when she looked at Jake, the smile disappeared.

Removing the paper carefully, he lifted the lid on the box and discovered the old book. Carefully he took the Zane Grey book from the box and opened it. A first edition. He looked up to tell her how wonderful her gift was, but Toby, turning the pages, spoke first.

"Mommy! Somebody wrote in the book. We have to get Mr. Jake another present. This one is messed up."

Jake looked at the page where Toby was pointing. The author's signature jumped up at him. He slowly raised his gaze to B.J., hoping she could see how much the gift meant to him.

"No, Toby, this is the perfect gift. That's the signature of the man who wrote the book." There were several gasps from those gathered around, but he ignored them all, concentrating on B.J. "Thank you. This is a magnificent gift."

She shrugged those shoulders again, and he thought he was going to explode. In spite of his enjoyment of his family, gathered around, sharing the moment with him, he wished he and B.J. were alone. He wanted to thank her again and again.

And he wanted to hold her. To feel her heat against him, to stroke that bare shoulder, to feel her lips move beneath his.

Chad moved to look over his shoulder at the signature. "Wow, I'm impressed. An autographed first edition. Where did you find it, B.J.?"

She suddenly seemed embarrassed. "It—it was my father's. Come on, Toby. Time to get you to bed." She rose, had Toby by the hand and was halfway out of the room before anyone else could move.

"Wait!" Jake ordered, putting his precious gift aside and rising.

She stopped and looked at him, but he could tell he wouldn't hold her long. Desperately he turned to Mildred. "Could you take Toby home? I need to speak with B.J. for a few minutes."

Red stood and pulled Mildred up from the couch. "We'll both take the little guy home and tuck him in. Okay with you, Toby?"

"No, that's not necessary. I can—" B.J. began, but Mildred cut her off.

"The least you can do is talk to Jake, B.J. He's been a good host tonight. And he's celebrating his birthday. Toby will be fine with us." Without waiting for B.J. to agree, she and Red crossed the room and took Toby's hand. "Tell everyone good-night, Toby."

He did as Mildred said, but when he got to Jake, he turned loose of Mildred's hand and ran back to Jake to hug him around his neck. "Happy birthday, Mr. Jake."

Jake loved the feel of Toby's arms around his neck. He

hugged the boy back. "Happy birthday to you, Toby. I'll see you tomorrow, and we'll try out that saddle."

Toby gave him his megawatt smile that warmed his heart and ran back to Red and Mildred. After the threesome walked out of the room, his brothers and their wives hastily began making excuses to absent themselves.

"It's all right. B.J. and I will go to the barn. We need a little privacy," Jake said in response.

"It'll be cold out there. There's plenty of room in this house," Pete assured him.

"It's not that cold out yet. Come on, B.J." He didn't want her worrying about someone walking in on them. And he didn't want to worry about it, either.

He wasn't clear about the need to see her alone. He didn't have any great plans. But he wanted to thank her for the incredible gift she'd given him. And he wanted to tell her she shouldn't flirt with those other men.

And he wanted to touch her.

"No, Jake, we should talk here," she insisted.

He ignored her, crossing the room and clasping her hand in his.

He led her to the kitchen, where he handed her her coat and grabbed one for himself. Then he took her hand again and led her to the door. Once they got outside, they didn't waste any time. The cold wind pushed them along.

"Man, I don't know how women wear skirts in winter," Jake complained as he closed the barn door behind them and switched on the light.

"Your legs get cold?" she asked, her voice husky.

"A lot more than my legs." He grinned at her, but then his grin faded as they stared at each other.

She abruptly moved away, wrapping her arms around her. "Why are we here, Jake? What do you have to say?"

"A lot. So we might as well get comfortable." He strode to the tack room at the back of the barn.

"It's late, Jake. I can't stay long," she called out, but he ignored her.

Several blankets were kept in the storage room for late nights if one of them had to stay up with a mare giving birth or a horse that was sick. He spread one out on a pile of hay and kept the other to cover with.

"Come on, B.J., sit down."

She shook her head no. "That would be like Hansel and Gretel bending over to peek in the oven. The wicked witch shoved them in."

"There's no wicked witch here, B.J. But I want to thank you for that incredible gift. And I'd like to keep my legs warm while I'm doing it. They're going to turn blue any moment."

"You're the one who wanted to come out here. And my dress isn't exactly suited to this weather, either."

"I know. It was a pleasure to watch you walk around tonight." He smiled but he hoped she couldn't read his mind. If she could, she'd be out of that barn faster than a charging bull.

"Jake Randall! You can't seem to keep your mind off— Never mind. You're welcome for the gift. I have to go now."

"I have something else to tell you," he said quickly. He breathed a sigh of relief when she turned around to face him again.

"What?"

"Come on over here and sit down. I'm not going to bite you."

She hesitated and then slowly walked toward him. He drank in the sight of her graceful movement, her silky hair, those long legs. When she sank down on the blanket, keeping several feet between them, he shook out the second blanket and let it fall over the two of them.

"What did you have to say?"

"Does your hair help keep you warm?"

"That's what you wanted to say?" she asked, almost outraged.

"No." He clasped her wrist to keep her from rising. "No, but it's so incredibly beautiful, I got distracted."

"Hurry up, Jake. I need to get home. Mildred will be waiting for me."

He dared scoot just a little closer, so that he could touch her hair. "I don't think you should've flirted with all those men tonight."

She jerked her head away, swinging her hair over her shoulder. "What? That's what you wanted to say?"

"Hear me out, B.J. I mean, you shouldn't mislead them like that." He was desperately trying to find the words to tell her the revelation he'd had tonight. A revelation that shook him to the core.

A revelation he wasn't sure he could handle.

But he knew she was his woman. As much as he knew he was her man. Everyone in the entire county knew it, too.

"I don't think I was misleading anyone," she told him icily.

He leaned over and kissed her gently, briefly, unable to keep from touching her.

"Jake," she protested warningly.

"Honey, you know you were. You and I—we're perfect for each other. And we both know it. Whenever we're close to each other, the rest of the world ceases to exist. There's an attraction—hell, more like a cataclysmic explosion—when we touch. Like this." He pulled her to him and let his lips do the persuading, the convincing. As always, when he touched her, she responded like the lover he'd never had. A lover who understood his needs more than him, who was as greedy for his touch as he was for hers. A lover who would never leave him.

She opened to him, accepted him, invited him. Her hands stroked his cheeks, his chest, as his did hers. The sexy, bare shoulder he'd lusted after all night welcomed his touch when he shoved off her coat. As his mouth greedily devoured hers, he managed to bare the other shoulder, as well.

"Jake," she gasped, pulling away. "We can't do this."

"Yes, we can," he whispered, and covered her lips with his again. Hell, they not only could—they *had* to.

Since her protest disappeared in a storm of caresses, he slid one hand up that devilish slit in her costume and stroked her long leg. She ran her hands over his bare arms, caressing his muscles until he thought they'd turned to jelly.

Slanting his mouth at a different angle, he devoured her all over again. She tasted of the sweetest honey, the ambrosia of life, and he thought he'd die if he couldn't taste her over and over again.

"It's not fair," she whispered as his lips sought the secret places along her neck.

"What, baby?" he asked between kisses.

"Your toga doesn't have any buttons." She was stroking his chest through his costume, molding and shaping. "I want to touch you."

He briefly pulled away. "A toga has one advantage over jeans. It's easily removed." Pulling the garment up, he ripped it over his head and tossed it away, leaving him clad only in his briefs.

She gasped, but she didn't pull away. Instead, like a magnet, her hands returned to his chest, her gaze following her hands' movement, and she smiled in pure pleasure.

"Hey, aren't you overdressed, Cleopatra?" he murmured. He'd pulled the other shoulder free, but her breasts were still covered by the white gown.

"Mine's not as easy to get off," she protested, her gaze never leaving his body, her fingertips learning him as if she were blind.

"I hope you like what you see," he teased as he reached behind her for the zipper he'd seen earlier. In only seconds, he showed her how wrong she was about her gown. It joined his toga somewhere in the hay, followed by a strapless bra. He cupped her beautiful breasts in his hands.

And knew he wouldn't be able to control himself much longer.

As if by rote, he put his hand to his back pocket for the condom he kept in his billfold. After all, he'd preached care to his brothers for years. And once he'd realized how tempted he was by B.J., he'd made sure he was prepared.

But he wasn't prepared for wearing a toga.

Damn!

Breathing hard, he pulled back. "B.J., honey...I'm not prepared."

Her eyes, heavy with desire, opened slowly, and he almost lost control at the wanting he saw there. "What?" she asked. Without waiting for an answer, her lips headed for his again.

He couldn't refuse the invitation. Not when he ached with desire, with the need for fulfillment. Not when he thought he'd die if he didn't kiss her. Their tongues danced with hunger, stroking and pleading. Their bodies pressed against each other, as if to imprint their shapes.

Their hands reached simultaneously for the last garments they wore, but that movement reminded Jake again of his problem. "Honey, I don't have any protection. I didn't think—"

She ignored him, and his briefs joined the rest of his clothes. When her hands explored the last secrets of his body, he thought he would explode. He slipped her panties down her long legs, aided by B.J.

"Now, Jake, now, oh please," she pleaded, almost sobbing.

Jake Randall, the sane, responsible older brother, the man who'd threatened and warned his brothers against carelessness, the one who'd planned never to put his heart on the line again, plunged into her, ignoring his own warnings.

And found heaven.

B.J. KNEW SHE'D DONE something terribly wrong. But she felt so good, so complete, that she told herself she must be mistaken. The demands of the day, a long, difficult one, coupled with the events of the evening, lulled her into a delightful place where only the warm body next to her had any meaning. Only the strong arms holding her were important.

Until she woke up a few hours later.

Something had disturbed her, pulling her from sleep. She snuggled against the warmth beside her, pulling the blanket closer to her. Arms tightened satisfactorily around her, and she almost drifted off to sleep again.

Almost.

Arms? Arms around her? Warm body next to her?

Comprehension returned instantly. And with it a sick realization of what she'd done.

Because as wonderful as last night had been, and making love had taken on an entirely new meaning to B.J., she'd made a mistake.

She couldn't have an affair with Jake Randall. For Toby's

sake, she couldn't be so irresponsible. And for her sake. Because her heart would break in two.

Even now, when she knew she had to leave him, she ached with longing. She wanted to have the right to awaken him and repeat the wonder of the night. She wanted to have the right to claim him as her own.

But he'd already told her that was impossible. He had no intention of marrying.

Even if he did, she'd have to say no.

She closed her eyes, shutting out the vision of Jake Randall, his features softened in sleep, his face darkened with a heavy shadow of a beard. How she wanted to feel those stubbly cheeks, but he would awaken. She couldn't risk that.

What was she going to do now? Live next door to him and stay in the perpetual hell of wanting him?

Leave, taking Toby away from his new home, his hero worship of Jake, his second mother, Mildred? Dear God, how could she have been so irresponsible? How could she have given in to desire at the cost of her son's…and her…happiness?

The pain her actions would cause gave her the strength to slip from beneath the blanket, to hurriedly but quietly search for her clothing and run from the barn into the early-morning winter of Wyoming.

It was no colder than her heart.

JAKE STIRRED, shifted against the blanket and reached for B.J.

She wasn't there.

His eyes popped open and he sat up, letting the blanket slide down his chest. He stared at the place she should be, but it was empty. In his mind, he traced their movement of the night before, wonder and happiness filling him as he remembered their coming together.

He'd never experienced anything like their loving. But he hoped to share it with B.J. again and again, for the rest of his life.

But where was she?

He gathered his clothes, hastily donning the toga. Before he could look for B.J., he needed to get back in his jeans, his boots.

Those loose, flowing garments the Romans wore didn't do much to help a guy stay in control. No wonder the Roman Empire had collapsed.

When he stepped outside, he realized the Romans had another problem. Sandals and short dresses weren't much protection against a Wyoming winter. He hotfooted it across the snow. As he burst into the kitchen, he discovered Red already there.

Damn! He'd hoped to slip in unnoticed.

"Well, well, well. Celebrate your birthday to your satisfaction?" Red asked, a knowing grin on his face.

Jake couldn't deny that the celebration had been spectacular. But he wouldn't feel easy until he found B.J. There were some things he'd forgotten to explain to her last night.

Chapter Fifteen

B.J. had no intention of talking to anyone this morning. She had no answers to the questions crowding her head. And she didn't want to answer anyone else's questions.

She took a quick shower and dressed in her customary jeans and shirt. Folding the costume from last night, she left it lying on her bed where Mildred would find it. Her aunt could return it to the Randalls later.

As she turned to leave the room, she noticed a piece of hay clinging to the white material. Quickly she plucked it off and threw it in the trash. There was no need to advertise her foolish behavior.

She reached the front door just as Mildred came down the hall, heading for the kitchen.

"Where you going, B.J.? You're out early."

"I've got a call to make. I'll check with you later."

"I didn't hear the phone ring," Mildred called, but B.J. ignored her aunt's words and hurried to her pickup. As she was getting in, Mildred opened the front door.

"What about breakfast?"

"I'll get something later," she returned, and started up the engine. With a couple of inches of snow on the ground, she had to give it a moment to warm up. Her eyes darted from her house to the Randalls', afraid someone would try to stop her. She felt as though she were escaping from a prison.

She headed into town to grab a bite to eat. It was much too

early to go to her first appointment. Besides, she needed some time to think.

What a mess she'd made of everything.

And the worst was falling in love with Jake Randall. She should've never allowed the movers to unpack their belongings once she'd met Jake. The awareness had been there even then. But she'd believed she could control it.

For nine months, they'd avoided each other, kept their distance. After all, she wasn't looking for a man. With Mildred's help, everything was fine.

But then Jake had wanted protection from matchmaking.

And he'd kissed her.

As if his touch had lit a slow-burning fuse, they'd come closer and closer to disaster. She had liked Jake. Now she craved his touch with all the desperation of an alcoholic searching for his next drink. She had admired Jake. Now she loved him until she thought her heart would break if she didn't have him.

And she couldn't.

He hadn't lied to her. He'd made his intentions clear. An affair would be welcome, a marriage would not. Last night he'd made his plans come true. She had no doubt that he'd make love to her again if she were here. They'd both shared their pleasure.

But she couldn't allow the incredible lovemaking to be repeated. It was too much. And not enough.

Which brought her to the most difficult decision she'd ever had to make. They, she and Toby, would have to leave. And she had to keep Mildred from coming with them.

The man she'd sold her practice to had written only recently to ask if she was settled in Wyoming. He had expanded the practice to the point that he was going to have to take on a partner.

She could return to her old job. Toby could rejoin his playmates. He'd gone to a little play school near their home two days a week. The place had child care most of the day, and her hours would be more those of a normal person.

They could make it.

They just wouldn't be happy.

A tear slid down her cheek.

EVERYONE WAS at the breakfast table by the time Jake got out of the shower, dressed and came into the kitchen.

"Your eggs are on the back of the stove," Red called from the table.

"Uh, I'm not hungry," Jake said, not slowing down.

"She's not there."

Red's quiet words stopped him.

"What are you talking about?"

"I saw her drive off just after you went upstairs. I guess she had an early-morning call." Red calmly continued eating. His brothers and their wives were watching the two of them. "Eat your breakfast."

Jake stood there, his hands on his hips, trying to decide what to do.

"You just get home?" Pete questioned, a grin on his face. "I'm going to have to have a talk with you about the hours you're keeping."

Jake snarled at him and turned to pick up his plate of eggs.

As if realizing taunting the tiger wouldn't be smart, they all turned their attention to their food.

Finally Anna said, "I hope you enjoyed your birthday, Jake."

"Yeah, it was the best birthday I've ever had, Anna. Thanks. You, too, Megan and Janie. And I love the saddle and the gloves." He stood and carried his plate over to the sink. The eggs he'd eaten were sitting in his stomach like leaden lumps.

He had to see B.J.

"That book B.J. gave you is incredible. Where are you going to put it?" Chad asked.

"I think I'll have a case made for it," Jake said as he turned around. "I want to be able to look at it, but I don't want it to be damaged."

"That's a good idea. One of the hands at Ben's place does some nice wood carving. Want me to ask him if he has any ideas?" Pete asked.

"Yeah, fine. I've got to go." Without waiting for any more chatter from his family, he slipped out into the cold morning. He intended to ask Mildred about B.J.'s early-morning call. He could follow her to whatever ranch had had the emergency. She might even need his help.

NO ONE SPOKE for several minutes after Jake left. Finally Megan asked, "Do you think he's all right? He seemed awfully… distracted."

Chad slipped his arm around his wife. "Yeah, he's distracted, all right. That's what happens when you ladies start messing around with our heads."

"I don't think his head is what got messed with," Red said dryly.

The ladies gasped in pretend shock, and Brett covered Anna's ears. "Please, Red, innocents are present."

Anna dug her elbow in his ribs. "So you think they, uh, made up?"

"I don't know. She sure lit out of here in a hurry this morning," Red said.

"But she would if she had an emergency call," Anna said. "That's what I do."

"Maybe you're right. But something don't feel right to me," Red insisted.

"Hey, that's the way I've been feeling for the last month," Megan protested, rubbing her large stomach. "Janie, I don't know how you managed to carry two babies around all the time."

"It was easier when I was pregnant than it is now." Then she grinned at her husband. "Except now Pete has to do part of the carrying."

The smile on Pete's face told everyone he loved toting his babies around, but he felt compelled to protest. "Man, Jake has no idea what he's getting into."

Red smiled at all of them. "Yes, he does, Pete. At long last, I think he does."

JAKE DISCOVERED Mildred had no more idea than he did about where B.J. had gone. When she led him to the table and poured him a cup of coffee, he took a sip and sat staring into space. Only Toby's arrival at the table woke him from his worrying.

"Mr. Jake! You remembered! I'm ready. I don't need no breakfast." He was already bouncing up and down in his pajamas.

Before Mildred could intervene, Jake hugged the little boy and then urged him to the table. "We cowboys don't go out in the cold without eating a good hot breakfast, Toby. And we sure don't go out in our pajamas. There's plenty of time, so eat."

Little conversation was necessary with Toby around. He asked question after question about Jake's horse and where they would ride.

After answering what seemed a hundred questions, Jake was relieved when Mildred interrupted Toby's inquisition. "If you don't go get dressed, you won't get to ride with Mr. Jake."

The boy jumped from his seat so quickly, Jake was afraid he'd hurt himself. To Jake's surprise, however, he stopped suddenly and looked at his great-aunt. "May I be excused, Aunt Mildred?"

"Yes, Toby."

In a flash, he was out the door.

"What a great kid he is," Jake murmured.

"Yes, he is. B.J. is a good mother."

He grinned. "You're preaching to the convinced, Mildred."

"Good. It's about time."

"So when are you and Red going to tie the knot?"

Her briskness disappeared, and Mildred began fidgeting with her fork. "Red wants to get married by Thanksgiving."

"Sounds like a good time to me."

"That's in three weeks, Jake. I can't marry him till I know B.J.'s settled." She avoided looking at him, but Jake knew what she was asking.

He stood, hearing Toby coming down the hall. "Make your plans, Mildred," he said softly, "because B.J. *is* settled. She just doesn't know it yet."

He caught Toby as he leapt toward him, and together the two of them went outside.

"YOU MEAN you've never done any riding?" Jake asked when they reached the barn. He had assumed that Toby had been introduced to horseback riding the past summer. He remembered the picnic they'd had by the lake when Brett had been engaged to Sylvia, the senator's daughter.

"I rode with Mommy. She said I was too little." Toby looked worried. "Am I still too little, Mr. Jake?" He stood there in his jeans and boots, his hat cocked at the exact angle as Jake's, an anxious expression on his face.

"No, son, you're not too little. But right now I don't have a horse the right size for you. Today you'll ride with me. But I'll start looking around for a smaller horse and a saddle just your size. We may even have some left over from when we were boys." "You mean I could use *your* little-boy saddle?" Toby said, his tone almost reverent.

"Why not? I've certainly outgrown it," Jake teased.

"That would be like I was your little boy," Toby said softly before covering his mouth with his hand.

Jake knelt down. "Would you want to be my little boy, Toby?"

The boy ducked his head. "Mommy said I can't be."

Jake's heart constricted, and he had trouble breathing. "When did Mommy say that?"

"After you bought me my hat."

Jake wanted to fold the boy into his arms, to assure him that he'd be proud to be his daddy. But until he talked to B.J., he couldn't. After all, B.J. should be the first to know he'd decided to marry after all.

"Tell you what, today we'll just be friends. But who knows what will happen in the future. Even mommies change their minds."

B.J. DIDN'T GO HOME for lunch. She grabbed a sandwich in town and then stopped her truck by the pay phone at the gas station.

Using her calling card, she reached her old animal hospital in Kansas City. Within a few minutes, she and Dr. Brown had come to agreement on her return to Kansas City. She promised to phone him again on Monday to work out the final details.

Hanging up the phone, she got back in the truck. But she couldn't find the energy to start the engine. She'd taken the first step to solving her problems. And the sandwich she'd eaten was threatening to come back up.

How could she explain their move to Toby? How could she convince Mildred to stay and marry Red? How could she survive without at least seeing Jake?

But how could she stay and not want him?

Tears slowly seeped from her closed eyes, washing her pale cheeks.

A knock on her window surprised her. She opened her eyes to find Ben Turnbull staring at her. Rolling down her window with one hand, she dashed away her tears with the other. "Hi, Ben."

"Are you all right, B.J.?"

"Yes, of course. I—I had a difficult case this morning and I was just collecting myself."

"Want me to call Jake? He could come drive you home."

She stiffened. Already people considered her Jake's property. Toby would think Jake was going to become his daddy. "No, thanks. I've got some more calls to make. Thanks for checking on me."

Without waiting for a response, she started the engine of her truck and pulled away.

Ben frowned as he watched her drive away. Something was wrong. Digging a quarter out of his jeans pocket, he reached for the pay phone.

"Red? Is Jake around?"

"No. He rode out with the boys to the west pasture. Wanted to make sure the herd was okay after the snow."

Ben stood there, undecided.

"Anything wrong?"

"I just ran into B.J. She was sitting in her truck, crying. Said she'd had a bad case this morning."

"Crying?"

"Yeah. I asked her if she wanted me to call Jake, but she refused and drove off."

"Do you know where she was heading?"

"No. She didn't say."

"Okay. I'll tell Jake. Thanks for calling."

"Sure. Let me know if you need any help."

RED AND MILDRED WERE sitting at the table having a cup of coffee when Jake and Toby returned to the house around four.

"Huh, here we've been doing all the work, Toby, while these two just sit around," Jake teased.

"Aunt Mildred works real hard, Mr. Jake," Toby said earnestly before smiling at his great-aunt and giving her a hug. "I've been riding Mr. Jake's horse, Aunt Mildred. He's great big! And Mr. Jake said he might find a horse just my size so I could ride by myself! Wouldn't that be neat?"

"Sure would, Toby, my boy," Mildred said, hugging him. "How about a cup of hot chocolate to warm you up? You're as cold as an icicle."

Toby giggled and climbed into a chair at the table. "Can Mr. Jake have some, too?"

"Sure. But he might prefer coffee. Jake?"

"Yeah, I'll take some coffee." He moved to the coffeepot and poured his own. "Have you heard from B.J. yet?"

Neither Red nor Mildred spoke, and Jake turned around in time to see them exchanging a glance. His breathing grew shallow as he stared at them. Then he said, "Toby, you'd better go wash your hands. I think Mildred is putting some cookies on the table."

Without any protest, Toby jumped down and raced for the kitchen door. He loved cookies.

"What is it?" Jake asked as soon as the swinging door closed behind the boy.

"Ben Turnbull called. He found B.J. sitting in her truck crying at the gas station." Red's matter-of-fact delivery didn't lessen the panic Jake felt.

"Why? What was wrong? Did he offer to help her?"

"Yeah. She said she had a bad case this morning. Then she drove off. Didn't say where she was going."

Jake looked at Mildred. "Has she called you? Have you been home to check for messages?"

"I have our calls forwarded over here every day. She hasn't

called once. And that's not like her.'' Mildred nibbled on her bottom lip, frowning, just the way B.J. did.

Jake began pacing the kitchen floor. ''Why wouldn't she call if she's in trouble? Do you have any idea who her appointments were with today? I mean, it's a Saturday. Doesn't she usually come home early?''

''Jake, you know how vets are. They're just like Doc Jacoby. They go wherever and whenever they're needed.'' Mildred brought Toby's hot chocolate, prepared in the microwave, to the table, along with a plate of cookies. ''I'm not surprised she's not home yet, but—but she doesn't usually cry.''

Jake paced some more.

''Uh, Jake, Mildred and I have been talking. We know it's none of our business, but—but exactly what happened last night?''

Jake turned to stare at him, and Red hurriedly added, ''It just seemed to Mildred that B.J. was acting funny from early this morning on. I mean, did the two of you have a fight?''

''No. We didn't fight. We made love.'' His bare-boned statement didn't begin to describe the events of the previous night, the wonder of their coming together. But Jake couldn't tell anyone about the emotions that filled him. At least, no one but B.J. He *wanted* to tell her.

If she'd just come home.

He ignored Mildred and Red and their reactions to his words. He didn't care what anyone thought. Except B.J. ''Should I drive out and try to find her? Have you called around to see if she's made any of her normal stops?''

''I'll make some phone calls,'' Red volunteered.

As he got up to go to the phone, Mildred added, ''It wouldn't do any good to drive around, Jake. She could be anywhere.''

Toby came running back in, his hands extended. ''See, Mr. Jake? I washed 'em good. Can I have some cookies now?''

''You bet, Toby. And Mildred's got your chocolate ready, too. Have you warmed up yet?''

''Yeah. I wasn't cold, 'cause you kept me warm. Mr. Jake put his jacket around me, Aunt Mildred. One of the cowboys said we looked just like twins,'' Toby bragged.

Jake sat down beside the little boy and shared a cookie or
two with him. All he could think about was B.J., however,
scarcely hearing Toby's ramblings.

He'd enjoyed the day spent with the child. More than even
he had imagined. He'd expected to like it. He couldn't wait until
his nephews were big enough to teach about ranching. But in
his mind, Toby wasn't a nephew. He was his boy. His very own.
Someone to pass on his legacy to.

He intended to marry B.J. And he hoped they'd have more
children. But none of them would be more precious than Toby.
Because he and Jake, along with B.J., all had chosen each other.

"I hear a truck," Mildred suddenly announced, cutting into
Toby's tale of his adventures that day.

Jake bounded up from the table and ran to the window. "It's
her. Keep Toby here." He grabbed his coat as he raced out of
the kitchen.

In his head, he was carefully preparing the speech he
should've made last night. It was past time to let B.J. in on his
change of mind.

When he reached the truck, just after it came to a halt, he
yanked open the door and pulled her into his arms. The speech
could wait. He had to taste her lips again.

They weren't warm and soft, molding to his, as he'd remembered. Her lips were cold and barely moving. Jake pulled his
head back to stare down at her. Her eyes were full of pain, her
cheeks pale.

"What's wrong, sweetheart?"

She pulled away from him. "I have a headache." When she
started toward her front door, he wrapped an arm around her,
pulling her close to him.

"I can make it by myself," she protested, but her voice was
weak, husky.

"No need to. I'll get you inside and fix you a cup of coffee.
After you take some aspirin, you'll be right as rain in no time."

She didn't say anything else. When they reached the kitchen,
he put her in a chair at the table and busied himself with the
coffee. Over his shoulder, he noted that she'd buried her head
in her hands.

As soon as he had the coffee going, he found the painkillers in a nearby shelf and grabbed a glass of water.

"Here. Take two of these."

She did as he directed, saying nothing. He moved behind her to massage her neck and shoulders. If nothing else, it gave him an excuse to touch her, and it might relieve some of her tension.

"Don't!" she ordered sharply, pulling away from him.

"Maybe you need to see a doctor. Do you get migraines?"

She'd lived there for almost a year, and he hadn't heard anything about migraines, but maybe she'd kept it hidden.

"No, I don't have a migraine. I just need to be left alone, Jake."

There it was again, that defeated tone in her voice that he thought he'd heard when she got out of the truck. He began to think it didn't have anything to do with her headache. "What's wrong, B.J.?"

"Nothing."

"Ben said you'd been crying."

"Ben's a big tattletale."

He poured both of them a cup of coffee and joined her at the table. "You told him you were crying because you had a bad case this morning."

She took a drink of coffee.

"Did you?"

"No."

"Were you crying because of last night?"

"Yes." No emotion was visible on her face or evident in her voice. Just a flat answer.

Jake sat there, unsure what to say. His planned speech didn't seem right. And yet he had to let her know how wonderful their future would be. "B.J., last night was—was incredible. I had no idea—"

"Yes, it was, wasn't it? Unfortunately we can't repeat it."

"What?"

"I told you I couldn't have an affair with you, Jake, so what I just said shouldn't come as a surprise." She stared straight ahead.

"I don't want an affair."

That remark got her attention. She stared at him, then rose from the table. "Good. Tell Mildred I'm going to take a nap."

As she reached the kitchen door, he finally got out the words he'd meant to say all along.

"I want to get married. I want to marry you, B.J."

She froze but didn't turn around. Finally, before she left the room, she uttered one word. "No."

Chapter Sixteen

B.J. reached her bedroom and grabbed for the doorknob. She wanted to shut out the world.

Unfortunately one stubborn cowboy had no intention of letting her do that. He grasped the edge of the door with one hand and her arm with the other.

"What do you mean, no?"

She swallowed and hoped that stupid sandwich was going to stay down. "No, I won't marry you."

"Why?"

Couldn't he leave her alone? Couldn't he take her answer at face value and go away? "I can't marry you."

"Look, B.J., I know I talked a lot of nonsense about not marrying again. But—last night I finally figured something out."

She didn't want to know. She wanted to cover her ears, close her eyes and hum. Anything to avoid the torture of hearing Jake's explanation.

She couldn't. Because Jake had released the door and her arm and cupped her face, lifting it closer, nearer, within reach of his incredible lips.

He went on without any encouragement from her. "Last night, I realized I loved you. It didn't matter whether I married you or not. I would still love you. Always."

She supposed he expected her to fall into his arms. Given a choice, that would be her reaction. But she didn't have a choice. She was a mother first, and a woman second, and Toby's best interests were paramount. "No.".

Shock, then irritation, crossed his face. He released her face and stepped back. "What do you mean?"

"I mean I can't marry you. Please go away." She turned her back on him. Seeing him only made her words harder to say.

Silence was her only answer. Then she heard his hard boots clumping down the hall, followed by the door slamming. He'd done as she asked.

She fell on the bed, her heart broken, tears streaming down her face.

JAKE COULDN'T BELIEVE IT. He hadn't been mistaken. Last night B.J. had shared the pleasure they'd had. She'd felt what he felt. He knew it.

But today she'd rejected him. Why? What had gone wrong?

He entered the kitchen, expectant gazes meeting his. He spoke to Mildred. "B.J. needs you. We'll keep Toby here."

"Is Mommy sick?" Toby asked, a worried frown on his face as Mildred hurried outside.

"Yeah. She has a headache. So noisy little boys need to stay here. Want to watch a video?" Jake couldn't imagine anything he'd like less, but he knew B.J. wouldn't want Toby near her right now.

He only wished she wanted *him* near her.

"You okay, boy?" Red asked.

Jake couldn't answer. His dreams had been shattered. Dreams he hadn't even realized he'd had until too late. He'd protested so much about marriage, he hadn't realized how perfect he and B.J. were for one another. Instead, he'd flaunted his refusal to marry in her face.

Was that the problem? She didn't believe him?

Hell, how could she not after last night? How could she think he could even think of another woman after holding her, loving her? How could she think he wouldn't want her at his side the rest of his life?

Because he'd told her he wouldn't.

He squared his shoulders. He wasn't going to give up. He and B.J. were meant for each other. He'd convince her. Of course he would.

"Jake?" Red repeated.

"Yeah?"

"You okay?"

Jake nodded. He couldn't bring himself to say the words, to give another lie. "Come on, Toby. Let's go watch a movie."

As he and the little boy, his hand resting in Jake's, left the room, Jake looked at Red. "Call me if you hear anything."

Red nodded.

Over an hour later, Red called them to dinner.

Jake stared at him, a question in his eyes. Red shook his head no.

"Maybe you should call."

"She hasn't switched the phone back. I tried."

Jake opened his mouth to offer another suggestion, but Red shook his head no again. "She'll let me know, boy. We just have to be patient."

Jake explained Toby's presence by saying B.J. was letting him pretend to be a cowboy all day, including eating with his cohorts.

Toby enjoyed the teasing he received. He also liked watching the twins as they took their bottles just before dinner. Janie even let him hold each one of them briefly, hovering over him.

"They're sure little," he said. "Was I that little?"

"I imagine you were," Jake agreed.

"Did my daddy hold me?"

Jake's heart twisted. "Yeah, son, he held you. Just like I held you today."

"But you didn't feed me a bottle!" Toby said with a giggle.

"Reckon he didn't change your diaper, either," Pete added, a grin on his face.

Everyone but Jake laughed as Toby gave a disgusted look. But Jake realized he wished he'd been there for Toby's beginning. He wished he'd fathered him.

If he couldn't convince B.J. to marry him, he'd have his heart broken twice. Once by B.J., and once by the boy beside him.

Then Mildred came in.

Jake leapt to his feet.

Red got up, too, and greeted Mildred with a kiss. "Hi, sweetheart. Want some dinner?"

"Yes, that'd be fine."

Jake couldn't wait, in spite of Red's attempt to make everything look normal. "How's B.J.?"

"She's sleeping."

"Something wrong?" Anna asked.

"B.J. had a bad headache."

"Shall I go check on her?" Anna's nursing skills frequently came in handy on the ranch.

Jake held his breath. He didn't think B.J. would want Anna to come, but he was worried about her.

"No, she'll be all right. She just needed some rest," Mildred said calmly. But Jake noticed she didn't meet his gaze.

He stirred his food on his plate, but he couldn't eat anything else. He was too worried about B.J....and their future. How ironic it would be if, after helping his brothers find love, he should be the one who crashed.

Dear God, help her change her mind.

B.J. WOKE UP around eleven o'clock.

The house was dark.

With a sigh, she pushed herself up from the bed. She needed a drink of water. And maybe a hot bath. And maybe a new life.

Mildred had appeared as soon as Jake left. B.J. knew he'd sent her, that he'd told her something was wrong. But Mildred had offered a wet cloth to soothe her headache. And she'd sat beside her bed, asking no questions.

B.J. had asked only one. "Toby?"

"He's having dinner with the Randalls."

So B.J. had closed her eyes and sought relief from the pain...in her head and in her heart.

The headache had gone, she realized as she made her way to the kitchen. The pain in her heart would never go away. Because Jake was right. They were perfect for each other.

Except for one thing.

Toby.

Jake wanted Randall blood, his blood, to carry on the name, the ranch. If she married him and they had children, he would be ecstatic. And Toby would be devastated.

He'd never had a daddy, as far as he could remember. He wanted Jake in that role. It would crush him if Jake didn't think of him as his son.

She couldn't do that to her darling child.

She was an adult. She could bear the pain of loss, of separation. She'd already done it once when she lost Darrell.

Hysterical laughter bubbled up inside her. How could she compare that pale affection she'd had for Darrell to the all-consuming emotion Jake evoked?

But she'd survive. Of course she would.

Turning on the light in the kitchen, she crossed to the sink and took down a glass.

The door opened behind her.

"How are you feeling?" Mildred asked.

"Fine, thanks. I appreciate your taking care of me."

"Want to talk?"

No, she didn't want to talk. She didn't want to tell Mildred that she was leaving, she and Toby. But she had to. The longer she waited, the more difficult it would be.

"Yes, let's talk." She pulled out a chair and sat down.

After Mildred had joined her, she said, "This is hard for me to say, Mildred, but—but our move here isn't working out for me. I'm going to take Toby and move back to Kansas City."

She saw the panic and devastation in Mildred's eyes. Pain pierced her, but she couldn't let it change her mind.

Finally Mildred said, "Okay." Her voice shook.

"You're not coming with me, Mildred," B.J. said softly, hoping Mildred would accept her words.

Mildred pressed her lips tightly together. "Of course I am."

B.J. fought back the tears and reached out to clasp Mildred's hands. "I want you to, Mildred. I don't know how I'll make it without you. Not because I can't manage, but because I love you. You've been my mother and Toby's grandmother. You've given us the love we needed."

Mildred's tears slid down her cheeks. "I love you both. We're family. Of course I'll come with you."

"No. You love Red now, too. I'd never forgive myself if I stopped you from living life to the fullest." Now B.J.'s cheeks were wet, too. "We—we'll keep in touch, write, call. Toby and I will be here for your wedding, whenever it will be." She swallowed a sob. "But I can't stay here."

"Are you sure?" Mildred pleaded.

B.J. looked away, unable to bear the pain in Mildred's gaze, and tried to smile through her tears. "I'm sure."

Before Mildred could ask her again, or ask for an explanation, B.J. rose and ran from the kitchen.

It was Sunday. Everyone slept a little later that one day of the week, rising slowly, leisurely. Jake could imagine his brothers lingering in bed with their wives.

He hadn't been able to sleep.

Red had found him hunched over the table, a cup of coffee in his hands, when he entered the kitchen.

Now the two of them, with nothing to say, sat staring into their mugs.

Until Mildred burst into the kitchen.

Red leapt up, and she ran into his arms, tears streaming down her face. "She's leaving," she gasped out.

Her words electrified Jake. He jumped to his feet.

And worried Red. "But you're staying?" he asked, hunger and hope in his voice.

"She won't let me go with her."

"What do you mean?" Jake demanded. "Where's she going?"

"Back to Kansas City. To her old job. She and Toby."

"When?" Jake's voice was hard, intrusive. He knew Mildred wanted to be alone with Red. But Jake had to know what B.J. had said.

"I don't know. Soon."

"Did she say why?" he asked.

Mildred shook her head.

He strode from the kitchen.

"She's still in bed," Mildred called.

He ignored her. Besides, he couldn't think of a better place for B.J. to be.

Leaping onto the porch, he was glad no one ever locked their doors. Otherwise, he'd have to break it down. Reaching into his back pocket, he pulled out his handkerchief. Without knocking, he threw open the front door and charged down the hall to B.J.'s bedroom.

When he opened this door, prepared to wake her, he discovered she was already awake, staring at the ceiling. He leaned against the wall beside the door after he shut it, afraid to go any closer. They had to get a few things straight before he could touch her.

"Jake!" she gasped, and pulled the covers to her chin.

As if he hadn't seen her gloriously naked already.

Instead of answering, he raised his white handkerchief in the air.

She frowned, a puzzled look on her face. "What?"

"Don't you recognize the universal sign of surrender?" he asked grimly.

"Surrender to what?" Her voice was tight, and she drew herself to a sitting position, leaning against the headboard.

"To whatever is keeping us apart."

Her eyes darkened, as if with pain, and she looked away. "I don't know what you're talking about."

"Yes, you do," he drawled. "I'm the one who's in the dark. I stayed up almost all night trying to figure out what went wrong."

She flashed him an angry look.

"I know I was arrogant," he admitted. Better to confess his sins than have her tell him. "Damn it, B.J., I didn't know!"

"Know what?"

"That it could be like this. That I could feel this way. With Chloe, I—I wanted her. But I didn't love her. And my wanting wasn't much. After we married, and I slept with her, I realized it was a momentary thing."

"Maybe this—this feeling will turn out to be momentary, too," she suggested, still not looking at him.

"Why won't you look at me?"

She flashed him another glare. Then looked away again.

"You know as well as I do that it's not momentary. You're as hungry for me as I am for you."

"Maybe I'm a nymphomaniac," she muttered.

"And you've kept away from men for four years?" Her suggestion was so ridiculous, it gave him hope.

"Go away, Jake."

He couldn't stay by the wall any longer. Crossing the room, he sat down on the edge of her bed. "I waved a white flag, Barbara Jo. I'll do whatever you want me to do. If you want to go back to Kansas City, then I'll go to Kansas City with you."

"Leave the ranch?" She stared at him. "Jake, the ranch is the most important thing in the world to you! That's why you found wives for your brothers. So the ranch could continue in the Randall name!"

"I want the Randall name to continue. I want the ranch to remain in the family. But that's all taken care of. You are more important to me than any piece of land."

"You'd be miserable in Kansas City," she muttered, her fingers picking at the bedspread, her gaze down.

"I'll be miserable without you wherever I am."

The tears began again, and he couldn't stand it. "Don't cry, sweetheart," he insisted, pulling her into his arms. "We'll be happy, I promise."

Her arms held him as much as he held her, and it filled his heart with joy. "You know how I realized things were different with you? Other than the fact that I couldn't keep my hands off you? You couldn't keep your hands off me, either." He grinned and lowered his head for a kiss.

"That's why I have to leave."

He'd begun to believe he'd convinced her. Until those words. Sobering, he said, "I think you'd better explain yourself."

Instead, she buried her head in his shirt and shook her head no.

"B.J., I love you. I want to spend the rest of my life with you. You've got to tell me what the problem is."

Finally she whispered, "Toby."

Jake frowned and pushed her back against the bed. "Toby? You think he's a problem?" His heart ached again as he considered her meaning. "He doesn't want me as a daddy?"

"Of course he wants you as a daddy," B.J. protested before a sob escaped. "But a real daddy. Not—not—"

"Not what? What are you talking about?"

"I don't want him to be second-best, Jake! I couldn't stand it!"

Completely confused, Jake shook his head. "Second-best to what?"

"Any children we might have. Any real children."

Jake sat back, stunned. Finally he said, "Dear God, B.J., is that what your refusal was for? Because you thought I couldn't love Toby as much as any other children we'd have?"

She nodded.

"I ought to pull you over my knees and paddle your behind! Except I might get distracted by your cute little rear before I got very far. Come here." He suited his actions to words, pulling her back into his embrace.

"But, Jake—" she protested, tears still falling.

"B.J., Toby and I already love each other. If you'll let me, I'll adopt him. Then he'll be a Randall in name. But he's already a Randall in my heart."

"Are you sure, Jake? He won't have your blood."

"Neither do you, sweetheart, but do you think that makes any difference about how I feel about you?"

A shining light was in her eyes, drying up her tears, and her hands slid around his neck. "Are you sure?"

"Very sure. And I'm ready to show you. How perfect that you're already in bed."

"But Toby—"

"I closed the door. And Toby has to learn that his daddy can't always be available." He covered her mouth with his and immediately felt his control slipping. She did that to him. "Especially when the distraction is his mommy."

"Oh, Jake, I was hurting so," she murmured as she surrendered to his kiss.

"Me too, Barbara Jo," he assured her huskily, "but nothing

is going to come between us ever again. The three of us. We're a family, the Randall family.''

She closed her eyes and hugged him tightly.

''And I'll never let you go,'' they both promised together.

Epilogue

Jake pulled his truck to a halt. He'd run into town to pick up some last-minute purchases B.J. insisted she needed.

Toby came flying out of the house, running in his direction, his hat sitting snugly on his head.

Jake grinned. About time for another trip to town. B.J. was right. The boy had outgrown his birthday gift in about a year. Today was only three days away from Halloween. And it was his and Toby's birthday.

Opening the door, he got out and caught Toby as he launched himself at him. If the boy got much bigger, he'd knock him over.

"Daddy! You're back."

"I am, son. How's Mom?"

"Fine. 'Cept Anna says the baby's coming."

"What?" Jake roared. He tucked Toby under one arm and ran for the house.

"Anna won't let me watch," Toby complained, his voice bouncing as much as his body.

As soon as he got inside, Jake set Toby down. "You stay here," he ordered, and rushed up the stairs.

He entered their bedroom, finding it full of people. Mildred, Anna and Doc were around the bed. He ignored them all, falling to his knees beside B.J. "Barbara Jo, how dare you start without me."

"I knew you'd get back in time," she whispered, a smile on her beautiful lips. "But it's a good thing you didn't take any longer. This baby is getting—'' She broke off to gasp as a pain seized her.

Stroking back her hair, he attempted to finish her sentence. ''Impatient?''

''Yeah,'' she said after the pain passed.

And she was right. Within minutes, as he watched and held B.J.'s hand, his precious daughter entered the world. When her frail cry signaled her protest, he buried his face in B.J.'s hair, hiding the tears.

''Well, well, well,'' Doc said, a smile in his voice, ''you have a baby girl, B.J. A beautiful baby girl.''

''Is she all right?'' B.J. asked, her eyes following Doc as he handed the baby to Anna.

Jake raised his head as Mildred, Anna and Doc all replied at once, ''She's beautiful.''

''Just like her mama,'' Jake assured everyone, a beaming smile on his face.

TWO WEEKS LATER, after he'd held his tiny daughter in his arms for the dedication service at church, Jake greeted his family and neighbors in the big living room on the Randall ranch.

''I'm not much for speech making, but as you all know, a lot of things have changed in the past couple of years.''

His gaze turned to his wife, sitting in a nearby chair, holding Caroline in her arms as Toby leaned against the chair. ''Two years ago, we were a bunch of bachelors living a pretty dull existence. Everyone teased me about my matchmaking, but it was the smartest thing I've ever done.''

''Here, here!'' Chad called, drawing laughter from the group.

''Now B.J. and I have been blessed, not only with the love we share, but also with two wonderful children. Janie and Pete have their twins, Chad and Megan have Elizabeth. Only Brett and Anna haven't— Yes, Brett?''

Brett had waved a hand at his brother, halting his speech. ''Actually that's not true, Jake. Anna and I are expecting our own Randall in about seven months.''

Anna's cheeks turned bright pink amid all the congratulations.

B.J. reached out and squeezed her hand, and Janie and Megan came over to kiss her cheek.

"Hey, how about me?" Brett protested. "I had something to do with this baby, too." The Randall women laughed and kissed his cheek.

"Well, it looks like we're celebrating more than Caroline. I guess that only leaves Mildred and Red. Got an announcement for us, Red?" Everyone broke into delighted laughter, and Mildred chastised Jake for his teasing.

Red, however, spoke up. "Me and Mildred will take care of the grandparenting, boy. You young ones just keep producing them."

"Yeah," Toby spoke up. "Next time we want a boy so I can have a brother."

"Next time?" B.J. asked faintly, but Jake heard her. He smiled, his heart full. In spite of her protest, he knew she'd welcome as many more children as God blessed them with.

Ben Turnbull called out, "Yeah, next time, B.J. You know how important it is to keep the Randall line going."

Jake nodded at his friend. "Yeah, I always thought keeping the Randall line going was important. But I've discovered something more important." He paused and smiled at his wife again. "I've discovered that the most important thing in the world is love. Love between friends, love between brothers, love between a father and his children—" he smiled specially at Toby, who glowed "—and most of all, love between a man and his wife."

He lifted his glass. "Here's to the happiness we've found."

Bending down, he briefly kissed B.J., Toby and Caroline, then raised his glass again before taking a deep, long drink, as his brothers did.

The Randalls had a lot to celebrate.

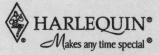

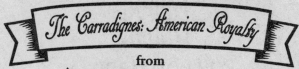

C'mon back home to Crystal Creek with
a BRAND-NEW anthology from

bestselling authors
Vicki Lewis Thompson
Cathy Gillen Thacker
Bethany Campbell

Return to Crystal Creek

**Nothing much
has changed in
Crystal Creek...
till now!**

The mysterious Nick Belyle has shown up in town,
and what he's up to is anyone's guess. But one
thing is certain. Something big is going down in
Crystal Creek, and folks aren't going to rest till
they find out what the future holds.

*Look for this exciting anthology,
on-sale in July 2002.*

Coming in July!
Top Harlequin® Presents author

Sandra Marton

Brings you a brand-new, spin-off
to her miniseries, *The Barons*

Raising the Stakes

Attorney Gray Baron has come to Las Vegas on a mission to find
a woman—Dawn Lincoln Kittredge—the long-lost grandchild of
his uncle Jonas Baron. And when he finds her, an undeniable
passion ignites between them.

A powerful and dramatic read!

Look for it in stores, July 2002.

HARLEQUIN®
Makes any time special ®

Visit us at www.eHarlequin.com

PHRTS